PRAISE FOR KRIS

"I adore Kristen Ashley's books. Her sto... page one and ... continue to dwell in yo... the story."

—Maya Banks, *New York Times*
bestselling author

"Kristen Ashley's books are addicting!"

—Jill Shalvis,
New York Times bestselling author

"Kristen Ashley captivates."

—*Publishers Weekly*

"There is something about Ashley's books that I find crackalicious."

—Kati Brown, *Dear Author*

"When you pick up an Ashley book, you know you're in for plenty of gut-punching emotion, elaborate family drama, and sizzling sex,"

—*RT Book Reviews*

"Reading a Kristen Ashley book, it's a journey, an adventure, a nonstop romantic thrill ride that is absolutely unparalleled in the romance world."

—*Aestas Book Blog*

"Nobody starts a book off better than Kristen Ashley. And while I'm on it, nobody ends a book like Kristen Ashley, either. Precious. Poetic. Perfect."

—*Maryse's Book Blog*

"Kristen Ashley books should really have a separate rating scale as they truly stand in a book universe of their own."

—*Natasha is a Book Junkie*

"Any hopeless romantic would devour everything Kristen Ashley has to offer!"

—*Fresh Fiction*

"My addiction to Kristen Ashley books intensifies with every book I devour."

—*Vilma's Book Blog*

"Kristen Ashley books should come with a warning that says, 'You may become addicted to KA books.'"

—*Night Owl Reviews*

Also by Kristen Ashley

The Deep End

the
farthest edge

KRISTEN

ASHLEY

ST. MARTIN'S GRIFFIN ⚜ NEW YORK

THE FARTHEST EDGE. Copyright © 2017 by Kristen Ashley. All rights reserved. Printed in the United States of America. For information, address St. Martin's Press, 175 Fifth Avenue, New York, N.Y. 10010.

www.stmartins.com

The Library of Congress Cataloging-in-Publication Data is available upon request.

ISBN 978-1-250-12113-4 (trade paperback)
ISBN 978-1-250-12114-1 (e-book)

Our books may be purchased in bulk for promotional, educational, or business use. Please contact your local bookseller or the Macmillan Corporate and Premium Sales Department at 1-800-221-7945, extension 5442, or by e-mail at MacmillanSpecialMarkets@macmillan.com.

First Edition: June 2017

10 9 8 7 6 5 4 3 2 1

This book is dedicated to Donna Soluri.
A woman who means a great deal to me.
And not just because we both like the F-word so much.
Thank God we met or I would have laughed a whole lot less.

acknowledgments

A girl's gotta have her cheerleaders, and for this series, my cheer-leaders are my editor, Rose Hilliard, who makes it an actual joy to read her edits, and my agent, Emily Sylvan Kim, who defies words to express how awesome she is.

Thank you both for believing in this series and for believing in me.

the
farthest edge

prologue

Of Course I'm Going to Kill You

Gerald Raines turned the corner into his bedroom and flipped the switch just inside the door that would illuminate the lights on the nightstand.

They didn't turn on.

His first thought was always his first thought when something went wrong.

To blame whatever wasn't working on his wife.

His second thought was always his second thought, or at least the one he'd had the last two years.

That being the reminder the bitch had moved out and divorced him.

He flipped the switch repeatedly, and when nothing happened, he stomped into the dark room, grousing, "I do not need this shit today."

"Not another move."

The voice came from the dark, rough, male, deep, quiet, calm.

Gerald's entire body froze solid.

He knew that voice.

Impossible. Totally impossible, he thought.

But what he knew was that if anyone could come back from the dead, it would be a member of that team.

That *damned* team.

Gerald didn't move even when the shadow formed in front of him, tall, lean. Healthy.

Impossible.

It got close, lifted its arm, and Gerald felt a circle of cold steel pressed tight to his forehead.

Not a ghost.

Real.

It couldn't be.

But it was.

"John," he whispered.

"I'd say you got nothin' to worry about," the shadow replied. "They're all dead. But you do got somethin' to worry about because, contrary to officially unofficial reports, I'm not."

"How did you——?"

Gerald stopped speaking when the cold hardness pressed deeper into his forehead, forcing him to arch back several inches.

In that moment, it took grave effort not to foul himself.

But when the voice came again, it was still eerily calm.

"You set us up."

"It was the mission," Gerald returned swiftly, raising his hands to the sides, showing he was unarmed, not a threat.

The shadow kept the gun to his forehead.

"You set us up."

"It's always the mission, John," he reminded him. "In the briefing notes, the estimates of success are communicated and they're never good." His tone turned from desperate to desperately flattering. "That's why we'd send your team. You had the skills to beat the odds. And you did. You always did."

Until they didn't because the mission had been designed that way.

"You set us up."

"It was the job, John. You know that."

"It was a goddamned," he pressed Gerald's head back with the gun as his shadowed face got closer, "*suicide mission.* With my team's corpses right now rotting in that fucking jungle, except Benetta and Lex, who were blown to fuckin' bits right in front of Rob and me, Rob dyin' in my goddamned fuckin' arms not two hours later, do not stand there lying to me, telling me it was *the job.* You . . . *set us up."*

Gerald tried for bravado, straightening his shoulders. "You understood the work we do, John. You signed up for it."

He took off the pressure of the gun and moved back inches, but he didn't leave Gerald's space nor did he drop the weapon.

"What I understand is that you had a shot at a deal with Castillo, he had a beef with the team because *you* sent us to take out his brother, somethin' we did, and Lex almost bit it during *that* mission, so you offered us up, ducks in a barrel, so you could use Castillo's network to get your arms where you needed them."

Jesus, how did he know that much?

Goddamn.

That team.

They could do anything.

And they did.

Even one of them surviving a mission that was designed to kill them all.

"Those fighters needed weapons and they're the only hope our government has to keep peace in that region without us engaging our own soldiers to do it at great cost of money and lives," Gerald shot back in his defense.

"So you set up your own fucking team to go down?"

"Castillo was an important asset," Gerald returned. "The only shot we had. Every mission, every move, we weigh the gains and losses, John, and you know how we reach those scores."

"We were your soldiers. *Our country's* soldiers. And you sacrificed us for a shot at a deal with a sleazy arms dealer? Who, by the way, fucked you the minute he could and didn't deliver one goddamned gun where you needed it."

Damn, he knew everything.

Gerald changed tactics.

"As far as your country's concerned, John, you don't exist. You gave up your lives. You kept your dog tags but gave up your identities. All six of you did. You were ghosts before you became *this* ghost."

"We were," he pushed the gun back to Gerald's forehead, "*your* soldiers."

That was true.

But in that game, it didn't matter in the slightest.

There were no soldiers.

In that game, everyone was a pawn.

"I have to make tough decisions every day," Gerald spat, losing patience so he wouldn't lose control of his fear. "You can't imagine, you can't even—"

The shadow cut him off, stating, "I got a tough decision to make too."

Gerald felt his bowels loosening.

God, he was going to die at the hands of a man he'd personally handpicked to be trained as a killing machine.

"Are you going to kill me?"

"Of course I'm going to kill you," the shadow replied calmly.

The bowels didn't go but Gerald felt the wet trickle down his leg.

There was the barest sneer in his voice when the shadow whispered, "Jesus, did you spend even a minute in the field?"

He smelled the urine.

Humiliated, terrified, Gerald stood there, staring into the dark, featureless face of a man who'd been trained to do a great many things, do them in a variety of ways, do them exceptionally well, and one of those things was to kill, and he said nothing.

"You didn't," the shadow kept whispering. "You sent us to dirty, rotten, stinking places, dealing with filth, doing shit that marked our souls, bought us each a ticket straight to hell, and you haven't spent a minute in the field. In your bedroom, you got one shot to be a real man, to die with dignity, and you wet yourself. Fuck me."

"Just get it over with," Gerald whispered back.

"One each," the shadow returned.

Gerald's head shook reflexively with confusion but when the gun pressed deeper, he stopped it.

"One?" he asked.

The shadow didn't answer.

"One what?" he pushed.

"One whatever I want," the shadow replied. "One day. One week. One month. One year. One for each. Five of them. Maybe a year for Rob. A day for Benetta. A week for Piz. A month for Lex. Another for Di. However I want it. You could have five years. You could have five days. Whatever I want. That's all you got. Then it's over for you."

And with that and not another word, the cold metal left his head, the shadow left his vision, and without a sound, he felt the presence leave the room.

And Gerald Raines stood beside his bed, his shoes sinking into the carpet in a puddle of his own hot piss.

one

BRANCH

Two years, three months later...
The man dropped to his feet.

Without hesitation, even though his jaw was hanging loose from its hinge, Branch kicked the man's face with his boot.

The head shot back, the body moving with it, but no noise was made, no movement outside what came with the kick.

The guy was out.

And Branch didn't give that first fuck if he ever checked back in.

Without another glance, he turned and walked away, doing so pulling his phone from his back pocket.

He kept walking, out of the building, right to his truck while engaging.

"Branch," Aryas said as greeting.

"It's done," Branch replied, beeping the locks on his truck.

"Message conveyed?" Aryas asked for confirmation.

"Absolutely."

"Good. Send me a bill."

"Will do. Later."

"Later."

Branch disconnected, swung up in his truck and drove away.

Eleven months later . . .

Branch parked directly in front of her house.

It had just gone two thirty in the morning.

He got out of his truck, his eyes to the home in front of him, not for the first time noting that the Willo Historic District of Phoenix was the shit.

Especially her place.

Second house from a dead end that led to a thick, tall hedge beyond which was a parking lot off Central. The location gave the property an odd sense of quiet, even right in the city, close to a busy street like Central, and also a definite sense of privacy on that dead end.

He kept his gaze on her place, the abundant tall trees and full shrubs around her house making it look like something not out of Phoenix, but from the East Coast.

Her water bill had to be off the charts.

She had a ton of planters bursting with flowers decorating the front steps of her bungalow.

Yup.

Definitely off the charts.

His eyes turned right.

She didn't have a garage, just a carport, but she didn't need one with those trees shading the house and her lot. When summer hit Phoenix and temperatures hit 115, her place would be thirty degrees cooler, a little oasis in a vast desert valley.

He walked up the front walk but took the path that led along her front porch to the side. Her drop-top white Fiat parked under the carport, Branch headed by it, seeing the interior was red and white, sporty, cute, such a girl car, it was a wonder it didn't reach out and smear lipstick on his jeans when he walked past it.

Two side doors to the house, one from the floor plan he'd down-loaded he knew led to a laundry room, the one closer to the back of her house let you into her kitchen.

He saw the moon gleam off the pool beyond the house, but just barely, due to the foliage and plant-covered pergolas that acted as covered pathways between house, carport and the small studio that stood at the back side of her property.

He stopped at the door to the kitchen and made a decision.

He'd inspect the studio later.

He picked the lock to her house.

He moved in and turned immediately to disable the alarm at the panel, feeling his mouth get tight when it didn't buzz.

She hadn't set it.

She didn't even have a badge in the window that said she had an alarm.

She also didn't have a dog.

And further, she didn't have motion sensor lights outside.

But she did have a fucking car that sat under an open carport that screamed a girl lived there.

He drew in breath, turned to face the kitchen, and went com-pletely still.

The floor plan showed the house had three sections of rooms, each section running the length of the house. One side office, laundry room, kitchen. Down the middle, living room opening direct into dining room opening direct into a family room. Other side, guest room, bathroom, small study, Arizona room jutting off the back. The bottom-level ceilings had been lowered so a master, with walk-in closet and master bath, could be set in the attic.

None of the rooms was big except the master.

But in that day of great rooms where kitchens were open, large and part of the house, Branch hadn't been prepared for this room to be so small, downright snug, filled everywhere, even if he was seeing it by moonlight, with shit that declared boldly a person who liked cooking lived there.

There was a small breakfast nook beyond the counter with the sink that faced the big picture window at the back of the house. There was a little table there, only space for two ladder-back chairs on each side. Plants hung from hooks in the ceiling and sat on high stands, making it look like gazing out the window was doing it through a jungle of leaves.

This was not a kitchen.

This was a kitchen in a house that someone had made a *home*.

Branch turned and exited immediately, pulling in oxygen when it seemed his breath might turn shallow, and his eyes hit on the studio.

A better place to start.

He moved there, noting the plantation shutters on the windows had been carefully closed. No one could see inside. Not from any angle.

He picked the lock, went in, pulled his small Maglite from his pocket and shined it around the space.

He knew this was her playroom before he'd entered but right then he saw that she didn't hide it under sheets and tarps, just behind shutters.

Branch shifted the light around, seeing a horse, a bench, a table, all of them good quality. It cost a mint to outfit a good playroom and she didn't make do. She'd been investing. Making smart purchases that would look good, stand strong during play and last a while.

Fashionable sink in the corner set in an attractive wood vanity, two matching tall, slim cupboards on each side.

He moved there, looked through the vanity and cupboards. Thick towels. Washcloths. Wet wipes. Soap. Bottles of foam anti-bacterial. Cleaning supplies. A large box of condoms. A little basket filled with some cosmetics—powder, lipsticks, gloss. Another filled with first-aid supplies—Band-Aids, bottles of antiseptic, tubes of ointment, gauze, cotton.

He closed the door to the cupboard he was inspecting, turned and shined the light around the room. Moving across the space, he noted hooks on the walls, in the ceiling, eyes in the floor, all looking sturdy. Whoever put them in might have wondered why or he'd been hers. But whoever that was knew what they were doing.

There was a tall cabinet and a large dresser across the room, both in the wood that made up the vanity and the cupboards. It all matched, was heavy and dark but attractive, giving the space the definite feel of a playroom, not a dungeon. It was stylish and handsome, even warm, somewhere you'd want to stay a while.

He didn't think on his last thought as he opened the top cupboard doors of the cabinet and shined the light in, feeling what he found there in his dick.

Cats. Whips. Switches. Flogs. Paddles. Some straps. Some harnesses. All hanging from hooks. All well organized and well maintained. All also excellent quality. Not many, but again, quality, not quantity, was what she was clearly going for.

He closed the doors and crouched down to the two drawers at the bottom of the cabinet, opening them. Top one had silk ropes, some chains, shackles, cuffs. The bottom drawer was full of leather straps with cinches attached.

Branch straightened, moved to the dresser. Nothing littered the top, so he opened the first drawer.

What he found there made his balls draw up.

Carefully placed in what looked like purple silk-lined, custom-made grooves were her toys. Plugs. Cocks. Vibrators. The first two in an impressive range of lengths, girths and shapes. If they had them, remotes were placed at the side of the toy they controlled. There was also a complicated cock ring, rabbit ears at the front for clit stimulation, and a strap that would lead between the balls to a bullet that could be inserted in the anus, all of it obviously vibrated—triple the fun.

She liked ass.

Not many of her kind didn't.

He didn't think on that either.

He closed the drawer, opened the next, and found baskets placed in, carefully organized and containing a large variety of necessary items. Lubes. Oils. Gels. Lotions.

Next drawer down he found scarves and eye masks, no sensory deprivation, no ball gags, no hoods.

Putting a hand in and touching the fabric, Branch noted she had a fondness for silk and all of them were either dark purple, deep blue or black.

He also noted in an intense way that almost made him feel something, not only in his dick and balls, but somewhere else, that she had her shit tight.

She knew who she was. She knew what she liked. And what she liked wasn't common or vulgar, as many people might see it (but he didn't, he still couldn't deny he liked the way she obviously played it).

There was an elegance to her style.

It wasn't about ball gags and he didn't find a single strap-on.

She got the life.

But she did it her way.

Yeah, that definitely almost made him feel something.

Almost.

The next drawer down, he found more harnesses, these for smaller uses, balls, cock, jaw. There were also two carved boxes he pulled out and opened; their original use was for rings or jewelry but she'd put four cock rings in the purple velvet in one, and a number of gleaming nipple clamps with and without chains tangled against the blue silk lining in the other.

He put the boxes back, closed the drawer, straightened and took one last look around.

It was a well-equipped playroom. She could get creative and be clean and safe doing it.

He cast his eyes down to the top of the dresser, lifted his hand

and swiped it along the top, shining his flashlight on his fingers when he was done.

Dust.

She hadn't been in there in months.

He drew breath in through his nose, switched off the light and turned his attention across the studio toward the wall beyond which was her house.

Aryas had made him an offer.

He needed to make a decision.

So he needed to go there.

He went there.

The inspection he made of her house was cursory. She liked furniture. A lot of it. She liked it to be comfortable. She liked knick-knacks, all of which, if he'd paid much attention, something he didn't do, likely had a story or meant something to her.

The Willo district might have been set with land purchases made in the Victorian era, but homes hadn't been added until the twenties and thirties. Her bungalow, his research had told him, had gone up in the late twenties.

Still, she decorated like that particular queen was going to rise up, make a visit and cast her judgment.

The heavy, cluttered, busy, flowery, frilly, fringy shit was not Branch's style.

Then again, he didn't have a style and he wasn't moving in.

He was just deciding if he wanted the woman who lived there to fuck him.

So how she decorated didn't factor.

On this thought, he moved from the living room up the narrow, steep-angled stairs that had been added at the front of the house when the attic had been converted.

The stairs led to a landing that had one of those plush lounge chairs women liked, a marble-topped table and standing lamp, all illuminated in that moment by the only window to the space that was original; the others were two sun lights set in the ceiling. Those sun lights would let in light, but with her trees, they wouldn't bake the room.

He turned to take the last, short flight of steps, which went from a right angle to the other stairs, and saw her four-poster bed.

It was colossal.

Definitely made for the space, not something you got in a store.

Branch wondered if she'd had it made.

Then he wondered why he wondered.

With that, he stopped wondering and walked to the bed.

She was sleeping, smack in the middle of it.

Her huge mass of dark curls were easily visible against the light sheets, and her small body barely took up any of the large mattress.

He looked away immediately and did the checks he needed to do.

Silk ropes hidden under the bed, tied securely to the feet of the footboard and headboard. Nothing but a vibrator for her in the left nightstand (also excellent quality and a premier brand).

The bathroom off the left side of the room was sunken, the ceilings in the eaves of the house, so the large, oval tub with jets at the end was recessed even further, in the floor and down two steps. The shower at the top, though, was big enough for two (or three).

And the room was pale green and baby pink and also decorated busy, frilly, flowery, so over the top, it nearly made Branch smile.

Nearly.

The walk-in closet to the other side of the room was close quarters, nowhere near as big as the bathroom (but still large), two steps down and stuffed full of clothes.

In fact, he'd never seen so many clothes. And shoes. Shelves and shelves of them. And handbags.

She kept her playroom neat and organized.

Her closet, however, was a disaster.

He found what he was looking for, silently slid it out, made sure the closet door was tightly shut and again engaged his flashlight to look into her toy chest.

He almost didn't bite back the low whistle when he saw how she liked to play in the intimacy of her bedroom.

Picking up a huge, black plastic phallus, he stared at it, his teeth in his lip to bite back his reaction.

"She likes to test a man's manhood, that's for fuckin' sure," he muttered.

Unbidden, thoughts of that cock shoved up his ass while he was in her massive frilly bed in her frilly room in her frilly house, maybe with his face stuffed in her wet pussy, Branch dropped the toy, closed the chest and pushed it back where it was meant to be.

Without delay, not looking at her sleeping in bed or making a sound, he exited the house, locked up behind him and walked to his truck.

He got in, fired his baby up, turned around in her drive without switching on his headlights, and he was all the way down her street before he turned them on.

He drove to his condo, parked in the underground parking and took the stairs at a jog up to the fifth floor.

He let himself into his place.

He had a TV. A DVD player. A sectional. A coffee table. Two stools at the bar (even if he was the only one who'd sat on either of them). And a bed in the one bedroom with a single nightstand and one lamp.

He had blinds.

He further had dishes. One pot. One skillet. One pint glass. And a set of four forks and spoons but only three knives he bought at Goodwill. He also had a bread knife, a butcher knife and a toaster.

These, and some clothes, belts and shoes in his closet, his truck and his gear, which was stored somewhere else, were all his worldly possessions.

He could move in with Evangeline Brooks in her frilly house in an hour, not needing his furniture, not having any problem at all with leaving it behind.

On that thought, he went to the packet on his coffee table and upended it.

One DVD fell out.

Aryas's handwriting in red marker was across the clear front. *Watch this,* it said, *and call me.*

He didn't go for the DVD.

He went to one of his unsurprisingly empty kitchen drawers, yanked it out, turned it upside down on the counter and ripped off the big manila envelope taped under it. An envelope that Aryas had given him eleven months ago.

The two DVDs in that envelope he took to his TV.

The one marked #1 on the front he pulled out, shoved in his player, and turned on his TV.

He went back to his couch, slouched in it, pointed the remote to the player and hit a button.

What filled his screen didn't stir him and not because these days it took some serious extreme to stir him, and even that often didn't work anymore.

No, it didn't stir him because he knew what happened two days after what was recorded on that tape at Aryas's club, the Bee's Honey.

And also because, the morning after that, the man on his TV screen being fucked up the ass by a Dom while he ate his Mistress's pussy, Branch had beat half to death. He'd then spent the next month dismantling his life so he was now living with his mother in Baltimore, unemployed, with a lisp that he'd never get around since he'd bitten off part of his tongue when Branch was kicking his ass, and he was totally broke in a way Branch had fixed it that it'd take some doing for him to stop being.

Aryas had told him to relay the message.

When a situation warranted Aryas not offering those communications himself but instead calling Branch in, Branch was always instructed to relay strong messages.

But the one Branch had delivered was not entirely Aryas's style.

And Branch had no qualms that he took that straight into overkill.

She didn't share, that fucktard's Mistress. Her slaves were hers alone. She might let people watch her work in a room at the club, but that was rare and that was all. She didn't even go to the social room at the Honey unless it was as an observer and she never went to outside parties except simply as a guest to be with her brethren, which meant for most of the festivities, also solely as an observer.

She played in a playroom at the Honey with the blackout, or if she was in a certain mood, the silhouette blinds down, her playroom in her studio, or in that huge-ass bed in her bedroom.

Her gig was intimate. It was just him and her. Every sub she had, Aryas had told him, it was that way.

But this sub in particular.

The fuckwad had wanted what Branch was watching on his TV. Begged his Mistress for it.

And Branch watched as he took his ass fucking and loved it. Even if the Dom's meat was impressive and the man wasn't holding back—the sub's ass had to be raw—he still lost his cool and shot his load on the floor before he was given permission.

The Dom he requested his Mistress allow him to serve didn't fuck around, which meant, as Branch fast-forwarded to it, he was made to lick his cum off the floor even while he watched the Dom eat his Mistress until she came.

The few times he'd watched that DVD, Branch had always avoided looking at her face when she came.

Alone in his living room, the night still on Phoenix, he finally allowed himself to look at her face, that unbelievably pretty face surrounded by all that dark, curly hair.

Then he turned off the DVD.

He hauled himself up and switched out the DVDs, went back to his couch and started her up.

As an exercise in control, he juxtaposed the retribution he'd doled out over the visuals he was currently seeing.

Branch had no idea what caused it. No one did. The sub had been servicing his Mistress—by that time exclusively—for seven months. They were an item, even outside the BDSM club they belonged to, Aryas's club, the Honey. They were liked, both together and separate. Members were talking about them moving in together. Maybe a wedding in the future.

It could be the guy couldn't come to terms with the fact he liked a real cock moving up his ass, even if he'd requested it his own damned self. It could be he wasn't big on licking up his own cum from the floor, even if the Dom he'd requested was known as a ball-buster, and in that particular Dom's case, that was literal. Not to mention, the asshole could have just used his safe word and all would stop. It could be he didn't like his woman being eaten out right in front of his face, and witnessing how much she liked it, even if he'd set that shit up his damned self too.

It could be something that had nothing to do with his kink.

But the facts of the matter were, he'd snapped, he'd done it during a scene, after he'd slammed her against a wall and dazed her, he'd wedged a bench under the door making it difficult for security to break in.

And then he'd gone apeshit and in the limited time he did have (because it might have been difficult to get in, but Aryas didn't fuck around with security, so they didn't fuck around getting in), he beat the fucking crap out of her.

Branch fast-forwarded again and saw the Honey's Queen Bee Dominatrix, Amélie Strand, holding her and cooing to her, as well as some sub he didn't know, who was a nurse practitioner in the real world, tending to her while Branch stood with Aryas across the room, getting his orders.

The sub by then had been hauled away.

She hadn't even looked at him.

He'd looked at her

And when he had, not yet even having seen that very tape, just seeing the results on her face, he'd felt the first feeling he'd felt since

Rob had died in his arms, after which all emotion fled and he'd gone cold inside.

Dead.

His only drive being vengeance.

And that feeling was fury.

He stopped the DVD, got up again and switched it out to the one with Aryas's handwriting on it.

He went back to his couch, took a breath in through his nose and turned on the DVD.

It was Amélie's pad. He knew it, even though what was being filmed had to be long ago since the woman who was on the screen had totally checked out.

Branch knew she was in Amélie's house because he'd been to the place, now that his friend Olly lived in it with Leigh.

She was standing by the floor-to-ceiling windows, the lights of Phoenix at night behind her spread out along the Valley, seeing as Leigh's place sat snug to the south side of Camelback Mountain.

She was in a little black dress, seriously high-heeled fuck-me sandals, the fingers of her small, delicate hand wrapped around a wineglass, the tips long and painted dark red.

She was petite. Maybe five-two. In those heels, he'd still tower over her. She was curvy. Fuck, lots of curves, *everywhere*. She even had a little belly that was so fucking sweet, he almost had to turn his eyes away.

And that hair. Dark, nearly black. And curly. Those thick, abundant, twisted, amazing, wild-ass curls no implement could tame, and thank God for that. They surrounded her head, fell in her eyes, bounced on her shoulders, tumbled down her back.

As the camera got closer to her, she turned her cute face with her perfect skin and brilliant blue eyes to it and smiled, little white teeth showing through the reddest, sexiest lipstick he'd ever seen.

Her makeup perfect.

Everything about her . . .

Perfect.

"You're a goof." Her voice sounded on the video, oddly low and sultry when she looked like the spunky high school cheerleader every guy was dying to fuck, her eyes sparkling at the camera.

"Be good and say hi to Sixx," Aryas ordered off camera. "She's missing us."

She turned her head slightly and looked out the sides of her eyes and gone was the spunky high school cheerleader.

She was just the woman every guy was dying to fuck.

"I'm never good, Ary," she said in that sexy fucking voice. "You know that."

"Then blow her a kiss," Aryas demanded.

Without delay, she lifted her hand and did just that.

Then she winked.

Branch's dick got instantly hard.

The visual of Evangeline Brooks cut away and a selfie video of Aryas Weather's big, black, bald head with his thick black beard filled the screen.

"You say no to that, brother, you're a lost fuckin' cause," he declared.

Then the screen went black.

Branch turned off the TV, tossed his remote aside and pulled out his phone.

He engaged it, went to his contacts and hit the button.

"It's just after four in the morning. You better wanna play, slave," Whitney spat as greeting.

"Get over here," he ordered and hung up.

She didn't waste time. For a shot at him, the bitch never did.

He opened the door to her and saw she'd brought a bag with her.

That was good. He didn't have his own toys.

He also didn't want to be surprised with what he got.

He needed it.

He moved away from her, barely looking at her, and headed to the couch, taking off his clothes as he went and making a point, like always, even if there was nothing to see, that that room was the only room in his place she'd be seeing.

He heard the bag drop on the sectional and only turned back to her when he was naked.

"You don't use lube, I'll break your neck," he told her calmly.

Her eyes flared.

She was very pretty. She had a great body, in the way every magazine, movie and TV show wanted you to believe.

For his tastes, she was too tall.

And too thin.

And she had fake tits, which sucked.

Since she rarely let him touch them, it didn't much matter.

He let her tie his hands behind his back with rough rope in a knot he could get out of in about four seconds, if he'd wanted to. He also let her gag him, shoving a small scarf into his mouth before tying another one around his head to hold it in.

She'd then taken his ass with a huge cock while he was on his knees in the seat of his couch, his face shoved into the seat cushions, his arms bound behind his back.

She'd used lube, thankfully. Sometimes she didn't bother, which meant Branch had to expend the effort to break the scene, break his bonds and get up in her shit.

But he'd shot his load not feeling her fuck him while smacking his thigh (Jesus, totally uninspired, but that was Whitney).

No.

He'd come, hot and hard, closing his eyes and remembering Evangeline Brooks blowing a kiss.

Half an hour later . . .

"Yo, brother," Aryas answered Branch's call. "It's early. What the fuck?"

"Brooks," Branch replied. "Set up a meet."

"Sweet," Aryas whispered, no longer sounding perturbed, now sounding pleased.

Branch hung up.

And before he could think about it—or think better of it—he hit his bed and went to sleep.

two

I'll Still Get Him

EVANGELINE

It was broad daylight when Evangeline walked up to the Bee's Honey, which was weird. Except for her interview to be a member years ago, she'd never been there in daylight.

It was actually just weird for her to be there at all.

It had been months.

But when Aryas had called her two days ago, asking to see her, telling her he had something important to discuss, she knew it was time.

Long since time.

She'd not only been avoiding the club, she'd been avoiding everyone in it and that was stupid.

They weren't Kevin. They weren't the life. They had no involvement in what had happened to her, the mistakes she'd made. They'd had nothing to do with it.

And each and every one, especially Aryas, Leigh and Felicia, had tried to stay close. Take care of her. Heck, Leigh *and* Felicia had both texted in the last couple of days to remind her the next book club meeting was coming up, and even though she'd missed nearly a dozen of them, they wanted her there.

But she'd pulled back. Stayed distant.

She wasn't mean about it. She returned texts. She made excuses. She didn't cut anyone out.

She also didn't let anyone in.

Now it was high time she let it go, and Aryas calling, telling her he had something important to discuss, was a reminder she had to pull herself together and reenter her life.

Not as it had been.

But these people weren't just Doms and subs she saw occasionally at her sex club.

They were her friends.

She knew what Aryas wanted to discuss. He owned the Bee's Honey not simply as a lucrative business venture but because he *was* the life. A super-snuggly, could-be-stern Dominant who wasn't defined by the fact he liked to spank his babies' asses while he had a vibrator working inside them. He was also a man who was committed to the mission of giving those like him and the people who liked to be played with somewhere not only safe but luxurious to go where they could be who they were at the same time be with others who understood them.

He would try to convince her to come back to the club.

That, she wasn't going to do.

He would also try to convince her to come back to her circle of friends.

That, she *was* going to do.

The one good thing—when your boyfriend and sex slave loses his mind during a scene, beats the utter snot out of you and you check out of life—was that you had to check into something else.

And Evangeline had checked into work.

She'd always worked hard. You couldn't mess around when you were a real estate agent. A sale never just fell into your lap. You had to make it happen.

But she'd had a decent work/life balance.

Not for the last year.

The last year she'd worked her behind off.

And so doing, she wasn't set up. She was *set up*. Credit cards paid off. Vacation fund (since she hadn't taken one in over a year) out the roof. Savings more than healthy. Max contribution to her IRA. And brokerage accounts going strong. New roof and everything in her house that needed fixing had been fixed. And she'd recruited so many clients, and kicked so much butt selling houses, they referred her to all of their friends in a way that she knew they'd refer her to their grandchildren.

All this so in thirty-five years she was going to retire, totally alone (and she was fine with that) but high on the hog. Cruises. A pimped-out pad. Cooking gourmet meals with every ingredient bought from AJ's Fine Foods. And not even a blink at dropping a load at Scottsdale Fashion Square.

That was her plan and she was going to keep working at it.

She just had to add her friends back into that mix.

The only things the last year she'd taken time out of work to do for herself were getting biweekly mani/pedis and massages, monthly facials, and carving out time to go to the gym. She'd dropped a ton of weight (especially for her on her small frame) when Kevin lost it on her. But she'd sorted that out since any free time she had that she wasn't working, getting a mani/pedi, massage, facial, or going to the gym, she was cooking.

So she'd gained it back.

C'est la vie.

She had no one to impress.

And she never again would.

Of course, none of these things offered her what she got from working a sub in a playroom at the Honey, or the one she'd been meticulously setting up in the studio at her house until it all went down with Kevin, or, if she'd let that sub into her life (and heart), in her bed in her home. But she'd have to make do.

She had been that girl who liked the feel of a crop in her hand and the results she got when she used it. She'd been that girl since those kinds of thoughts could enter her mind in a way she could try to process them. She'd never had an issue with being that girl. It was just who she was.

But that wasn't the girl she was going to be anymore.

Not after Kevin.

She opened the door to the Honey, and in her current frame of mind, the hit of walking into the luxe foyer that was no less attractive lit brightly with daylight wasn't as big of a hit as she'd prepared for it to be.

It helped that Aryas was walking down the back hall behind the reception area toward her.

She smiled.

He was a big, beautiful black man. Huge. He towered over almost everyone.

As she moved to him and he continued to move to her, neither stopping, he did what he always did even if she was in four-inch, black suede Alexander Wang pumps.

When he pulled her into his arms, her cheek hit his pectorals and he dwarfed her.

Considering her height, it was not surprising her father and two brothers weren't much taller than her (and her mother was an inch shorter).

So she'd always loved getting a hug from Aryas, being engulfed in his strong arms, pulled to his big, warm, hard body, not feeling tiny and vulnerable, feeling safe and loved.

Kevin had not been a big guy. She wasn't into big guys. But considering what happened, it was good Kevin had been even smaller, leaner, only five foot seven, a great body he maintained, but he wasn't a powerhouse.

Aryas was a powerhouse in all its forms.

But right then, getting her first hug from him since the one he gave her two days after it happened, assuring her all had been "taken care of," she was all about the physicality of his powerhouse.

And as she used to do, she let herself drink it in.

He pulled back slightly, not letting her go, and dug his chin in his neck to look down at her.

"Got a nonfat iced mocha waiting for you in the office, my sweet," he shared.

He so knew her and not just the way she played.

In life.

Her smile got bigger and she hid the hurt inside it caused when she watched him take in her smile and then watched relief flood his face.

She'd done that to him.

She'd made him feel to blame when he wasn't.

She'd taken too long to show him she was all right.

"You know all my vices," she teased.

He finally gave her a big grin. "That I do." He let her go only to take her hand. "Come on. Let's sit. Those pretty shoes aren't for standing."

She could run a marathon in these shoes and he likely knew it.

He was just a gentleman.

That was part of what Aryas was too.

He had her in his office, had gone to the gleaming wood console at the back wall to open a hidden refrigerator to get her mocha, getting his own slim can of lime Perrier, and he sat in the expensive black suede chair beside her, not opposite her behind his desk.

He popped the cap of his drink as she took a sip from the straw of hers and he gave her a top-to-toe in her chair.

"Lookin' good," he stated.

"Feeling good," she told him, her lips still curved up.

His face got serious.

She didn't like the look of it and immediately leaned toward him, reaching out a hand to curl her fingers around his knee.

"Don't," she whispered.

"Baby—" he began.

She shook her head and squeezed his knee. "I'm all right. I threw myself into work, which is good, I needed it and you know me." She wiggled a foot, sending him another smile. "I like my shoes. And handbags. And the entirety of the Nordstrom accessories department. More money never hurt anyone."

"Evange—"

She gave his knee another squeeze as her smile faded. "I left it too long. I got involved in work, in life, and I just left it too long. And the longer I left it, the deeper I got into what my life had become, it became harder to find ways to reconnect and that's on me. It isn't on you. Everyone tried to pull me back in and it just became habit, being out. *I* did that. I didn't even want to but I did it. And I'm so glad you called, Ary, because it's time I put a stop to that and you gave me an excuse." She offered him another smile, this one smaller, taking her hand from his knee and sitting back. "And I'm starting with you."

"Honored, sweetheart," he murmured.

"You shouldn't be. You're my man. Of course I'd start with you," she returned, injecting a lilt into her voice in hopes of lightening the atmosphere.

"You need to call Leigh. Felicia. Mira. Things are happening."

That didn't sound good.

"What things?" she asked.

"Penn and Shane are getting married."

That got him another full smile as she thought of the Master and his slave whom she knew in and out of the life, how long they'd been together, how good they were together in all ways and how happy she was for them.

"I know. Shane texted. I texted back but haven't connected other than that. I'll give him a call. It's so exciting!" She ended that with a genuine jump in her seat because she loved Penn and Shane, she was thrilled for them and it was about time they made it official.

"Leigh is living with her man, Evangeline," Arya continued. "His name is Olly. Solid guy. Yin to her yang. She's all class, as you know. He looks like a bouncer at a bar run by the Irish mafia. But what he is, is a firefighter. She's deep with him, over the moon to be right there. For his part, she lights his world and he doesn't hide it."

Evangeline couldn't be happier for her friend. Amélie had been looking for that and Evangeline was glad she'd found it, mostly because she was a good woman, a good friend—she deserved it.

"I know that too, Ary. Leigh told me. Left a few voicemails. I e-mailed her back. Also Felicia, Mira, Romy, they all told me, and I could go on. Everyone's thrilled for her so I look forward to meeting him."

"Mira's also got a man," he continued.

She shifted, suddenly ill at ease.

Life went on.

And she was missing it.

Deliberately.

Oh yes, she had to pull herself together.

"I know, honey," she said softly. "Mira called. Left a voicemail. I've been meaning to call her and I will. Right after this. She and her man are both putting their houses up for sale and they're buying something together. They want me to list them and show them some places. I need to get on that for them."

In her defense, something she wasn't going to share with Aryas because it was lame, Mira had only called about this three days ago.

But in her job, three days was two and three-quarter days too long for her to return the call.

"Sixx is back," he shared.

"I heard that too," she replied uncomfortably.

Aryas tipped his head slightly to the side, his gaze on her becoming intent.

"You here, does that mean you're coming back to the club?"

She straightened, shaking her head slightly, and lifted her plastic cup to take a sip before she answered.

"I don't think that's something that's going to be in the future for me, Ary."

"Evangeline—"

She lifted a hand but lowered her voice. "Love you. Love that you're looking out for me. Feel like an idiot and worse, a jerk for going into my head then falling into work and not reaching out to everyone. Sorting myself out. And I'll be reconnecting, with everyone. But that . . . ," she shook her head, "that part of my life is behind me."

Arya's face turned hard with concern. "That part of your life is part *of you*."

"Ary, I messed up."

"Leenie, *he* was messed up. That was not on you."

"I don't know that for certain. What I *do* know for certain is that it wasn't on *you*."

His face closed down.

"It wasn't, Ary," she stressed.

"I should have read it on him," he returned. "Fuck, I should have smelled it on him."

"I didn't and I spent much more time with him."

"You had other things on your mind."

She did.

Love.

Marriage.

Babies.

A life together.

God, she'd been such a fool.

"I think he surprised everyone," she told Aryas.

"He did. Everyone. But it's my job *not* to be surprised."

"Ary—"

This time, he lifted a hand.

And he was better at it.

She snapped her mouth shut.

Aryas spoke.

"Babe, you gotta let me carry that load because no way in fuck there's a thing you can say or do to make me let it go. You walk in that front door, you depend not on the person you're with to keep you safe, you depend on *me* to keep you safe. You're not answering an ad and taking the risk with whoever shows. You're not at the Bolt and needing to worry about how they clean or even *if* they clean up after the ones who went before you. The Honey is your sanctuary. And it's on me to provide that."

Evangeline didn't reply so Aryas kept speaking.

"He's taken care of. I told you that and it's true. He won't hurt you again. He won't hurt anyone again. I saw to that. That's done. But I gotta live with the blame so I stay sharp in order to make certain it doesn't happen again."

Evangeline had no idea how Aryas had taken care of Kevin. She held some guilt about this too. Kevin clearly needed help.

It was just, with what he'd done to her, she'd made the decision that it wasn't her that should help.

She doubted Aryas got him into counseling.

That said, if ever there was a time to pull your own self together, examine what was going on in your head—beating the crap out of, not your Mistress, but your girlfriend, was that time.

In other words, at least she'd forgiven herself for not assisting in that and doing so, had allowed herself to move on and heal. After Kevin did what he'd done, she knew that whatever happened to him was not her concern.

She'd been falling in love with him. Thinking about a future with him. And he'd been right there with her. So she couldn't stop herself from hoping he'd gotten help and feeling some remorse that she hadn't stepped up to be a part of that.

But the first time his fist connected with her face, he lost the right to expect her to be there for him.

And she gained the right for that to be okay.

"I'll give you that," she said softly.

"Obliged," he replied with a quirk to his lips. But immediately after that, he pushed, "Be more obliged, you came back to the club."

She sighed and began, "Aryas—"

"Get you don't want to and won't push it. Hope you do. Hope you get over it. Hope you come back to us and to *you* in all the ways you *should* do that. You can't find that in you . . ." He shrugged but didn't stop coming at her. "That's the way it is. I can't push that. You gotta find that in you. But connecting with you. Seeing where you're at. Getting you to come back to the family. Taking your pulse is only part of why I asked you here. I also got another reason."

Evangeline took another sip of her coffee before she asked, "And what's that?"

"Got a sub for you."

She blinked and her stomach pitched.

"Sorry?" she queried.

"Perfect for you. No strings. No boundaries. This guy is not looking to connect. He's not looking for a relationship. Hell, sheer number of Dommes he goes through, you might only get one crack at him before he vanishes from your life. But at least you'll get off the way you like it that one time. And if you can keep him around awhile, you might have some fun, break yourself back in, give yourself what you need, without any baggage."

Um.

Whoa.

That all sounded way too good to be true.

But still.

"I'm not . . . I don't think . . ." She swallowed. "I'm not ready for that, and to be honest, Ary, I'm not sure I'll ever go back there."

"Fool thing to think, more fool thing to do," Aryas returned instantly. "Especially when you got a chance to have a go with this guy. You got a shot at a guy like this guy, you should take it. And I mean that for *you*. Only for you. For where you're at. For what I suspect you need about now. He doesn't want to hold hands. He doesn't want to share a drink in the hunting ground. He doesn't want you to give him your number or stake your claim on him in the club or anywhere. He wants you to get him off and he's open to anything you wanna do to pull that off."

He's open to anything you wanna do to pull that off.

She fought squirming in her seat and it made her angry.

This was not a part of her life anymore.

This was something she was never going back to.

She'd said that plainly to Aryas and he shouldn't push it.

"Aryas, please, seriously. I think I learned my lesson with Kevin and Damian."

"Damian's back too."

Evangeline went still.

"He wants to see you," Aryas went on.

"Oh my God," she whispered.

She hadn't heard that.

"Couple of days ago, he contacted me to share he was back in Phoenix," he carried on, "and he'd be coming back to the club. He didn't want to do that until he saw you. Spoke to you. Made sure you're all right."

Evangeline said nothing but what she thought was, she should talk to him. Damian had sent flowers every week for three months after it happened. He'd shown up at her door half a dozen times, three of which she'd let him in to talk to him, show him she was okay, the swelling was down, the bruises were healing, *she* was healing.

The other three times, she'd hid like a coward and not answered the door.

His e-mails often went unanswered. She'd answer enough not to seem like a loser.

She needed to reconnect with him too. He didn't need to be let off the hook. Damian didn't play it that way. He never expressed guilt for what happened (which was good, because he didn't hold any), just concern for her.

Her eyes dropped to Aryas's thigh and she murmured, "I shouldn't have let Damian touch me."

"That was the scene Kevin wanted."

She lifted her gaze to his. "I shouldn't have let him have it."

"It had nothing to do with you or Damian. It was fucking *Kevin* and only *Kevin*." He leaned across the arm of his chair toward her. "Damian doesn't hold guilt. Damian doesn't feel the burden of blame.

Damian has his shit together and he knows takin' that motherfucker's ass and eating your pussy and making him watch had nothing to do with that asshole losing his mind. You were all-in a controlled situation where *Kevin* held the control. He was not gagged. He had a safe word you both knew. He could have ended that scene at any minute. He didn't end it. He *got off on it.* You gave him what he wanted, what the motherfucker *asked for.* That isn't on you. That isn't on Damian. It's partially on me because I didn't see he had it in him to have that kind of break. But don't lay that shit on yourself, Evangeline. And don't lay it on Damian."

She simply stared in his eyes.

"Nod, baby, so I know you got me," he ordered.

Weakly, she nodded.

She also noted Aryas didn't like the "weakly" part of that and didn't hide it, but he accepted it.

"You got guilt because you got a thing for Damian?" he asked quietly.

She did and she didn't.

The man gave great head and he was beautiful to look at.

But she was a Domme and he was a *Dom*, pure and true. His work hit extremes but more often than not it was a thing of beauty.

Those two didn't go together even if she wanted them to, which she didn't.

She needed to crack the whip.

But now, doing that only in her mind with her vibrator held to her clit.

"He's gorgeous and he's very good at what he does, but no." She lifted her shoulders slightly. "It was just the scene. I was just caught up in Damian and the scene."

"He's got that way," Aryas muttered.

"The Honey's subs all over the city will have spontaneous orgasms, knowing he's back in town," she muttered back.

Arya's face cracked in a grin and it didn't leave, so it was a surprise attack when he went back to his earlier topic.

"I want you to look over my guy."

She sat back in her chair and shook her head. "Ary, leave this alone."

"No club, unless you reserve a playroom in the off hours, you both enter at different times and there will be no cameras."

She stared at him.

No cameras?

A year ago, the cameras in Aryas's playrooms that, as policy, he always had monitored might have saved her life.

He kept talking.

"He's not that, Leenie, and no way, and you know this to your soul, no fuckin' way I'd set you up for that again. This guy is solid. Unshakable. No other man I'd choose for you."

She again said nothing, but if he believed that about this man, it was true and she knew that to her soul.

Aryas didn't say nothing.

"You do him at yours. You sign an NDA. You don't talk to anyone about him, using his name or in any way. He's adamant about his boundaries. No one watching. No one in attendance. No one but the two of you participating. I arrange a meet, here, when no one's around. You look him over. He looks you over. You want a trial session, we make this meet at a time where you got some of it to spend on him. Blackout blinds down on the room. You two take it from there. And from there, I'm out."

"He requires a nondisclosure agreement?" she asked, more than a little stunned at this prerequisite.

"Even if you'll meet him here, this is not club play, Evangeline, and he needs to know he can trust you in all ways, but especially with that. It's not my place to get into why he needs that and I'll just warn you, he's not gonna get into *anything* personal with you. That's not yours to have. He just needs it and that's all you need to know. And you need to take care of that for him, keep him safe with that. If you don't, you talk, he won't sue you. But, baby, mark these words, you sign that NDA, you take him on, you keep what happens and

everything to do with the two of you under wraps because I don't
know what his consequences will be if you don't. He'd never hurt a
woman, physically, I said it before but right now, of that I swear."

He crossed his heart and lifted his hand, two fingers up like he
was a Boy Scout doing a salute.

He dropped his hand and finished on a whisper, "But he'll destroy you."

"Who is this guy?" she whispered back.

"You won't know that until you," he leaned forward, tagged a
piece of paper on his desk and sat back, offering it to her, "sign this."

It was then she understood his game.

*Hell, sheer number of Dommes he goes through, you might only get one crack
at him before he vanishes from your life.*

He's open to anything you wanna do to pull that off.

He's not gonna get into anything personal with you.

If you don't, you tale, he won't sue you . . . But he'll destroy you.

Aryas knew her.

He knew what she liked.

He knew how she played.

He knew exactly what would make her squirm in her seat.

And he knew precisely how long it had been since she'd had her
kink.

"You're throwing down the gauntlet," she accused quietly.

"You feel like picking up the glove?" he shot back, shaking the
piece of paper at her.

She stared into Aryas's eyes.

No strings.

Anything she wanted to do to get him off.

When he was done with her, he'd vanish from her life.

Her gaze dropped to the paper.

"Bet you, and we'll make it interesting, lay five grand on that
fucker, he'll give you one go and then he'll move on," Aryas pushed,
but it was a dare.

She looked back at him.

A dare.

Yes, he knew her.

"No reflection on you and your skills, which are sublime, my beautiful baby." He grinned a wicked grin. "Just that this guy is unbreakable. There's no edge for him any Domme can get anywhere near to push him off and that's what he's looking for. Being taken to the farthest edge and shoved right the fuck over."

Taken to the farthest edge.

Evangeline was not into that. She wasn't into extreme. Not like many who were into that in the life.

No, the edges she coasted were exactly what Aryas wasn't quite saying, but she read this guy couldn't handle.

Unless he had the right Mistress to lead the way.

Damn it all, she was getting wet.

"Five grand?" she snapped.

Aryas pressed his lips together and she was too peeved to get *more* peeved that he did it to suppress his amusement.

He unpressed them to confirm, "Five grand. But Leenie, babe, just to get it straight, he walks away from you at first meet, we're even. It's only if you get a crack at him the bet is on."

She lifted her nose at the same time she snatched the paper from his hand, declaring, "He won't walk away."

"He might," Aryas said gently, and his sudden loss of humor and careful tone made her focus on him again. "Beware of that. He's done it before. In some ways, he doesn't give a shit about anything. In some ways, he can be frustratingly choosy."

"If I want him, he walks away, I'll still get him," she announced.

Aryas stared at her, a light in the backs of his eyes gleaming.

"You and Sixx and our Leigh. You beauties love your challenges," he finally muttered.

She leaned forward, slapped the paper down on the desk and grabbed a pen lying close. She set her drink on a coaster, and not reading a word of it, she signed the paper, snatched it up, as well as her coffee, sat back and crossed her legs like she was spending all day in his office.

She turned back to Aryas, offering the agreement to him.

"I want a copy of that," she demanded.

"I'll get on that right away," he replied, his words shaking with humor, his generous lips surrounded by his thick, black beard tipped up.

Aryas took the paper, got up and walked out of the office, likely to find a copy machine, because it was doubtful the man had ever done his own copying.

When he was gone, Evangeline hauled in a deep breath before she took another long sip of her coffee and wondered what the heck she'd just done.

three

Fun and Done

EVANGELINE

"Okay, just as long as you don't mind I'm only on chapter three of the book," Evangeline said in her car, hesitantly.

"My darling, if you're back at our book club, you can set fire to the book, we girls won't care," Amélie replied.

Evangeline felt warmth fill her chest.

Even so.

"Leigh, I—"

"Don't, *chérie*," Leigh interrupted her, hearing the tone of her voice, and as a talented Dominatrix, but mostly as a friend, Leigh read it even over a speakerphone in a car. "We take up where we left off. You must know all of us understand."

"Thank you," Evangeline replied quietly.

"Please, don't say that. There's enough gratitude everywhere. It doesn't need to be verbalized. You're feeling it, and we are too, now that you're back. Just show up at Romy's and again we're a big happy family."

Emotion overwhelmed her, which probably wasn't good, considering she was on her way to the Honey to meet Branch, Aryas's "guy" (she'd been let in on his name, only the first one, after Aryas had given her a copy of the NDA, something she'd eventually read, which she knew from all the legalese she had to go over with her work was exhaustive and ironclad).

However, Amélie had phoned her on the way there to follow up on the text Evangeline had sent sharing she was coming to the book club meeting the next evening, even though she probably wouldn't finish the book.

Evangeline had missed enough calls from her friend ("missing" meaning she'd avoided them by not answering). That was done. She'd taken the coward's way out, texting in the first place.

It was time to be a big girl.

In a number of ways.

She pulled herself together and said, "Okay. Agreed. One big happy family. I'll call Romy to see if she wants me to bring anything and I'll see you tomorrow night at seven."

"Can't wait, darling."

"Me either, honey."

"Until then," Leigh bid as farewell.

"Yes, until then. 'Bye, Leigh."

"Goodbye, Leenie."

She drew in breath, heard the disconnect and focused on what was to come.

She had a clear slate, no meetings, no showings, no work, not for the next three hours.

If this guy struck her fancy, she had a small bag of goodies sitting next to her on the seat that would be used for the first time in nearly a year.

And the dratted part of it was, she was looking forward to it.

She didn't want to be. She wanted to be able to tell herself by *showing* herself that she could move on from this. She could live this part of herself in her mind with a toy in her hand and be good with that.

She'd taken that risk, thinking she'd had it all with Kevin, a sub who could also be the man in her life. Take out the garbage (which he did, though with some coaxing). Set up appointments to have her tires rotated (which he did, with no coaxing). And get in her face about keeping it because apparently tire rotation and anything to do with a car was the end-all, be-all of living an ordered life.

They'd been talking about moving in together.

Now, okay, in thinking on it (almost nonstop) the last couple of days, maybe it was extreme and perhaps even ridiculous to say she'd never have another man in her life.

And in the last couple of days Evangeline had given in to those thoughts and she'd found she was okay with moving on with that in her head, and maybe in her life.

But more, she'd come to understand that Kevin was screwed up. That was abundantly clear. And to allow whatever was twisted in his head to twist her life so she didn't find some kind of happiness with a man in it was weak and just plain wrong.

But the man she might find might be into a little bit of kinky. A little bit of fun. A little bit of different.

And she hoped he was.

But she wouldn't count on it and she wouldn't look for it.

If he wasn't, she'd settle for vanilla.

And find a waterproof vibrator so she could have her fantasy life in the shower.

Yes, with all the thinking she'd done the last couple of days, she decided she may have a go again at finding someone, but she was firm that someone wasn't going to be in the life.

Maybe that was extreme too.

But when your man slams you into a wall, cracking your head against it so stars explode in your eyes as pain sears through your skull, and then smashes his fist in your face repeatedly, and his (thankfully bare) foot in your stomach (and face), Evangeline felt it was okay if she shied away from opening herself up to that kind of relationship again.

She knew she wasn't screwed up. She'd been intrigued by the life since she was fifteen, when she found her mother's copy of *Goodbye,*

Janette, read it on the sly and she just knew. Who she was. How she was. What she wanted.

Seeing as her mom had that book and read it openly in the house, it never occurred to Evangeline that what was in it and what it made her feel might not be "right" or "normal." It was just what it made her feel, and from the time she could, she sought out more of it.

That didn't mean everyone in the life was like her, like Amélie, Aryas, Damian.

Sure, it could be said that men out in the mundane world could have triggers to trip where they'd lose their minds.

But it wouldn't be *her* tripping those triggers. It wouldn't be *her* holding that guilt she'd led someone she loved to a dark place.

Amélie had told her that it had taken less than five minutes for Aryas's men to break into that playroom.

And in that time Kevin had broken her nose, cracked four of her ribs, and both of her eyes had been swollen shut for over twenty-four hours (she hadn't been able to see out of the left one for three days because it took that long for the swelling to go down). She'd also had a fractured cheekbone and a mild concussion.

All this damage in five minutes because she'd flipped a switch that she should have seen, not as a girlfriend, but as a Mistress, she shouldn't have flipped.

Meeting Aryas's "guy" and having a little fun with a man that she knew would be nothing but fun, as well as her type, because Aryas wouldn't offer up anything else for her . . .

Well then . . .

Wonderful.

No strings.

Fun and done.

Anything beyond that.

No go.

Still, she wished she wasn't so excited. She wished the hunger she used to so enjoy hadn't set upon her. But there it was gnawing pleasantly at her insides in anticipation of goodness to come, start-ing the instant she walked out of Aryas's office with that NDA folded and tucked in her purse.

She wished she could take it or leave it.

It stunk that she couldn't.

But the fact was, she couldn't.

And now she was where she was.

So onward.

She drove into the Honey, seeing the parking lot empty except for Aryas's black Cayenne and a black GMC SUV, feeling that hun-ger grow.

Right.

Fine.

Fun and done.

All good.

She grabbed the handles of her small bag before she opened the door and threw her leg out.

As instructed (by Aryas), she parked close to and approached the back door to the club.

As expected, it was open.

She moved through the halls, keeping centered and focused so as not to have any kind of freakout that the last time she was there, she'd been carried out by Aryas, beaten to hell and not giving a damn.

Because she might have been beaten to hell.

But the worst of it was, her heart had been broken.

She walked directly to Aryas's playroom, known as the red room since it was decorated in reds, and the opaque shades that could be drawn down over the wall of windows to black out what was inside were the only shades in any of the rooms that weren't black, they were red.

As she approached, she saw the red shades were drawn down.

She kept her gait steady.

It had been a year and the last scene she'd had was a bad one. She'd been assaulted at the same time she'd had a relationship end very, *very* badly with a man she'd thought she'd loved and was considering spending the rest of her life with.

That happened.

A year ago.

This was now.

It was just a look-over anyway. It might be she wouldn't like what she saw. Or he wouldn't. And then giving any headspace to worrying what came after that was just a waste.

She was a Domme.

She'd trained under Mistress Sixx *and* Mistress Amélie, the two finest Dommes Evangeline had ever had the honor to see at play.

And before Kevin, even if she'd only been in her late twenties, she was one of the most sought-after Dommes at the Honey.

Now she was just thirty years old and she made good money. She took care of herself. She was successful. Educated. She wasn't hard to look at. She had her own style in looks, clothes (and play) that she was honing to perfection.

She could do this.

She totally could do this.

She opened the door, stepped in and saw him.

Oh my.

She was *so totally going to do this.*

She closed the door behind her, dropped her bag and stood right where she was.

Aryas's red room, known as his because this was mostly where he took his slaves, looked more like an opulent boudoir. Plush. Sumptuous. Heavy, carved furniture. Big, posted bed dressed in red and topped at headboard and ceiling with mirrors. Candelabrums everywhere.

No candles had been lit right then. The scene was not set, only red-shaded table lamps here and there were illuminating the space.

It still gave it a feel.

And that feel was good.

But more, the man before her was *amazing.*

Tall, not insanely so, still, she could be wearing six-inch platforms and she'd be able to force him to bend to her.

Black hair, a thick shock of it. It was groomed, but still somewhat long. It was clear he did not pay for expensive haircuts and he got them only when such a menial chore eventually caught his attention. Something that should have happened perhaps a month ago but didn't so it was brushing the collar of his untucked, long-sleeved, burgundy shirt.

And that shirt was a cargo shirt, sturdy, hard-wearing, this to go with his khaki cargo pants with all their pockets.

Boots on his feet.

Skin tanned.

The long body underneath was obviously lean and fit. Covered completely with loose-fitting clothing, she still sensed the power he packed and knew he likely kept it cut, but not because he liked to maintain a pleasing physique. Because it was part of whatever made him make her sign that ironclad NDA.

She especially liked his broad shoulders.

And his beefy thighs.

Not to mention hands she wanted to order him right then to use to do a variety of exceptionally delicious things.

But his face.

As unimaginative as the word was, it still worked: chiseled. His features were chiseled to the point they were downright harsh.

He'd lived. He'd seen a lot in his life. Things she didn't want to know, which was good, because they weren't hers to have.

Lord, but Evangeline could look at that face for hours, watch it flush with need, that strong, dark-stubbled jaw turn hard at the effort it took not to come or to bite back the pain, the utter blank he was treating her to right then as he stared back at her growing intense through an orgasm and then lax through the aftershocks.

However, the bottom line was the eyes.

Those eyes were what it was all about for her.

Everything.

What she needed through blood and bones and soul right down to her pussy.

Surrounded by long, curling lashes, they were a glacial blue that took aloof to the highest of heights.

He wasn't remote.

He wasn't icy.

He was marble.

Aryas was right.

This man was unbreakable.

She might be able to give him an orgasm, but that was simply biology. Enough stimulation, it was going to happen.

She'd never break behind those eyes.

She'd never get inside.

And Evangeline felt the wet gather between her legs at the hunger now clawing inside her just to get one . . . single . . . shot at attempting to do just that.

Breaking this magnificent specimen of a man.

"Undress," she demanded.

It was risky, making the demand. No cue from her, and definitely not him, had been given that they were moving on.

But he needed a firm hand.

She knew it to her soul.

And Evangeline had one.

She'd been taught by the best.

Still, she had to hide the fact that she was holding her breath the five seconds (she counted) it took him to lift his hands to the buttons of his shirt even as he shifted his feet to flip off his boots.

Relief and want both sluiced through her, drenching her panties, making her nipples tighten.

Heck, she actually felt her palms start to itch.

Even so, in acquiescing to her command, he gave her nothing. Not a flash of desire. Not a hint of humor. Not a nuance of need.

Nothing.

His expression didn't change at all.

But within minutes, it happened.

He was standing naked before her and she'd been right. He was cut. Sinewy, solid muscle that was in no way bulky, but also it was not in question the power behind it.

And his cock.

God, his cock.

A good length, but a *fabulous* thickness, formed so well, it was only semi-hard in that moment, but it was a thing of beauty.

And the high, tight ball sac behind it?

Sublime.

However, she'd had training and practice. The naked human form in its many varieties she'd seen hundreds of times and she'd come into intimate contact with a number of them.

So she knew what she was seeing.

And what she saw didn't come from the life. Subs could go to great lengths to get what they needed. Marking was not unusual, even commonplace in the temporary reddening of a paddle or striping of a whip, strap, switch or other.

But it could go deeper.

Fire. Branding. Tattooing. Cutting.

Blood play happened even at the Honey (and incidentally, Damian was a master at that too).

But Evangeline knew, without saying a single word, the man called Branch was now sharing with her the things she didn't want to know about the life he'd led.

Two scars, both nasty and looking like they hadn't healed quite right, both at his left shoulder, about three inches apart. She had no idea what they were but if she had to guess, she felt she'd win a bet for accuracy they were bullet wounds.

A scar slashing across his abdominals from right to left, long and nasty, clearly stitched together in a way that, if the doctor who did it was an actual doctor, and a Western one, this man called

Branch should be living in a mansion due to winning the malpractice suit.

It was healed but it still looked a mess.

Five scars riddling his thighs, both front and sides, three on the left, two on the right, in various shapes and lengths. She didn't know what made them but the wounds had clearly been deep and also not tended well.

All of this seemed to highlight the now-healed tears, cuts and slashes all over his arms, ribs and legs that were far more minor but so abundant, it felt like each and every one of them were opening on her skin, wide and gaping, causing her pain, making her bleed.

"Jesus, fuckin' Aryas," his deep, grating voice sounded in the room, yanking Evangeline out of the frozen stupor she'd fallen into and hadn't even noticed while examining him, "he can pick 'em."

He was moving, turning, dressing again and Evangeline saw his back.

She sucked in an audible breath.

Now those, those *could* be from the life.

Crisscrossing his back and some on his upper thighs (but oddly, none over his ass) were profuse signs he'd been whipped.

Repeatedly.

Over a length of time.

And severely.

When he yanked his cargo pants over his ass, she came back to the room.

And herself.

"Did I say you could dress?" she asked.

He turned to her, shrugging his shirt on. "I wanted a bleeding heart to kiss my scars, I'd pay a whore."

She stared in shock at his words.

This guy was a sub?

"What did you just say to me?" she demanded incredulously.

"You heard me," he grunted. Shirt on but unbuttoned, he bent to pull on his socks and boots.

"Stop moving and hear *me*," she snapped.

He straightened and stalked her way.

She felt a curl of fear sicken her stomach even if his gait wasn't aggressive.

He was getting close.

And he was a man in a playroom at the Honey.

With her.

And no cameras.

"You're in the way," he bit out, coming to a halt in front of her.

Quickly, Evangeline sorted herself out.

"We're not done here," she told him.

"We're totally done here."

"I like what I see and I'm in the mood to play," she pushed.

"Sorry, don't give a fuck," he returned.

"Step back, Branch," she said softly, holding his eyes, "and take your damned clothes off."

"I'm thinkin' you don't get this so I'll spell it out for you," he stated.

And it was then she noticed he wasn't angry. He wasn't impatient.

He wasn't anything.

He was just looking down at her and speaking.

"I don't need your brand of lame-ass shit," he finished.

Ouch.

She suffered that without a wince but marked the fact that an insult hurt worse when it was delivered by an amazing-looking man who looked like he not only didn't care that he hurt your feelings, he didn't care you existed at all.

Unfortunately, he wasn't done.

"What gets me off, you don't got in you to give me."

"You won't know that unless you," she leaned toward him, "*step back and take your fucking clothes off.*"

"I'd laugh, but you playin' Mistress isn't that funny."

Her head moved like she'd been slapped.

"Now, woman, stop wasting my time and get outta my way."

She stared in his eyes.

They were void.

She stared some more, doing it harder.

And at what Evangeline saw (or more to the point, didn't see), she made a decision.

A decision she knew might change her life.

But staring in his eyes, even with all that had befallen her with Kevin, in that moment, she did not care one . . . single . . . bit.

She stepped out of his way.

He sauntered out like he was leaving a fast-food restaurant once he'd been given his burger and fries.

She stared at the door he'd casually tossed closed behind him.

"You're terrified," she said to the door and stood there, breathing deeply. "Utterly paralyzed by it," she whispered.

She stopped speaking and drew in an annoyed breath.

Aryas.

Damn the man.

Damn him.

"I have exactly what you need and it scares the pants off you," she told the absent Branch whatever-his-last-name-was (if Branch was even his real first name).

She continued staring at the door, knowing she'd been played.

Played by Aryas Weathers, her friend and the man who wanted to see her be exactly who she was meant to be.

And find her way to happy.

But she didn't care.

No way it was going to be fun and done with Branch whatever-his-last-name-was.

No way he was going to walk out of that playroom without looking back and vanish from her life.

No way.

She was going to hunt that big boy down and she was going to tear him open and then she was going to *shatter him*.

He liked to be pushed to the edge?

She was going to take him there.

Shove him right over.

And go over with him.

And when they landed, they both were going to explode.

All over the place.

And love every bit of it.

four

The Pound

EVANGELINE

Evangeline got out of her car and threw her door shut.

She stood in the graveled lot in the dark of night in the pit of nowhere that was whatever the area of Arizona was called beyond Buckeye.

And she stared across the vast space filled with cars at the large, dilapidated warehouse, the only building within *miles*, and decided if Branch whatever-his-name-was wasn't in there, when she eventually found him (and she would find him), she'd do something she vowed she'd never do.

She'd strip her own scars into his back.

(But of course, she'd make him come while doing it.)

With that thought, she stomped in the gravel in her platform heels toward the building.

To say the last month had been frustrating was an understatement.

It started with an idea.

A good one.

No.

A *delicious* one.

One she carried out immediately after book club the night after her failed meeting with Branch.

A book club, incidentally, that had been precisely what Amélie had said it would be.

Taking up where they left off.

One big happy family.

No one said a word or cast a glance.

Sure, the hugs Evangeline got when she arrived were longer than they'd normally be. And perhaps Mira's eyes had teared up a little.

But after that, it was just . . .

Family.

Book discussion had ended, wine consumption and life discussion had ensued, with Romy yanking out her laptop and sharing a new online store they all *had* to know about immediately.

She was not wrong.

It was tremendous. Nirvana in the form of a discreet, online adult store.

The wares were pricey, but they were fabulous, and in some cases, works of art.

One case in particular, Evangeline had to have it.

She had to.

And she had to have it to make things clear to her submissive (who didn't yet know he desperately wanted to be her sub, but she was going to show him the way if it killed her) just how things were.

And so, when she got home, she didn't hesitate to go right to her office, fire up her computer and then take forty-five minutes adding and deleting from her basket two different styles of the same toy.

One had an ice-blue jewel at the end of it, much like the color of Branch's eyes.

One had a sapphire-blue jewel at the end of it, much like the color of Evangeline's.

In the end, the heavy, sleek, gleaming aluminum plug she'd bought had the sapphire-blue jewel because, she decided, it was going to be *her* she'd slide inside him. It would be *her* that filled him. It would be *her* he'd hold deep.

It cost a mint, and when it arrived, she found it was hefty and slightly larger than she expected, but Evangeline decided that was perfect too.

He wouldn't forget she was there.

Right there.

Buried deep.

And as she took her nights to search for him, she kept it in its custom-made velvet bag in her glove compartment.

Ready to stake her claim.

The problem with this plan was that Branch wasn't at any of the clubs.

Night after night, she trolled them—the sex ones and the vanilla ones besides—and he was not to be found.

Which at first was annoying.

Then it was frustrating.

Through this all, it was tiring (she was a girl who liked her sleep and dropping into bed at three in the morning was not her idea of living the high life, especially when she did that not having anything to show for it).

Eventually, she realized this failure was unsurprising.

Branch was not the club kind of guy, in any of a club's varieties.

She couldn't ask around for him because she'd signed that damned document and he wouldn't have asked her to sign the damned thing if he frequented places like the Bolt.

No, but she knew he was a man and men found what they needed. So Evangeline also knew he got what he needed (if not what he *needed*) somewhere and if it had to be on the deep, down low so no one would know, he'd have to get creative.

Thus she scoured the ads trying to decipher if he'd put one in and finagled herself (through her friend Josh, who was only a loose

friend, mostly because he could often be a douche, but he was a friend
because he could sometimes be a decent guy, and he was also a part
owner of the Bolt) an invitation (and paid the fee) to the only private party that had happened in the ensuing weeks.

Unfortunately, after striking out at the party, and during it
having to scrape off a variety of subs who made it plain they liked
the look of her, she wasn't beneath hitting the last known place she
thought Branch might hit to get his kink.

And, if she was honest about it, she knew it was the first place
she should have looked.

This being going to a Pound.

Evangeline would guess everyone in the life in Phoenix had heard
about the Pound.

She'd also guess that anyone with membership to the Honey
would go nowhere near it (and, perhaps, speak those words with a
sneer to their lips even though they all practiced nonjudgment not
only because it was right, but because they eschewed judgment due
to their way of life—that was how bad a Pound was).

And lastly she would guess that Josh was a frequent attendee.

The Pound, as local lore had it, was a traveling BDSM scene.

Not a club, it didn't have its own structure.

A *scene*.

No one knew when the next opening would be. Or where. All
they knew was, when it happened, the text would go out and be for-
warded to those who desired it, the cover charge would be hefty, the
security would be extreme (but only to keep the police from catching them) and anything went.

A total free-for-all.

Orgies.

Booze.

Drugs.

Cum, sweat, puke and blood everywhere with no cleanup crews.

The lot.

One didn't pass out at a Pound or they'd wake up on a dirty

mattress (the last if you were lucky), seeping from every orifice without any memory of what had occurred.

It sounded dismal.

Heinous.

It was also an edge Evangeline knew to her bones Branch would seek out to skid right along, thinking he was proving something to himself.

And maybe not aware he was failing miserably.

So when she struck out yet again in the vain (she knew) hope that Branch would check out the talent at the Bolt, she charmed the knowledge out of the front desk kitty-baby that Josh was up in the office with one of his partners.

And she made her way there.

Once she'd arrived she found the office at the Bolt couldn't be less like Aryas's office at the Honey.

A large desk that had once been grand but now had copious deep grooves and chips at the edges that Evangeline couldn't fathom how they'd been made.

And the room was painted oppressively in a very dark blue (something she didn't like even though that was one of her favorite colors). It was also filled with slouchy, ludicrous, legless furniture that made bile race up her throat, thinking what might have happened all over it (and she was a Dominatrix, so that extreme of nausea at the very thought said something).

The partner she didn't know and Josh didn't introduce her to (so she introduced herself) was named Barclay.

"But friends call me Clay," he'd said on a sweet smile and a firm handshake that made her think he was more like the decent side of Josh and didn't have the douche part in him.

"Nice to meet you," she'd replied on a squeeze of his hand and they let go, no lingering, just a friendly introduction (indicating more decent from Barclay). She'd then looked to Josh but said to them both, "I don't want to take a lot of your time, but I wanted to know if you knew when the next Pound would happen."

Josh, with his mess of sandy-blond hair (that was not attractively overlong, like Branch's, it was just a mess) and blue eyes that made it clear he'd taken something, lit up.

"Coolio, bitch!" he shouted. "Want me to go with?"

In other words, she had not been wrong that Josh was a frequent attendee.

And oftentimes a douche.

Geez, how did this guy run a business?

It was on this thought that Evangeline realized she did not feel excitement coming from Barclay.

Thus she avoided looking at him.

But she had some idea how Josh ran the business.

He collected the money, offered up his loopy charm to keep the members happy and this Barclay guy did the tough stuff.

"No, I just want to check it out," she answered Josh.

"You should let Josh go with you," Barclay entered the conversation.

As it would be rude to continue to avoid him when he spoke directly to her, Evangeline looked to him to see him regarding Josh.

She also saw he was rather handsome, in an understated way. His hair was dark, his frame was slight and his brown eyes were kind.

The last meant, she hoped, Dom or sub (for the life of her, when she was usually really good at reading that kind of thing, she couldn't read on him which way he swung, so maybe he was a switch, in other words, swinging both ways), he'd found someone he liked to play with in the life and in life.

"And bud, you go with her, you go clean and sober, man. Yeah?" he ordered.

"What's the fun in that?" Josh returned moodily but instantly brightened. "Oh, right. I can score at the Pound."

"No, Josh," Barclay said firmly. "You're with her, you keep your shit together."

"She's a Domme, dude, she can take care of herself," Josh shot back.

At this, Evangeline fought a sigh.

In the beginning, before being a member at the Honey, when she found what she was looking for other places, learning, before the intense training she'd been given at Aryas's place, she'd often been mistaken as a sub because first, she had a vagina, and second, she was petite.

The hunting ground at the Honey meant this didn't happen. When she was there, she occupied one of the booths, not the hunting ground, like all the Doms. Thus there was no misinterpretation.

It was irritating to have it happen again.

"I get that," Barclay surprised her by saying. "But doesn't matter and you know it, Domme or not, her first time, *dude*, you keep tight until she gets into the swing of things."

"It's just booze, sex and drugs, with house music rather than rock 'n' roll," Josh replied.

"It's a fucking wasteland *way* beyond Thunderdome, asshole, the apocalypse that happens *after* the apocalypse that people go in, they don't know what they're getting into, they won't come out." Barclay looked to her. "Or at least, the person who comes out won't be the one who went in."

"I've heard all about the Pound, Clay," she said quietly, trying to communicate she was grateful for his concern, but it was unnecessary.

"You could have heard it, Evangeline, but that doesn't mean you won't be shocked stupid when you experience it. That shit's fucked up, babe. And if Josh won't go with you, much as I hate that mess, I will."

That was sweet.

But also unnecessary.

"Like Josh said, I can take care of myself," she assured him.

"Where do you play?" he asked.

"I don't play," she told him.

His brows went up. "A voyeur?"

"I'm taking a break," she allowed herself to share.

He shook his head. "Seriously, Evangeline—"

She assumed her Mistress voice and retorted, "Seriously, Clay. I'll be smart because I *am* smart. I'll stay safe because, I'll repeat, *I'm smart*. I may not have been there but I can imagine what I'll find there and if it's worse than that, so be it. But there's a reason I have to go and it's important, or trust me, I wouldn't go. I'll do what I need to do and then I'll get gone."

He studied her and assumed (correctly), "You're lookin' for somebody."

Evangeline didn't answer.

"Please tell me it isn't a sister," he said quietly.

Yes, Barclay was of the decent variety.

"It isn't," she promised.

"Take Mace," he ordered. "And a crop or a baton, preferably a baton. And not to let it be known which way you swing but to use it if you need to. And Evangeline, babe, *use it if you need to.* You can beat someone bloody in that scene and they'll likely be so hopped up, they won't feel it but they *will* come while you're doing it."

She tried not to sneer but failed.

He caught her sneer and mumbled, "Yeah. No connections there, beautiful. It's not about the beauty of the life. It's the embodiment of why the vanilla world thinks we're all fucked in the head."

"If you're done doggin' my people," Josh cut in and Barclay and Evangeline looked his way to catch him looking at Evangeline, "I'll text you when the next one is happening. And if you want me to go with you, I'm there and I'll do it straight and score after you leave."

And there was the decent Josh.

"Thanks, Josh."

"You want me too, darlin', I'm with you. I'll give you my number," Barclay offered. "Just call and I'll be there."

She took Barclay's number because these two were the only two who would know she'd be going. She didn't intend to go with either one of them because she couldn't. If she found Branch there, the

NDA precluded her from approaching him if anyone she or he knew was around.

But she'd never tell Aryas, Leigh or anyone else in that circle she was going to a Pound. They'd lock her in a playroom at the Honey and torture the idea out of her head (perhaps in ways she might eventually find lovely, but she still couldn't have it).

So these two—especially, she sensed, Barclay—knowing she was going and on the other end of a phone should things get hairy were better than no one.

So she'd take them.

It took nearly a week for Josh to text her the details that a Pound was happening that very night.

She had a client that she'd set up five showings for the next day, these starting at nine. This meant getting her game face on and her morning business done after however long it would take her to sort whatever she found (or simply to find it), and probably getting very little to zero sleep was going to hurt.

But in the end, she told herself, it would be worth it.

She knew if she explained what she was doing to anyone, hunting Branch, it would seem crazy to some, creepy to others.

It was only to her however, that it had to make sense.

But she knew.

Kevin nearly twisted the life she was meant to lead away from her.

She was not hunting Branch with the ludicrous desire she'd move him into the amazing bungalow she'd managed to score in a downturn in the market in the awesome Willo District of Phoenix. After which she'd coax him to take out the trash and honor the appointments he set up to rotate her tires while wearing his rings and planning their future together over *Monday Night Football*.

What she expected to do was use him to heal her last wounds.

And do it healing his.

All this so they could both move on, perhaps not whole, because she'd only had a chunk taken out of her, but she knew in that one meeting with him that he'd had great masses torn away from him.

But they would still move on.

If that was together, and he turned out to be the guy who deserved it, she'd be open to it.

If not, they'd still both come away, if not whole, then resurrected.

It was a miracle she even wanted that for herself.

What was more, and what she needed to accomplish to heal herself, it would be an even bigger miracle if she could pull it off for Branch.

Therefore, after negotiating the massive gravel lot in her platform pumps, and handing over two hundred dollars in cash (criminal), she entered the flashing lights and hammering music of the Pound.

She did this without even a single one of the seven enormous security guys who loitered outside the side door to the premises giving her anything but leers at her ass, breasts and hair.

Not one of them even held a metal detector wand.

Which meant there could be anything in there.

Drugs, she knew.

Booze, she was told was sold at a makeshift bar.

But also guns (it *was* Arizona).

Anything.

She just hoped like heck Branch was also in there.

So she could get him the fuck *out*.

five

Ma'am

EVANGELINE

It would seem Evangeline had a vivid imagination, because nothing in the Pound shocked her stupid.

Although it was loud and dark (when the makeshift lights weren't flashing), filthy and crowded, it was all actually humdrum.

It was simply the sheer numbers of people engaged in all of it that was kind of shocking (not to mention, she couldn't imagine how any of them had come up with two hundred dollars cash just to get in).

But nothing she saw was enough to shock her stupid.

Of course, she'd never seen a drug sale go down in her life so she was a little taken aback when she saw her first, then her second, and her third (all this before she carefully traversed the length of just one side of the warehouse).

But other than that, she'd seen all the positions, the multiple partners, live fellatio and cunnilingus, toy play, blood play, burn play, cat/whip/crop/switch play, homosexual, heterosexual, pansexual activities at the Honey.

And it was far more beautiful to watch there than here, with sweating, grunting, glassy-eyed subs *and* Doms clumsily careening to lazily navigated orgasms that meant absolutely nothing.

No.

It wasn't shocking.

It was sad.

And although she did carry a small can of Mace in the sleek black handbag with its short strap that kept it tucked right under her arm, as well as a baton in her hand, as Barclay had advised, she had nothing to worry about.

At five foot eight (but only because she was wearing her six-inch aubergine platforms), she towered above these BDSM heathens not due to her increased height.

Like she was a goddess in tight leather pants and a black Chantilly lace blouse with the boned, silk strapless bustier underneath it.

No one approached.

If any of them were aware enough of their surroundings to catch sight of her, they stared at her like it was Aryas Weathers himself who was there to inspect the minions, tutting at how his flock had been lost, offering salvation with a look.

This made the whole thing even sadder.

And it made her stomach roil in fear that she might actually find Branch here. Tall and fit and beautiful in his broken way, his cavorting with these lost souls would be a travesty.

As much as it would be frustrating she'd driven all the way out there, handed over two hundred dollars of hard-earned cash and been subjected to this wretchedness, she felt, after pass two around and through the warehouse with no sight of him, her heart getting lighter.

She didn't condone it (far from it) but he could probably find a prostitute to give him what he was looking for.

As for her, if the night was a bust, she had one final resource to tap.

She'd been avoiding it but the only one who knew about Branch was also the only one who'd probably know how to get in touch with Branch.

So she was going to have to do some fancy footwork to get Aryas to lead her to Branch.

And she had a feeling this would need to be *serious* fancy footwork because if Branch didn't want anyone to find him, Evangeline had a feeling even Aryas would think twice (or five times) about going against his wishes.

She was making her third pass, going down the outside wall of the warehouse, trying to decide if she wanted to take another pass through the bodies, clearly-dump-acquired furniture and frighteningly stained mattresses to give it another shot when she saw the clumsy whip work of a pleather-wearing Domme.

One really should not wield a whip after taking Ecstasy or shooting heroin or whatever made someone wobble like that (and by "wobble" she meant the woman's head; the rest of her body was weaving—she was barely keeping her feet).

However, she did manage to crack the whip, doing so falling out of the top of her bustier, both breasts, exposing it all, and not looking at her target, but stupidly staring down at her breasts like she forgot they were there.

Lord.

This wasn't a wasteland beyond Thunderdome.

If the ghosts of Sid and Nancy stumbled sluggishly out of the ten-person orgy happening on two stained twin-bed mattresses beside her, swearing (Sid) and screeching (Nancy), she wouldn't be surprised.

Evangeline tore her eyes off the woefully-lacking-in-skill Mistress to glance at her poor sub when she stopped dead in midstride.

She'd seen it once and she'd know that back anywhere.

Branch.

Branch with his T-shirt not even taken off, just pulled up and off his arms, the material hanging around his neck. His cargo pants were also up, hanging loose at his hips as that was the way he wore them even if he was also wearing a belt. His hands were not bound but they were up, fingers curled around a hook that looked like, without much effort at all, he could tear it right out of the wall.

Heck, it looked like *she* could tear it out of the wall (if she could reach that high, which even in her pumps, she couldn't).

But his back.

The wobbly Domme had been too close to him and too high (the last of the drug-addled variety).

She'd opened skin.

Twice.

Evangeline saw red fog her vision as the music and noises all around her muted.

Then she saw the Mistress, who'd stuffed herself back in her bustier, starting back for another go.

Without thinking how crazy, and possibly dangerous, it was, Evangeline darted forward, arm raised.

By nothing other than a miracle, the length of the whip moved through the webbing of her thumb and forefinger, giving her a bite, but nothing more.

Instantaneously, she curled her fingers around the tip before she could lose her chance and she gave it a rough yank, pulling the handle clean from the befuddled Mistress's grip.

She wobbled and weaved, looked around idiotically, then glanced up and focused with effort on Evangeline.

Baton now tucked under her arm with her purse, Evangeline was coiling the whip in her hands.

Surprisingly, the other Domme stayed focused.

"Hey, what the fuck?" she demanded, only slightly slurred.

Evangeline looked to Branch.

He hadn't moved, turned to look over his shoulder, nothing.

"I said," it came from closer and Evangeline cut her attention back to the Domme, "*what the fuck?*"

"You touch what's mine?" she asked.

"Ain't me who's got their hands on my whip," the Domme fired back, still advancing and not understanding the point Evangeline was making.

Evangeline retreated, warning, "Don't get closer."

"Give me back my fuckin' whip."

"I said, do not get closer."

"And I said," the woman started rushing toward her, "give me back my fuckin'—"

But Evangeline had uncoiled the whip and started rounding it in a circle at her side to get a feel for its weight.

However, as the woman kept coming, she stopped it just beside her head and lashed out, cracking it at the woman's high-heeled, thigh-high pleather boots.

The woman jumped back.

Evangeline struck out twice more, now advancing, the other Mistress retreating, the tip of the whip striking within inches of the woman's toes.

It was then she executed an overhead crack, landing the tip near the woman's midsection, which made her stumble back, nearly losing balance, her face getting pale with fear in the darkness.

"I told you," Evangeline snapped, deciding to mentally thank Sixx for her excellent whip-cracking tutelage later, "do not get closer."

She dropped her whip arm, if not the whip, and looked to Branch, not surprised to see him turned, his shirt still bunched around his neck, but his arms were crossed on his chest and he was watching the Domme who'd been working him with a bored expression on his face.

Not looking at her.

Not indicating in the slightest he was stunned she was there.

Or glad.

Or anything.

In fact, it was like she wasn't even there.

A month she'd searched for him only to find him in this cesspit, his back opened by a whip that had Lord knew how many germs infesting it, and he looked bored.

And *he'd* called *her* unknown ministrations "lame-ass"?

Right, she wasn't going to open up his back (that had already been done, and not by someone who knew what they were doing . . . or had earned that privilege).

She was going to tan his ass.

She stormed up to him, and as she did, in a way that was reflexive only due to the fact that a human being was aggressively approaching him, his attention shifted to her.

But it was only a cut of his eyes. He otherwise didn't move.

Yeesh, he was something.

She kept moving anyway, right at him. She got close, whereupon she transferred the whip to her left hand and reached out with her right, firmly cupping his package.

His lower half jerked back, his crossed arms slightly loosened against his chest, and she saw in his eyes that she now had his full attention.

"Not even hard," she hissed, tightening her hold on him to see in the flashing lights only his lips thinning in response. "She opened you up," she jerked him by his crotch, "and you're not even *hard*."

He hadn't been but she felt him stirring in her hand as his eyes bored into hers.

She released him and ordered, "Put your shirt on, we're going."

"Listen, lady, no trouble. He's yours, he didn't say. No trouble. I just want my whip back."

Because she was angry, she turned, stepped well free of Branch and did another overhead crack, followed by a quick flick, totally showing off and not caring, especially when the woman cowered in front of her.

She then, handle down, spun the whip in a circle in front of her before she sent it spiraling and skidding across the floor to the other Domme.

She turned back, hoping to God Branch had pulled his shirt on because she'd lose her mind if he'd disobeyed her.

He'd put his shirt on.

"End of your belt out of the loop," she bit out.

He studied her silently but his hands moved to pull the end of his belt out of the loop.

His easy acquiescence was a shock she didn't allow herself time to fall into the wonder of it.

She approached him again, latched onto his belt and tugged him hard, stomping toward the door.

Those close who'd watched the show got right out of their way.

Those who were not as close and involved in whatever they were doing didn't even notice them so it took some zigging and zagging to make it to the door.

Evangeline made as short a trek of it as she could.

And then they were free.

She thankfully breathed in clean air and pulled him into the gravel, hoping to all that was holy that her talents in heels led her through the stone without her turning her ankle, going down and breaking her wrist, which would mean annihilating her ego.

"Not surprised that one scored a tight ass," one of the "security guards" muttered loudly.

She ignored him and kept dragging Branch, who was letting her, something she wasn't concentrating on or she might not turn her ankle in the gravel. She might do something wholly un-Mistress-worthy and sink to her knees in gratitude.

Once free of earshot if not eyeshot of security, she yanked him to a stop and turned on him.

"Where's your truck?"

"You wanna lead or you wanna follow?"

He didn't sound amused but somehow she got that from him.

And it ticked her off.

She let go his belt but grabbed his crotch again and squeezed.

His jaw went tight.

Oh dear.

That sure was pretty.

"This once, handsome, I'll repeat myself," she snapped. "Where. Is. Your. Truck?"

He jerked out his chin. "Last row, under the trees."

She loosened the pressure but didn't release him, smiling sweetly, and all fake, saying, "That wasn't so hard, was it?"

Of course, he made no reply.

She grasped his belt again and stormed through the gravel to the last row, well away from the warehouse, close to where she'd had to park but because she'd gotten there late.

She had no idea if he came late too.

She also didn't care.

When they arrived at the last row, she thanked the heavens there was only one GMC SUV to be seen, and led him there, right around it, to the hood.

There she stopped, lifted a hand and shoved it with all her body weight into his chest.

He went back against the grill, lightly, but at least her shove wasn't for naught.

She got in his space.

"Beep the locks."

He stared down his nose at her.

She pressed closer, doing so pushing her breasts to his chest.

"You wanna ride the edge, Branch?"

He kept staring down at her.

She tossed her head toward the building they'd just vacated. "You think that's riding the edge? That Domme taking a whip to you, out of her mind on junk, wasted? Is that what gets you off? Not the 'lame-ass shit' you think you'd get from me?"

He said nothing, just continued staring down at her.

She again cupped his cock and balls, hard, knowing from what she'd felt before what she'd find.

He'd been getting hard before. Now he was fully hard, straining against her hand.

So who was lame-ass?

She almost smiled.

She did not.

She pressed closer and tightened her hold.

"That's not what gets you off," she whispered, dragging the apple of her palm along the length of him. "And it's not what you need."

She couldn't be sure but she thought she heard him drag in a breath.

She decided to go with that.

"You've been bad, baby," Evangeline kept whispering, rubbing her palm along his still-growing dick, feeling his physical excitement start to throb between her legs. "And even big bad boys get punished, yes?"

He said nothing.

"Yes?" she pressed, verbally and physically.

"Yeah," he bit out.

"Yeah what, handsome?"

He didn't reply.

She gripped him didn't go lightly, and enjoyed the heck out of watching his jaw get hard again.

"Yeah, *what?*" she demanded.

"Yes . . ."

She waited for it staring up into his eyes, but he didn't give it to her.

He finished with "Ma'am."

Not "Mistress" as he should do (and he knew it).

He'd called her "ma'am."

It wasn't what she wanted or what she deserved, liberating him from that cesspool and simply being who she was.

But from him, she'd take it.

"Beep the locks, Branch," she demanded, releasing him. "Then turn and put your hands to the hood of your truck."

He hesitated, but only a second, before he dug into his cargo pants and pulled out the keys.

He beeped the locks.

She snatched the keys from his fingers and took a step back, crossing her arms on her chest, her baton still tucked with her purse.

He didn't hesitate again.

He turned his back to her and put his hands on the hood.

When he'd done that, she went directly to the driver's side, opened the door, threw her baton on the seat and pulled her purse down her arm.

She opened it and dug in.

She left the Mace where it was tucked inside.

The other things she brought with her (outside her ID, phone, cash and credit card) she pulled out, and shielded by the door so Branch couldn't see, she tucked them into the back waistband of her trousers.

She then slammed the door, pocketed the keys and walked back to Branch, who watched her do this with a vacant expression on his face, but he hadn't moved.

Evangeline did, settling in right behind him, and she didn't delay in reaching around, finishing releasing his belt and going for the button and zipper of his pants.

She did this rough and close, her breasts brushing his back.

And she did it talking.

"I'm annoyed with you, baby," she told him quietly. "Annoyed enough at you being naughty not to wait. You get your punishment here. Right here. Take a step back so you're bent into the hood and spread your legs out."

To her astonishment, he did as told immediately.

So she returned the gesture, rocking his hips to yank down his pants and boxer briefs, exposing his ass.

Tremors shot up the insides of her legs as his pants caught on his spread, solid, honed upper thighs.

She'd been taking so much in the first time she'd seen him naked, she hadn't taken in just how fine of an ass he had.

But right then, in the moonlight, she saw it.

It was so beautiful, it could be pitch black and she'd simply *sense* its sheer perfection.

Nothing could make that ass better.

Not a thing.

Except the sapphire of her plug winking at her.

Which she was going to witness that night.

Fuck yes, she was.

Through the shadows between his legs she saw his balls high and tight, but full, and got a hint of the length of his cock, hard and heavy.

"Give me your ass," she snapped.

Again, without delay, he tipped for her.

Her legs trembled.

God, God, *God*, she'd missed this.

The control. The hunger. The excitement. The wet gathering between her legs. The thrum at her clit. Her breasts swelling, nipples hardening. The gorgeous sight of a sub obeying. Ready to take what she had to give.

Moving for it. Tipping for it.

Asking for it.

Needing it.

How could she ever think she could live without it?

And God, *God*, *God*, taking him in, she'd never had the kind of beauty that was Branch being hers to do with as she wished.

Damn, but she wanted to sink down and bury her teeth in his ass, crawl under him and draw his sac in her mouth, grasp his dick and swallow it.

She didn't do any of those things.

She positioned at his side.

Then she reached out.

And she spanked him.

Hard.

Fast.

Loud.

And she kept doing it, in quick succession.

She cracked his ass relentlessly, to the point she felt the heat and pain in her own hand.

But she didn't stop.

When she noticed his legs were braced strong, he'd pressed his thighs out further, his pants biting in, she knew it was time.

So she kept at his ass, reached in front and grabbed his thick, hard cock.

She stroked, tugging down, holding firm, and watched his head fall back, his back arch, his ass tip up, his roughened jaw a line of granite in the moonlight.

God, what kind of beauty was this that was Branch?

She didn't know. She'd never had it.

And, Lord help her, she could lose herself in it.

She kept stroking, and tanning his ass, as she asked, "You like being bad, Branch?"

"Yes, ma'am," he ground out between clenched teeth, head still back, taking his spanking gloriously.

Getting off on it.

Yes, she could get lost in him.

She knew but asked anyway.

"You like being spanked?"

"Yes," he pushed out.

"Have you been naughty enough to deserve more?" she demanded, still working him, cock and ass.

"Yes," he grunted.

"Say it, Branch. Tell me you've been bad."

"I've been bad, ma'am."

Lord, beautiful.

"How bad, Branch?"

"I deserve more."

Still working him, she forced it.

"Ask."

He didn't make her wait.

And his tone was low, almost hoarse, as he gave her what she wanted in more ways than one.

"Please, ma'am, spank me more."

Unbelievably amazing.

It had been so long, it was going to take everything not to come simply by giving him this.

But she held back and pushed it.

She had to, he needed it, *they* needed it.

But mostly he did.

And she had to give it to him.

So she jacked his cock and spanked his ass until her hand stung so badly she couldn't do it anymore, which was at the same time his head dropped.

Only then did she move in, pressing close to his side, gripping his dick in a tight hold at the base and sliding her flattened hand from the small of his back downward, digging her middle finger into the crevice, finding his hole and burying her finger to the second knuckle.

A noise sounded in his chest, there and gone, but as elusive as it was, it exploded between her legs like she'd made him roar with his orgasm.

Her legs were shaking but she had to go on. It was crucial.

Or she'd lose him.

So she did just that.

"I'm claiming you, Branch," she told him, shocked her voice came out as strong as it did when it was taking all she had to stop her entire body from trembling, or instead climbing on the hood and ordering him to fuck her silly. "I don't care you don't want my 'lame-ass shit,' you're taking it because right now, I own you."

He stayed still, her finger up his ass, her hand wrapped around his dick, his head bowed.

Amazing.

Maybe the most exquisite thing she'd ever seen.

"Do you understand me?" she asked.

He took a breath she could feel him take as her body moved with it.

Then he said, "Yes."

"Who owns you?"

"You do, ma'am."

"Yes, I damned well do," she forced out, extricated her finger but started stroking his cock as she reached back to the waistband of her trousers.

She unscrewed the cap with her thumb, letting it fall to the gravel, and still stroking his cock, she squeezed the lube down his crevice and she did that generously. Tossing the lube aside, she went back to him. Gathering it, she used it to ease her way as she fucked him with her finger, shallow, shallow, deeper, deeper, stroking at the front faster, harder.

All the while talking.

"Now, baby, I like how you take a punishment and can admit to being bad. So, we're going to get in your truck, and when you walk to the passenger side, I want you to pull your pants up but when you position in the truck for me, I want your cock and balls out for me to see, to touch if I want, you got me?"

"Yes, ma'am," he said tightly as pre-cum hit her fingers.

Pre-cum.

She'd earned his cum.

That Domme inside hadn't even made him hard.

Now, after just a jacking, a spanking and a hint of a fucking, she had his cum.

A drop.

But she was damn well going to take it.

And get more.

Her pussy quivered, her lips curled up and she kept stroking and fucking while talking.

"I'm going to drive us back to my house and then you're going to show me you can be a good boy. Right?"

"Your car," he bit off.

She slid two fingers inside him, drove deep and heard his bitten-back snarl.

Brilliant.

She pressed herself closer to his side as she pushed him further, fucking him harder, jacking him faster. "Don't worry about my car, baby. I got it covered."

She didn't but she hoped Josh and/or Barclay had their phones close, were light sleepers and could lend her a hand for the promise of a generous gift card to wherever they wanted.

"Ma'am," he grunted in a way she focused sharply on him.

It was a warning.

"You need to come, handsome?"

He puffed out a shallow breath as answer.

An answer she correctly guessed was yes.

She tightened her hand on his cock and quit stroking as she slid her fingers out of his ass.

"No coming, Branch. Not until I say."

"Yes, ma'am."

"Now, one more thing before we go."

She couldn't see it, but she felt it.

He braced.

She was taking him there.

He was fighting it.

But he wanted to go there.

She felt like screaming in glee.

She didn't.

She reached behind her and slid the plug out of her waistband.

Staying pressed close, she got up on tiptoe, kept hold of his cock and slid the tip up and down his crease.

"Look at me, handsome."

It took a moment but slowly, unbelievably slowly, he turned his head and looked down his shoulder at her.

She felt his eyes.

She felt his need.

She felt everything.

Now it was her job to make him feel the same thing.

"You feel that?" she whispered, gliding the plug back and forth through his lubed crack.

"Yes," he whispered back, that tone she'd never heard whispering over her nipples, her clit, beautiful agony.

"That's me, baby," she told him. "The woman who owns you, it's me. And you're going to take me inside. I'm going to fill you with me, Branch. You're going to sit beside me in your truck with me inside you, seated deep. And when we get to my house, you're going to wait until I pull you out of this truck by your cock and I'm going to pull you into my house by your cock because that's how I want to lead you into my house the first time I take my big boy there. Then I'm going to let you go. When I do, you're going to walk to the front of my house, up the stairs, take off your clothes and lie in my bed, naked on your belly with your legs spread for me, so when I follow you, the first thing I see is your ass with me planted deep."

"Yes, ma'am," he replied without hesitation.

She caught the tip of the plug at his hole and held his gaze.

She felt him go slightly up on his toes.

Heck yes.

He wanted that.

But she had to be sure he knew what he was getting.

"Do you understand what I'm saying to you, Branch?"

"Yes, ma'am."

"No, baby," she pressed closer, got up higher on her own toes, sliding the plug in barely half an inch. "Are you going to take me inside?"

She felt him still.

She also felt his silence cover her, shroud her, shroud them, as his eyes looked into hers in the moonlight.

The silence lengthened and that shroud turned heavy and suffocating.

And just when she thought he'd pull away, he said low, "Yes, ma'am."

No.

Now was when she felt like screaming with glee.

But it had to be him.

She would help and did, sliding the plug in another half an inch.

Then she ordered, "Take it."

He stayed still and stared at her.

"Take it, Branch," she demanded.

He didn't move.

"Take it," she whispered.

"Fuck," he bit out.

She twisted it lightly. "Take me inside."

His gaze burned through the moonlight.

Then she held his plug steady as he eased back. She watched his white teeth appear, sinking into his bottom lip, and she experienced a heady, sweet, convulsive mini climax as he opened for her then closed around her as he took her inside.

She cupped his ass, feeling the cool of her jewel against her fingers and thinking it might be the loveliest thing she'd ever touched.

But she didn't dally.

And she didn't care a bit her voice was breathy when she ordered, "Pants up, handsome, climb inside. Cock and balls available for me to play with on the ride. Let's go home."

six

He Was Fucked

BRANCH

He was fucked.

Totally fucked.

As he lay on his stomach in her huge-ass frilly bed in her frilly bedroom, naked, his plugged ass pointed toward the stairs, his rock-hard cock in agony trapped under him, his balls hanging so heavy, they didn't need a weight tied to them to bring the pain, he knew without a doubt he was fucked.

She was good.

With a lot of things.

Damn, with *everything*.

This included with a whip.

Christ, watching her wield one, it was a wonder he didn't get instantly hard and come in his pants.

And she was good with the boss.

At first it was cute, that little thing with her bouncing curly hair dragging him around by his belt, rapping out orders.

But it wasn't cute.

She had a grip of steel.

It was fucking *hot*.

But Jesus, when she got down to business, she was *hands right the fuck on*.

And fingers.

He should have pulled away, cut her verbally like the first time, dug his own keys out of those sweet, tight, leather pants, swung into his truck and left her standing there.

But did he do that?

Fuck no.

He'd slid her plug inside his own damned self.

And he'd loved taking every inch.

That bitch was heavy up his ass, tight, cool, fucking amazing. He had no idea what it was made of but he'd never felt anything like it.

Nor anything quite as good.

Even better with his ass still hot from her spanking.

The woman had magic hands. He didn't know a single Domme who could withstand delivering a tanning that thorough without needing to stop it to end her own pain.

Evangeline did, though. She kept at him until the sting of each crack felt like a detonation in his balls.

It was a miracle he didn't blow.

Hell, sitting in the passenger seat of his own truck, cock and balls out, ass hot from his punishment, full of whatever she'd given him, trying not to fidget or wrap his fist around his dick and take care of business, he got even harder just watching her standing at the hood, head bent to her phone, texting then talking—she was so easy to look at. To watch.

All this before she swung in *his* seat, pulled that fucker all the way forward so her legs could reach the pedals (seeing as she'd kicked off her shoes) and she'd started *his* baby up, reversed out and headed them to Phoenix.

But her torture wasn't over.

He should never have called her lame-ass.

He should have just walked out of Aryas's red room.

She was on a mission.

And he was fucked.

He knew this because he didn't sit beside her, exposed to her, and she ignored him like many Dommes would do to lengthen his punishment.

Oh no.

Fuck no.

The woman played with him nearly the entire way. Stroking him. Circling the tip. Cupping his balls. Squeezing gently. Whispering, "Lord, my cock is so very pretty," in that voice of hers.

And once, at a stoplight, she'd opened her purse, used the rearview mirror to put on that deep red, sexy fucking lipstick of hers.

Then she'd dropped the lipstick in her purse, tossed it in the backseat, turned to him and declared, "Something's missing, handsome."

And with that, she undid her seatbelt, bent right over him and took him inside, tightening her lips around his dick.

As soon as she was there, she was gone, leaving a red ring of lipstick just under his cock head.

Marking him.

That move might not have been inspired.

But the way she did it, where he was, how he was positioned for her, his ass heated and full . . . Christ.

The woman was genius.

And he was fucked.

He had no idea how he held himself from blowing all the way to Phoenix.

What he did know was that she was good to her word.

She drove them to her house, parked under her carport, reached to the backseat and grabbed her purse, put on her shoes, jumped out and rounded the hood. When she got to his side, she pulled him out by his dick, led him in with his dick, and then let him go before she lightly smacked his ass and declared, "You know what I want, baby."

She'd then thrown her purse on the near-minuscule island of her kitchen and gone to the fridge.

He should have walked out the door.

Instead, because he was fucked in a number of ways, including, it would seem, the head, he walked through her house, up her stairs, found she'd left a light on by the bed, got naked and got in position for her.

He needed to come.

He needed to come and then go.

Then he needed to get his head screwed on straight and find someone other than Whitney to take care of business.

Not through Aryas.

Yeah, he needed to make that happen however that had to happen.

But never again through Aryas.

And he needed to make sure Evangeline Brooks didn't cross his path again.

What the fuck she was doing at a Pound, he couldn't believe.

But he knew.

She was out for him.

He didn't know how to take that and with his cock throbbing, his balls aching and his whole focus centered on hearing her come up the stairs so she could make him blow, he didn't have it in him to consider it.

He needed to come.

And then go.

He felt her before he heard the soft footfalls of her feet on carpet.

His head to the side, he saw her enter his vision, come right to him and sit down on the bed by his hip.

As he was becoming accustomed, she didn't fuck around being hands-on.

She reached between his legs, gently cupped his balls and ordered softly, "Scooch over to the middle a little, handsome."

With her still having a hold on him, he did as told.

When he did, she slid into the bed further, but only to stay seated at his side.

However, her hand slid up and he felt her cover his plug in his ass.

"Do you know how pretty this is?"

He just looked up at her, arms crossed under him on the pillow, cheek to them.

"It's got a blue jewel at the hilt," she shared.

He thought of seeing her sweet ass plugged with something like that and his hard-on raged harder.

But a talented Domme with her sub plugged like that?

A sub who'd slid her inside himself?

Fuck.

He was fucked.

Her attention moved to his ass as she stroked along the cleft, murmuring to herself like he wasn't there, "God, baby, I want to eat you all around that, feel it against my tongue."

Branch closed his eyes so he wouldn't thrust into the mattress or open his mouth and beg her to do just that.

Her little mouth shoved up his ass?

Fuck.

Her hand moved, tenderly caressing his ass cheeks, he opened his eyes and she kept murmuring toward his backside.

"You're all red, Branch. So unbelievably pretty." Her attention came back to his face. "I'm afraid I like it so much, I might spank you even if you haven't earned it."

Before he could react to that (thankfully), she bent toward him suddenly, her hand going between his legs to cup his balls again.

"But you'll be bad, won't you?" she asked close to his face.

"Probably," he answered.

She grinned.

Cute and hot.

Damn.

"I'm sure you will. But be very bad, Branch. I like the way you take your punishments. but more, I have a feeling you can take a lot and I want to see how far that will go."

He wanted that too.

So much, he felt his balls tighten at the thought.

Something she undoubtedly could feel too.

He decided not to speak again.

"Open your legs wide for me," she ordered.

He slid his legs open wide.

She massaged his balls and his eyes slid closed at the feel but he snapped them back open.

"You can like that baby," she cooed.

Branch remained silent.

"Now he's being bad," she whispered, still massaging him.

Christ, he needed to thrust.

"Do you like what you're feeling, Branch?" she pushed.

"Yes," he bit out.

"Lift up a little bit at your knees, I want your cock."

Goddamn it.

He wanted her to want his cock.

And he wanted her to have it.

He did as told.

She went right in.

He couldn't stop his eyes closing at the beauty of her firm, strong, little hand gently jacking him and he decided to keep them that way even if in his mind's eye he could see those long, red-tipped fingernails on her small hand wrapped around his dick.

Still, it was better if he couldn't see the real her.

Just feeling her was bad enough.

"I'm going to fuck you like this, handsome. Take your ass and stroke your cock. No, make you fuck yourself while you fuck my hand. Actually, both."

Right, she also needed to quit talking.

"Do you want that, Branch?"

With a goodly amount of effort, he held onto his control and opened his eyes. "Right now?"

Another small smile. "Not right now, baby. You haven't earned a good fucking."

"Too bad," he muttered, dropping his gaze to her tits, which was a bad place to put it, so he closed his eyes again as she kept at his dick.

"I'll take that as a yes."

She knew what she was doing, telling him what she was going to do . . . later.

Making him want a later.

And he had to keep his shit so he wouldn't lose the strength to get his head together and end this.

He'd take tonight.

And that was it.

"You can settle back down, Branch," she said, her hand drifting away, over his balls, through his ass, along his right cheek and over, down his other, and soothing the back of his thigh as he regained the agony of lying on his raging hard dick.

Then she slid off the bed.

He watched her walk to the bathroom—eyes trained on her ass in those pants—before he lost sight of her.

She came back with the lace shirt off and a wet washcloth in her hand.

She sat back on the bed and put the warm cloth to his back.

"Get this cleaned and get ointment on it," she said quietly.

"You don't need to—"

"Shut up, Branch."

He shut up.

She cleaned the marks that he knew didn't need it. He'd had worse. A lot worse. They weren't deep or long. They wouldn't heal great, but he didn't give a shit.

When she'd done that, she went back to the bathroom and

returned with a tube of ointment. She sat again beside him and carefully oozed it on, spreading it along his cuts.

He closed his eyes and tried to force his mind to a variety of things.

All he felt was her touch.

Not sexual.

Nurturing.

Goddamn her.

And, likely because of the feel of it, something he hadn't felt in a very long time, for the first time in years, he thought about Tara. His first real Mistress, and she would have been his last if he hadn't fucked it up.

They fell into it so easy. The life and then their lives.

So he wasn't equipped to handle it when it got hard.

And then she was just . . . gone.

He opened his eyes.

Evangeline finished, and without a word, slid off the bed.

He watched her walk away, focusing on her now, Evangeline.

His one-night-only, seriously talented Mistress.

He'd give himself this.

Come and gone.

He didn't deserve it but fuck it.

Too many shit scenes with Whitney and the like of her. Aryas playing his games thinking Branch wouldn't cotton on, every once in a while taking what they could give and getting the fuck gone.

Yeah.

Just like that.

He'd let himself have Evangeline.

One night only.

Then he'd get the fuck gone.

She came back and he blinked.

No leather pants or silk bustier.

No makeup.

She was in a dark-blue, satin nightie that barely covered her pubis.

His cock might have been calming down but it pulsed at the sight of her.

She went right to the nightstand and turned out the light.

The room blackened then opened up slightly when he became accustomed to the moonlight streaming through the windows in the ceiling.

He heard the nightstand drawer open and close and watched her shadow move into the bed on her knees.

She got between his legs.

He stiffened.

But he went solid when he felt her lips brush his ass cheek. The small of his back.

Up.

Along a scar.

Another one.

Up.

She kissed his shoulder.

Up.

Her lips slid along the side of his neck. Her thighs now pressed into his ass, he could smell her.

Her perfume was faint, but, damn, it was pretty.

Shit, she was unraveling him.

"You're being so good, just a little fucking, baby," she whispered in his ear. "Like before, slide your knees up a bit."

Damn, she wasn't unraveling him.

She was going to kill him.

And the shit of it was, he wanted to go at her hands.

He slid his knees up.

He felt the curls of her hair glide along his skin as she moved back down.

She took hold of his plug and with the other hand reached under and cupped his balls.

"Want this?" she asked.

Goddamn her.

"Branch, do you want this?"

"Yes," he ground out.

And fuck him, he didn't.

He needed it.

"Ask for it."

Goddamn her.

"Fuck me, ma'am."

"As you like it, baby," she whispered, her hand moving to his dick, the plug gliding out, and Christ, beautiful, so goddamned sweet, she glided it back in.

So.

Goddamned.

Sweet.

She stroked his dick and she fucked him rhythmically, gentle but deep, doing it in an outstanding way Whitney couldn't dream of offering, but she didn't do it long.

Not nearly long enough.

She filled him, her hand left his dick and then he heard her vibrator turn on and felt her fingers curl into his still raw ass, her nails digging in.

She was making herself come between his legs so he could hear, he could sense, but he couldn't see or feel.

"Stay in position, handsome, I want my jewel winking at me."

God.

Damn.

Her.

He needed to thrust.

He needed her to take his ass.

He needed to drive his cock inside her—mouth, pussy, hole, he didn't give a fuck. He needed to *move*, not lay there slightly up on his knees, listening to the hot noises she made as she took herself there, undoubtedly staring at the plug she'd planted up his ass.

And he was entirely, thoroughly, totally fucked because he needed something else more.

And she knew what that was.

She knew he got off on every fucking second of staying in position for her, helping her take herself there.

Lame-ass?

Christ, he was a moron.

Her nails scored through the sensitized flesh of his ass cheek when he listened to her slip over the edge and he had no fucking clue how he found the control not to roll over just to watch, it sounded that damned gorgeous.

She fell forward when she was done, her forehead to his back, side rib cage, her hair tumbling all around, obviously not giving a shit about the ointment in her curls. The vibrator went off but her hand slid around his hip, to his dick, and closed firm.

"Relax, baby," she whispered against his skin, her low voice wispy, sexy.

Beautiful.

He lowered his hips and she lazily stroked him against the mattress as he felt her breath even against his skin.

When she'd recovered, gently, she released him, moved. He felt her on all fours over him and he braced, waiting, even fucking hoping.

But all he heard was her putting her vibrator on the nightstand.

Then she shifted to his opposite side, the bed moving slightly with her, and she curled a thigh over the top of his ass, pressed herself against his side. He turned his head her way and looked down to see her arms up, neck bent, her face resting on her hands that were resting at his lat.

And he heard her mouth murmur, "Sleep now, Branch."

Was she fucking kidding?

"Ma'am."

She hooked her calf around the side of his hip and rubbed her pussy against the other side. He could feel the wet silk of her panties and he almost didn't swallow his groan.

"You didn't think I'd let you come tonight, did you?"

Goddamn her.

He didn't reply.

"Sleep, handsome," she said on a leg squeeze of his hips.

With his cock that hard, his still-stinging ass full, his legs spread, aching balls hanging in the breeze, and her wrapped around him, she wanted him to sleep?

"Do you need covers?" she asked.

"That'd be good," he grunted.

"Don't move," she ordered.

Terrific.

He learned his mistake when she did move, disengaging to get on her knees beside him.

She yanked the covers out from under him, this scoring through his dick like a hot poker traced along it, and once she'd freed them, she pulled them out from under her knees, settled in just as she was and flicked the covers high over both of them.

Wrapping them in her frilly covers in her frilly bedroom with her little, warm, sweet body tucked tight to his side.

He should have let them sleep on the covers.

It took her seconds to melt into him in sleep.

He liked her feel.

Her smell.

Her weight.

His body trapped by her thigh.

And there it was.

Yup.

He was fucked.

Branch woke to Evangeline stroking the back of his thigh.

"Wake up, handsome," she whispered in his ear.

Jesus.

How did he sleep?

"Roll over, baby, I feel like sucking cock," she ordered.

Jesus.

He didn't hesitate, he rolled.

She moved too, tossing the covers off them, but he was already hard with a morning erection, head foggy with sleep and full of the memories of what she'd done to him the night before, he didn't feel the cool air hit his skin.

She shifted between his legs.

Then she put her hands behind his knees as he stared to the windows in the ceiling and tried to assess what time it was.

It was February. Sun still not out too early, light in the sky, but it was barely dawn.

These thoughts flew from his head as she put pressure behind his knees and his eyes moved to her.

"I want them up and cocked for me, please."

He did as told, lifting his knees and cocking them.

She moved her hands from behind his knees to the sides when his calves would have trapped them.

"Wide," she demanded.

Fuck, she was good.

He opened his legs wider.

"More, Branch," she said, giving a slight press to the sides of his knees.

He opened them wider until he felt a stretch down the insides of his thighs. It didn't hurt, but he couldn't ignore it.

And it went right to his balls and hole.

"That's it," she whispered.

Replacing her hand at his left knee with her mouth, she trailed it down.

Down.

Before she got to him, she lifted her gaze and caught his.

"I want you watching."

Oh, he'd be watching.

"Yes, ma'am."

She grinned, slid just the tip of her tongue out and grasped his cock in her fist.

She lifted it from his stomach to her tongue and touched it, tip to tip.

He bit his lip.

God, fuck, shit, he hoped he'd earned his orgasm.

She ran the tip of her tongue down to the base, between his testicles, and up.

Then she gobbled him deep.

Fuck, he'd never seen anything that pretty.

And the feel of her?

Christ.

The brilliance of it made him do something else he hadn't done in years.

Lose control and close his eyes as he dug his head into the pillows. He couldn't help it. Her sweet, hot mouth was something.

She raked her nails down the back of his thigh and he lost her mouth.

"Did I say watch?" she asked when he looked between his legs.

"Yes, ma'am."

"Then watch, Branch," she demanded.

"Yes, ma'am."

Hands on, and apparently mouth on, she didn't hesitate again to suck him deep and God, fuck, *shit*, it took all he had to watch her pretty curls, pretty mouth, and pretty face bobbing on his dick, taking him deep, the tip of his cock hitting the back of her throat, and not throw back his head and groan.

Phenomenal.

She kept going as she ran her hands up his thighs, pressing them wider, the stretch deepening, the pain coming, his ass lifting, his cock gliding into her mouth.

Magnificent.

Pure, fucking glory.

He took it and he took more and he watched the whole show, his ass tightening around his plug, his balls hanging heavy, he couldn't help it and didn't care she ended it and tanned him again.

He started rocking into her mouth.

She slid up and breathed, "*Yes*," against the tip and went at him again, this time now with her hand, meeting it with her lips. Hand up, lips down, hand down, lips up, all the while he added to the sweet torture, rocking into each stroke.

Fucking ecstasy.

He took it and he took more and he loved every goddamned second.

And he did it until he could take no more.

"Ma'am," he grunted.

She released him and looked up.

"My big boy need to come?"

"Yes," he puffed out.

Suddenly, she was between his legs, her warm, soft pelvis resting on the heated hardness of his, her face in his, her hand wrapped around the side of his neck, fingers back in his hair, holding his head up.

"In ten minutes, you're going to leave," she declared and he just managed to bite back an oath. "You keep me inside you. You can slide me out to shower and get on with your day. I'm going to give you my number. At nine o'clock, you text me. Then you slide me back in and you take your fist to your cock but you do not come, Branch. You text me when you've had enough. You slide me out. You go about your day. At one o'clock, you text me back. You take me inside. You jack your cock for me until you're about to come but you do not come, handsome. You text me when you're done. You slide me out. And at seven o'clock tonight, you come to me, full of me, and then, my big boy, I'll take care of you."

She had him.

Christ, shit, fuck.

She had him.

"You'll make me come, ma'am?" he bit out.

"How do you want it?" she asked.

"Like you said."

"Say it."

"Fuck me, jack me."

"By then, you'll have earned it. So that's what you'll get."

"Then give me your number."

She smiled brilliantly at him and the world shrank.

There was nothing.

Nothing but her pretty face and that brilliant smile lighting a soul gone dark.

His soul.

His soul that had been dark far longer than it took Di, Piz, Lex, Benetta and Rob to die.

No, it had gone dark years earlier, after he'd finished it with Tara and she'd fucked up by placing an ad and getting herself a "sub" who wasn't big on people who liked kink so the motherfucker had caved her head in.

All that burned away with the brightness of Evangeline's smile.

Shit.

"I'll give you what you want, handsome, but I'm me. I might have to get creative."

"You let me blow, you can do whatever the fuck you want."

Her smile got bigger.

Oh yeah.

Shit yeah.

Totally fucked.

And he knew it more when, ten minutes later, he walked out of her house to his truck, clothed, still plugged, her number written in dark red lipstick on his chest, his cock ringed with the same.

He knew it even more when he got off on the feel of her everywhere, inside him, the rasp of his still-hard dick against his fly, and the first thing he did (after shifting the seat back) was lean over, open his glove box, find a pen, some paper, and open his shirt so he got her number down before it smudged.

But he knew it the most when he finally got his shit together enough to buckle in, start his baby up and back out of her drive, feeling relief that, by some miracle wrought by an enchantress, her Fiat was parked at the curb.

seven

Domesticity

EVANGELINE

Evangeline stood at the stove, stirring the meat sauce, her head bent to her texts.

Not a problem, read Barclay's text, which had just come in as a late reply to the one she'd sent that morning expressing gratitude for him coming to her house, grabbing the key to her car, which she'd put in a pot outside, then driving all the way out to fetch it and return it. *And don't worry about the gift card. Just tell me you found who you were looking for.*

Definitely.

Barclay was the decent kind of guy.

But now what did she do?

People at the Pound saw her with Branch and she didn't know those people. She didn't know if he knew those people. She didn't know if that was going to be a problem for him.

What she did know was that she was precluded from talking about him in any way.

And Barclay was obviously worried about the unknown person someone he barely knew was concerned about.

It's all good. And again, I really appreciate you helping out. If no gift card, then I'm making you dinner. And trust me, I love cooking and I'm good at it. I'll make it worth a way too early in the morning drive out to no man's land, she texted back.

She put the spoon aside for the meat sauce, looked at the clock and turned on the flame under water she'd already boiled so when she needed it ready to roll, it would be.

Her phone buzzed in her hand and she looked down at it to read Barclay's reply of, *You're on, beautiful.*

She grinned.

Then she moved her thumb on her phone to get to her list of texts and touched the listing titled "MBB" (My Big Boy).

The text string came up.

9:01: *Starting.*
9:13: *Done.*
1:03: *Again.*
1:12: *Done.*

Branch whatever-his-name-was.

Man of few words, even in texts.

Reading it (again), Evangeline's grin turned into a huge smile.

She'd had hope, but she couldn't be sure. He'd left with her toy inside him and a promise to text and come back that night to let her finish him off.

This could have been a tactical error. He was no novice submissive. He would know, regardless of her assertions she owned him, that her giving him instructions to carry out during the day meant something deeper. And he'd know what that deep meant.

And for Branch, that could be a big problem.

Not to mention life, separation and time had ways of messing with your head. Considering what Evangeline had run into last night at the Pound, Branch's head was already messed up with something she'd decided *she* was going to straighten out.

It wouldn't be a stretch to think that, being away from her, he'd let that mess talk him into not coming back to get what he needed.

But he'd texted. He'd done what she'd told him to do (she was sure of it—if he wanted to be a good boy, she was realizing he could be *very* good).

Even so, between 1:12 and—she checked the clock again—6:52, he could change his mind.

Her heart was telling her he wouldn't.

Whether it was his heart, his head or, the biggest probability, his cock telling him to come back, she would probably never know.

But she was betting one of them would.

On this thought, she started to put her phone down in order to pick up her wineglass to take a sip when it rang.

She looked at the number. It was out of state and she didn't recognize it, but seeing as her business was her business, that happened often, therefore she answered the call with, "Evangeline Brooks."

"Evangeline."

Damn.

She knew that voice.

"Damian," she replied.

He'd gotten a new number, e-mailed it to her, but she'd never programmed it in.

Obviously he hadn't lost her number.

"How's it going, my beautiful girl?"

She looked to the clock again, not needing to be on the phone with Damian when Branch arrived but needing to do a variety of other things to finish off dinner and she had to have it all as ready as possible when Branch showed.

She was suspecting he wasn't big on domesticity and getting-to-know-you activities so she had to be resourceful, because to break through why she was guessing he'd formed that marble around him she had to find a way to make this not (entirely) about how hard she could make him come.

She had to make it about who they were and how what they had could fit into life.

"It's going good, Damian," she replied, rechecking that the oven was preheating for the bread. "Aryas told me you were back in town."

"Yes. I'll probably be here for a year, depending on how this project goes, maybe longer."

"It'll be good to have you back."

"It's good to hear you say that, Evangeline."

She drew in breath and tucked the phone between ear and shoulder so she could dress the salad, doing so now not only to have everything ready when Branch arrived but also to avoid her guilt that she'd given Damian any impression she might not want him back in her life.

"Listen, I've got something happening in about five minutes so it's great to hear from you, honey, but I can't talk long," she gave him the truth, if not a detailed one. "Maybe we can do lunch sometime soon? Catch up?"

"It's good to hear you say that too, sweetheart," he murmured, sounding like he meant that a good deal.

She drew in another breath.

Damian kept talking.

"Aryas said you'd checked out. Word is, you're checking back in."

"Yes, well, it was time," she shared. "It was actually time months ago but I got addicted to selling houses and being able to pay for the new shake-style roof my house needed about seven years ago that looks so amazing, if I wasn't scared of heights, I'd climb up a ladder and kiss it, so I let it go but, well . . . now I'm back."

"Glad of that, Leenie."

"So we'll do lunch."

"You should come to the club."

Damn it.

"Damian—"

"Aryas says you've checked back in but not that far in."

"Taking baby steps," she lied.

Last night, she'd taken one giant leap for Mistress-kind.

"Take one with me. I'll hit the Honey. Find a sub. Let you know. You can come, outside the glass, Evangeline. Watch me work." His voice lowered. "I know how you like to watch me work." Before she could get a word in, his tone returned to normal, with a hint of amused when he finished, "Get your juices flowing again."

She cut her eyes to the door when she saw headlights beaming along her driveway.

Oh, her juices were flowing.

Damn it!

"We'll talk about it later."

It was like she didn't say anything. "Or we can watch Leigh with her stud and do it together. I hear the work she does with him is sensational."

This made Evangeline press her lips together.

Although it could not be said she didn't like to watch (because she very much did), she, personally, was not into exhibition. It was just something she wasn't big on doing. If a sub had earned a punishment, she might work with them with the blinds up in a playroom at the Honey, but she, herself, would not perform. She'd make them perform.

But this kind of occasion was rare.

When she interacted with a submissive in any real, intimate way, she wanted privacy, for her, for her sub, for the focus she wanted them both to have on each other and what they were doing, feeling, sharing.

She had seen Amélie play with many of her toys.

But the idea of watching her play with the man she lived with, the man who, if how she talked about him, how she looked when she talked about him, and how others looked knowingly at her when she talked about him, would be in her life for the rest of it, didn't appeal to her in any way.

Both, she would assume, very much enjoyed showing off the beauty they could make together.

It was just Evangeline that felt that was an invasion she couldn't perpetrate.

"I'll call you," she said hurriedly, moving to the packet of spaghetti to put it in the water. "We'll make lunch plans. Talk about it then. But now, Damian, I'm so sorry, but I have to go."

"All right, Leenie. Dinner, sometime soon."

Dinner?

She didn't say dinner.

"I'll call you," she promised.

"If you don't, I'll find you."

She stilled

He'd *find* her?

" 'Bye, Leenie."

"Goodbye, Damian."

He disconnected.

She tossed her phone down, dumped the entire packet of spaghetti in the rolling water (who knew? Branch wasn't a huge guy but he still had a lot of muscle to fuel, so he could be a huge eater) and the door to the kitchen opened.

Branch walked in and stopped dead, hand on the door handle, not even closing the door, eyes to the stove, nostrils flaring at the smells in the air, the entirety of his manner alert and on edge.

Nope.

Not into domesticity and getting to know you.

His gaze cut to her. "Dinner?"

"I'm hungry," she replied.

"Evangeline—"

"I got home only half an hour ago."

Lie.

For the herbs and diced pepperoni she added to her meat sauce, that enhanced the flavor exponentially, to do their job, it needed at least that amount of simmering, usually more. She'd been home an hour and a quarter and hadn't even taken off her skirt and blouse (but she did take off her shoes) before she started cooking.

"If you've eaten, you can hang out while I do it. If you haven't, you can eat with me," she finished.

"I can also come back in an hour," he said low.

She locked eyes with him.

He needed it played this way?

She'd play it any way he needed.

"No, you cannot." she replied just as low.

They battled with their eyes.

When he didn't back down, she asked softly, "Do you want to experience what I've decided to do to make my big boy come for me?"

His delay in reply lasted too long, forcing her stomach to twist as panic edged in.

But finally, he answered curtly, "Yes."

"Then you wait until I eat. Now, Branch, have you eaten?"

His gaze moved back to the stove before returning to her. "Not anything that was as good as that looks and smells."

He had no idea, but she was about to rock his world.

This being, of course, before she hoped to God she *rocked his world*.

"Then come in, grab a beer. Dinner will be ready in ten minutes."

She wasn't about to tell him she didn't drink beer. The five varieties currently in her fridge she'd purchased guessing he did, but not knowing what he liked.

Instead, she got busy finishing the meal, and as she did so, she came to understand the flaw in her plan.

To Branch, what was going on between them was not about getting to know you. She could have no idea what Aryas shared, but her guess was that Branch would need some kind of assertion that the Domme Aryas was setting him up with would know the score. Therefore, he would assume Evangeline knew the score (and she did).

She was just changing the score.

Something he didn't know and she couldn't let on.

Therefore, after he got his beer (he was an ale drinker, good to know) he moved (no cargo pants this time, just an olive drab cargo shirt and jeans, both looking awesome on him) to the island and she had no conversational gambit.

And as she carried on sorting out dinner, he didn't offer one.

Instead, she realized with some disquiet, he stood still at the island with his hand wrapped around the beer bottle and stared out her kitchen window, looking both oddly uncomfortable and like the view to her pool was not fascinating, but a lifeline.

Surreptitiously watching him, suddenly she was questioning the wisdom of forcing even half an hour of domesticity on Branch whatever-his-last-name-was.

At least this early in the game.

Just as suddenly, she had an idea that segued into the idea she'd had earlier that would make all of this possibly easier on him.

So after she pulled out the bread, drained the pasta and turned to him to hand him one of the two plates she got down, she declared, "Usually, I eat in front of the TV. Go ahead and dig in."

And with that, she piled up her plate, topped up her wineglass and went to the TV.

By the time he joined her (with double the food on his plate— apparently whatever he had for dinner *really* didn't cut it), she had a DIY program on that she was hoping they'd both find interesting enough while she wowed him (she hoped) with her cooking and then got him into the zone where he was clearly far more comfortable being.

"You put pepperoni in your tomato sauce?" he asked.

With her feet up on the coffee table, nestled in the corner of her couch opposite Branch, who was sitting both feet on the floor in the corner of his, hunched over his plate like he was going to dine and dash in her home, she looked to him.

"It isn't tomato sauce, as such. It's *meat* sauce," she answered.

He looked back to the TV, shoveling in spaghetti and muttering, "Now I get why you got that ass."

For a second, she froze at what sounded like an insult.

"Next time, double it," he kept muttering.

She grinned at her fork before she pushed it into her mouth.

Apparently, she wasn't the only one who liked ass.

"Can you give me the secret to this bread, or if you do, will you have to kill me?"

God, he was being funny.

Which meant he was killing her.

In a good way.

There was nothing better than a man who was funny.

Except a beautiful man with a great ass who liked her ass and her cooking *and* her playing with him the way she liked to play ... who was funny.

"I brush it with olive oil and a little truffle oil before I sprinkle on the cheese," she answered.

See?

She'd definitely not been home just half an hour.

"Shit's amazing," he mumbled.

She felt like doing a cartwheel.

She kept her seat and kept eating.

"My guess is, the answer is a yes," he went on, still eating, eyes to the TV, "but to confirm. You come lookin' for me at the Pound last night?"

"Yes," she answered immediately.

His gaze slid to her. "Why?"

Her gaze stayed on him. "Because you're mine."

He seemed to consider that, but only for a few seconds, before he returned, "Not then."

"Oh yes you were, handsome," she replied quietly. "You just didn't know it yet."

He adjusted his ass in the seat, the only time he showed physically that he'd come to her as told, and murmured, eyes back to the TV, "Well, I do now."

"Excellent," she murmured back and resumed eating and not quite watching the TV.

But as she did, a thought occurred to her and, although it was risky, she decided to go with it.

"I'd been looking for you a long time, Branch," she admitted.

His attention came back to her but he said nothing.

"You weren't easy to find."

"Stunned you managed it. Think you can guess I'm a man who, if he doesn't want to be found, makes that so."

"It took me a month and I had to attend a Pound to manage it," she shared.

"Determined," he replied.

"I told you I liked what I saw in the red room," she reminded him. "If you didn't learn this last night, I get what I want and I don't mind being creative in doing it."

There seemed to be humor there and gone before he noted, "Saw you wield that whip, so obviously you can take care of yourself, but before that, would have said you showin' there wasn't real smart."

"There was no threat there," she returned. "People so zoned out they can barely stand are hardly in a position to bother a sober woman with a baton even if she isn't exactly a hulk and she's wearing six-inch platforms."

"It was a tame night."

She felt her eyes grow big.

"And it was early," he continued.

Early?

It'd been after one in the morning.

"What'd I miss?" she asked, curious.

"Catfights. Overdoses. Voyeurs hearing about it, showing, thinking they can watch and getting sucked in, then freaking way the fuck out either because of a bad trip or, say, they're a chick and it strikes them all of a sudden that they might not have wanted to eat some passed-out junkie's pussy."

Her lip curled.

Branch watched it with no expression before he spoke on.

"Yeah, like I said," he looked back to the TV, "last night was a tame night."

"Do you go there often?"

"Nope."

That was good.

"You don't go there at all now, Branch."

Still hunched over his plate, facing the TV, his gaze slid to hers. Before he could respond, she kept at him.

"You have someone else that takes care of you?"

"Evange—"

"She's gone," Evangeline stated quietly, but firmly. "Be she one or multiple, Branch. When I said you're mine, you're mine, handsome. I do not share."

He held her gaze

Then he looked away and murmured, "Not a loss. She sucks at it."

Evangeline carefully and silently let out a long breath of not only relief but exultation because he didn't fight it and the "She sucks at it" inferred that he felt Evangeline did not.

He finished his food first and she took her time finishing hers, doing this purposefully, regardless of the fact that he seemed uncomfortable again, sitting on the couch with her, still hunched over his now empty plate like he didn't know what to do with himself.

And watching him without letting on she was, she had the troubling thought that maybe with this beautiful man she'd bitten off more than she could chew.

It was time to get him to a place where he felt safe.

She took her feet off the coffee table and stood up.

His head tipped back and he straightened in the seat when she did, watching her and looking like he'd join her.

Evangeline went right to him and took his plate but bent over him.

"Now, Branch, I'm relaxed and in a place where I'm good to spend a lot of time on you without anything but you on my mind. So I'm going to go tidy up, you're going to prepare for me and I'll explain," she told him. "When I get back, I want you naked, on this couch, displayed for me. Your back to the corner, legs and feet up, one calf on the back of couch, the other thigh splayed wide to the side. I want your arms out, one down the back, one down the arm, and when I get to work, you'll keep them there. When I return, baby, I wanna see all of you with easy access, I want you hard for me and I want to see my jewel buried deep. Do you understand your instructions?"

He slid immediately into his role and he did it with a brief, flashing flare in his eyes that, although brief, said everything she needed to know.

He was in his safe place.

He was hers.

"Yes, ma'am."

She nodded and bent closer. "Right, now, before I go, we have to have two quick chats. One, what's your safe word?"

"Don't have one."

"Everyone has one."

His gaze went intent and he enunciated his next two words precisely. "I don't."

He knew it but she felt it pertinent to say regardless.

"You have to know with your experience that that's not smart."

"What I know with my experience, Evangeline, is that works for me."

Evangeline tipped her head slightly to the side. "Anything goes?"

"You wanna do it to me, I can take it."

She had no doubt.

Or at least the things he thought she might do.

Sitting with her and enjoying a meal she cooked while doing something normal like watching TV, not a chance.

They'd get to that.

Maybe.

If she managed to wring a miracle and broke through.

"Right," she carried on, "as that's the case, the second part of our chat might now be moot but I'm going to ask it anyway because that's how I play it. Are you trained?"

"Been in the game a long time. Anything you want, I'll do it."

She bent even closer. "Your ass, Branch. I mean your ass. You've been very good. You requested a fucking. You're going to get one. How much can you take?"

Another flare, less brief this time, and she felt her pussy quiver.

"Whatever you wanna give me, Evangeline, I will take it."

"I feel like testing you, baby," she warned.

"I'll pass," he growled. "So bring it on."

Her big boy.

Raring to go.

Lovely.

She nodded and straightened. "Prepare for me, handsome."

With that, she walked away.

She did the dishes then she slid her feet in her flip-flops and went out to her studio to get what she needed.

When she was in her playroom, she didn't think of having Branch out there, something she hoped to have, and soon.

Now, she wanted to take him in the intimacy of her home. She wanted him surrounded by her in that way, not her playroom, *her*, her life, her things, making him a part of it.

Evangeline took her time with all this. She wanted Branch to understand he was worth that time, and more, she would be worth the wait.

Finally, after returning, having flipped off her shoes, on slightly shaking legs, more than ready to get on with the evening's festivities, she went back to the family room and rounded the couch on her side so she could see him fully positioned in the corner of his.

He was exactly as she'd told him to be, and that was an extraordinary sight to see.

But he was also more.

He was displayed for her on her couch, legs up and open, cock hard, balls heavy, plug winking, eyes on her, alert, exposing some arousal in his expression (if not all she'd like to see, but that, she was learning, was Branch—she'd get him there with that too), and he had no hang-ups.

He didn't look anxious. He didn't look tense. He didn't look embarrassed.

He looked ready to play.

He was a thing of beauty.

She put the stack of towels down on the coffee table, the toys she'd selected hidden among the folds, and turned back to him.

Shimmying up her tight skirt a smidge, she entered the couch on a knee between his legs.

She leaned in close to his face but not touching him.

"Now to get you ready, handsome," she whispered.

He just held her eyes.

She moved down his chest, ignoring the scars she'd like to soothe with her fingers, her lips, she kissed his right nipple. His left. Down, she kissed his belly. Down, she kissed the tip of his hard cock. And down, she kissed his sac, giving herself the pleasure of drawing in his scent there, something she'd discovered that morning during her blowjob she very much liked.

Back up, she went to work on his nipples, nibbling, tonguing, sucking. She engaged her hand on his other one to twist and pull.

She knew he was feeling it when he squirmed under her.

With all his experience, he was still sensitive there.

Excellent news.

She switched nipples, mouth and fingers, and kept at it until she got more squirming.

Only then did she lift slightly away and reach out to the towel. Flipping over an edge, she exposed what he'd be getting that night.

And heard the light hiss of his breath.

Her big boy could take what she could give?

They would see.

She fought a smile and nabbed a nipple clamp.

Holding herself away, she pinched and pulled a nipple, her gaze to his face.

He held hers like it was a dare, only a slight clenching of his teeth exposing she was affecting him.

Being a bad boy, holding back.

She'd get him.

She clamped the nipple and did it so tight, his jaw hardened.

God, she loved the look of that.

"Is that okay, Branch?"

"Yeah," he pushed out.

He felt pain.

But he liked it.

"Good," she murmured and went to work on the other nipple.

The instant she finished clamping it, she wrapped her hand around his dick and pumped.

A muscle jerked up his cheek.

She allowed her eyes to wander him, splayed for her, nipples clamped, cock thick and reddening, and she saw his ass clenching around his plug as her hand stroked.

And she knew she could have that moment and that moment alone, he could get up and walk out, and she would be okay with it.

For an instant.

But then she'd realize he was like a drug, and once you got your dose, you were good. You were brilliant. You were flying high.

But when it was gone, you needed more.

She did not let this thought alarm her.

She rode it, reached out, tweaked his nipple hard and he sucked in an audible breath.

Her gaze moved to his. "You're so pretty."

He didn't reply but there was a flush to his cheeks, a heat in his return gaze.

Oh yes, she was affecting him.

She bent closer, stroking him deeper, tighter.

"I'm going to fuck you now, Branch," she whispered.

"As you like it, ma'am," he ground out.

"I like it rough, Branch. Can you take that?"

"Told you, take anything you wanna give me, you make me come doin' it."

"You'll come, baby," she cooed, bent closer, almost like she was going to kiss him but instead she brushed her lips along his rough jaw, feeling the bristles against her lips score down to her clit. She slid her mouth down his neck, gentle, sweet, so it made him jump slightly when she glided down and took a fierce nip at his clamped nipple. "Lovely," she breathed.

Making quick work of it because to do it she had to stop stimulating his cock and she wanted the stimulation not to cease, she prepared the toy thoroughly then came back to him.

Capturing his gaze yet again, her unoccupied hand went to his plug.

"Slide down a little, handsome."

He slid down, his chest rising and falling, no longer able to fully hide he'd seen what was coming.

But she knew by the look in his eyes he wasn't fearing it.

He couldn't wait to get it.

And that "it" was a lot. He was going to be stretched wide and filled deep.

And he was going to seriously get off on it.

God, he was a thing of beauty.

She carefully slid his plug out and swiftly set it aside on the towels.

Then she went back to him. The thick head of the toy to his anus, her hand back to his cock, she leaned over him, close, so all he could see was her, all he could smell was her, but he would still feel *everything*.

"What do you want, Branch?" she whispered, putting pressure on the toy against his hole.

"I want that," he growled.

"What, baby?"

"Fuck me with that, Evangeline."

She pressed and his body tensed, the cords in his neck stood out and she sensed his fingers digging into the couch.

"Shh, handsome." She stroked his cock gently, still putting mild pressure on at his ass. "Relax."

"Shove it deep."

Oh yes, her big boy couldn't wait to get fucked.

Her panties drenched.

"Take it slow," she coaxed, feeling him open.

"Fill me," he grunted.

"Baby—"

"Fuckin' fill me," he bit off.

She pushed the cockhead of the toy in, Branch closed around it, then in a smooth, slow thrust, she glided it home.

When she did, his head dropped back, his chest arched forward and his ass sought her hand as a low groan rumbled up his chest and filled the room.

Evangeline convulsed all over, nearly orgasming at witnessing the depth of his pleasure.

Then his head came up, his cool-blue gaze slapping her with an ice burn that sent her shivering with anything but cold.

"Take my ass, Evangeline," he growled.

She was so excited she didn't make him ask twice or say please.

She moved closer, working him, cock and ass, her face in his, their eyes locked.

"Faster," he grunted.

She ramped him up every way she could, faster, harder, tighter, deeper.

His head dropped back again so all she saw were the muscles of his neck standing out in tense relief, the strong line of his jaw, and he started to move.

His fingers clenching the couch, his head thrown back, he jacked his own cock viciously in her hand at the same time rocking the toy up his ass, the sub who was a master, Evangeline along for his wild, beautiful ride.

"That's it, baby, take yourself there," she encouraged breathlessly.

"Fuck," he grunted.

She put her weight into it, she put all she had into it and he fucked her fist and rode his toy even harder.

"Yes," he hissed out between his teeth.

"Don't come, handsome, so beautiful, I want more," she ordered, watching him, taking it all-in, letting his show drive her higher.

"Ma'am," he groaned, now bucking in her couch.

Utterly dazzling.

"Give me more," she demanded.

His head came up, his eyes unfocused, the need stark on his face.

She'd done it.

God, *God*.

Dazzling.

"Evangeline," he whispered.

"More," she pushed.

"Need to blow."

"More, Branch."

"Fuck," he bit out, head falling back, he gave her more.

"That's it, baby, ride it, earn it, that's it."

Then it came.

Low, guttural, tortured.

Perfection.

"Ma'am, please."

"Come," she commanded.

Instantly, he blew. Bucking violently underneath her, his cum jetted up his chest as she kept at him, staying in sync with the intensity of his orgasm.

And he came more, milky gushes shooting out, wave after wave splashing on his boxed abs.

"Fuckin' *fuck me*," he groaned. Brutally jacking her hand with his hips; he kept coming to the point Evangeline knew she needed to lead him down.

Carefully, slowly, she glided the toy out and tossed it to the towels.

She shushed and cooed at him as she gentled her fingers around his dick, swiftly unclamping his nipples. She soothed them with light petting from her thumb before she soothed his neck, his jaw. Milking the last weak bursts from his cock, she was resting her body against his side, in the bend of his hip and thigh, gently stroking his cock.

Finally, his head lolled and she just held him warmly at the base and watched his face, the harshness softened to an almost unbearable beauty in his aftermath.

"Okay?" she whispered.

He turned his head to the side so he could look into her eyes.

"Too bad I'm not into exhibitionism so we don't have a witness to an undoubtedly record-breaking orgasm in length and amount of cum."

A joke.

Again.

Branch could joke.

She smiled at him.

As he had that morning, his eyes grew unfocused as they fixed on her mouth.

And damn, she wanted to kiss him.

But she needed something else.

And after his show, that something else had to happen immediately.

So she lifted up off him, grabbed his hand in hers and yanked up her skirt with her other hand.

That got his attention. The usual alertness (and then some) returned to his face just as she slid his hand, with hers, into the front of her panties.

She bent over him again, her other hand braced in the seat between his body and the back of the couch, put her face close to his and rubbed his middle finger, hers covering his, against her clit.

The feel of his strong, long, calloused finger rasping over her tight nub made her head snap back and she needed more.

So she gave herself more.

Manipulating his fingers, she touched herself, fucked herself (with her finger and his), rode their hands and took herself there (with a good deal of his help—he took the guidance, but he added his own pressure and it . . . was . . . *divine*).

And she came on her knees, bent over him, spasming against their hands, her forehead nearly resting on his, her delicate puffs of breath and soft moans landing on his lips.

Jerking lightly through some aftershocks, she cupped herself with their hands and let her forehead float down to hit his shoulder.

She'd done it.

She'd earned his cum (a good deal of it). She'd earned the beautiful climax she'd just had that came from watching him perform for her. She'd earned this man jacking himself at her command twice that day and texting her that he did, then watching him walk in her kitchen door while she was making dinner. She'd earned him lying under her, his hand in her panties, the massive load of his cum still exhibited over his torso.

She'd earned this.

She'd earned *him*.

But as she came down, she realized there was something she hadn't earned.

The scene was done. They'd both come. It was over.

And now, he could clean up, get dressed and walk away.

He could also wrap his arms around her recently orgasmed, sensitive, relaxed, heated body and hold her to him.

Or touch her.

Or stroke her.

Or show her some affection.

He did not.

She held his hand against her sex and she knew the only reason he kept it there was because his Mistress was making him keep it there.

They'd just shared everything.

But they had nothing.

And then he gave her something.

His mouth to her ear, his fingers at her pussy giving a tender squeeze, Branch whispered, "Okay?"

It was only a little bit of something.

But Evangeline was going to take it.

She nuzzled her face in his neck and whispered back, "Yes, honey, okay."

She felt a tenseness hit his body when she said the word "honey," but it was there and gone in a way she wondered if she'd felt it at all.

Because she sensed it was paramount to keep him focused, she didn't delay in lifting her head and looking into his eyes.

"Now, my big boy, it's time to take care of you after you gave me such an amazing show and then get you ready for bed."

The eye flare that got was also brief.

But it was closer to the surface.

Progress.

So she'd take that too.

eight

Asshole

BRANCH

Branch woke the next morning perfectly aware of where he was.

That being as Evangeline had positioned him after the warm bath she'd given him, this being after she'd fucked him on her couch.

He was tied to her bed with silk ropes at his wrists and ankles, on his stomach, arms spread wide, legs spread wide, hips up on a soft, cylindrical bolster, ass in the air, all of him covered in her sheets with her tucked tight against his side, her leg wrapped around the back of one of his thighs.

It was still mostly dark. He saw from the light in the room that dawn was just touching the sky, and he didn't even try to stop his mind drifting back to all she'd given him the night before.

It went without saying, the woman knew how to take a man's ass. She'd used a thick, long, rigid, sweet cock he'd feel for the next week.

And totally get off on it.

And he'd come harder, and needless to say, longer than he'd ever come in his whole fucking life.

Close to the end of it, he thought he might not ever quit coming.

And he didn't fucking care.

Evangeline kneeling between his legs, taking him there, her face not hiding the fact that she seriously dug the show, he'd do it again. He'd do it hourly, if his ass could hack it, just to get off that fucking huge.

Just to know she was getting off right along with him.

But it was arguable if that was the best part.

No, even after the most phenomenal orgasm he'd ever been given, his fingers deep in her sweet, wet pussy, watching her take herself there couldn't have been better.

Fuck, so damned pretty he'd never forget it. Never forget watching her eyes darken, her cheeks get pink, feeling the little gusts of breath she pressed out against his lips.

But even with all that, one could say he was not a big fan of coming to her house and discovering he had to sit for dinner and small talk (though her cooking was unbe-fucking-leivable—it was spaghetti but it was amazing).

He couldn't have felt more awkward, a man like him being in the kitchen of a woman like her. A kickass Mistress.

But so much more.

She'd built her own business. Bought herself a sweet house. Had good friends who felt everything for her. Created a home that might be frilly and busy and flowery, but it was also warm and inviting, comfortable, and a place where Branch had not earned the honor to hang.

Unless he was giving her something, like allowing her to fuck him because she loved doing it and loved that he loved taking it, and letting her use his fingers to make her get off.

But he had to admit that she somehow made even hanging in front of her TV eating dinner not as bad as it could have been.

If it had been as bad as it could have been, if anything could make him walk away from Evangeline Brooks, that would have done it.

He couldn't say during that time he shared with her eating in front of her TV that he ever felt like he was right at home mostly because it had been years since Branch had felt right at home anywhere.

He could say the longer he was with her, the easier it got, and once she'd unwound from her day, she didn't fuck around being how she was.

Hands seriously on.

After the scene on her couch was over, she didn't invite him kindly to leave and he also had no opening to do that himself.

Not that he'd want to.

Her version of looking after him included a warm bath in her big, oval sunken tub that comfortably fit two, the jets on. A bath that smelled of lavender and mint, where she got in with him, bathed him and petted him and stroked him. And the warm water, his huge orgasm and her attention, with her curls stacked in a mess on top of her head, some hanging down on her shoulders getting wet, far from sucked.

Not to mention, his ass needed it. He liked rough. She liked rough. And she could give it rough, but more, be right there as he rode himself raw.

After the bath, she'd toweled him off, made him stand there while she did the same with herself, giving him time to take her in naked, something he'd only seen briefly as she joined him in the tub, a spectacle that was as he'd expected it would be.

Seriously fucking sweet.

She'd then pulled on another nightie (this one gray with lace, but just as short as the other), no panties, and led him to a bed where she'd already swept the covers down and laid the bolster.

She gave him his instructions, he carried them out, then he got languidly hard again as she'd tied him down.

Once she had him down, she put more antibiotic ointment on the cuts on his back that didn't need it, but this time, he didn't attempt to share that info.

After that, with his ass in the air, the room dark, was when she quietly, efficiently and tenderly took care of business he'd not once allowed anyone to do for him, not even Tara, inserting a capsule of some gel up his ass that instantly eased his jacked hole.

After doing that, she kissed each cheek, the small of his back, the area between his shoulder blades and the side of his neck.

Without a word, she'd pulled up the covers and settled tucked into his side.

He was learning she could fall asleep at the drop of a hat.

What shocked him was that, tied to the bed in a position that wasn't exactly uncomfortable, but it hindered all movement, her sweet body pressed close, within minutes of her dropping off, he could do the same.

Now he was awake and Branch had a decision to make.

She'd claimed him at the Pound. He'd let her spank him with him braced against his truck (and he'd let her drive the damned thing, and no one drove his baby but him, even if he had someone in his life he could allow to do that). She'd staked him with her jewel. She'd sucked him. Jacked him. Fucked him. Bathed him. Tied him. And he'd filled himself and jacked himself at her command, texting her he'd done it.

He'd come.

So the time had also come for him to decide if he was done.

The right choice was clear.

Get the fuck out of her life.

He was a dead man with a mission and so much baggage, she'd get crushed under it if she knew.

In his research before deciding whether or not to meet her, he'd learned she had a mother and father and two brothers, all living, none of them living close (she grew up in Wisconsin), but she was still close to them, with them talking frequently and visiting each other when they could.

She had a life.

She probably wanted marriage. Kids. Soccer games and dance lessons and family vacations to Disneyland.

Branch could give her none of that.

He didn't even have a social security number.

The government had killed him off once, not a loss to his

drink-addled mother and drug-dealing older brother, two of the three reasons why he'd escaped and joined the army at eighteen in the first place. The third being his father, who had showed in their lives often enough to teach Branch how not to treat a woman, and this not only the lesson of You Shouldn't Take Your Fists to Your Wife, but a shitload more, before he'd disappeared altogether.

His computer geek buddy, and partner in a variety of literal crimes, Gerbil, had made certain Branch was well and truly dead, no one could trace him, no one could track him, no one even knew there was a him to track.

Regardless, Branch remained off the grid. No bank account. Cash-only payments for business. No foreign travel. Condo and truck owned under a shell that could, if given a year and a team of forensic accountants to find it (Gerbil was that good), be traced to a man from Monaco who'd died three years earlier.

Nothing else.

No trace of Branch Dillinger.

He breathed, he didn't exist.

Gerbil told him he could get on the grid. No one was looking but it didn't matter. Gerbil could make it so he could live a real life and no one would find him.

But until Gerald Raines was dealt with, Branch was going to remain a ghost.

After he was dealt with, Branch was going to take the cash he'd been carefully accumulating and go somewhere no one could find him, and more important, he couldn't fuck up anyone else's life.

No family trips to Disneyland in the cards for him.

And none of that even scratched the surface of why he'd checked out in the first place. Joined Raines's team. Happy to leave his life behind in a permanent way as a living ghost who was sent on government missions they'd deny any knowledge of if the team fucked up. This after he'd ended things with Tara because he was young and stupid and hadn't learned relationships were compromise.

He'd had a shit life. He just wanted easy and a paycheck and not to bicker about stupid shit. Like how it pissed him off she left rooms where she didn't turn out the light and she threw it in his face he made more money than her but that didn't mean he got to make all of the rules when she wasn't trussing him to their bed and giving him what they both needed.

This leading her to take stupid risks to get her kink when she didn't have him at the same time make a point to Branch which got her dead.

He had a lot of blood on his hands, Tara's was the most indirect, but hers was the blood he knew he'd never wash off.

Yeah, the choice was clear.

He should get the fuck out of Evangeline's life.

He drew in a breath that drew in the scent of her hair.

And he suddenly was unsure if he was a bigger asshole for breaking up with Tara about stupid shit, this act leading to a violent, ugly death where, before it came, she'd had to have been terrified out of her mind. Or knowing down to his balls there was no way in fuck he was done with Evangeline, and he knew beforehand him just breathing her air meant her life might unravel too, since he seemed to have a knack for causing that.

The breath he took must have been big because it stirred her.

Her hand slid down his side, along the small of his back to his ass.

"Branch?" she called sleepily.

Sleepy. Turned on. Just talking, she had the prettiest voice he'd ever heard.

"I'm awake," he answered.

She shifted, touching her lips to his lat and murmuring, "Did you sleep?"

He really wished she'd quit with the lip touches, the kisses.

The affection.

And he really wished she'd *not*.

"Yeah."

"Good?"

After coming that hard and a bath with her?

He'd slept like the dead he was.

"Yeah."

"Good," she whispered, tightening her leg around his thigh. "You doing okay?"

She meant being tied.

He'd stay tied for her for a year, if she liked him this way.

And not because she fucked him better than anyone who came before.

Which was also not the reason why he knew he was going to be a tremendous asshole and keep it up with her for as long as she'd have him.

The reason why was because he didn't know if he'd be able to keep breathing if he lost the shot at witnessing another one of her happy smiles.

And this was because he hadn't done much good in his life and seeing that happy come in a way he knew he gave it to her was something he'd never experienced but had known immediately was precious.

That thought in his head, his voice came out soft, "I'm yours, Evangeline. I'm okay any way you want me to be."

Her hand at his ass gave a squeeze and she pressed herself closer, murmuring another "Good." She cupped his crease and whispered, "Here?"

"All good," he muttered.

"It needs a break today."

She was probably right.

That still didn't mean it wouldn't suck he'd walk away from her house not having her inside him.

Fuck, he was an asshole.

She glided her lips up his lat to his back, her hair sliding with her, as she said softly, "I'm going to have to be creative with how I'm going to make sure you're reminded of me all day."

Christ.

His morning erection grew bigger.

It was then she began, giving him a screaming indication he should let her have what she was going to take from him in her bed that morning and then he shouldn't only disappear from her life, but get the fuck out of Phoenix so he didn't have the urge to come right back in.

At the same time she made it utterly impossible for him even to think about that option.

Lips, hands, tongue, and gentle with the teeth, she explored his body, every inch of it that she could get to. Arms, neck, shoulders, back, ass cheeks, thighs, calves, ankles, and then in a cute, sweet, hot burrow, laving his balls in a way he knew she was knelt between his legs, her touch almost reverent, like she was worshiping his sac.

His cock hard and hanging heavy, brushing the soft cotton of the bolster, it was beautiful torture, every second.

It got better when she made her way back up to his neck, working there, her body straddling his, warm, her tits soft against his back, he could feel her wet seeping into his skin.

Suddenly, she was gone, her fingers gripping his hair, and she pulled his head back, swung in front of him, thighs over his biceps, and she shoved his face in her pussy.

Shit, but she rocked it.

"Eat, baby," she breathed.

Fuck yes.

Her hand still gripping his hair, his body unavailable to him, not able to touch her in any way but with his mouth, he ate Evangeline like hers was the last pussy he'd ever be offered.

And life had saved the best for last.

She smelled good and she was sweet there too, sweet and so goddamned wet, what he felt last night was not a one-off because she liked watching him take his fucking. She was drenched.

And it was awesome.

He took her with his mouth and listened to her noises, driven to make them more urgent, licking, sucking, tongue fucking, biting her clit. Finally, he heard her find it and he felt his cock throb in a way he worried he'd shoot as she rubbed his face in her cunt through her orgasm.

When he felt her quiver through the aftershocks, he turned his head and brushed his mouth to her thigh, hearing her whisper, "You're good at that."

He said nothing.

But he was fucking thrilled she thought so.

She stroked his hair and kept talking, her voice still low and breathy from coming. "Now, I've got a quandary."

Branch had a feeling, whatever her quandary, it was him that was going to have to work it out for her one way or another.

This was why his balls got tight.

"You see, baby," she kept talking, now also stroking his shoulders, "you've been very good. And usually, I reward very good. But in being very good, we've made a part of you unavailable to me so you can't take me away with you like you'll normally do."

"I hear you," he murmured, liking lying with his face in her pussy and liking that she was perfectly cool with letting him do that after she'd come when a lot of Dommes finished their business and then got on with shit.

It was who he was. It was how he was. And there was beauty to a scene lingering, the intimacy of such a position, and for him, getting to experience the service of being laid out for her, at her mercy, even just to allow her to show affection.

He also didn't like it.

And that last was mostly because he liked it too fucking much.

"So, I'm afraid, handsome," she went on, "that I'm going to have to leave my mark on you in a way you'll feel it all day."

Automatically, his hole tightened and he rubbed his dick against the bolster.

Fucking brilliant.

"But don't worry," she kept at it, "I'll take care of you after you take that."

"You wanna give it," he turned and touched his mouth to the juncture of her hip and thigh, not a kiss but as close to one as he felt he could give, "I'll take what you can give."

"So good," she whispered, wispy and sweet. "That earns your choice, Branch. Strap or switch."

Fucking *brilliant*.

"Switch," he answered immediately.

"My big boy," she purred with approval.

With that, gently, she lifted his head, rolled away from him and he felt her exit the bed.

She came back and he saw her, knees to the bed at his side.

She smoothed a hand over his ass. "Ready?"

"Always."

She kept running her hand along his ass.

He wrapped his fingers around the silk cords in preparation.

Then he demanded, "Test me."

"Sorry?" she asked.

"Test me."

"Branch—"

"Every time I move all day, I want the burn of you driving through my balls."

She emitted a feminine growl he felt shooting right up his ass.

"You say when," she ordered, her voice having gone throaty.

"I won't say when. For me, there is no when. You stop when you're done."

Suddenly, her shadow blocked out the dawning light in the room, her hair was all over his neck and shoulders, and her lips were at his ear.

"When I'm done striping you," she said in his ear, "I'm going to jack you and squeeze your balls, milking every bit of cum you have out of you. And tonight, when you come back to me, I'm going to blow your fucking *mind*."

If she had better to give him than last night, he didn't doubt it in the slightest.

He pressed his pulsing cock against the bolster.

"Stripe me," he bit out.

Another growl from Evangeline that ended with her sinking her teeth in his earlobe, a sharp bite that radiated down his neck, spine, through his ass and right to the tip of his cock.

Then she was gone.

An instant later the switch landed on his ass.

If the woman could give a spanking, and she really could, she *rocked* a fucking striping.

Fucking, *fuck*, she thrashed his ass, the backs of his thighs, the pain, so elegant, so exquisite, so perfect, drove up his balls, his hole, through his dick.

He found her rhythm and lifted for her every stroke, meeting it, his cock rubbing against the bolster, and he heard the switch hitting his flesh mingled with her noises, not of effort—hot sweet noises of getting turned way the fuck on, all of it dragging him right along with her.

She took him to where it hurt like fuck and she took him beyond to where it burned like hell and then she took him beyond to where he was going to have to blow.

"*Baby*," he groaned, not even in his mind, all about his ass, thighs, cock and sac.

The switch was tossed aside and she was between his legs, stroking his dick and squeezing his balls.

"Fuck yes," he grunted, his fingers clenching on his bindings, his hips pistoning into her hand. "Fuckin' fuck, fuck yes, make me blow."

"God, could you be more beautiful?" she asked, voice filled with wonder.

"Squeeze, Angie."

If he wasn't skimming the edge of a colossal orgasm, he would have noted the husky beauty of her "Honey."

But instead, ass slicing through the hair, cock thrusting into her tight fist, she tightened her hold on his balls, his head shot back, he yanked at the posts of her bed with his grip on his ties and his grunt scored a path from cock to throat as he blew into her sheets.

She milked him, squeezed him, did as she always did, keeping true to her promise, wringing every drop of cum out of him, and his body juddered through a string of shattering aftershocks before he could do nothing but go slack.

She let him go, crawled up him and straddled him.

Dripping pussy to his back, the rest of her surrounding him, she stuffed her face in his neck and whispered, "You're so damned amazing, it's like I dreamed you."

Right.

Branch was done.

Done fighting it.

Just *done.*

"Untie me."

Her body stilled, but probably thinking he'd had enough, it was the Domme she was that she moved swiftly, near to frantically, untying his right wrist, right ankle, over to his left ankle and left wrist.

Once fully released, immediately he rolled, avoiding his cum. Hooking her by the waist, he pulled her under him, gave her some of his weight, lifted his head and froze solid.

He had a lot on his mind. Gratitude for another fucking unbe-lievable orgasm. A driving need to touch her, something she'd never allowed with any freedom but he sensed she wanted.

But mostly, after that, hearing how much she enjoyed it, *feeling* how much he did, tasting her pussy still on his tongue, hearing her come now three times, knowing she'd given him two orgasms and they'd been the two best of his life (by a long shot), and eating her goddamned, fucking spaghetti, Branch had the driving desire to share with his Mistress that he needed to fuck her.

Not then.

But she had to know that was what her sub wanted, that seed needed to be planted in her head because with all he was getting, he *needed* to know he'd soon get her pussy.

Get *her*.

He'd been inside only a handful of women since Tara and none of them had done it for him.

But he knew Evangeline would do it for him.

And he wanted that.

However, in the dawning light, what he saw was Evangeline, hand planted firm in his chest, body stiff and inert, eyes wide and fucking terrified.

He'd freaked her.

She'd had a sub snap on her and he was now her sub and he'd freaked her.

Fuck.

Branch kept one arm wrapped around her but slowly lifted his other hand and for the first time directly touched her hair, tangling his fingers in it tenderly.

Damn, it was soft.

"I'm not gonna hurt you, Angie," he whispered.

"Y-you move fast."

Fuck.

Shit.

"Never hurt you, honey," he told her gently.

"Y-y-you, I . . . I . . . you moved really fast."

Fuck, he was a moron.

"I liked that, baby," he shared.

"I . . . okay, good," she pushed out.

"I wanted to touch you."

She nodded, staring into his face, and he could see her fighting it and losing.

"Hold you," he explained. "I've never really touched you."

She kept nodding but her hand planted in his chest loosened.

"Oh-okay."

He should tell her he knew. He should tell her he'd been there but she'd been so messed up, she didn't notice. He should tell her he'd seen it all, all of it, on tape. He should tell her it was him who dealt with Kevin.

He should tell her.

He didn't tell her because he didn't want her to know the monster in her bed.

He touched his forehead to hers, looked into her frightened eyes, felt that look burn in his gut, and he whispered, "Never, not ever, not fuckin' *ever*, Angie, would I hurt you."

She stared into his eyes.

"I'm trained," he found himself saying.

Christ.

Blurted it right out.

"I know. I know you're an experienced sub."

"I am that, absolutely, honey. Had my first Mistress at nineteen, had a fair few in between, and I'm far away from nineteen."

"Right."

"I mean, I see your reaction and I can guess where it's coming from and you need to get I'm trained. That training meaning, feeling you freeze in my arms, look at me like that, I'm not up and out of this house, hunting down the dickhead who made you think I'd ever hurt you. I'm in check. I'm here. With you. *That's* what I mean by trained. I did not lie. You got a style. It's different than any Domme I've ever seen. It works on me, fuck, Angie, beauty. But I've been switched worse than that, not as good as that, but *worse*. Whipped worse than what you saw the other night. Nipples practically twisted off. Cock in a vise. Weights hanging from my balls. Had bitches fuck my ass who had no clue what they were doing. When I say there's nothing I can't take, there is *nothing I can't take*. And because of that, the way you give it, I love taking what you've got. But it's more. I've learned control in a variety of ways, Angie, as a sub and a lot more, and you never have to worry about me losing it, no matter what we do."

"I . . . you're right."

He was relieved when she melted underneath him, her hand sliding up to curl around the side of his neck.

He was not relieved when she spoke again.

"That was actually insulting, me reacting like that. He's . . . you . . . the guy, he's not you. I'm sorry."

"Do not ever fuckin' apologize for having an honest reaction, Evangeline," he clipped.

She blinked.

"Angie, you fucked me on your couch last night, I shot a load that coulda been collected and used to populate an island the size of Great Britain, and I'm not sorry I got off like that for you, on show for you, it's who I am, it's what I like, it's the way it is. And right now I'm pissed because my ass burns like fuck, I fuckin' *love* it, my balls are wrung dry, and I love that too, and I should be enjoying that, holding you in my arms, telling my Domme I want her to find a time she'll let me fuck her. And I'm not doing that. Instead, you're annoying the shit out of me apologizing for giving me a piece of you. Showing me who you are. Offering me the opportunity to share with what we got, two days, you can't have missed I feel totally safe with you so it means everything to me to know you feel the same with me."

"I feel safe with you, Branch."

"Don't say shit you don't mean to make me stop being pissed, Evangeline."

"I actually *did* feel safe with you until you, um . . . got pissed that I apologized then made an irate speech about wanting me to feel safe with you."

"Now don't say shit that's cute that just serves to piss me off more."

She clamped her mouth shut.

He glared at her.

She let him.

This went on awhile.

Eventually, she opened her mouth again.

"Just to say, I agree with your assessment of the load you offered last night, Branch, but I don't think the world's population of females is ready for a whole country of Branches. Forget about it for Dominatrixes. Thank God you want this all on the hush-hush. If I had to claim you in the hunting ground at the Honey, I'd have to beat them all back with my baton."

And the woman just got cuter.

He couldn't hack it.

He let her go, rolled to his back and wished he didn't because it brought the pain in his ass up acute, that feeling might make him hard again, and if she saw it, she might feel inclined to do something about it.

He did not lie, she'd wrung him dry, and he might get off on her fucking him on her couch while she watched. he would not be down with her witnessing a lame-ass spurt of cum for any of her talented efforts.

She rolled with him, pressing down his side and laying a hand on his chest.

His eyes slid her way and the look on her face . . .

Fuck him.

Fuck him.

Staring at it he knew without a single doubt that was the last vision his brain would call up before he left this earth.

Playful. Sweet. So damned pretty.

Amazing.

"I didn't know you had that many words in you," she teased.

"Shut up, Evangeline."

"And I promise never to apologize again. For anything," she kept at him.

"Your ass can get red too," he warned.

The grin flirting at her mouth became a smile.

Fuck him.

"Last, I'll take your request to fuck me under advisement."

"Appreciated," he grunted.

"And feel free to hold me whenever you want, that being when I haven't ordered otherwise. I promise not to freak out again either."

"Evangeline—" he growled.

"Okay, okay," she lifted her little hand with her red-tipped nails and waved it, still smiling, "I'll stop busting your balls. Until, of course, I have you tied down again. Then all bets are off."

He rolled his eyes to the ceiling.

She lowered her tits to his chest, he felt her face get close to his, her hair brushing his skin, and he'd gone through the most intensive training a man could face, and that not being as a submissive, but he'd pretty much checked all the boxes on that too, and he still didn't have the control not to look into her eyes.

"I'm really glad you like what we do together, Branch," she said softly. "Because I really like it too. It's been a while for me, and I won't get into that, some of it you've obviously guessed, but I'm super-happy that the man I found to break that seal I wound tight around that part of me was you."

He needed to kiss her.

Needed his mouth on hers, to know the taste of her there, to connect with her the second most important way a man could connect with a woman physically.

He hadn't kissed a woman since Tara.

But he needed to fucking kiss Evangeline.

She stayed close and he knew, he knew in her eyes she was waiting for it.

Wanting it.

Maybe even needing it too.

He rounded her waist with an arm and gave her a squeeze, saying gently, "I got shit to do today, Angie. Fucks me but I gotta get this raw ass on the road."

He had to give it to her, she did her best to hide it.

But he still saw the disappointment.

And it cut like a blade.

"Okay, honey."

"Okay."

"You'll be back tonight?" she asked.

"What time?" he asked back.

"I don't know," her lips twitched, "it's you making dinner."

Fuck him.

"When will you be home?"

"Six?" she said like he could confirm.

"I get dressed, you get me a key. I'll have dinner ready when you get home."

She blazed him with a smile.

Oh yeah.

Fuck him.

"Anything you don't eat?" he asked, fucking his own damned self because right then, even if he got in a shootout five minutes before—and the shit he was into, that could happen—he'd still make it to her house with groceries in time to feed her.

"Celery. Green peppers. Red peppers. Yellow peppers. Any peppers that don't pack a punch are useless. Zucchini. We'll just say squash in all varieties, except cucumbers, if that's a squash, because I love those. Spinach, if it's cooked. If it isn't, I love it. Iceberg lettuce, I'm uncertain why it exists, it tastes of nothing and I avoid it unless it's slathered in blue cheese dressing and sprinkled with red onion and bacon bits. No lamb, because I always think of those fluffy little darlings following their mummies and I want to create an anti-lamb-eating collective à la PETA and go on a militant rampage—"

So cute.

She was killing him.

Branch interrupted the cuteness because he could take no more.

"Rewind, what *do* you eat?"

And she kept fucking smiling.

"Mostly everything else."

"I'll figure something out," he grunted.

"Branch?" she called.

He focused on her.

"Thanks for liking getting your ass whacked."

Shit, he was going to kiss her.

To stop himself, he rolled, taking her with him, surprising an adorable little "*Eek!*" out of her, and he set them on their feet beside the bed.

There, he smacked her ass and ordered, "Key."

She slapped her ankles smartly together, saluted and rapped out, "Aye, aye, Captain."

Then she shot him a grin and strolled to the stairs as he muttered, "Smartass."

"Until the day I die," she called, skipping, *goddamned skipping*, down the stairs.

Narrow stairs.

Shit, she was going to break her neck.

He'd have a word with her about skipping on those fucking stairs.

And setting her alarm.

And getting motion sensor lights.

He took a second to take a breath before he enjoyed the burn in his ass as he walked to the bathroom.

He looked in her mirror that had curlicues etched into all its scalloped edges.

Curlicues.

Not one inch of her house wasn't decorated.

"Jesus," he muttered.

He took in his reflection.

"You're an asshole," he said.

His reflection shared that he was totally goddamned right.

And still.

He didn't give a damn.

nine

Hope for Something

BRANCH

Branch got out of his shower and inspected his ass in the mirror.

He saw what he felt.

It was red and raw.

He shook his head because he got off on the look of it, mostly because he got off on the memory of how it got that way.

He also shook his head because he knew he was taking being an asshole to the highest heights, seeing as, even an hour after leaving Angie, time he should have taken to get his head straight, he still didn't give a damn.

What he did give a damn about was the fact that the ring of red lipstick she'd planted around his cock, yanking him out of his jeans and dropping in front of him to do it before he'd walked out her kitchen door, had been washed away in the shower.

He didn't like losing it but with some of the shit he had to do that day, it wouldn't be good he smelled of lavender, mint and Evangeline.

He wrapped a towel around his hips, walked into the kitchen to see if he had any food (this would be a negatory, but he could always hope there was a stray leftover, fast-food chicken tender that didn't need to be thrown away a month ago), his phone chirped on the counter and he looked down at it.

He picked it up, engaged the screen and realized, with all things Evangeline, he hadn't checked it since he hit her pad last night.

He had three missed calls from Aryas, one from Gerbil and two voicemails.

Shit.

He went to the voicemails.

Aryas's was first.

"Call me as soon as, brother," he demanded.

Gerbil's was second.

"News, no biggie, I don't think, but you'll wanna know."

Neo-Nazis could take over the world and Gerbil would describe it as "no biggie" because he lived in a bunker and had enough freeze-dried rations for him and five generations of his spawn (if he ever got around to making any) to wait out a nuclear strike. So his message could mean anything.

Since it was Aryas's third call that was the last that came in, Branch started with him.

"Yo, thank fuck you called. I'm about to board a plane to Seattle and I got some worries I don't want to take with me," Aryas stated as greeting.

"Hit me," Branch replied, staring at his countertops empty of anything but his toaster and mail, all of it fliers to "Occupant" because no one knew he existed.

Still, there was a shitload of it.

He didn't need mail.

He needed a coffeemaker.

And a bagel.

"Word came in. I know you buzzed her but contacts of mine shared someone fitting the description of Evangeline was seen entering the last Pound. Won't mean contact for you with her, but I gotta know if my girl is taking risks for reasons I gotta shut down. So gotta ask you to get on her."

Damn.

"You with me?" Aryas asked when Branch didn't answer.

"Someone's reporting to you about her?" Branch asked, not liking that idea at all.

"Not a lot of petite, curly-haired Dommes who look like they got their outfit off a Dolce and Gabbana catwalk hit the Pound, brother. A boy of mine calls one of the Pound's security an acquaintance. They were having a beer. Shit was shared. Tweaked my guy. Don't even know if it was her. So yeah, in a roundabout way, if she's doing something seriously stupid and it was her, someone's reporting on Evangeline."

That wasn't a problem. At the Pound, she'd cause a stir even if she hadn't given a skilled demonstration on how to wield a whip.

"She was there for me," Branch told him.

"Say again?"

"Apparently, she didn't agree with my decision not to go there with her. She found me. Shared that. I've spent the last two nights at her place."

A sucking void of silence.

"It's good, Aryas, and she's fine," Branch assured.

"Best five grand I ever spent."

"Come again?"

"Nothing. Last two nights, you say?"

Branch had been in the army and he'd worked on a "government task force" that was mostly men.

Regardless, the women he'd worked with usually knew how to keep their mouths shut and listen.

The men ran their mouths like idiots and felt knowledge was power, no matter how inane that knowledge was.

And if it was gossip, they fell on it like vultures.

And that never changed.

"We're not talking about this," Branch warned, going to the pile of mail and sweeping the lot of it in the trash bin at the end of the counter, the bin half full and not that wide, this meaning some of it fell on the floor.

"You got plans of going back?" Aryas pushed.

"Again, we're not talking about this."

"You do."

Fucking Aryas.

"So you finally got your head out of your ass," the man noted when Branch again said nothing.

"Did I say we're not talking about this?" Branch asked.

"How is she?" Aryas asked back, his tone losing the wiseass quality, concern hitting it.

Branch was not going to share his fuckup of that morning.

But he was going to share that Aryas had nothing to worry about.

"Back in the saddle like she never left it."

"Which means you're getting your shit jacked and good."

Fucking Aryas.

"We're done," Branch stated.

"Wait," Aryas said quickly. "While I got you, Nibs is out on paternity. Pedro's lost a friend, cancer, bad shit. He has to drive to New Mexico. Tyler's got some food poisoning that's fucking his shit up, he's been out two days and it looks like he's not coming back for a few more. Which means Tina Marie letting Jake go on that mini-cruise with his girl was poor timing. The boys in the booth are scrambling to cover. It'd be good, tomorrow night, you could help out."

It would not be good.

That meant a night away from Evangeline.

But Aryas was one of the only people in Phoenix he could call a friend.

And he paid in cash.

He also didn't blink at Branch's fees.

Not to mention, saving for a lifetime of living in a shack on some unknown beach in some unknown country far away meant Branch needed to take all the cash he could get. He was good with a shack but he also felt it important to eat something other than coconuts he could shake from his own trees once he got there.

"I'm there."

"Thanks, brother. I'd say say hi to Leenie, but I figure you'll tell me to go fuck myself."

"You'd be right."

There was laughter shaking his "Later, Branch."

There was none shaking Branch's "Later."

He disconnected and waited to call Gerbil until after he'd pulled on some shorts and jeans and a comb through his hair that he really needed to find time to get cut (something, if Evangeline was in his life how she'd claimed him, he should ask her if she wanted—Dommes had a thing about hair, as evidenced with how Angie had used his that morning).

He heard a click, a pop and two more clicks before his untraceable call to Gerbil went through and the man answered with a deep baritone, "Wassup?"

Gerbil was not called Gerbil for any reason a man could be called Gerbil.

He was called Gerbil so people who'd never met him would think there was a reason to call him Gerbil, thus making them vastly underestimate him.

He was actually a six-foot-tall, ripped black man who, before he'd slipped off the grid, had more than once been asked to be on "Men of . . ." charity calendars.

One thing Branch had not done as a submissive was take a man.

One thing Branch never would do, seeing as the only stipulations to his play were single-partner, nonexhibition (unless he was at a Pound, but that was over) Femme-Domme play, would be take a man.

He liked his ass fucked solely if a woman was behind the cock.

Hell, it could even be he liked his ass fucked *because* there'd always be a woman behind the cock.

Still, he could say feeling no hits to his manhood that Gerbil was the handsomest man he'd ever seen.

He was also the genius who'd been recruited from the marines to be their tech and comm support for tactical missions before he got fed up with smelling the stench of the shit they did and disappeared off the face of the planet.

But he'd kept in touch with Branch, Rob and Lex.

So when Branch, injured and weaponless, needed an extraction out of a jungle after his own command had set him up to be taken out, and he miraculously came upon a working pay phone in a septic tank that sad country called a town, his first and only call was to Gerbil.

And when Gerbil found out what had happened to the team, he was all-in to assist Branch carrying out what needed to be done.

"What's up is you called me," Branch told him.

"Yeah. Right. Blips, man. About fifteen alerts," Gerbil replied. "No, make that twenty."

"I don't speak geek or read minds, man, fill in the blanks," Branch returned.

"'Course," Gerbil said good-naturedly. "See, I got tags, you know, on all the files that have anything to do with anything I give a shit about, right?"

"I'm with you."

And he was, but barely.

Gerbil, as usual, didn't care.

He kept going.

"Which means I get alerts on any files that are accessed that I've taken an interest in. Which means I got tags on all the files that were buried, but not deleted, because Raines is a fucktard, but that's beside the point and you already know that. I digress. In short, this meaning I got tags on all the files on all the missions Rifle Team took on. And twenty of them have been accessed."

Branch grew deathly still.

This was because he had been the lieutenant in charge in the field of the government's officially unofficial elite cleanup squad, a squad called Rifle Team.

"And?" he clipped when Gerbil said no more.

"No one has touched those files in over three years. I did some digging. There's a new man in town, this being the replacement to the replacement that Raines handpicked when he retired, the first replacement having been asked to kindly pack up his shit and get the fuck out before he fucked any more shit up. And we'll just say from some of the shit they uncovered that even I haven't seen that it's seeming Raines didn't have the approval from higher-ups to green-light some of the things you guys did. It's also seeming the asswipe took some not-so-small amounts of cash for favors, sending the team into action on these missions that not only had no green light, no one knew fuck-all about them, and other things, which I find unsurprising and I've told you that's been my theory since—"

"Gerbil, focus," Branch bit out. "What does this mean?"

"Right, John. Just to say, they can't open an investigation because no way the government could expose that shit without huge threats to intelligence, but more, foreign relations. But Raines has gone off radar."

Cold carved through his stomach.

"What the fuck?" Branch bit out.

"Not from me, brother. Relax," Gerbil assured. "I know exactly where he is. But retirement stopped bein' as cushy as it seemed when he was unofficially officially asked to haul his ass into the office to have a few chats."

"Fuck," Branch whispered.

"No matter, John. Retirement wasn't cush anyway, seein' as he's scared shitless any day you're gonna rise from the dead, *again*, and make him eat a bullet. By the way, did I tell you he got another Rottweiler? Another Rottweiler. Now he has four. Didn't take much when he bailed but took all four dogs with him. Like a dog can stop you. It was like he fell asleep the day they outlined your training."

For some reason, this made Gerbil burst into deep, booming laughter.

Branch didn't find shit funny.

"What's your read on this?" he asked into Gerbil's laughter.

Gerbil was still chuckling when he replied lightheartedly, "Welp, way I see it, no governmental investigation, but serious mishandling of government assets and traceable linkage to unofficially official activities in foreign territories that, if discovered, means some relations that are iffy at best might get iffier, those files won't get redacted. They'll be destroyed. And another team like Rifle Team will be dispatched to deal with anyone who could be considered a vulnerability. So, seeing as you're dead, and I'm also dead, even though I enjoyed Christmas with my folks in the Bahamas, thank you for not asking, the only one left is Raines."

Damn it to hell.

Gerbil kept talking.

"Raines sees the writing on the wall and he's done living in terror behind his gazillion-dollar alarm system that I set off occasionally for shits and giggles and his *four* Rottweilers and his seven thousand guns, lying in wait in a puddle of his own piss for you to take him out. He's disappeared."

Shit.

Gerbil wasn't done.

"What I need to know is, do you want me to keep track of him, which isn't hard but I can't say our new man in town is finding it as easy as I am, or do you want me to leak his whereabouts so you can strike the task of blowing his head off when you find a free day from your to-do list?"

"Death is relief. It's the fear that's the vengeance," Branch reminded him.

Gerbil fell silent.

"Why didn't he destroy the files himself?" Branch asked.

"That'd be a good question if he didn't have someone *almost* as good as me to bury them. And encode them. Though, even buried and hard to crack, it was still fuckin' stupid. The problem is, the new man in town might not be able to find Raines, but he's no dummy and he's got someone *almost almost* as good as me who dug them up.

And by the way, that someone *almost* as good as me that worked for Raines is now MIA. My guess, weighted to the bottom of the Potomac."

Christ.

"Why?" Branch asked. "And why now? If no one knows there's something to dig up, why are they suddenly digging?"

"Good question."

"Can you find out?"

"Brother, I can do anything."

He said no more.

Branch sought patience.

Gerbil was a genius but like all the ones Branch had met, and there'd been a few, he was both ragingly eccentric and not real good with common sense.

When he found his patience, he ordered, "Well then, Gerbil, *find out.*"

"On it," Gerbil muttered. "Now, what do you want to do with Raines?"

"Living in fear of a U.S. government kill squad finding him *and* me coming after him, what do you think I want to do with him?"

"Let him lie in wait in a puddle of his own piss for when he'll buy a bullet," Gerbil deduced.

"They don't call you genius for nothing."

"Mensa cried the day they thought I died."

"Every single member or are you talking figuratively?"

"That's always been you, John. I'm pretty and a mastermind and you've only ever just been pretty so you try to make it up by being a smartass."

Branch found his mouth actually forming a grin.

It felt rusty and wrong so he stopped doing it.

Then he stood halfway to the door to his bedroom and realized he had a decision to make.

Considering he was going to her house that night and cooking dinner, though, he actually didn't.

"I have something to share," he said, walking back to the kitchen.

"I'm all ears."

"There's a woman."

Another sucking void of silence.

"It's very early," he continued. "And it's going nowhere. But she's in my life. No idea how long it will last but want you to keep an eye out for her."

"John, you're dead," Gerbil said quietly.

"I know that, man."

"No one is looking for you. You can have a woman, brother," he said quietly. "I keep tellin' you, you want it, I can give you an entire life."

"They find Raines, he could give me up."

"John, *you're dead*," Gerbil repeated. "Raines is living in fear because you came back to life once. They killed you then *I* killed you and I do it better. He's got four Rottweilers because he believes in ghosts since he's seen one. But he sent men to look for you, files, by the way, he also didn't destroy, but I did, even if they all reported the John Doe cadaver found in that Chicago morgue was irrefutably *you*. There's no trace because *I* left no trace. You're home free."

"I'm home free, why is someone uncovering those missions, Gerbil?"

"I'll find out."

He would.

And Branch would have to wait.

But right then, he also had to explain.

"When I say Evangeline and I are new, I mean really new. But she's a good woman and I don't want my shit to fuck up her life any way that might conceivably happen."

"You left your shit in a jungle, John."

Branch didn't say anything but he wished like fuck that was true.

Gerbil, as was usual, did say something.

"Evangeline is a pretty name."

"Last name Brooks. Phoenix address. And if you can't find her, I'll give you her address."

"If I can't find her, *puh*," Gerbil scoffed.

Right, now *he* was acting stupid.

"Just, you know, tag her files or whatever voodoo you do to make sure no one's getting up in her shit."

"Consider her covered."

"Thanks, man," Branch muttered, opening his fridge and deciding it was high time to throw out the moldy block of cheese that was the only thing, except for a crusted-lip ketchup bottle, that was in it.

Fuck.

He shut the door.

"Jesus, brother, she's pretty."

He'd looked her up already.

"Those curls, whoa. Nice eyes too," he went on.

"Just tag her files, Gerbil," Branch sighed.

"Well, you have fun tagging *her*. Can see why you quit abstaining to take a shot with this one."

"I haven't been abstaining."

"I mean *relationships* not sex."

"We've been seeing each other two days. It's not a relationship."

"You want me to look out for her, John. Two days shmoo days. If you want *me* to watch over her, it fucking *is*."

Christ.

"Can I stop talking to you now?" he asked.

"I hope you don't 'slam, bam, thank you, ma'am' her like you do me," Gerbil razzed.

He called her ma'am but the one doing the slamming was her.

That was something Branch was not going to share.

"Can I give you a new name when I give you a new identity you can use to set up house and make babies?" Gerbil asked.

At that moment, Branch didn't want to make Gerald Raines eat a bullet.

He wanted to make Gerbil eat one.

"You picked it, brother," he reminded him.

"I was having an off day setting up fake identities," Gerbil mumbled.

Christ, maybe he didn't want to kill Gerbil.

He wanted someone to kill *him*.

"Just find out why those files were opened. I'm hanging up now."

"John," Gerbil called.

"What?" Branch asked impatiently.

"You're allowed to be happy. We were all fed the same line of bullshit to enter that fucked-up game. The majority of the missions were solid. We helped people. We saved lives."

"We took them too."

"It's the job of a soldier, brother."

"And some of the jobs were dirty."

The words were heavier when he said, "That's the job of a soldier too."

He unfortunately wasn't wrong.

"Think about it," Gerbil urged. "This pretty girl of yours, if she's a good woman, give her a straight shot to try and make you happy."

This from a man who'd yet to make spawn because he rarely left his bunker because he knew precisely just what was in the dark that should terrify you out of your mind.

"I'm not sure happiness is in the cards for men like us, Cameron," Branch replied quietly.

"That might be the straight-up honest truth, brother, but the true death is the death of hope and you die that death still living, you might as well just be dead."

"Are you writing a self-help book in your spare time?" Branch joked to lighten the mood.

"Don't bust my balls, man, 'cause if you . . . *you* find it in yourself to hope for something, then go for it, your black brother from another mother might feel the strength to resurrect his own hope. And maybe, just maybe, we live the lives Rob, Di, Benetta, Lex and

Piz weren't given a shot at, this world might turn out not to be the shithole I know it to be."

And after delivering that, Branch knew the conversation was done.

Because Gerbil hung up on him.

ten

I Don't Regret It

EVANGELINE

Evangeline speared some leaves in her huge salad, lifted her fork and looked to Amélie before taking a bite.

"Let me think about it," she said.

They were having lunch. Leigh had called that morning to ask if she had free time. And fortunately, because she enjoyed having lunch with Leigh and hadn't in a long time, she did.

This invitation, Evangeline knew, came because Amélie had her back and was wasting no time in making sure she was dug in.

And Evangeline was delighted to dig right in.

After her friend, who worked at a vet that also had a small no-kill shelter for animals, just shared pictures of two dogs and three cats who were looking for a home, this lunch was also, Evangeline discovered, about trying to get her to adopt a pet.

She did not find this annoying and she also didn't find it a surprise. This was Amélie's way.

Not to mention, Amélie knew Evangeline's dog had died of cancer about a month after she'd met Kevin. He didn't like animals (she should have known then he was screwed in the head) and their relationship at the Honey and in life had progressed swiftly. So even though, back then, Leigh encouraged her in a gentle way to get a new member of the family, she'd held back because of Kevin

She hadn't done it since him because she got caught up in other things and didn't think she had the time and attention required to welcome a new pet.

"All right, *chérie*. Dr. Hill's practice is there when you're ready," Amélie replied.

"How many furry babies do you have now?" Evangeline asked after taking her bite, chewing, swallowing and while forking up some more.

"My two feline beauties that you know who miss you, so you must come visit, and we got a dog for Olly. He'd lost his and the time was right."

Amélie's cat Cleo probably missed her, that kitty was sweet and social. Her Stasia had been so sadly abused, she took a cat's aloofness to new levels so she probably never even knew Evangeline existed.

"Things good with your Olly?" Evangeline asked, sparking a smile at her before taking another bite of her salad and watching Amélie's face turn to sheer beauty as it got soft with thoughts of her lover.

"They are," she replied, her voice as soft as her expression.

"I'm happy for you, Leigh," Evangeline replied quietly in return.

"Me too. I was beginning to give up hope. He was a dream come true."

Those words hit Evangeline in the stomach in a way she couldn't quite decipher if it was very good . . . or very bad.

"I'm glad and I can't wait to meet him," Evangeline said.

"I can't either, darling." Her look changed slightly, but Evangeline caught it. "And I'm looking forward to when you return to us at the Honey."

Evangeline shifted in her seat and also straightened in it. "Leigh—"

Leigh lifted an elegant hand (the only thing she *could* do—every-thing was elegant about Amélie).

"That's all I'm saying, Evangeline. No more on that topic. You know you're welcome. You know we all want you back. You know we all want you to heal. And you know, I, personally, feel it's crucial to you in a myriad of ways to return to your true self, your passions, who you are, to complete that healing. It's up to you to decide when it's time or if there is a time. But I'll say to you now, if a hurt that cannot heal was delivered to you, that's understandable too. A break of trust like that in our world is very hard to overcome. There will be no judgment. We all will understand that too. And we'll take you however you give yourself to us."

God, she loved Amélie.

Which made it immensely difficult to sit there and listen to her saying the things she'd just said without sharing that she needn't worry. She was taking steps to heal that hurt.

But more, it was difficult to sit there and not talk to a sister in the life about the path she'd chosen to do that, the partner she had in that effort (who didn't know he was her partner in that sense) and the new kind of difficulties she'd bought herself in trying to perpet-uate a vital break in a man who might prove unbreakable.

Which might again break Evangeline's heart in a way she sensed already in what she had with Branch, especially after what he gave her that morning, would be far harder to heal than what Kevin had done to her.

Amélie would have good advice. She'd listen and she'd share. Or she'd just listen, if Evangeline simply wanted a sounding board.

But she couldn't say a word.

And it stunk.

Damn, but she hated Branch's stupid NDA.

All she could do was look in her friend's eyes and say, "I think I'm making some strides in that too."

Relief rushed swiftly through Amélie's eyes and Evangeline knew her friend was trying to protect her by trying to hide how deep that went.

Which deepened Evangeline's disappointment she couldn't talk to her friend about all that had happened the last few days.

"Either way, Leenie, either way," Amélie replied.

Evangeline smiled at her and again tucked into her salad.

That evening, in her car, Evangeline turned the corner on her street holding her breath.

Hers was one house from the end. It wasn't a long street, and she expelled her breath seeing Branch's truck parked in front of her home.

She drew in a breath again and tamped down the hope.

This had been her struggle all day.

She'd lost hold on it that morning after what had happened with Branch. His taking her in his arms. His sharing all he'd shared. His words. His irate concern. His exposure of hints of his personality. His calling her his Domme. His request to connect with her physically in a deeper way. His calling her "baby" and "honey" and . . .

Angie.

No one called her Angie.

That was all Branch's.

And she loved it.

But a day had passed, and outside of striping his ass, telling him he was making dinner and stopping him right before he walked out her door to leave her mark on his cock with her lipstick, she had not left him with any instructions. She had not made certain that he checked in so she could be certain she was on his mind in an effort to make sure that mind didn't take him places she didn't want it to go.

So seeing his truck in her drive was a huge relief.

But she knew she had to go cautious and keep her expectations low.

Giving a man, even one like Branch, two orgasms he clearly enjoyed and perpetrating a mild break to the point, after he received one, he couldn't wait to pull her into his arms was a step in the right direction.

That didn't mean he didn't have a whole day to retreat.

One obstacle down, she thought as she parked under her carport, *he's here.*

Now, onward.

She grabbed her purse and attaché, opened her door and threw her legs out.

She experienced another hint of relief when she entered the house and saw him strolling, wearing cargo pants again, this time switching it up by wearing a navy tee that did very nice things to his eyes, from the family room to the kitchen.

The TV was on and the air was filled with delicious smells.

She looked at his face.

Damn.

He'd used that time to retreat.

He was there. He'd clearly cooked. He'd made himself at home, watching television while waiting for her to arrive.

But he was not relaxed and at ease.

His discomfort was not awkward like it had been the night before, but it was there.

And his expression was remote.

No "Honey, I'm home!" then.

And no welcome-home kiss.

She sensed Branch didn't kiss even if this was an intimacy that usually the Master or Mistress would prohibit or grant during play.

But they were not in a club's playroom, where the scene was all there was.

They'd been in her bed and on her couch in her home.

He'd had opportunities to take a kiss.

He'd had opportunities to show he wanted one.

He'd taken neither.

Evangeline did not allow the depth of her disappointment at this to pierce the carefully controlled bubble of hope she was nurturing.

But she still recognized the disappointment.

"Hey," she called, giving him a small grin and tossing her attaché and purse on the counter by the door before she cleared it and closed it behind her.

"Hey," he replied. "Work good?" he asked.

"Yes. Busy. Maybe too busy. I need to slow down."

He made no reply, just stopped by the island and regarded her.

She advanced slightly, getting close-ish, putting a hand on the island to brace herself to lift a foot and slip off her slingback. "You? Good day?"

"Good as they can be."

That wasn't a very upbeat answer.

"Started out all right, though," he continued.

She slipped her other shoe off and gave him a look and a raised brow.

"All right?" she asked.

His mouth moved not exactly in a grin and he gave one shake of his head before he changed the subject.

"Chicken enchiladas."

She stared. "Homemade?"

"I got a dick but that doesn't mean I can't cook."

"Of course not, a number of the best chefs are men."

"A majority number," he returned.

"That's only because when something as," she lifted her hands and did air quotation marks, "*common* as cooking hits *elite* status, men horn in and take all the glory when there are thousands, probably millions of women who could kick their ass given just a toaster oven to build miracles."

"Don't doubt that," he muttered, the blankness in his eyes no longer totally blank.

There was a light there, dim, but with anything Branch gave her, she'd take it.

"Is dinner ready?" she asked.

"Whenever you are," he answered.

"Great, honey," she whispered and watched the light in his eyes flash out instantly.

She stood, feeling its absence like it lit her soul and all had suddenly gone dark, but she powered through that quickly, trying to figure out what flipped that switch to "off" while continuing to speak.

"I'm going to go get changed. You want to dish up? I'll be back in a second."

"Got it covered," he muttered and started moving around the kitchen.

She carried her slingbacks up the stairs and quickly changed into a slouchy, dip-backed knit top in electric blue and a pair of dark-gray, drawstring, soft-knit yoga pants

She piled her hair up on her head and psyched herself up all the way down the stairs to persevere.

It was day three. She was a recently-brought-back-to-life Mistress with the most challenging sub she'd ever had on her hands. He was an experienced sub so her challenge was not about that. Her challenge was vastly different and vastly more important. And she was facing it coming off another sub whom she had not read was also challenged.

One of the totality of differences between Branch and Kevin (for they were not alike in any way) was that, whatever was screwing with Kevin's mind, he'd hid.

Branch wore the fact that he was damaged and he didn't want to be fixed like a badge.

She turned the corner of the stairs and saw him on her whiskey-leather, deep-seated couch in front of the TV.

Her plate was sitting on the coffee table and there was a glass of red wine beside it. Steam was coming off the plate, and as she walked toward him, she saw the humongous portion he'd served on it looked delicious.

She also saw Branch had not achieved a new level of comfort in her house after spending time in it, cooking in it, hanging in it and being played with right in that very space he sat, on the edge of his seat, again hunched over his plate, eyes to the TV.

He looked to her and she saw in the time it took her to go upstairs and change, the blank he'd slammed down had turned void.

He'd retreated since that morning.

But in the last ten minutes, he'd withdrawn.

Damn it.

She didn't do anything but walk around the back of the couch, take her seat and claim her plate.

"Looks good," she murmured.

"Good," he murmured back.

"Thanks for pouring me some wine," she said.

"Not a problem," he replied.

She took a bite and watched him eat, eyes to the TV.

Wow.

It *was* good.

"Delicious, Branch."

"Glad you like it, Evangeline."

Evangeline.

Not Angie.

Damn.

His gaze turned her way and he said, "Don't have HBO. Heard this was good. Been wanting to catch it for a while. Is it cool with you?"

She looked for the first time to the television and saw there was an episode of *True Detective* on, first season.

He'd pulled up HBO GO.

She'd never watched it but had always intended to.

She looked back to Branch and said, "Yes. Haven't seen it but I've wanted to."

"Want me to start it at the beginning?" he offered.

She shook her head. "I'll catch up later."

He did nothing but dip his chin and resume his attention on the TV.

She ate. She sipped her wine. She couldn't eat but half of the portion he gave her even if it was exceptional, the chicken so tender and flavorful, she wanted to know how he managed it.

She didn't ask.

She let him watch his program, and when she'd finished what she could, seeing he'd finished his plate, she'd unfolded out of the couch and got up.

He looked up at her.

"Keep watching, Branch. I'll deal with this." She took his plate. "Do you want more?"

"Nope," he said.

"Another beer?"

"That'd be good."

She nodded, tagged his empty bottle and walked out of the room.

Now she was perplexed.

She was more perplexed when she came back, gave him his fresh bottle of beer to a mumbled "Thanks," and resumed her place and her wine sipping.

He was still on the edge of his seat like he was about to get up and sprint out.

But he was sitting there, not giving her any vibes he wanted her to get the lead out, start a scene, take him to where he needed to be to feel safe.

Still, the awkwardness had settled back in. He didn't want to be there and he wasn't making it obvious but it was a feeling so entrenched in him, he couldn't hide it.

She didn't get it and she didn't know what to do about it mostly because he also actually looked like he was into the episode.

However, when the credits rolled, he picked up the remote, stilled them and turned directly to her.

She opened her mouth, ready to slip right into it, get him where he needed to be.

But he beat her to it.

"We got a few things to chat about."

She shut her mouth.

She opened it to say, "Okay."

"Right," he stated and stopped.

She waited.

It hurt to watch but it looked like it actually took effort for him to straighten and sit back in his seat and she didn't think that effort was about the fact the striping she'd delivered that morning was surely still burning the flesh of his backside.

He twisted his torso to her.

"This morning, when I told you to get me your key..."

Oh boy.

He'd demanded her key himself.

It was way, *way* too early in what they had for a demand like that, be it in play but especially in life.

Even so, she'd been beside herself with glee he'd made it.

Now he was freaked about it.

"...you skipped down the stairs," he finished.

Her head shook slightly in confusion.

That wasn't what she expected to hear.

"Sorry?"

Finally, he rested back against the couch, laying his arm along the back, and for a moment, she was bedazzled simply because he was so very easy to look at, especially on her couch in a casual position she hadn't ordered, turned to her.

"Evangeline, that upstairs room is an add-on to this house."

Now she was more confused.

Why was he telling her this?

"Yes. I know."

"And those stairs weren't meant to be there. They were put in a space inadequate for them so the risers are too high and the steps are narrow."

This was very true. When she'd bought the house, it took a long time to get used to those stairs.

"Yes," she said slowly.

"And you skipped down them this morning."

"I did?"

"You did."

She probably did. She'd been so high on thinking she'd made huge strides with Branch that was something she'd do.

Idiot!

"Well, I—"

"Don't do that again."

She closed her mouth.

"It's dangerous," he declared. "You could fall and break your neck."

Her heart thumped in a way it was a wonder it didn't leap out of her chest, springing back, just like in a cartoon.

"I've been negotiating those stairs for three years, Branch," she told him quietly.

"Don't do it again, Evangeline."

Still Evangeline.

Not Angie.

And right then, him clearly having thoughts all day of her falling down her steps, and worried about it enough to boss her around, she didn't care.

Maybe she *had* made great strides with Branch in their short time together.

"Okay," she agreed. "I won't do it again. Or I'll try to remember not to do it again."

"Just don't do it again."

She fought a huge smile and said softly, "I won't do it again, Branch."

A mixture of things passed through his expression that were elusive, there and gone so quickly, she couldn't say for certain she'd seen them.

But it looked like shock, disbelief, even puzzlement, like he thought she'd bear down and start an argument about something that might seem ridiculous, but in the end it was him looking out for her and it meant something to him, but it didn't to her, so there was no reason to argue.

He got over it but did it making it clear the discussion wasn't over.

"And you need to engage your alarm when you're not in your house but mostly when you are. And lock the doors when you're here. You didn't lock it when you came in which is cool, because I'm here, but it is not cool if I'm not."

"Well, I—"

"Just engage the alarm and lock the doors like I said, Evangeline."

She was finally getting it.

And she needed to allay his concerns.

"What happened to me that you guessed this morning happened at the club. It didn't—"

He interrupted her. "We'll talk about that in a second."

She shut her mouth again.

"Use your alarm," he demanded. "And lock yourself in. Even if I'm here, it's smart. Get in the habit. And you need motion sensor lights outside."

At that, she shook her head.

"I don't like them, Branch. They switch on when anything passes, even the critters or the wind—"

"They're a deterrent to assholes who're intent to do asshole things. Those assholes are gonna do those things no matter what. It sucks they might pick a neighbor to do them to if they get spooked by your lights or see you got an alarm. But at least it won't be you who has to deal with assholes."

"I still don't like motion sens—"

"You don't buy them, Evangeline, I will and I'll install them. This isn't a request."

She blinked.

Right, there was something she hadn't yet quite understood

about Branch that had been staring her in the face, heck, *slapping* her across the face since the first second she'd laid eyes on him.

He was a submissive.

But he was an alpha-submissive.

Which might not be mutually exclusive to the kind of submissive he was and the kind of man he was, though she couldn't know because she'd never paid attention to that kind of thing.

But Branch bossed her around even when she was working him and she hadn't even noticed it, likely because it was such an integral part of him.

And he was bossing her around out of a scene, in her family room, just in life. Not to mention, that spilling out all over the place in her bed that morning.

So he was just a straight-up, somewhat-in-your-face *alpha.*

She'd never had one of those. She'd only seen alphas at work as Doms.

And realizing it, *experiencing* it, she felt the area between her legs get tingly.

"Okay, handsome. I'll go shopping."

"Good," he bit off and instantly adjusted, wincing very slightly, but she felt that wince tingle between her legs too.

That feeling was gone when he looked away only to look right back.

The determined expression on his handsome face had disappeared. Now it was closed off.

"I got something to share and I'll preface it by saying, I share it, you want me gone, I'll just go. I'll get it and it'll suck because this is good. I'd like for it to last awhile. But you gotta know who you're fucking."

Evangeline didn't move and it wasn't a surprise because, at his words, all of a sudden it felt like her insides were frozen solid.

When he didn't go on, it took a good deal, but she forced out, "Okay, Branch. I'm listening."

"I know what happened to you at the club because I was there," he announced. "Aryas called me. I do jobs for him and that night after it happened, he called me. You didn't see me because you were fucked up. But he called me and I was there. In that room. With you."

The chill she felt became a deep freeze and she just stared at him.

"Shoulda told you this morning and I wanted to but I didn't and I wish I could say I didn't because I was looking after you. I'd freaked you and you didn't need anything to freak you more. But I didn't do it looking out for you. I did it because I like what we got and I was weak. I didn't want to lose that. But I've been thinking about it today and the right thing is that you should know."

"Okay," she whispered.

"I'm not done," he shared curtly.

She stayed silent

"That night Aryas called me and it wasn't to get a lock on Kevin. He already had a lock on Kevin. It was to deal with Kevin. And I dealt with Kevin."

Evangeline felt her breath go funny.

"It isn't mine to give about Aryas's business so I won't give it," he stated. "What I will say is, most the time Aryas has got a message to convey, it's the kinda man he is and the rep he's got that he's good with delivering it. Sometimes, he wants to be certain that message isn't forgotten. That's not all the work I do for him or that I just do, but in a case like that he calls me in."

When he didn't go on, feebly, she nodded.

So he went on.

"He called me in. And I conveyed his message. That being, beating the shit out of that asswipe and then destroying his goddamned life."

"Oh my God," she breathed.

He continued like she hadn't said a word.

"It's important you know with your relationship with Aryas that that wasn't the message he wanted delivered. But so you understand completely what I'm saying to you, I'm gonna give you a little piece of me."

Oh my God.

That time, she didn't verbalize it.

But she felt the words thrum deep.

"I knew a woman and she was important to me. She fucked up, did somethin' she knew was stupid, and she got her head caved in by some asshole who I don't give a fuck what his issues were, acting on them, there's no one with a decent soul on the planet who wouldn't think he'd done wrong. Even if she liked to tie men up and spank their asses. So when I got a shot at Kevin after what he did to you, I took it further than Aryas required and there was motivation to that. What you gotta know is, I get there was motivation for that. No trigger had been tripped. I knew precisely what I was doing, why I was doing it, and I did it deliberately."

When he paused, Evangeline just nodded, feeling a lot—utter sadness at the story he had to tell about the woman he knew—and a lot more about all the rest of it.

"But she wasn't the only motivation I had," he carried on. "I saw you, bloodied and fucked up and havin' trouble breathing because he'd cracked so many ribs, little thing like you, in that room where trust is paramount and he broke it in one of the worst ways imaginable. But it was worse. You cared about the guy and he snapped on you, so my motivation was also you."

Oh my God, she thought again.

"Okay, Branch," she said quietly.

He kept speaking.

"And again, I didn't lose control. You should know for more than one reason it wasn't about losing control. You should know because you've been sleeping beside me and you gotta have the information you need to decide whether you wanna keep doing that, that the man you sleep beside is capable of what I'm capable of, doing it with a purpose and fully cognizant of what I was doing."

He took in a breath and finished.

"Now, you got a decision to make but I'll share a couple more things before you do that."

Again she nodded.

Again he went on.

"One is to confirm what you know. Kevin is taken care of and he's not a threat to you nor will he ever come into your life again. Two is that, like I don't have an issue with who I am and how I am with what I like to get me off, in that kind of job, I do not have that first fuckin' issue with what I did. There are things I've done that I regret in my life, but that's not one of them. I don't give that first fuck what might have been behind that man losing his shit and taking it out on you. You do not harm someone who doesn't deserve to be harmed. You absolutely do not take your fists to a woman. And you categorically do not hurt someone who's put their trust in you and has given you a place in their heart. I figure, if every motherfucker who took his fists to a woman or a child or anyone who loved them got his jaw broken and his life dismantled, that shit would stop. Since that doesn't happen, it goes on. But I was in a position to make certain the man who harmed you learned a lesson. So I gave it to him. And I don't regret it."

He stopped talking and Evangeline just sat there.

Well, she didn't just sit there.

She sat there with words racing through her brain.

You skipped down them this morning . . . Don't do that again.

Just engage the alarm and lock the doors like I said, Evangeline.

You don't buy them, Evangeline, I will and I'll install them. This isn't a request.

You cared about the guy and he snapped on you, so my motivation was also you.

But I was in a position to make certain the man who harmed you learned a lesson. So I gave it to him. And I don't regret it.

And . . .

I'll get it and it'll suck because this is good. I'd like for it to last a while. But you gotta know who you're fucking.

"You need to make the choice right for you, Evangeline," Branch cut into her thoughts and she focused on him. "You want me to go, I'll go. You want time, I'll go and you got my number. If you can handle who I am and what you now know and want us to keep going, you call me and I'll come back. But you can't, like I said, it'll suck, but I'll get it and I'll honor whatever decision you think is right."

"I'm uncertain," she said quietly, "that the domestic violence shelters should change their mission statement to 'Healing through breaking his jaw and dismantling his life.'" She paused and concluded, "But they should."

The remoteness left his face and she watched the stiffness in his body that she hadn't noticed before begin to slightly relax.

So she instantly set her wineglass aside and rolled up to her hands and knees in the couch.

She crawled the short distance to him, coming up and sitting back on her calves when she got close and then lifting a hand to curl it at the side of his neck as she brought her face near to his.

Stroking his jaw with her thumb, she whispered, "Thank you for that honesty, Branch."

He stared into her eyes and said nothing.

So she did.

"Without a lot of time to think on it, having known Kevin, and you're right, caring about him, I have to admit I hope he found the strength to work through whatever was troubling him to make him do what he did. But even so, I'll share I also don't care what it says about me that I don't have to think too long to understand that I'm totally okay with the lesson you taught him because I *did* care about him and he had every opportunity to share with me what was troubling him and he didn't. He hurt me. If I was a different person he could have changed the course of my life in irrevocable ways that would have been tragic. And actions deserve consequences. Maybe, if I could choose, his consequences might not have been that extreme. But I wasn't the only one he hurt, whose trust he broke, who was affected by his actions, so I'm not the only one who gets to say what his consequences were."

She adjusted her hand to bring it to his jaw so she could rub her finger along his lower lip and she felt her belly melt when she saw his eyes react to her touch.

But she didn't bring his attention to it.

She kept talking.

"I think it's also important for you to know that I suspect that wasn't easy to share but, honey, I'm so glad you did because until I sat there listening to you, I hadn't worked all this out in my head. His issues that he made mine were still shaping who I was becoming, how I was living my life and who I thought I was. You've just made me realize I need to let that go. It was him. Everyone said it but it really *was* just him and I had nothing to do with it so I also have to thank you for leading me to that because it feels flipping *awesome* to finally let that go."

"Angie," he whispered.

She had it back.

And she rejoiced.

But she didn't let it show except to share, "I like what we have too, Branch, and I don't want it to end so please don't walk out the door. Because, although I promised to rock your world tonight, I've since decided I'm going to take my time doing that so I'm just going to sway it a little bit and let you enjoy the anticipation until I'm ready to roll."

That got her his beautiful eye flash, much closer to the surface, and she really, *really* wanted to reward that by kissing him.

But he might not want that so that was no reward.

She'd have to give him the reward he'd want.

She lifted her other hand to his jaw, murmuring, "Thank you again, baby."

"You're thanking me for beating the shit out of your ex-boyfriend."

She shook her head slightly.

"I'm thanking you for not keeping from me the fact you did. I'm thanking you for, perhaps unintentionally, but it still happened, making me look at what happened from a different perspective. One that was meaningful. A way to look at it that I needed. I'm thanking you for being honest and letting me know who I have in my bed so *I* can make the decision if I wish him to remain there, something I can imagine you have some sense is important to me."

She stroked his cheekbones with both hands and kept speaking.

"If you think in future I'll have issues about the fact you've got no regrets for carrying out the kind of lesson you taught Kevin, that you're that man, then please, don't worry, Branch. In our short time together, you've shown me the kind of man you are in many ways, nothing hidden. You did what you did. You had reason. You shared with me those reasons. And though I might not completely agree with it, you have no regrets and it's not my place to give you any because I also don't completely *disagree* with it. I've only known you three days and I'm aware there's a lot of you I'll never get. But I like what I have, maybe especially what you gave me tonight, and I'm not just talking about the enchiladas, which were superb. So I'm good, handsome."

His eyes dropped to her mouth, he seemed to sway toward her, she held her breath as a curl fluttered in her belly, but his eyes cut back to hers and he growled, "I need you to sway my world right about now, Angie."

In his safe place.

Where he could be who he was and show it without holding anything back (or, at least, without holding *everything* back).

But he'd called her Angie.

And that worked for her.

"Okay, baby," she whispered, "I'll sway your world."

His eyes dropped again to her lips but only briefly before they returned to hers.

It was time to take him to his safe place.

"I'm hoping I've taught you that good things come to those who wait so we'll see how well you can wait. I want you to turn off the TV. Then I want you naked, Branch, standing by my side of the couch. I feel like reading and having a few glasses of wine tonight, handsome. But I'm sure there'll be the occasion where I'll also want to look at that lovely cock of yours, touch it, kiss it, suck it, your balls too. So position for me, legs slightly apart, so I can also get to your ass if I want to, hands linked behind your head. I want you hard when I return. I'm going to clear up the kitchen now, but before I go, I need to know, is all that understood?"

She knew it was by the heat he wasn't *quite* hiding building in his eyes.

But he answered anyway, "Yes, ma'am."

She gave him a smile.

She wanted to give him something else. At least a small peck on the lips.

Instead, she let him go and moved back, ordering, "Please don't delay, Branch. I'll be watching you preparing for me from the kitchen."

She got out of the couch and so did he.

She went to the kitchen and tidied.

She also watched.

And she let her mind filter over what had just happened.

You skipped down them this morning . . . Don't do that again.

He cared.

He cared about her.

He cared she was safe. He cared she looked out for herself. He cared enough not just to chat with her about skipping down the stairs but that and the alarm, locks, motion sensor lights . . . and not hiding who he was. Making sure she knew, perhaps not in a thorough way where he'd laid his heart bare and shared every second of his history, but he still gave her what she needed to understand who she'd let in her bed.

After Kevin, it was a gift.

Branch being Branch, Evangeline knew just how precious that gift was.

And it gave her hope. Much more than his texting her after he'd done as she'd instructed. Much more than him showing at her house to make dinner and enduring his discomfort at being in a situation he found awkward so he could be with her.

Yes, much more.

Much, *much* more.

She was terrified she was all kinds of stupid to feel it.

But even if she put all she had into it, she couldn't stop it.

Later that night, after arming the alarm (she'd had to look up the code, that was how long it had been since she'd used it), Evangeline walked up the steps, turned at the landing, and her eyes hit Branch as she'd left him.

Tied down, hips on his bolster, as she'd had him last night and as she'd left him half an hour ago.

Her clit quivered, her nipples hardened and her lips curled in a smile as she approached the bed, seeing his beautiful cock hard and resting against the cotton, his balls drawn up tight, and some lovely, fading pink marks on his ass and thighs where her switch had bitten into him that morning.

She wasn't surprised that even with the time she'd been away he was still hard. From the time she went to the couch with her book and a refreshed glass of wine, to the time she tied him to the bed, he'd stood beside her, hands linked behind his head, and she'd read (not really taking anything in because she had a tall, handsome man with a big, beautiful, hard cock standing beside her) and sipped her wine.

And played.

It wasn't relentless.

It was a delicious realization that he was also the kind of sub who liked that kind of play because the longer it lasted, the harder he got, the bigger reaction she'd get when she eventually touched him, to the point the last several times he couldn't hold back his groans.

And right then, as sheer the perfection was that he was, she approached the bed carrying the things that would complete that to finish preparing him so they could go to sleep.

She touched a hand to the back of his ankle and her grin got bigger when she saw the bunched muscles of his calf and the sinews at the back of his thigh clench.

A light touch and he was reacting like that.

Her big boy was ready for her to get serious.

Climbing into bed on her knees, she ran her hand up his calf, his thigh, to his hip and she set aside what she'd brought with her.

"I want a day, Branch," she whispered, lighting her hand on the back of his other knee and gliding it up his thigh, "where I tie you down like this for me and you stay positioned for me all day. Whenever I fancy, I can come up, play with your balls, stroke your cock, spank you, eat you, fill your ass, fuck it."

She planted both hands in his ass and massaged the cheeks deep with her thumbs, hearing his grunt of pleasured pain as she pressed into the strips from his switch, and feeling that noise in her pussy.

"Maybe harnessed." She slid one hand down and stroked his sac and watched his ass jump at the touch.

Yes.

Sheer perfection.

"Balls and jaw," she kept at him. "Force your head back. Make you stay arched for me for hours."

"Pick the day," he grunted as she lifted her hand back to his ass and kept massaging, "I'm here."

More from Branch.

She took it.

"So good," she murmured, digging her thumbs in and widening the space she attended, massaging his ass, his upper hips, the muscles beside his spine at his lower back, then she came back down and spread him open hard.

"Fuck," he hissed.

"Have I swayed your world tonight, Branch?"

"Yes, ma'am," he bit off.

"I'm not done."

"Fucking great," he muttered, sounding like he meant it but was still bracing for it.

She loved that about him.

Fucking loved it.

She let him go and tucked the two washcloths she'd brought under the bolster because he wasn't moving tonight but her big boy could shoot a load and she'd already changed the sheets that day, she didn't feel like doing it again or having his cum seep into the mattress pad so she'd have to wash that too.

Then she squeezed a liberal dose from the tube she'd brought on her fore and middle fingers and trailed it up his crease, not hesitating when she'd reached her destination to dive both right in.

The headboard swayed as his hands wrapped around his ties jerked it and his head shot back.

Oh yes, she was going to harness that jaw and make him stay arched for her.

God.

Gorgeous.

"Feel good?" she asked unnecessarily.

"Fuck yes," he puffed out.

She fucked him with her fingers and watched his entire body strain against his bindings, taking it and liking it.

"God, I could watch you take a fucking for hours," she whispered reverently.

"Then do it," he challenged, but his voice was gruff.

"We'll find that time, baby, I promise," she whispered, withdrawing her fingers, and he expelled a breath that sounded very nice, but also disappointed.

Yes, he'd liked it.

She took up his jewel, used a hand to spread one side open and put the tip of the plug to his ass.

"You're missing something, handsome."

"Yeah I am," he grunted.

"You want it back?"

"Fuck yes."

God.

She loved that too.

"You want to be filled with me?"

"Fuck *yes.*"

Loved it.

"Ask for your jewel, Branch."

"Plug me, Evangeline, fill me with you. Give me my jewel. Ma'am, please."

She slid it slowly inside, watching his ass tip up to help and his head arch back as it opened him, and when he closed around it his face dropped to the pillows and he pushed out another breath.

She took in his ass filled with her.

Yes.

Now he was utter perfection.

"Now, I want my show," she whispered, wrapping her hand around his rock-hard dick. "Take yourself there, Branch. Flaunt my jewel for me. Show me how beautiful it is, what's mine. And come whenever you're ready."

He said nothing.

But he did as told.

And watching him fuck her fist tied to her bed with her jewel winking from his ass, she wished she hadn't decided that she too was going to wait for her own climax so when the time came to rock his world, she could rock *both* their worlds.

When he finally blew, it might not have been as outstanding as the first two orgasms she'd given him, but it was still magnificent.

And that was the point. When the real goodness came, he needed to be ready.

Anyway, she couldn't force that out of him each time or he'd eventually not have the strength to function and that'd be no good at all.

She milked him dry, gently withdrew her hand and folded the cloths over on each other, pulling them away.

She then put her hands to his ass, one thumb to his plug, and kissed the small of his back, pressing in lightly with her thumb, and said there, "You sleep with my jewel, baby."

"Fuck yeah, Angie."

She grinned against his skin.

He liked her inside.

And she loved that too.

She made short work of preparing for bed.

And joining Branch there.

eleven

I Do Not Share

BRANCH

"Good?"

"Fuck yes."

"More?"

"Fuck yes."

"Take it, baby."

"Give it, Angie."

Fuck, fuck, *fuck.*

She did, with him untied, cheek in the pillows, knees slightly pulled up, as he'd been ordered, she took his ass with his plug while he stayed in position to take it, unmoving, as he'd also been ordered.

"My cock needs you, Angie," he grunted.

"Hmm."

"Please, ma'am."

"So sweet."

She went faster.

He pushed his palms into the mattress as his head tilted back.

The tip of the wide plug slammed right where he needed it again and again and shit, fuck, he was gonna blow.

"Ma'am."

"You like to get fucked, don't you, Branch?"

"Fuckin' love it how you do it, Angie."

"Take more."

"Let me jack my cock."

"Not yet."

"Fuck," he hissed.

She kept at him and, without his permission, or hers, his hand shot out, bracing against the headboard, and when it did, she demanded, "Up on your knees, hands behind your head."

He came up on his knees, feeling the plug sink into place, and she was behind him, one hand cupping his balls, the other hand wrapped around his cock and pumping, and he linked his hands behind his head.

"Let go," she whispered.

He did, thrusting into her hand.

"Need to come," he grunted.

"Do it," she whispered.

He arched, she pumped, squeezed, and he shot across the towel she'd slid under him when she'd positioned him.

His body jerked, his cock thrust through her fist, and he kept jetting across the towel until the orgasm shifted to shudders and he fell forward on the bed.

She kept hold and went with him, neither hand moving, just holding him warm and sweet, like her body was curled over him, tits pressed to his back.

Warm and sweet.

"I hadn't meant to let you come, hoping to get you primed for later, but you're just so pretty when you blow, baby," she whispered against his skin. Her tone moved from awed to amused when she went on, "Good I had foresight just in case to lay that towel. After witnessing that, I'm not in the mood for more laundry."

Shit, he hadn't told her later would be *later* because he had to work for Aryas that night.

Now was not that time.

Now was the time to feel fucking great after she'd worked him, get his wits together and allow himself a moment to feel her, warm and sweet, all around him, her hold claiming on his junk, so he could pretend for a time he was the man who could give it to her in a real way and then take out that memory later, when he needed it, having it forever.

Eventually, he murmured, "Need to see to you, Angie."

"I want you primed, Branch, but I want to be primed too, and if you keep giving me this goodness, when I let you give me *the* goodness, I might pass out from my orgasm."

Fuck, he couldn't wait to see that.

"I'll be there to revive you."

"Yes, you will," she whispered, kissing his back.

Branch closed his eyes.

Evangeline laid her cheek to his skin. "As much as I'd like to stay here like this with you forever, I probably should go get ready to sell some houses."

"Yeah," he muttered and didn't hide, like she didn't, that he didn't much like agreeing.

He lifted up and she went with him, her hands leaving his groin so she could wrap her arms around his middle.

He stilled.

She rubbed her face in his back.

He closed his eyes again and memorized all of that too.

"Okay," she gave him a squeeze. "We should probably get out of bed now."

Branch took her hand, moved out of in front of her, turned and swept her with an arm before rolling out of bed.

He set her on her feet in front of him, her hands now on his chest, her head tipped back, the dawning sun no match to her dazzling smile that felt like it lit the dusky room.

"Now that's the way a woman wants to be pulled out of bed every morning," she said through her smile.

"So noted. Shower?" he asked.

She leaned into him, pressing her breasts to her forearms against his chest.

"Definitely."

She whooped as he swept her up in his arms and carried her to the shower.

And hearing it, having her where she was, he almost smiled.

Almost.

"That's not good news," Evangeline said.

No, it fucking wasn't.

They were in her kitchen. She was putzing around. He thought it was cute. And she'd just pushed a travel mug of coffee in his hand because he was dressed, had her lipstick around his cock, her jewel still up his ass, and he was about to walk out the door.

But he'd told her tonight was out because he had work.

"I'd say I'd come to you when I'm done but I won't be done until at least four, four thirty."

She stopped what she was doing and looked to him, her eyes big.

"Yowza."

Fucking Evangeline.

No end to the cute.

He ignored that and carried on.

"I don't want you to have that hassle. I'll go home and sleep it off and see you tomorrow."

"You can sleep it off here."

"Come again?"

She shook her head and he felt it in his gut with how she looked away and mumbled, "Nothing." She raised her voice and went back to pouring milk into instant oatmeal as she said, "Work is work, Branch. I get it. A lot of the time I have to work nights and weekends too." She put the milk aside and turned to him with a small grin. "More time to get primed."

He wasn't feeling like her change in subject.

"You want me to sleep it off here?"

The grin faded and she shook her head. "After working all night, you don't want to sleep tied to a bed, not that that was what I meant," she said the last hurriedly. "You could just sleep. After working that late, you'll need to get rested. Just that, well, it just came out. I mean, you probably have a nice house and a nice bed and—"

"My condo's a dump and my bed is lumpy."

She said nothing and just stared at him.

"Except for when I show, will you even be here?" he asked. "You'll have to get to work and I'll still be wanting some shut-eye."

"It just came out, Branch. I wasn't thinking."

"I'll show and you won't work me. Just crawl into bed with you and sleep here?" he pushed.

"I know what this is," she whispered suddenly, locking like he'd never seen her look.

Miserable.

"Don't worry," she continued. "I know what this is. Aryas made that clear. But while I have you . . ." she trailed off, shook her head. "I just like you around and I didn't think. Just let the words come out."

Branch stood there, feeling too much, and stared at her.

But in all the too much he was feeling, the thing he felt the most was hating like fuck that look on her face.

She tried to force it off with a smile but he knew her smile. It was burned into his soul.

And the one she was giving him was fake.

"Tomorrow, after dinner, I'll introduce you to my playroom."

"I like that you like me around."

Yup.

He'd just said that.

Fuck.

Something like wonder filled her face.

Fuck.

"Tell me the code to your alarm, Angie, because you're gonna set that fucker and I don't want to set it off at five in the morning when I show."

That made her face light and he wasn't an asshole.

He was a motherfucker.

Because he wanted to sleep in her bed with her, even if for an hour, then stay in it after she left because she wanted him to and not because her bed was comfortable, even if he was tied to it.

But because he was going to give it to her because *she* wanted it and he couldn't hack her looking like she'd looked, thinking she'd fucked up, thinking she wouldn't get what she wanted because he'd made it clear it wasn't hers to have.

Christ, he could barely sit on her couch without bolting.

And he couldn't believe he was standing in her kitchen with a travel mug of coffee in his hand that she'd made like he was her man and he'd earned the privilege to stand right there.

And now he was going to let himself in and crawl in bed with her like he belonged there.

Giving her indication that might be someplace he'd eventually belong.

Yep.

Total motherfucker.

"Eight, two, eight, eight," she stated immediately.

All other thoughts fled as Branch felt his brows snap together. "You got a security code with three of the same digits in it?"

"Oh no," she fake cried, "not another heartfelt lecture about how I need to stay safe. I already promised not to skip down the stairs and I *like* skipping. I can't take more, Branch."

"Total smartass," he muttered.

She gave him another happy smile.

He did his best to ignore it, a best that was not good enough.

"Change the code, Evangeline. But do it tomorrow, so I can get in without raising a holy racket and waking that sweet ass of yours up."

She kept smiling.

He wanted to walk to her and kiss it off her face.

Instead he turned to the door.

"Branch?" she called.

He had it opened and turned back.

"Your ass is sweeter," she declared.

"Love you love my ass, honey," he said low and watched his tone register in her face, seeing it soften, and knowing the mother-fucker he was he'd give her that again too so he'd see more of that look. "And it loves you. But trust me on this. I might not have got my hands on it yet, but still. Your ass is *way* sweeter."

He didn't let her say dick.

Before she could crawl deeper into his soul, he walked out the door.

"It's cool you doin' this, Branch," Pat said.

Branch was in the control room at the Honey. The large bank of monitors that filled one wall were all either showing active play-rooms, static views of the area around the building, reception, or two wide angles that offered views to the entirety of the large bar space the members called the hunting ground. There were also monitors with constantly shifting views of the maze of halls, and also two with views of the smaller bar that was deeper in the building, the social room.

"Not a problem," Branch replied, walking in, eyes to the monitors, seeing Olly and Leigh sitting in a booth, curled into each other and chatting.

Ol had been trying to get hold of him now for weeks. But his head had been fucked from the minute he'd walked out of Aryas's red room, turning down the promise Evangeline had written all over her, and he'd avoided his calls.

Ol was in love, living with his woman, and he had it all. A classy Mistress that did it for him and an amazing lady in his life, sharing his home and bed with her, who also did it for him.

In that state, anyone wanted to spread that goodness.

And Ol had been riding his ass, if cautiously and being cool about it, but he didn't let up about Branch finding the same since the minute, in a moment of weakness (something he seemed to be getting way too fucking much lately), Branch had shared they were brothers in more than the fact they both had a dick.

After walking away from Evangeline, he couldn't deal with more of that.

Now, he definitely couldn't.

"Shit doesn't happen much," Pat said and Branch looked back to him. "Only need one man on the monitors. You'd think it'd be awesome, but you get it night after night . . ." He shrugged. "So we usually trade off. Half hour on. Half hour off. You're out of this room, you patrol. Hunting ground. Social. Halls. Outside. Rich, the bartender in the hunting ground, and Matt, a server assigned to social tonight, can be called in if shit goes down, which it won't 'cause it never does, but it's in their job description. I'll take first shift on monitors and you patrol."

"Right," Branch muttered, not sharing what Pat already knew.

He'd done this before.

He knew the drill.

And it wasn't hard.

"You're scenery, man," Pat kept at him. "I know you've done this before but a reminder. None of the members see you, if you can manage it, or even sense you, if you're good at it. Just keep an eye. Don't stay in one place too long. Especially in social. If the impossible occurs and something goes down and you're not in that room, I don't see it on the monitors and haul ass or Matt isn't on it, the male Doms'll be all over it. Don't watch. Patrol."

He knew how to patrol and he knew how to become scenery and he knew a fuckuva lot better than Pat knew either.

He didn't share that.

Because he also wasn't a big fan of having simple shit repeated to him, because he might not help with security at the Honey often, but he'd done it twice in his memory in the short year Pat had been working there. So he didn't need this guy sharing he thought his balls were bigger by treating Branch like he was a moron or like he was some asswipe who got his rocks off watching people play when he was supposed to be protecting them.

So he gave the guy a look that said all that even as his mouth moved.

"Yeah, man, like you said, I've done this before."

But he didn't need to say the words. The way Pat's head jerked to the side and his torso swayed slightly back showed he was alert and he'd read the threat of pissing Branch off.

Branch lifted his gaze to the clock at the back wall.

He glanced at Pat, shoving the earpiece in his ear that had a mouthpiece he could activate in the cord that control used to communicate to security on patrol, and said, "Half an hour."

Then he walked out.

The half an hour went fast and was boring as hell, considering the alternative was watching television while eating Angie's food (or her eating his) then letting her sway or rock or shatter his world, he didn't care which it was.

It would be with her.

The next half an hour wasn't any better considering it was early and most everyone was still in the hunting ground, or just preparing to go to the social room, so there wasn't a lot of activity except people drinking, some subs preening, some playing it cool, and Doms watching.

Very little action on monitors or patrol.

He went through three back-and-forth shifts, noting that Ol and Leigh were hanging, Queen Bee Mistress and her prince of a sub holding court, Masters and Mistresses sliding in their booth, chatting, sliding out, making an approach, standing at the side.

But most of the time, they just cuddled together, smiling a lot, touching a lot and sipping at their drinks, being together and also heightening the anticipation for what was to come.

After his third patrol, he came back, tugged the piece out of his ear, jerked his chin to Pat and Pat took off.

Branch settled in.

Olly and Leigh were still there, she was turned nearly fully into him, grinning up at his face because he'd just thrown his head back and laughed.

Pain sliced through Branch's gut.

He knew his friend understood the importance of all he had.

He still didn't.

His eyes scanned the monitors and he took note that in the last half an hour, people were getting down to business.

He didn't watch. He was on the job. He just assessed it was copasetic, and it all was, so his gaze moved on.

He caught it at the end of a flash of a hallway.

He reached forward immediately and hit the dial that would turn the monitor back to the view it'd scrolled out of.

And he stared.

"What the fuck?"

He couldn't believe his eyes.

But there was no denying there she was, in a hot, tight purple dress, high heels, hair piled high on her head like she'd worn it last night after she'd changed from her work clothes (and like she'd worn it in their bath) but more styled.

She was standing with the Dom who'd fucked her ex-boyfriend's ass after which he'd eaten out her pussy.

Evangeline.

"What the *fuck*?"

He leaned forward, pulled out his phone and tore his eyes from the monitors to scroll down his contacts.

Evangeline wouldn't have her phone as most of the women left their purses with reception so they didn't have that hassle, but also, he saw on the monitors she didn't have a purse. Or her phone.

The men usually didn't check anything at reception, they'd put it on vibrate, which was probably Aryas's policy, but they'd have their phones with them.

He found Olly's contact and hit "Go."

The hallway view had switched again so his eyes went to the hunting ground view where Olly and Leigh were sitting.

He saw Olly pull his phone out of his inside jacket pocket, check the screen, look at Amélie, say something then take his call.

"Hey, brother, what—?"

"Right now, I'm in the control room at the Honey and I saw Evangeline in the hall with a Dom. Go get her, Ol, and bring her to me."

He watched Olly's head jerk before he heard, "Uh . . . what?"

"I'm. In. The. Control. Room. At. The. Honey. Evangeline is there. In the halls. With a Dom. I cannot leave my post. Go *get* her and bring her to me.'

"Evangeline?"

"Olly," he bit out.

"Are you . . . ?"

Branch watched Ol drop his phone and listen to Leigh before he said something to her.

Amélie turned and looked directly at the camera, her striking face startled, before her lips quirked and she turned back to her man and said something in reply.

Olly lifted his phone to his ear. "Branch, bud, are you and Evangeline—?"

"She's with a Dom who's tasted her pussy when she's supposed to be home waiting for me. Go. *Get. Her,* Olly."

If he was close, he might be moved to punch the huge grin that spread on his friend's face.

Fortunately quickly, Ol replied, "Right. Going now. Hang tight."

He disconnected and watched Olly and Leigh both slide out of the booth, Leigh doing so because she was sitting on the outside. Amélie slid back in, watching her man walk toward the door that led to the playrooms before her eyes came back to the camera and Branch saw her cat's smile.

He looked away and scanned the rest of the screens, turning his mind while he waited.

He saw Olly approach the Dom and Angie, who were both at some windows, watching a scene in a playroom, and the screen scrolled. When he saw that view again, the Dom was standing alone, staring down the hall, his face not hiding he was pretty fucking ticked.

And Branch knew, looking at him, he was not ticked that a sub came and collected the Domme he was enjoying a scene with.

He was ticked because he liked the taste of Evangeline's pussy.

He scanned the screens and waited, coming slowly out of his chair in an effort to keep his cool when the knock sounded at the door.

He opened it and looked down at Angie's pretty face all made up, making it, if not prettier, definitely hotter, and noting distractedly her body looked even better in that fucking dress when he could see it close up.

"Branch," she breathed, then her eyes grew big.

She looked at Ol, at Branch, at Ol, then at Branch again.

Fuck, she was cute even when he was seriously fucking *pissed at her.*

"Thanks, Ol, got it from here," he stated.

Leaning in to nab her hand, he pulled her in the room.

Then he shut the door on Olly's smirking face.

He turned to her, and before he could open his mouth, she was there.

"What are you doing here?"

"That was my question to you," he shot back.

"I . . . well," she shook her head, "I'm a member. Well, I mean, my membership has lapsed, because it's a whopper of a fee and I had a roof to pay for, among other things, and I wasn't coming here, but I don't think Aryas will mind this once, since he wants me back in the fold, so—"

With his hand in hers he drew her closer and growled, "Angie."

She looked to the screens then to him.

"Oh," she whispered. "You're doing a job for Aryas."

"He needed cover," Branch bit out. "Now, baby, answer my fucking question."

"My friends wanted me back," she said.

"And the guy you're sharing your bed with thought your ass was at home, watching TV."

"Branch—"

"But instead, he saw you on the monitors hanging with a Dom who wants another crack at your pussy."

She swayed back.

He pulled her forward.

"I know all that happened, Evangeline."

"Okay," she said softly.

"And I know that guy doesn't give a shit you're a Domme. He'd go sub for ten minutes to get on his knees and beg you to partner with him."

"I don't think Damian—"

"He wants you, Angie. Doms work together all the time, that work gets hands-on between the Doms and you know it and he wants that with you. Again. And again. And a-fuckin'-*gain*."

Her eyes drifted to the screens as she murmured, "I was kind of getting that when he said he wanted to have dinner with me."

Branch's vision exploded.

"Say *what?*"

She gave her attention back to Branch. "*I* said lunch. *He* said dinner."

"Babe, you're not havin' lunch with this guy."

"I—"

"Repeat after me, 'Branch, honey, I am not havin' lunch or dinner or *anything with this guy*.'"

She went still and stared up at him.

"You're not repeating after me," he warned.

She jerked like he'd forced her from a stupor and shifted toward him, putting a calming hand on his chest.

"Branch, honey," she started in that sexy voice of hers, "I'm not having lunch or dinner or anything with Damian."

"You are correct. You're not."

"We're exclusive," she said, and Branch was too pissed to hear that it came shyly. "I don't share. And clearly, you don't share either."

"Correct again. I do not share. Not you."

She went silent and stared up into his eyes, standing close, smelling good, her hand on his chest.

Branch just stared back, trying to get a lock on his temper.

Eventually, she spoke. "You're hot when you're being all alpha-possessive."

"You can show your appreciation of that by fucking me raw and draining my dick dry when I'm not this pissed at you."

Her head tipped to the side with curiosity and not a hint of fear. "You're pissed at me?"

"Angie, you were in the hall of a sex club with another man."

"He invited me to watch a scene. Sixx is working."

"Angie, you were in the *hall* of a *sex club* with *another man* when I thought you were at home, alone, waiting for me."

Understanding clearly fully dawned because she gave him that look he'd only had once, but he'd become addicted to it at a glance, the soft one, before she got closer, slid her hand up to his neck and whispered, "I'm sorry. You're right. I thought, since you were out working, not knowing you were working here, obviously, that seeing as everyone has been asking me to come back, and to make them feel better and think I *am* back, I'd take this opportunity to come into the Honey. Gab with some friends. See and be seen. Then go home." Her hand at his neck gave a slight squeeze. "I wasn't going to do anything, not with Damian, not with anybody. I didn't even think I'd go back to the playrooms. But Sixx is working and, well . . ." She grinned. "Watching Sixx, a girl could get ideas."

"It goes without saying I'm all about you feeding your imagination, Angie. But if I've got shit to do that takes me away from you, you wanna hit the Honey, you let me know. I won't hit it with you but I got an in to keep an eye on shit, and if it goes south, I'll get a call so I can get my ass here."

Her fingers at his neck squeezed hard, and for a second, what was wafting off her filled the room.

Then it cleared away.

"Nothing will happen to me here, Branch," she said softly.

"I know," he returned firmly.

She quieted but that soft look came back, it was also warm, and he felt both in his gut, his dick, his balls and all through his chest.

It felt phenomenal.

However.

"Are we understood?" he pressed.

"We're understood, Branch."

Hearing that, he walked direct to the wide-seated, comfortable rolling desk chair he'd vacated, dragging her with him. He sat in it, pulled her ass into his lap and leaned them both forward to turn the knob that would open comms to the earpiece Pat was wearing.

"You keep patrol until I tell you you can come back," he ordered into the room.

"Sorry, repeat?" Pat's voice could be heard asking.

"You keep patrol until I tell you that you can come back."

"Doesn't work that way, Dillinger."

"Does tonight."

"Dude—"

"I got someone in here with me and we're settled in."

"That is *not* on, Dillinger," Pat returned irately. "No one but security and staff in—"

"You call Aryas right now and ask if he's cool with me sittin' the night in control with one of his members. He'll know what you're sayin' and he'll tell you that you keep patrol until I tell you that you can come back. Now are you comin' here and gettin' in my face about this so we call Aryas together so he can tell you to back off and be pissed you interrupted him in whatever the fuck he's doing right now? Or are you gonna keep patrol?"

There was silence.

Then Pat replied, "I'll keep patrol."

"Good call."

He turned off outbound comms, sat back and looked to the screens.

Evangeline fiddled with the collar of the dark-blue dress shirt he was wearing.

He was dressed like a member, suit jacket, slacks, nice shirt, nice shoes that weren't all that comfortable. None of it was. He couldn't imagine working in an office.

But to be part of the scenery, you had to wear camouflage.

"Your last name is Dillinger," she whispered.

It was now.

"Yup."

A beat of silence ensued before, "You look nice dressed up, Branch."

He glanced at her to see her eyes to his shirt then he turned back to the screens.

"I'm counting the minutes I can rip this shit off."

He heard her giggle and that hit warm in his chest too.

"You're definitely a cargo pants and jeans guy."

He grunted because he felt it unnecessary to put too much effort into agreeing to the obvious.

"Um . . . so, can you, well . . . *explain* what just went down with Amélie's Olly?"

He looked down at her. "He's a friend."

Her brows rose. "He is?"

"A good one."

"Oh," she mumbled.

He turned back to the screens.

"I'm thinking he knows about us now," she noted.

She was undoubtedly right.

And damn if he didn't give a fuck about that either.

"Ol isn't stupid, so yeah."

"And he'll tell Leigh."

He didn't have to.

She knew too.

"Yeah."

"Are you okay with that?"

He looked down at her. "Those two. And you should know, Aryas knows."

"Oh," she mumbled again.

"Those two and Aryas only. I'll have a word with Olly later. I'll tell him to have a word with his woman. Tell them to keep it to themselves. But only those three, Angie."

She nodded.

No discussion. No pushing.

She just nodded.

Like when he started their chat last night and he told her not to skip down the stairs. She seemed confused, but when she got it, she got it, agreed to be safe and there it was.

No argument. No bickering.

There it was.

She also didn't push to know what was behind what he was saying now.

She simply settled in his lap and fiddled with the buttons of his shirt.

She felt made to fit there.

Fuck.

"You want me to call, have a server bring you a drink?" he offered, eyes to the screens.

"I'm good, honey."

She sounded it, quiet, content.

Gorgeous.

Fuck, he just kept pushing it further, dragging her right along with him.

But he didn't set her off his lap.

He wrapped his arms loosely around her.

She snuggled closer.

Gorgeous.

Fuck.

"Just to say, good call sending a sub the size of a house with his Domme's command to come and get me. Things might have gotten hairy with Damian if I walked off with a sub who'd come to fetch me if that sub didn't belong to Amélie. He's kind of a stickler for the rules."

"I just told him to get you. I didn't tell him how to do that. It would have been me if I could leave this room. I can't. So it was Olly."

"Well, he was clever about it," she muttered.

Whatever.

Branch had gotten what he wanted. He didn't care what shit went down to get it.

"That's the first time I met Olly," she shared.

Branch said nothing.

"He's perfect for Leigh. Like he was made for her."

Branch knew how that felt.

Shit.

"Now I'm even more pleased for Leigh," she murmured.

"You should be," he replied. "They're happy."

She snuggled closer.

They sat in comfortable silence for a good long time before she murmured, "Sixx is a master."

Branch's eyes went to the Mistress she'd mentioned and he couldn't disagree. He'd seen the woman work more than once. But he'd turned down the opportunity for her to work him when Aryas made it some time ago, not because the woman didn't know her shit and explore it on a variety of different levels. There was just something about her that hadn't done it for him, something off, something that made Whitney seem, regardless of Sixx's obviously superior talents, warmer and fuzzier.

In a big way.

He tightened his arms slightly.

"No, Angie, she's a Mistress."

"Yes, she is."

He watched Sixx at work and saw again that she was very good at what she did.

But she was no Evangeline.

More silence then she said softly, "It's beautiful."

"Sixx?"

"Leigh with her Olly."

Olly and Leigh had finally hit a playroom.

His eyes moved up to the screen with a view to Ol's room.

Like Evangeline, when she was ready to roll, Amélie didn't mess around.

His bud was strapped to the floor, arms out in front of him, forehead to the wood, on his knees, calves and ankles strapped down set wide, long pony's tail up his ass, body glistening with oil, his enormous cock hanging hard and heavy, getting his back and ass and thighs curried by his woman.

Branch moved his eyes away.

Not because it wasn't beautiful, like Angie said. It was.

Just that was his bud and he knew Olly no longer gave that first fuck people watched. He liked it. Was proud of it, what he could give to his woman. What he'd earned in return. Got off on it. He'd shared all this with Branch.

It was just that Olly wouldn't care if Branch saw, but Branch would care if Olly saw. That had never been his gig. And so he felt the need to return a favor that didn't need returning.

Still, he did it.

"Feels weird, watching them," she noted. "Like an invasion of privacy."

"I hear that."

"You probably can't turn off their monitor."

He gave her a squeeze. "Sorry, baby, no."

"I get it."

She did more than anybody, even though hell would freeze over before Olly hurt Amélie in any way he could do that.

"They don't mind," he told her.

"I know."

"He's proud of it. He likes that she shows him off."

"Really?"

"Yup."

"So you guys *are* close."

He glanced down at her to see her gazing up at him. "Yeah."

She grinned.

He tore his eyes away and looked back at the screens.

"She's never tailed anybody that I know of," she murmured.

"She has now," Branch pointed out the obvious.

"Saved it for the right one."

"Mm," he hummed.

There was more silence, it lasted awhile, it felt good, right, but it was no surprise Evangeline broke it when Ol started humping the air, head back, the tail clearly jacking his hole in a way he liked.

Branch wondered if he looked like that when Angie was working him.

He hoped so. Even watching it come from his brother, Branch hoped he gave even a little bit of that to Evangeline.

What he knew was Angie's face looked like Leigh's.

Sweet.

And hungry.

She shifted in his lap. "I can't wait to get you in my playroom."

He drew her closer. "Me either, Angie."

He held her longer and silence set in, lengthened, when finally she tipped her head back and kissed under his jaw.

Branch closed his eyes.

"I better go. Leave you to it. Need some sleep, honey. I'll see you when you get there."

He looked down at her soft, contented, pretty little face and there'd been a number of times when he could kiss her, when he knew they both wanted it, and now was one of those times.

He didn't kiss her.

He whispered, 'See you when I get there."

She didn't quite hide the disappointment but smiled, lifted her hand to run her fingers down his jaw, then scrambled off his lap.

Branch watched her walk to the door and he watched her open it.

And his soul lit again when she turned and blew him a kiss.

She winked, walked out the door.

And Branch manipulated the screens so he followed her, step by step, as she went to reception to get her purse then made it to her girly-ass car and drove away.

twelve

See the Light

EVANGELINE

The bed moved when Branch got in it.

"Branch?" she mumbled.

"Yeah, Angie, shh," he shushed her, drawing her into his arms, into his body, covering her slightly with his weight and warmth.

She felt her lips curl up, thought to say something, touch him, and began to slide an arm around him.

Then she fell asleep.

Evangeline woke, thankfully, before the alarm.

She shifted slightly and tipped her head back when the arms around her tightened.

She saw Branch's face in sleep, the still-shadowed room not hiding what wasn't surprising.

Even in sleep, he looked alert, like he could wake and be ready to face an attack without even blinking.

Evangeline wanted to soothe that, soften it so the expression on his face showed nothing but ease and serenity.

And not just in sleep.

But she'd take just sleep.

However, that might be an even more herculean task than the one she'd assigned herself so she decided to just stay on target . . . for now.

She could up her goals later.

And after how he'd behaved last night, just seeing her standing in the hall with Damian, then everything that came after, she was beginning to believe she might get the chance to do that.

Smiling to herself, she started to move out of his arms carefully, not wanting to disturb him.

But like a cat, his long body stretched even as his arms convulsed, pulling her back into his embrace, all this automatically.

She waited it out as he gathered her closer, still asleep, and tried not to let her smile split open her face.

When she again attempted to pull away, she watched his eyes flicker open.

"Sleep, baby, but I have to get up."

He blinked, gave her a squeeze, muttered, "'Kay," and let her go.

Rolling, he nabbed a pillow and pulled it to his chest, hitching up a leg, and she watched him fall back to sleep.

Lord, she didn't want to leave him.

But she had a meeting with Mira and Trey to go through their houses and set up their listing and she couldn't let her friend down.

So she got out of bed and was as quiet as she could be getting ready for work.

And so she wouldn't break down and bail on her friend, as she tiptoed, shoes dangling from her fingers, to the stairs, she only allowed herself a glance at Branch's amazingness as he slept in her bed. His black hair and tanned skin a shocking contrast against the pillows and sheets. His muscles still defined even in rest. And even with all the frills, flowers and ruffles, his body looking made to sleep in her bed.

She did her thing in the kitchen, leaving it tidy, but setting it up for when he got up and writing a note.

Then, with another smile on her face, she unarmed and rearmed the alarm, unlocked the door, locked it behind her and walked to her car.

She was in her office, working on Mira and Trey's listings, when her phone went.

It was Amélie.

Oh boy.

She took the call, answering casually, "Hey there."

"Hey there?" Amélie asked instantly, and somewhat irately.

She straightened in her chair and started, "Listen, Leigh—"

"We all must live our lives, Evangeline, and we do things for reasons that not everyone understands. But you sat there listening to me share my concerns about you turning away from your nature and you didn't say a thing. Your business is your business, *chérie.* However, I was open with my concern and I must admit to feeling some hurt you didn't find some way to assuage it."

Now she felt like a bitch.

"Leigh—" she tried again.

"Are you and Branch together?"

With that, she felt some surprise.

"Do you know him?" she asked.

"Of course, he's a good friend of Olly's."

This was something that came as a shock to her even though Branch had shared the same thing, and as Leigh and Olly were together, it shouldn't.

However, Branch seemed so impenetrable she couldn't imagine him having friends.

But he did.

Olly, as Branch had said last night.

And thinking about it, it was clear with the situation as it stood, Aryas was much more than someone who came to Branch for "jobs."

Aryas might own a string of exclusive sex clubs across the Western United States, but he wasn't a pimp. If he was looking for Dommes safe for Branch, he wasn't doing it to pay a marker or because he was the benevolent god of all who practiced BDSM and he worked tirelessly to make sure all his subjects got their kink.

He did it because he cared for Branch.

And now another friend (possibly), Leigh.

It was almost like Branch was a normal person (in the way Branch could be—that along with being unfairly gorgeous, a screamingly possessive alpha and a god among subs).

"We, well, we're . . . ," she tried to explain.

Together?

They were. They absolutely were.

They were exclusive.

They also weren't.

Together, that was.

The message Branch delivered last night was clear, however. The exclusive part was not in question.

She felt a happy tingle but ignored it.

"Listen," she went on, "you can't tell anybody."

"Why not?" Amélie asked.

"Because that's the way Branch wants it."

Amélie didn't reply.

"He's private about that," Evangeline explained.

"Understandable but I'm afraid, *chérie*, that cat is out of the bag."

Damn.

"How? Have you said something to someone?" she asked.

"No. Though we'll just say Damian wasn't all that pleased I sent my Olly to go fetch you and he came back to the hunting ground to share this with me. Since Olly was engaged in delivering you to Branch, Stellan overheard him and felt, as I was unprotected, regardless that I don't need protection, that he had to come to my rescue. This is good, in a way, we've been distant for a while. But it was also bad, because it caused a little hullabaloo."

Fabulous.

A hullabaloo at the Honey, little or not, was never good.

Leigh spoke on.

"Not as big a hullabaloo as you being back in the first place, which had interest piqued already. But Olly marching you through the hunting ground wasn't missed by anybody. Further, his escorting you to the control room wasn't missed by some arriving subs. This was shared and I'm afraid, my darling, that, although Aryas's security is very good, they aren't invisible. So although I don't think many of them know who Branch is personally, they saw him around last night and have seen him around at other times. He's not difficult to look at, among other things, so we'll just say he's rather unforgettable. And for an experienced Master, Mistress or sub, he's not entirely hard to read. They saw the other one was not the one in that room with you. So talk ran rampant, and correct, I'll note, assumptions were made."

Damn.

"Okay, Amélie, I'll warn Branch." Not a conversation she was looking forward to, though it *was* him who'd had her dragged to that room in the first place. "But please, can you try to keep a lock on it from now on?"

"If this is how you and Branch wish it, Leenie, then of course."

Evangeline let out a breath.

"How long has this been going on?" Leigh asked.

This was her new quandary.

He'd said only Aryas, Amélie and Olly.

But did he mean she could talk freely?

Or did she still have to honor the nondisclosure agreement even though they all knew?

Better safe than sorry.

"Like I said, and I'm sorry, Leigh, but Branch is really private."

"I don't find this surprising. What I will say is, I find it hopeful."

Evangeline felt warmth hit her belly.

"I didn't know Kevin that well outside the club," Amélie continued. "What I knew I liked, personally, and for you. But I didn't know him well. Branch, however, I like unreservedly."

More warmth hit her belly. So much it felt hot.

And good.

"Really?" she asked softly.

"Really, my darling," Amélie replied in the same way. "He's quiet. I can't say I know him very well either. But he's got a lovely manner. He's respectful. I'm uncertain how to describe it but he makes it clear his friendship with Olly is meaningful and, obviously, with Olly what he is to me, that means a good deal to me. And Olly thinks the world of him."

All this wasn't good.

It wasn't great.

It was *wonderful*

"I like him," she whispered, like Branch could hear her sharing.

"I'm glad." Amélie matched her tone. It was cute and sweet and felt beautiful.

"He's . . . he's . . . very honest, Leigh. In *everything*."

"That's a delight to hear, Leenie."

"We haven't been together long and he's, well . . . there are things—"

"You needn't say more or break whatever trust he has in you, Evangeline," Amélie assured. "I've been around him often. I understand what you're saying."

Evangeline knew she would.

And being able to talk about it, if not thoroughly and totally openly, felt marvelous.

Especially getting Amélie's opinion on Branch.

She only really needed Aryas's.

But Amélie concurring meant everything.

"I'm scared," she admitted.

"This also isn't surprising," Leigh replied gently.

"Of a lot of things," Evangeline carried on.

"My darling Leenie, the beauty of you is you feel that and you've still carried on. You don't have to share, I've not had what happened to you happen to me. I can't understand, I can just imagine how difficult it is to sally forth after what Kevin did to you. And you should feel exceptionally proud of yourself that you did that, Evangeline. Exceptionally proud."

Evangeline rubbed her lips together, liking hearing that too.

Leigh kept talking.

"And also, doing that with one such as Branch, who I can imagine is quite the match for you. I won't break the trust Olly has in me, and thus the trust Branch has in Olly with what he's shared that Olly has given to me. But I will say that I not only hope you best that match for you, I hope you do it for Branch. Olivier is worried about Branch finding happiness. However, I know, if anyone can bring that about, it's you."

"Thanks, Leigh," Evangeline whispered.

"Don't thank me for sharing the truth, Evangeline. Now, I'll just have to hope that you make great enough strides in that so the two of you can come over for dinner. Olly is over the moon that Branch has found somebody, especially after I've shared so much about you and he knows how lovely you are."

She grinned.

She couldn't help it.

But still she warned, "I wouldn't hold your breath for that, Amélie."

"I won't, Evangeline, but I'll still hope."

Evangeline would too.

"And I'll do my best to keep gossip curtailed while you do your work," Leigh went on.

"Thanks, Leigh. I appreciate it."

"Don't mention it, darling. Now you enjoy yourself and we'll have lunch again soon."

"Absolutely."

"Take care, Leenie."

"You too, Leigh."

They hung up and Evangeline looked to the clock on her computer.

It was just after noon. She had no idea if Branch was awake and taking on the day or not.

But she didn't want to wake him if he was not.

So, her lips curled up, her heart feeling light, she went back to her listings.

BRANCH

The phone ringing woke Branch up.

He opened his eyes, hauled his body the *long* way to the side of the bed and tagged the jacket he'd dropped to the floor last night.

He pulled out his phone and scowled at the screen.

Then he took the call.

"What?" he asked, trying to force the sleep from his voice but not quite succeeding.

"Brother, it's past noon and I woke you up? Did she jack your shit and good when you made it back to her and you're still recovering? Or did she paddle your ass for dragging her away from Sixx's scene, the burn didn't let you get to sleep and you're still recovering?" Olly harassed.

"Fuck off," Branch muttered, rolling to his back and pushing up so his shoulders were against the headboard.

"Thanks for the opportunity, Branch. Leigh was so pleased I delivered her friend to you, she *did* jack my shit and good, so when we got home I slept like a baby."

Unfortunately, Branch had witnessed that very thing.

He didn't share that.

Then again, Olly knew he was in the control room so he knew he did. He just didn't give a fuck.

"You're obviously not fucking off."

Olly's voice got low. "Bud, I'm so fuckin' happy for you, I don't even got words to express it."

Branch dropped his head but opened his mouth to speak.

"Don't get excited, Ol, we've been together just days and it isn't going anywhere."

Olly didn't hide he didn't like that.

"Why the fuck not?"

"She's a good woman."

"Then I'll repeat. Why the fuck not?"

"She doesn't need my shit."

"If she hasn't had the chance to give it to you, it's not mine to give. We'll just say I just met her last night but I know a lot about her and she's a strong woman, Branch. My guess, strong enough to take your shit."

"I know how strong she is. I know her story. And that might be the case, she still doesn't deserve it."

"I don't get this, man."

"You don't need my shit either."

"Well then, brother, let me give you a crash course in friend-ship," Olly returned with a sudden bite in his tone. "It isn't about the good times over beer. It's about the shit times and being able to stand strong by your boy when he's having them or after he's had them or whenever it hits. So I might not need it and I might not want it but I'm *your* boy, so if you ever feel like giving it to me, I'm no brother at all if I don't take it."

Branch rolled his neck, feeling so much, he didn't speak.

He didn't need to.

Ol wasn't done.

"And same thing if you find a good woman. You said she's a good woman and you know better than me. But Leigh doesn't suffer fools gladly so I also know your assessment is true so my guess is, you give her your shit, she'll take it, help you get past it and then maybe you can find your way to happy."

"My brand of shit, Ol, you don't know, but no one needs it."

"You know because I told you that I landed *my* brand of shit on

Leigh and it was a load, Branch. It nearly buried us both. But she was falling in love with me and saw the promise we had so she found her way through it and look what I got."

"Ol—"

"No," Olly cut him off. "You mean something to me, Branch. You were there when I needed you and I don't give a fuck you were being paid. What you made happen was meaningful to me and you got my trust, brother, and you earned a place in my heart, so I can't listen to this shit anymore. I know a lot of men who are good men, relatively decent men, but they're still dicks. I know two men who are good men, decent men, right to their balls, and they deserve to be happy. Clay is one. You're the other."

Ol was talking about the situation Branch helped out with when a maverick Domme at the club injected her poison into a variety of lives, including Amélie's.

He was also talking about Barclay, part-owner of the Bolt, who was now a friend of Branch's because Olly was a friend and Olly's assessment of that man wasn't wrong.

"Find your way past this, Branch," Olly urged. "And if I can help with that in any way, you know, but I'll say it again, I'm here."

All Branch could give that was a "Right."

That was when Olly lowered the boom.

"And just sayin', you can't, don't know this woman, just know she means a lot to Leigh, so if you can't sort your shit, cut her loose because she doesn't need to be played that way."

"I can't."

Fuck.

He was so fucked in the head, he couldn't even control his own goddamned mouth.

"Then don't," Olly whispered. "And be fuckin' *happy*."

It was safe to say he'd had enough.

"I need to be done with this chat," Branch clipped.

"I'll give you that."

"And I need you to keep a lock on this. What Evangeline and me have is ours. You know. Amélie knows. Aryas knows. That's it, man."

" 'Fraid it's too late to flip that lock, Branch. You know the Honey but figure you don't know that about the Honey. Evangeline is popular and it's a wonder balloons and confetti didn't drop when she hit the hunting ground last night. The one and one that equals the two of you might be more like algebra. But those people are used to figuring out complicated equations. And they want good for her. So a whiff of it, they were all over it."

Fuck.

"Then just do your best to stem that tide, Ol. Want her and me to be just her and me but it's not anyone's business the way I play it."

"You got it, bud," Olly muttered.

"Just got up. Got shit to do. I dig what you've said, man, and time comes I need that, I'll take you up on it. Just need you to know now, it's appreciated."

"And that's good to know."

"Talk and beer later."

"Yeah. Later, Branch."

"Yeah."

They disconnected and Branch pulled himself out of the bed, throwing his phone on the nightstand and heading to the bathroom.

He used the toilet, washed his hands, splashed water on his face, and it had been so long since he'd spent the night at a woman's home in the way he'd done last night at Angie's, putting him where he was right then, not getting his ass dressed and out the door, he hadn't thought to bring a toothbrush.

She had an electric one. He found a replacement head. Went for it. Then headed back to the bedroom and got dressed.

He was in the kitchen when he saw a large, square, neon Post-it stuck to the coffee machine.

He went there, ripped it off and read:

MBB,

MBB?
What the . . . ?
His mouth twitched up in an almost grin.
Her big boy.
He read on.

Hope you slept well.
*   Help yourself to whatever. I set up the coffeepot. The switch on the front, flip it to on.*

Branch needed some coffee so he did just that.
Then he read on.

I've got a late-ish showing tonight but I should be home around 6:30. Maybe latest 7:00.
*   My turn to cook, if you don't mind eating late. If you do, we'll get takeout and I'll pick something up to bring it home with me.*
*   See you later, handsome.*

*   xxx E*

Her turn to cook.
He'd wait.
And not let himself think about how easy he was letting him-self fall into shit like it being her turn to cook.
He also didn't let himself think about moving around her kitchen as he searched for some bagels, didn't find any but did find some English muffins so he loaded one in the toaster.
While he was getting out butter, his phone went again.
Unknown call, no number, no location, nothing.
Which likely meant Gerbil.

Good timing.

If word spread about him and Evangeline, it increased his vulnerability.

And hers.

There was a reason there weren't a lot of people in his life and this was for his safety.

And theirs.

A dead man didn't have friends, but Branch had allowed himself a few of them he knew he could trust.

But that man absolutely didn't have a woman.

"Yo," he answered Gerbil's call.

"Piz," Gerbil replied.

Branch stilled on the short trek from fridge to counter with the butter.

"What about Piz?"

"You know that crazy-ass bitch he married and divorced who was most of the reason why he didn't mind becoming a ghost to be on Rifle Team?" Gerbil asked.

"Yeah," Branch answered.

"Well, the crazy-ass bitch was more like a cunt. She divorced his ass and didn't share she did it pregnant with his kid."

Branch unfroze and made his way to the toaster, saying, "You're shitting me."

"Nope. A little girl. She's almost seven now. And crazy, bitch-ass mama has decided the government is going to set them up so she's all up in their shit, threatening to sue, saying Piz died the first time he died, that being the fake one, due to negligence. This being why he was traced to Rifle Team and the files were discovered."

"I can't fucking believe that woman was pregnant. If Piz knew—"

"He'd be alive, a part-time daddy, because if he knew he had a kid, he'd never sign on to Rifle Team," Gerbil finished for him.

They both fell silent, thoughts of Piz alive, the man they knew who they also knew would kick ass as a father and love doing it weighing heavy over the phone line.

Gerbil broke it.

"From internal memos, they're gonna pay her off to shut her up. So she'll go away. And outside Raines being screwed that audit brought his shit to light, everything's all good, brother."

At least there was that.

"Thanks for lookin' into that," he said, the muffins popping up, he put them on a plate and got a knife.

With that, he stilled again.

Because he knew right where her knives were.

Shit.

He reactivated and moved back to the muffins, asking, "And Raines?"

"Well, just because I like how you mete out vengeance, I'll have to admit to making it a little tough on the new guy's team in finding him. You say the word, I'll make that easier."

"I feel like saying the word, I'll do that," Branch replied. "Now, I gotta share that things with me and Evangeline aren't under wraps like they used to be."

"Under wraps?"

"No one knew about us."

"Why?"

Not a-fuckin'-gain.

"Do I need to explain?" he clipped.

"Yeah, you do," Gerbil retorted.

"No, I don't," Branch ground out. "I made more enemies in those missions than just Raines, Cam."

"And they all think you're dead, John."

"Let's keep it that way. And now we gotta keep Evangeline safe. Because the circle I got is tight. And it seems the circle she's got is tight. But shit happens."

"For the most intuitive field operative I met in the entire fuckin'

United States intelligence corps, you're one dumb motherfucker," Gerbil fired at him.

Branch's back shot straight.

But again, as usual, Gerbil didn't let up.

"Two days ago, you tell me you're with a good woman and you want me to help you keep her safe. Now you tell me word's getting out in your circle. If you don't see what's happening to you with her, John, I'm gonna have to come out of my bunker and slap you upside the head so I can rattle it loose."

"Don't piss me off, Cameron," Branch growled.

"I'm a thousand miles away from you and even *you* couldn't penetrate the Gerbil Shelter even if you *could* kick my ass in about three seconds so don't mind if I do piss you off, John, so you'll see the fuckin' light."

"Last woman I gave a shit about I broke up with and a week later she went out and got herself dead."

"Fuck," Gerbil whispered.

"Head caved in with a baseball bat."

"Holy fuck, John, *fuck*."

"She would not have done the stupid shit she'd done to get herself in that position if I hadn't ended it with her so do *not* fuckin' tell me I need to see the light. Even if you don't get why I feel I have to do it, you need to get I feel I have to do it so I'm protecting Evangeline and I'm asking *you* to help me protect Evangeline and that's the last we'll talk of it. If you don't wanna help with that, *brother*, then just don't and shut the fuck up."

"I'll help, John. Of course. I'm here for you, always. Team, man. Brotherhood. Always."

"You got any more to give me?" Branch demanded.

"No."

"Then later."

With that, he disconnected.

He stared at the muffin, suddenly not hungry.

And his phone rang.

"Goddamn it," he bit out.

He looked at the screen and relaxed when he saw the name of a colleague he sometimes worked with, a man named Tucker Creed, on his phone.

Then he took the call.

And with all the shit he'd been getting that day even though he'd only been awake less than an hour, he needed time to clear his head.

So even though it meant missing Evangeline's cooking, the job Creed asked him to help out with, he took it.

EVANGELINE

After finishing up Mira and Trey's listings, Evangeline was about to head out the door to find some lunch.

But when her phone rang and it said Branch was calling, she didn't even bother playing it cool.

She snatched it up, took the call and put the phone to her ear.

"Hey," she greeted.

"Hey, thanks for making coffee."

She felt the smile split her face.

"Did you get some food?" she asked.

"Muffin," he muttered then spoke more clearly, "Listen, Angie, this sucks but a friend of mine called. His usual partner is his wife, don't ask, she's arguably more badass than him, but that's beside the point. They've got a job and they can't find a babysitter and it's her turn to watch the kids. He's asked if I'd take his back on it tonight and we trade favors. I gotta do it."

"Oh," she whispered.

"It's gonna run late, I don't know how late."

"Oh," she repeated.

And waited.

He had her key.

His job had run late last night too, but he'd come to her and pulled her in his arms when he'd crawled into her bed.

This after he pitched an alpha fit at seeing her with another man.

But she waited.

And he made her wait.

And then she waited more.

And he said nothing.

"So, well, okay," she filled the silence. "Tomorrow?"

"Yeah."

"It's Saturday but I have an open house so I won't be home until maybe six."

"Fine. Be here then."

She was going to sleep alone.

Okay.

Right.

Maybe he needed this and maybe she needed to pull back and give it to him.

And also, maybe she needed some time too.

But she had more to say, things he wouldn't like, and she might as well get it over with.

"You should know, I spoke with Amélie and she said—"

"I know," he cut her off. "Ol called. I asked him to nip it in the bud the best he could."

"I said the same to Leigh."

"Good."

He said no more.

She waited again.

He still said no more.

Evangeline again filled the silence.

"Okay, then, I'll see you tomorrow."

"Tomorrow, Evangeline."

With that, she heard the disconnect.

She stared at her phone.

It wasn't like she didn't expect a fight. A wild ride. Ups. Downs. Steps forward. Steps back.

But after last night, first sitting held in his arms in his lap at the Honey like they'd done it thousands of times before, then being pulled into his arms in her bed, she thought . . .

It didn't matter what she thought.

She needed to stay strong.

She was getting in there.

She knew it.

And she'd come to know that Branch was worth the ups. The downs. The wild ride.

The fight.

She just needed not to give up.

thirteen

Evenly Matched

EVANGELINE

At nine o'clock Tuesday night, Evangeline heard the kitchen door open.

She was sitting in her couch, back to the door, not exactly watching the fourth episode of *True Detective*.

She looked not over her shoulder toward the kitchen door, but down to her phone that was sitting on the seat of the couch beside her, which she activated.

The text string came up.

Saturday at 6:23 p.m.: *Not going to make it. Tomorrow.*
Sunday at 5:40 p.m.: *Tonight's not good. Tomorrow.*
Monday at 6:57 p.m.: *Tonight won't work. Tomorrow. Seven.*
That day at 7:47 p.m.: *Be late. Around nine. All right?*

She hadn't answered.
Because she was a woman.
A woman who met a man who, in his way, had told her the score.
Okay, she'd changed that score.
But fuck it, he didn't fight too hard.

And he'd done some adjusting of that score too because it was *him* that staked *his* claim with the Damian incident.

And he blows her off for work (understandable), twice (understandable) but *then* he blows her off not giving any reason, again *twice*. And *then* he texts, already late, to say he's going to show at nine at night on a Tuesday?

She looked at the time on her phone screen.

It was nine thirteen.

And after all that, he shows even later.

She looked back to the TV.

She saw out of the corner of her eye Branch enter the room. He stopped and she kept watching the TV so she didn't see what he was doing or what he was looking at.

He took his time before moving to the armchair that was angled toward the TV beyond the couch and he sat on its arm.

"You didn't lock the door, Angie."

Was he serious?

With that, she looked at him.

God.

Why did he have to be so gorgeous?

"You need to lock the door," he pushed, face inscrutable but nevertheless alert and watching her closely.

She looked back to the TV.

"You're pissed," he muttered.

He was a sharp one.

She said nothing.

He let the silence linger before he broke it.

Speaking quietly, he shared, "I needed time to clear my head."

"You have my number," she replied, still looking at the TV. "You could share that. Just like that. 'Evangeline, I need some time to clear my head.' You can speak the words or text them." She faced him and finished, "It's been intense, I know, Branch. I was there too. So I'd get it and you know I would."

"I know you would and I shared it just now."

She wasn't playing that game.

She grabbed the remote, paused the program, tossed the remote aside, then looked back to him.

"I like you," she stated baldly.

He winced and looked to the side.

God.

Branch.

"Sorry that hurts, Branch, but I like you," she kept at him. "You're handsome and you're honest and you can be funny and you can be sweet and you're strong and protective and possessive and your alpha tendencies are all kinds of hot and you make fabulous enchiladas and you're fucking *amazing* to play with. I love how you put yourself in my hands. I love how you react to me. I love how much you can take, how you let me be free to let go, how you trust me with you, how I can trust I can let go with you and we'll both get something beautiful out of it."

He looked back to her but made no reply.

"I get what this is," she informed him. "I told you, Aryas made it clear. Even so, that doesn't mean I'm not allowed to like you. Enjoy being with you. And I do. With both. But I'm a human being. I can't stop myself from feeling something for you, and to return the honesty, even though I sense you can't hack it, because of feeling that, hoping for something more. And more honesty, even though you're not stupid so I'd guess you already know, I pushed that. And even more honesty, Branch, I might have been muddying the waters but *you* did your own muddying, holding me in your lap at the Honey. And with all this honesty I'm giving you, you should know, I can't stop myself from feeling, and I also can't stop myself being a woman, and not only knowing I deserve some respect, but demanding it."

"I respect you, baby," he said, the words soft even with his gravelly voice so they were also sheer beauty.

"Don't be sweet," she whispered, the hurt filtering her tone,

damn it, and she saw him wince again when he caught it. She shook
her head. "My fault. Branch, I signed on, literally, to be your unpaid
Dominatrix whore. But to give you more honesty, with that, I'm not
sure *I* can hack it."

"You aren't my whore," he ground out, face now hard.

She tipped her head to the side. "No?"

"No," he clipped.

She sat still and waited.

Damned waiting.

It had only been four days but she was fed up.

She wanted to be strong, not to give up on him, but four days
of hurt and worry that he had four days to coat that marble with
more ice, or worse, he was going to vanish from her life, was four days
too many.

God, why had she even started this?

She'd known from the beginning there was a bigger chance at
failing than succeeding and with every minute she spent with him,
she knew there was more and more to lose.

So maybe she should cut *both* their losses.

"I think maybe—"

"That woman who I told you about, she was mine."

She snapped her mouth shut.

"She was not my first girlfriend," he held her gaze direct, "she
was not my first Mistress. But she was my first real one of both.
We lived together for two years but were together for four. We broke
up. Strike that," he spat out the last two words in a way that had
her, already alert, go straight to wired. "*I* broke up with her and she
didn't want it. It hurt both of us. She was sure we could work it out.
I was pissed about I don't know what the fuck but whatever it was
it wasn't worth digging my heels in. I dug my heels in. She could be
petty, something I know now we could have worked on because she
was young too, younger than me, and to make me pay, she answered
an ad from a sub. By the time he caved her head in, he'd taken out
three others. Not Dommes. Prostitutes, escorts. But she was his last.

They caught him after her. He's on his fourth appeal on his wait to get injected."

This was like a story out of a book.

A sad one.

Tragic.

Brutal.

It couldn't be real.

But looking into his eyes, she knew it was real.

"Branch," she whispered, her heart squeezing.

"I have fucked and been fucked by a lot of women but I've only had one relationship that mattered. I loved her, Angie. We had a lot of good times. But when life settled in and it wasn't all just good and easy, I didn't have the tools to pull my shit together and grow the fuck up. Met her when I was twenty-three, she was twenty-one, lost her when I was twenty-seven, she was just twenty-five. I'm now thirty-eight and I've lived with being young and stupid and proud and stubborn and what all that meant to her for a long time."

She turned to him, lifting a leg on the couch and started, "Honey, you didn't—"

"I've fucked and been fucked by a lot of women," he repeated, speaking over her. "And not one, not even her, gave me what you do and I do not only mean the way I love how you fuck my ass or switch it raw."

Evangeline held her body still as she felt a tickle slip up her spine, doing this also holding his gaze.

"I got so much baggage, honey, not just her, I'm just scratching the surface," he whispered. "You're so tiny, it'd crush you."

She felt tears sting her eyes.

He wasn't damaged.

She didn't know what he was. She'd never seen it.

The only way she could describe it was that he'd been *destroyed*.

"Please, Branch—" she began to whisper back.

"What I'm saying is, I like you too. But I can't give you dick. Only this. Only what we got now. But Angie, you gotta know, for your sake, for yours only, when I feel I gotta disappear, I gotta do that . . . for you. And if you can't take what I have to give, just take what we have and enjoy it while we've got it, then it'll fuckin' kill, but for you, right now, I have to walk out that door."

"I don't understand," she said softly.

"I can't explain and that's for you too."

She put a hand on the couch and leaned toward him. "I might be small, handsome, but don't let that fool you."

He shook his head. "Just know I know what I'm doing and know it's not for me, because if I was the motherfucker I could be, I wouldn't give this to you. I wouldn't warn you. I'd take, and when the time came, I'd leave. But you've got your warning, honey, and it is what it is and that's all it can be. So what's it gonna be?"

Evangeline stared in his eyes and gave him her own warning, "I know what it's going to be, Branch, but you need to know I'm not going to stop trying to break through."

He nodded. "I get that. I'll take it. Because I'm not the mother-fucker I could be, but I am the one I am. But just to say, baby, you fight that battle, you'll lose."

"I'm stubborn."

It almost looked like he was going to smile.

"Think I got that."

She continued staring into his eyes and promised, "I'm going to make you happy."

"I know."

She felt like an arrow pierced her heart, her body actually jerked with it.

She was giving that to him already.

But they were still having this conversation.

"I'm still going to walk away," he told her gently, confirming her thoughts.

Eyes locked, they both fell silent.

It was again Branch that broke it.

"So what's it gonna be, Angie?"

She saw him, not hiding he sat tense, waiting.

He didn't want her to tell him to go.

And at the same time, he did.

"You've thrown down the glove, Branch," she informed him.

Sadness filled his eyes.

She hated to see it.

But by damn, she was going to obliterate it.

"Be smart, baby," he whispered. "And be stronger than me because I don't have it in me to walk out that door. I'm here because I couldn't stay away. Four days I've been fighting the pull that's you and," he tossed up a hand to indicate himself sitting on the arm of her chair, "I lost. You say I'm protective but now I'm telling you, you have to protect yourself. You've gotta tell me to go."

She ignored his entire speech.

"And I'm picking it up."

He closed his eyes and looked away.

She sat still and silent.

He opened his eyes and looked to her.

"That wasn't smart, Evangeline," he said, still whispering.

She didn't reply.

Something moved over his face that twisted the tip of the arrow, tearing a hole, gaping.

"Because I'm weak, because I'm a motherfucker, and because you're all that's you, I need more so I can have it when I don't have you so it isn't me that's going to save you . . . this time," he shared.

Good.

Fucking *excellent.*

Perfect.

Evangeline got up and walked to him.

He kept his seat but tipped his head when she got close.

She put both hands to his cheeks and dipped her face to his.

He was so long, her feet were bare, but even standing with him sitting, she didn't have far to go.

She loved that.

And she loved that he'd given her time.

Because she was going to take it.

And then she was going to do what she told herself she'd do from the very beginning.

She was going to guide him to that edge, the one he wouldn't go near, the one that was farther than he would allow himself to see, and she was going to take them both over.

She slid her nose along his, tipped her mouth like she was going to kiss him, but held back.

He let out his breath and she felt it against her lips.

Almost as good as a kiss.

But not quite.

"Thank you for my warning. Thank you for more honesty," she whispered. "I hurt for you, what happened to your woman. I hurt for her. Even if it means I'd never have you, I wish I could erase that so I could erase the pain it caused, that pain that still lives in you. But as crazy as it may sound with how hard that had to be to share, how hard I know it was to hear, I still thank you for giving that to me."

She stroked his cheeks with her thumbs and slid her nose up the side of his and down again, continuing to stare into his eyes.

"But if you need more, baby, I'm here to give you what you need," she murmured. "I get the score. Don't you worry. But don't you underestimate me either. Because I get what I want and if I want you, in the end, you're going to give yourself to me. And it's not just that. It's also that if you want me, and you're right here, you're back, you said it yourself, you couldn't stay away, so I know you want me, and that means I'm going to give myself to you too."

He put his hands to her hips, gliding them up over her waist until he closed his fingers around her ribs.

"Not a smart decision but you're a smart woman, Angie. You know the score. And in any game evenly matched, no one ever knows which side will win."

"Then we'll see."

He looked like he didn't want to say it but he still muttered, "Yeah, we'll see."

She couldn't help but smile.

The ice of his eyes instantly melted.

And seeing that, she thought, *God, he has no clue.*

But some surprises were good.

And when she took him over the edge, his surprise was going to be a doozy.

She rested her forehead to his and slid one hand up and into his thick, soft hair, stroking it, and the other one she slid down to his neck.

"Now, there's some world rocking I've been intending to do, and I'm annoyed at it being delayed, so my advice, big boy, is not to make me wait any longer."

"Angie—" he murmured.

She gripped his hair in a loose hold. "Your game, Branch. My rules. Agreed?"

His gaze stayed fixed to hers.

"Don't hate me when I'm gone."

God, she was going to have to go all-in, even more all-in than she'd been, to get him out of whatever that hellhole was where he lived in his head.

And she would do it.

Fuck yes.

She'd do it.

"I won't, because unless that happens under mutually agreed circumstances, you're not going."

It was then he tipped his beautiful lips, touching them to hers, at the same time wrapping a strong hand around her neck.

She froze.

And against her lips he demanded, "Promise me or I walk out that door." He gave her neck and ribs a squeeze. "Don't hate me when I'm gone, baby. I can't have you the only way I'll have you when I'm gone knowing I did that to you. So promise me."

He played dirty.

She could too.

She gentled her hold on him and gave him the truth.

Because he wasn't going anywhere.

"I won't hate you when you're gone, Branch."

He studied the look in her eyes before his forehead rolled against hers with his nod.

She took him back to her earlier subject.

"So, are we agreed?"

"We're agreed . . ." He let his fingers drift along her jaw before he dropped his hand to curl his fingers at her hip and he tensed them in as he finished, "ma'am."

Game on.

She closed her eyes, slid her lips to his ear and stroked his hair.

"Sit on the couch, Branch, and get comfortable. I want to finish watching this episode."

He slid a hand into her baby doll tee, ran a finger under the waistband of her faded jeans from spine to hip and he replied in her ear, "Yes, ma'am."

Yes, he was going to play dirty.

But she could play dirty too.

If the game was worth winning, she could do anything.

And without knowing how she knew, deep inside her heart she still knew Branch was worth winning.

She lifted away, letting go, and stepped away so his hands would drop.

They stared at each other another second before he straightened from the armchair and did as he was told.

Evangeline grabbed the remote and moved into the couch.

Not in her corner.

She laid on her side, settling her head on Branch's thigh at the juncture of his hip.

He didn't hesitate to put his fingers in her hair, gliding it off her neck, then back, stroking.

It felt amazing.

Yes, he was going to play dirty.

She hit "Play" on the TV and muttered, "I'm farther than you got but you're going to have to suck it up."

"I'll live," he muttered back.

She grinned, curled her hand in front of her on his thigh and watched the program.

He stroked her hair, played with it for a while, and finally, he let his arm rest along her side, fingers trailing lazily on her hip.

She let him settle in, she waited until she felt him relax, and she gave it more time, enjoying being like this, on her couch, with him.

But eventually she moved her hand to his fly, unzipped him, and feeling the relaxation leave as his thighs and abs tensed all around her, she dug her hand in, pulled his dick free, adjusted her head and slid him, soft, into her mouth.

She sucked.

He hissed, "Fuck."

And he grew.

She sucked harder.

He grew more and his fingers at her hip pressed in.

She laid there, pretending to watch the TV with his now hard cock in her mouth, sometimes sucking, sometimes rolling her tongue around.

He remained tense around her, his fingers digging into her flesh.

The episode ended and she dug into his fly again, his hips flexed and they didn't relax because she cupped his balls, squeezed and sucked.

"Jesus, fuck," he bit off.

She released him quickly and rolled to her knees in the couch, hand to his stomach, and looked into his eyes.

"Playroom, Branch. Naked, and drape yourself belly to the horse. I'll be in, in a minute."

He stared at her as she pushed away from him and sat back on her calves.

Then he angled out of the couch, tucked himself in his pants and sauntered through the family room, the kitchen.

"The key is on the hook by the door," she called out just in time.

Without breaking stride, he nabbed the key from a hook that was behind the door and then he walked right out.

Damn, he was not even doing that.

Four days ago, Evangeline had readied the playroom for when they were supposed to be playing in it, so all was prepared.

She'd had it all planned out, including her outfit, which didn't include the tee and loose-fitting hipster jeans she was wearing.

Or the underwear, that wasn't her worst, or her best.

So she dashed up the stairs, pulled off her clothes, exchanged underwear and decided to pull the same clothes back on.

It didn't matter anyway. It wouldn't take long before he wouldn't notice at all what she was wearing.

She started to dash back to the stairs, but stopped herself and walked calmly down them, grinning at herself as she did.

Oh yes.

Branch Dillinger had no clue.

She slipped on her flip-flops by the door, grabbed her keys and locked the door after she left.

She could see the light from the playroom eking through the firmly closed slats of her plantation shutters.

And she forced herself to take her time walking the short distance between house and studio.

She stood outside, hand on the handle, and took a breath, two, four, six.

She had to make this good.

And then, when she had him ready, she had to make it the best.

On that thought, she opened the door.

She was always excited to play.

She was always exceptionally excited to play with Branch.

But seeing him naked, ass to the door, draped over her high saw-horse with its wide, padded bench, his cock still hard and hanging low between his spread legs, his balls beautiful, heavy and tight, she felt a drench of wet hit her panties and a weakening of her legs.

She sorted herself out, closed and locked the door, slipped off her flip-flops and moved to the dresser to drop the keys on the top and gather what she needed.

She nearly stutter-stepped when she saw, on top of the dresser right in the middle, her jewel.

He hadn't worn it to her.

But he'd brought it with him, to leave behind, or to offer her to again stake her claim, she had no idea.

It didn't matter.

It was hers.

But it would always only be his.

She put the keys down and moved to the front, side of the horse, where she saw him lying with his cheek to the blue leather of the padded bench, his gaze on her.

She got close and crouched so she was eye to eye.

"Okay, baby, tonight, you don't get to talk. You can grunt. You can groan. I like your noises. But no words, yes?"

Heat drifted into his eyes as she spoke and he replied, "Yes, ma'am."

She nodded and continued, "In a second, I'm going to start your preparations. I want you to put your arms and legs along the legs of the horse. Do that now."

He shifted as she'd asked, though he was mostly in that position already, at least his arms were dangling down the front legs of the horse. His legs weren't spread that far apart.

Now they were.

"Excellent," she breathed.

Having watched him position for her, her attention came back to his face.

"No moving. You won't be able to soon, but no moving until I make that so."

She saw the flash in his eyes at the hint of what he'd be getting but other than that, nothing.

She'd get something.

She'd get everything.

Because she was going to take it.

She touched her finger to his nose, his lower lip, his chin, then she lifted up and moved to the dresser.

First, she started with the oil. She smoothed it all over, massaging it into his flesh, taking her time, doing this to soothe him and herself, break them both in, only begin to build the burn.

When she had him oiled and glistening all over, neck to shoulders, down his arms, back, hips, ass, thighs, calves, ankles, the entirety of his delicious body gleaming and glorious, she went behind him on the horse.

She oiled his cleft, not inside, and decided it was time to get serious.

Liberally dosing her hand, she massaged his sac, watching his chin dip into his shoulder, his eyes close, and feeling his feet roll up.

"My big boy's balls are almost as pretty as his cock, almost as pretty as his ass," she whispered.

Branch kept his eyes closed, his legs tensed and up on the balls of his feet, and as she kept at him, she saw his jaw tense.

That was pretty too.

So pretty.

She went for his cock and watched him clench his teeth as she stroked, firm and deep, slow, and back and again and again.

She slid the oil into her pocket and engaged both hands, massaging balls and stroking cock.

He allowed a bitten-back grunt, but she knew what that meant.

She kept at him until she saw his legs start to tremble and his teeth come out to bite his lip.

God, he was amazing.

Time to move on before she got too involved in this part and had him roll over so she could do the same as she'd been doing, but sitting on his face.

She let him go and watched his back move as he puffed out a breath, his feet rolled down, and she went to her cupboard.

She got what she needed and returned.

She didn't make light work of it, she didn't make short work of it and she didn't relent as she did it.

She strapped him to the horse, every few inches, ankles to thighs, his hips free to move (slightly, they were resting against the horse but he could pull them away), upper waist and up his back, wrists to under his arms. She did this touching him, petting him, cooing to him, sliding her fingers through his hair, through his ass, over his balls, stroking his cock.

His breaths were coming heavy and she knew her big boy liked to be tied down, but strapped down and nearly completely unable to move, he *loved*.

"I see you like that, baby," she whispered, bent over him, lips to his ear, fingers running lightly over the skin of his ass.

As told, he said nothing.

"Being good, and good gets rewarded, and I know how you like it, Branch."

She slid her hand in his crease and circled his anus with her finger.

She watched his jaw get hard and felt her clit pulse.

"So fucking pretty," she whispered.

She kissed his ear, his shoulder, still circling at his ass, before she drifted slowly away and went back to her dresser.

She got what she wanted, a vibrating cock ring that had ears at the front for clit stimulation when she rode him while he had it on (or, more importantly, when he rode her). It also had a tail that also vibrated with a small bullet that reportedly (she'd bought it but never used it) packed a punch up the ass.

She'd soon find out.

She prepared the bullet, moved behind him and slid the ring up his cock, needing to go hard as he was so distended it was a tight fit. She seated it to the base.

Then she dropped to a crouch and fed the tail in his ass, sliding the lubed bullet inside.

His ass cheeks bunched and again he rolled up to his toes.

"Now you get a tail, handsome," she said, not hiding the marvel in her tone at all he could do to her with just a few movements, how pretty he was, his cock ringed, the vibrating cord nestled through his balls and leading into his ass. "But I like yours better."

After she fed it inside, she slipped her finger in gently, feeling his body give a slight jerk as she made sure the bullet was positioned where she wanted it.

When done, she fucked him lightly, careful not to move the toy, and watched his hands clench around the legs of the horse.

"You missed getting fucked, didn't you, Branch?" she asked.

He huffed out a breath.

She grinned, slid her finger carefully out and went back to the dresser.

She grabbed the remote, turned, leaned her hips against the bureau and allowed the visual of her handiwork to glide languidly up her pussy, enjoyed it several moments longer just because she could, then she flipped the switch to low.

His head shot back, then forward, pressing his forehead against the padding, his fingers tight around the legs of the horse, his feet up on his toes.

Yes, it appeared that bullet packed a punch.

Astounding.

She moved to him, legs trembling, nipples so hard, even the soft silk of her bra was too rough, and crouched in front of him.

"Look at me, baby," she urged.

He put his chin to the pad and caught her eyes, his heated, dark, liking what he was getting so much he was finding it hard to focus.

Her clit quivered.

"Did I hit the spot?" she asked.

He jerked up his chin.

She moved up the vibrations.

His teeth clenched and the horse jumped an inch.

Her lips parted and it took all she had not to take a handful of his hair and stand in front of him, making him watch while she shoved her hand in her jeans to take herself there.

Instead, she got in his face and announced, "Now you know I like your ass red, and you like your ass red, so let's get on to that, why don't we?"

He hissed a breath through his teeth. She smiled at him, leaned in, touched her mouth to the side of his lips and moved away.

She went back to the cupboard, grabbed a leather strap, thick with nice edges, and moved back to him.

"Ready?" she asked.

He didn't move.

She slid the setting higher on his tail.

The horse lifted off the floor and landed hard and she watched his head jerk back and then fall forward.

"I'll take that as a yes," she murmured, knowing her panties were drenched, her jeans were probably getting drenched, and hoping she got to the end of this scene without breaking it just to give herself what she needed.

It wouldn't help, doing what she was going to do, liking doing it, liking watching him take it, and knowing how much he liked it too.

But she had a battle to win.

And she was going to give it all she had.

So she strapped his ass, hearing his burred hiss as he took the first blow, his second, his third, all at his ass, she didn't deviate. And she kept at him, loving delivering every stroke, loving watching his head jerk back and stay back, his jaw carved in granite, a muscle jumping in his cheek, his ass tipping to get it, loving just as much getting every stroke.

No, her Branch, her big boy . . .

He had no clue.

She ratcheted the vibrations up his ass, through his balls and at the base of his cock, higher and higher as she strapped his ass and she kept doing both . . .

Until he broke.

Bucking against the table, thrusting his hips, fucking nothing, he groaned, "Fuck, Angie, fuck, *fuck.*"

She landed three more lashes then she dropped the strap and grabbed his cock.

He kept thrusting through it.

She bent over his back as best she could.

"Do you want your plug?"

"Fuck yes," he grunted.

"With the tail?"

"Both," he ground out.

She moved to the dresser, lubed the plug and brought it back.

He was still slightly bucking, forehead to the table, groaning, "Fuck, shit, *fuck.*"

She touched the plug to his hole.

Branch twisted his neck and speared her with his eyes.

"Drive it deep," he growled.

She drove it deep and his head jerked back, eyes closed, his entire body tensed, all the muscles growing defined, as a forced, slow, guttural "Yes" rumbled from his throat.

That was when she knew it was time.

Fast, she tore her clothes off, leaving them in a puddle on the floor.

After that, she swiftly released the straps from his back and arms, but not his legs.

"Up," she ordered.

He pushed up to straight with his legs strapped to the horse, his engorged, rock-hard cock bounding free of the edge of the horse, standing proud in the nest of black hair between his legs, his balls separated by the vibrating cord, flushed and heavy.

Unbelievable.

Magnificent.

She climbed on the horse.

She'd intended to offer herself to him then order him to take her. But she didn't get that chance.

Before she could get in position, his hands clamped on her hips, hauling her between his legs.

That was not on. A sub didn't take over. Not unless told.

She should have reprimanded him, ordered him to stop.

She was too caught up in his reaction, the power of him, everything about him, she didn't even consider it. The thought didn't cross her mind.

If she was in her mind and not all about her body, him, what was happening between them, she would be shocked about this.

She was a Domme.

But she wasn't shocked because she was too busy *totally* getting off on it.

He took both of her legs and wrapped them around his hips. Then he gripped his dick, positioned it, took hold of her upper hips in both hands, and his flaming eyes locked to hers, rammed her down as he drove inside.

Taking him, being full of Branch, her back arched, neck arched, head pressing back into pad.

"Who likes to take a fucking?" he growled, pounding inside her, deep, he was so thick, God, *God.* "Look at me, Angie," he ordered.

She forced her eyes to him. So beautiful, he kept thrusting inside her, the horse jolting with every stroke.

"Hands up, baby, hold onto the horse. Arch for me," he demanded.

She didn't even hesitate.

She did as told.

"That's it." He kept driving deep, faster, harder, his cock slamming into her clit and the vibrations of the ring at the base of his dick unrelenting.

"Branch," she gasped, her head arching back again.

"You like to get fucked, Angie?" he asked.

Alpha-sub payback.

God, glorious.

"Yes," she whispered.

She felt his hand leave her hip and then she felt his fingers twist and pull her nipple and her entire body spasmed, arching further, tightening her legs around him, driving her own hips into his thrusts.

"Look at me," he bit out, pinching her nipple, the sting scoring a line of fire from breast to clit, and with effort, she did. "Say it, baby," he kept at her. "Tell me you like to get fucked."

"I like to get fucked, Branch."

"How do you like to get fucked, Angie?"

"Hard, Branch. Rough."

"Yeah, you like it how I give it, don't you? Any way I wanna give it."

"Yes, I like it how you give it," she forced out.

"And who's fucking you, baby? Whose cock are you taking?"

"Yours."

"Mine," he clipped. "And whose pussy is taking my cock?"

"Mine."

He drove in and ground in.

Hard.

She moaned.

Loud.

"Whose?" he asked.

"Yours," she pushed out. "Your pussy, baby. You're taking your pussy."

He again started thrusting

"Yeah, I fucking am." He bent over her, gripping her at her neck and powering her down into his drives, grinding out, "Tell me how much you like your fucking."

"I love it, baby," she breathed. "Fucking love it. Don't stop."

He pounded into her.

"Don't stop, Branch."

"You gotta come, Angie," he grunted.

"Baby," she breathed.

His hand went into her hair and his lips brushed hers.

"Come, Angie," he whispered and ran his tongue along her lower lip.

She came.

And he kissed her.

Gasping into his mouth as he slid his tongue inside and she moaned against it, thrilling at finally getting the taste of him, arching into his body, engulfed by all he was giving, all she was feeling.

She was still consumed by her climax as his grunts filled her mouth and the horse moved under them as he drove them across the floor, slamming into her, coming inside her, driving his orgasm up her cunt and down her throat. It retriggered hers and she wrapped her arms around him for something to hold on to as the world fell away and they both slipped over the edge.

Vaguely, still trembling through powerful aftershocks, she felt his kiss gentle, turn soft, sweet, before he slid his lips along her cheek, her jaw. They went away and she felt his hand leave her hip. He made a low noise, his cock slipped out, but it slipped back in, without the vibrations, and she knew he'd pulled off his ring and tail.

Then he pushed his hand under her, wrapping his arm around her, and pulled her into his body even as he rested some of his warm, heavy weight on her.

Her head had fallen naturally to the side so Branch took what she unwittingly offered and slid his lips up her neck to her ear.

"You play dirty," he whispered.

Evangeline felt a lazy grin curve her lips.

She turned her head.

He lifted his and she caught his eyes, the look in them what she felt through her whole body right down to her bones—languid, sultry, dreamy. Spent.

Who knew it felt that good to take a plunge, land and shatter?

"Pretty little thing," he muttered, his eyes moving over her. "Never prettier than when you come, though. Never seen anything that pretty. Now I've felt it, never felt anything that pretty either."

He'd been kissing her.

Finally kissing her.

But he'd been watching.

God.

Hot.

She slid a hand up the ridged scars of his back, under his lat and up his chest to rest it on his jaw.

"You aren't pretty when you come," she told him. "You're hot."

His lips quirked, another almost-smile, before he shook his head. Then his eyes grew serious. "What am I gonna do with you?"

"Well, you aren't going to fuck me again anytime soon," she replied, ignoring the serious that stayed and the concern that filtered into his gaze as she spoke. "Because you're a battering ram and my nether regions need a break. At least until tomorrow."

The concern fled, another lip quirk with a brow lift. "Nether regions?"

"Nether regions."

"You said pussy when I was fucking you," he pointed out.

"You were fucking me," she retorted.

"Right, so you can slip a tail up my ass before you strap it but you can't say 'pussy' when I'm not fucking you?"

She lifted her head, her lips against his, her gaze holding his, and whispered, "Pussy."

His hips flexed into hers as his eyes flared.

She pulled back half an inch, sliding her hand to his neck and stroking his jaw with her thumb.

"My big boy likes dirty talk," she murmured.

"Your big boy likes everything you do to him."

She smiled at him.

His eyes dropped to her mouth and he muttered, "Especially that."

"Branch?" she called.

He looked back at her.

"I win," she whispered.

Humor and frustration and gravity warred in his eyes, right there for her to see.

Not hidden.

In full view.

Yes.

She'd won.

"That's game, Angie." His arm around her held her closer even as his mouth warned, "You haven't even won a set, so be careful, honey, don't think you've won the match."

She said nothing.

Just smiled at him.

His fingers tangled deeper into her hair as his eyes warmed.

God, no clue.

All she had to do was smile at him.

And it was match point.

Every time.

fourteen

A Good Man in Her Life

BRANCH

The next morning, Branch walked into Evangeline's bathroom while she stood, wearing nothing but a pair of dark purple, lacy underwear, her hair wet but still curly, the ringlets springing back as it dried. She was bent over the basin to put her makeup on.

He felt the view of her round, sweet ass in his dick and reminded himself for the fifth time that morning that he'd given it to her.

She understood the game. She was aware of the stakes. He'd laid it out straight and she'd made her decision.

He reminded himself of that but he still knew he was a motherfucker.

He slid the mug of coffee on the counter beside her and watched her in the mirror as she looked down at the cup then up at him, also through the mirror, her lips curving up.

"Thanks, honey"

He didn't feel that in his dick.

He felt it somewhere else.

Tara had called him sweetie.

She'd also called him slave.

He hadn't gotten off on "slave" since and had been relieved when Evangeline didn't use that word.

He preferred "handsome," "baby," and being her "big boy."

And he preferred "honey."

The first time Evangeline had used it—knowing that endearment didn't have anything to do with how they played, it was just a sweetness about her that she gave away—and like everything that was Angie, it dug right into his soul.

In the four days it took for him to try to pull his shit together, attempting to come to terms with the fact that the best thing for her was never to see him again so he should stay the fuck away, and failing spectacularly in that endeavor, he'd also struggled with the fact that he liked her "honey," her "handsome," her "big boy" and everything else more than what he'd had with Tara.

That felt like a betrayal of Tara, her memory and the history of them.

But Tara had not been an experienced Mistress. They'd been learning the life together.

And the sweet feel of Evangeline in his lap, the brilliance of her smile, Branch knew it wasn't about time passing so the intensity of what he and Tara had had faded.

Angie didn't dig in about stupid shit. Angie didn't bicker.

Angie listened.

Not only that, Angie didn't fall apart when she hit the hard and then panic, that making her hackles rise and her mouth open to say shit she didn't mean because she was scared. This meaning he'd be right there with her, and things would escalate to a place they couldn't pull them back.

No, Angie got what was important—like him treating her with respect and not just as his Mistress, and her finding a way to break through because they both knew this was something different, something special. And when their shit hit the hard, she didn't back down or panic. She listened and communicated.

What they had was good. What they had was worth developing. What they had, he knew, if he was a different man and these were different circumstances, he wouldn't be the one to break it off when the going got tough. He wouldn't find reasons to dig in. He wouldn't feel down deep the frustration that, even with the good, something wasn't clicking.

So the past four days he'd struggled with understanding that maybe it wasn't youth, stupidity and stubbornness that led to his ending it with Tara.

It could be, if he and Tara both had given it more time and grown up, they would have found where they needed to be.

It could be, the man he was, he needed an Evangeline.

"Got something on your mind?" she asked softly, taking him out of his thoughts.

Standing behind her wearing just his jeans, Branch focused on her in the mirror to see her *very* focused on him.

He didn't give her his thoughts. She had enough ammunition to wage her war already, a lot of it he'd given to her. He didn't need to give her more.

Instead, he gave her other thoughts.

Turning at her side and leaning his hip against the basin, he looked down at her direct.

She tipped her head back and gave him her gaze the same way.

"You took me there and it was pretty much an impossibility for me not to go right where you took me instead of doing what I should have done. But that's beside the point. It's also a piss-poor excuse. The discussion should have been had when I asked for what I wanted, and I should have started it. It's too late now but just so you know, as a requirement for Aryas to do his thing for me . . ." He let that lie, knowing she'd get what he was saying and she did. So when she nodded, he went on, "I gotta get tested and do it at the Honey just like a member. I'm clean. No worries with taking me ungloved." He lifted a hand and tugged at one of her curls before he finished, "You let your membership lapse, but are you still——?"

She interrupted him. "I'm clean, Branch." She then turned fully to him and put a hand on his stomach. "There's been no one since Kevin and I'm on the Pill."

He was glad to know she was clean and protected.

But although he'd already guessed it, the other wasn't great, especially for her. She had a libido that equaled his.

"Bet that sucked for you," he muttered.

She pressed into his stomach with her hand as she leaned her body into his, grinning up at him. "Yes, well, the drought is over."

"Yeah," he replied, and it fucking was.

Being inside her . . .

She could spank his ass, fuck it, suck his cock, jack it, all of that magnificent.

But the feel of her pussy was unparalleled—tight, hot and so wet. It had been heaven thrusting inside her last night.

Even so, that was something else that had been dragging on his mind that morning.

"Have you ever . . . ?" he began.

Branch didn't finish even as she tipped her head to the side and asked, "Have I ever what?"

"Nothin'," he muttered, looking down at her coffee and then to her. "Gotta get on the road, Angie. You cool with me taking another travel mug?"

"I have five thousand two hundred and twelve of them, so yeah, I'm cool."

He felt his brows rise as his lips hitched. "Five thousand two hundred and twelve?"

"Okay, maybe about five thousand one hundred and ninety-seven of them."

"Right."

"So take what you need," she offered.

That was Evangeline, always giving him what he needed.

Damn, he thought.

"Cool," he said.

She leaned closer. "I've got a late showing tonight. Probably won't be home until seven thirty, eight. You should get yourself some dinner. I'll grab something somewhere along the way. But, handsome, I'd like you to meet me here at—"

"I'll have dinner ready when you get home, honey."

She shut her mouth and her eyes warmed.

She thought she had him.

But Branch intended to give her as good as he had it in him to give for as long as he had it in him to give it to her so he could leave her with what he needed to leave her with when he was gone. Good memories with a sub who did it for her, ending her drought, and more, a man who gave a shit about her and she got to do that too in a safe place that would set her up to trust whoever came next.

It might make him even more of a motherfucker than he already was and he couldn't even think on the idea of her moving on with another guy.

Branch had had a gun to his head on a variety of occasions and managed to hold his shit, but for the life of him, he knew, even with a gun to his head, for a shot to be with Angie, he couldn't do anything else.

She rolled up on her toes, her hand not at his stomach catching him around the back of the neck and pulling him down.

He was going to have her mouth again, not because it was clear she was intent on taking his.

He was going to take hers.

He bent to her, wrapping his arms around her, pulling her soft, little body into the curve of his, and he kissed her, tasted her with his tongue, took his time and drank his fill.

When he broke away, she was gazing up at him, eyes soft and vague, not quite like when she'd come but not far off, and just like everything with Angie when he knew he shouldn't, he couldn't stop himself.

That look, he took her mouth again.

She'd melted in his arms and had a hand clenched in his hair when he broke away again and forced himself to say, "Really gotta go, baby."

"'Kay," she murmured.

"Text me when you're on your way home."

"All right."

"Later, Angie."

"Later, Branch."

He let her go and moved away, doing it swiftly. If she called him back, ringed his cock with her lipstick, planted her jewel up his ass, he might not go at all.

He had a travel cup of coffee in his hand and was walking down her drive to his truck at the curb when he noticed her neighbor pulling out and he glanced that way.

Normally, Branch would avoid eye contact. To stay safe but also to do the jobs he took, he needed to be vapor. You couldn't be vapor catching anyone's attention. Eye contact was still contact and Branch didn't make contact with hardly anybody.

But the way the woman was waving at him and the fact that she was Evangeline's neighbor, he couldn't be a dick and ignore her.

So he caught her eye, jerked up his chin, noting her big smile, and then he looked away and kept walking to his truck.

He got in, secured his coffee, belted up, started her up and turned around in Evangeline's drive, knowing as he rode down her street he should drive on and keep driving until he hit Alaska, he was well away from her and the way he knew he'd fuck up her life.

He didn't do that.

He drove to his condo to change clothes as he'd showered with Angie.

And then like he had since he'd moved to Phoenix two years ago, he took on his day.

Branch sat in his truck in the parking lot, watched the man walk into the smoke shop, and he wondered not for the first time at the extent of people's stupidity.

First, how the guy hadn't spotted Branch's tail, he didn't know. He'd been following him in the same vehicle on and off for the last

week, doing it less and less cautiously because the man was clueless.
Branch could actually tailgate him and the guy was so deep in his
own world, he'd have no idea.

But that wasn't the worst of it.

If he was skimming off the top of a guy like Fred, Branch's
client—and although a good client, he was very much not a good
guy—Branch would not be walking in broad daylight into the front
door of the business owned by the dude who was assisting him in
doing this.

Then again, if he was one of Fred's boys (not that he'd ever be
one of Fred's boys), he'd never consider skimming off the top. Fred
would have his balls. Literally. He collected them from morons who
he felt deserved to be liberated from that part of their anatomy and
kept them in jars of formaldehyde in his office.

Seeing this the first time he'd been contacted to discuss a job
had made Branch think twice about taking said job.

Since Fred not only didn't blink at his fees and his strict demands for autonomy, he also paid bonuses if the job was done quick
and clean (which was the way Branch worked), he'd taken the job and
several since.

But now he wasn't watching the door to the smoke shop thinking of having to go to Fred, sit in an office where there was a lit shelf
behind Fred's desk holding five jars filled with men's testicles.

He was watching the door to the smoke shop upending his
phone in his fingers, and again, and again, wondering if he should
make the call he wanted to make, and if he did, which one of the three
men he could call that he actually *should* call.

If he made the call, Aryas was likely out.

He didn't know if the man was back in town and this conversation should be face-to-face.

However, if he had this conversation with Aryas, other things
might be communicated that Branch didn't want communicated,
these things could be interpreted erroneously, and that could cause
future problems.

So in town or not, Aryas was still out.

Erroneous things he didn't want communicated was why he couldn't call Olly either.

"Shit, fuck, shit," he muttered. Eyes remaining on the door to the smoke shop, he engaged his phone and muttered in it, "Call Barclay."

The phone did its work and rang three times before Barclay answered, "Yo, bro. You been MIA so long, thought you'd dropped off the face of the earth."

"I haven't," Branch replied.

"Seeing as I'm talking to you, I got that," Barclay said, laughter shaking his words.

Listening to it, it wasn't the first time Branch wished he'd had even a little bit of the life that Barclay led.

Life was just good for Barclay and he let that show. The guy was honest but cool about it, even if what he had to share could be prickly. He had a great sense of humor. He liked what he did. He had good friends and a goodly number of them (not surprising with how he was). And he laughed a lot. His business partners could often drive him up the wall, but other than that, life was good and he didn't take it for granted. He was appreciative and he had no problem putting in the work to keep life just that way.

Branch hadn't thought about having a good life, not since Tara's had been taken.

Since then, he hadn't looked into the future. He hadn't considered the idea he should be content with his present. He hadn't hoped or wished for anything.

He'd just been breathing.

Branch stopped thinking about that shit and asked, "You got time to have a beer tonight?"

"You and Olly meeting up?" Clay asked back.

"No."

Another sucking void of silence.

Although Barclay reached out to him every once in a while, usually to include him in a beer he was having with Ol, Barclay and Branch had never had a beer together, sharing time on their own.

And clearly, Branch suggesting this surprised Clay.

"So you got time?" Branch pushed. "There's somethin'..." Fuck, how did he say it? "Got a question about something and thinking you're the go-to guy on it."

"Well, yeah," Barclay replied tentatively. "I'm free. Sure. I'm cool. You got a question and I can answer it, I will. You wanna hit PV Tavern?"

That was their usual place, a bar in Paradise Valley that wasn't trendy or up its own ass. It also wasn't a dive, it wasn't all about sports and it wasn't all about bikers. It was quiet. And it wasn't a firefighter bar so Olly could get a break from his brothers who were brothers but that didn't mean he wanted to spend every waking minute with them.

"Not PV," Branch answered.

He gave no alternative because he knew no alternatives. He met the guys irregularly, not habitually, to throw back a few and watch the game. He didn't unwind sitting at a bar, sharing the shit of his life with a bartender. He didn't go on the prowl, positioning himself someplace for the sole purpose of evaluating the women in his sights to decide who he wanted to take home and fuck.

He worked.

He slept.

He sometimes met Olly for a beer at PVT and sometimes Barclay joined them.

And now, for as long as it took for her not to get totally torn up when he took off on her, he spent time with Evangeline.

"Uh...," Barclay mumbled before he suggested, "The club?"

No way was he going to the Bolt.

Unless he was on a job, Branch didn't get near Clay's club, the Bolt. Too many assholes who went to Pounds hit the Bolt and Branch didn't need that hassle.

He also didn't need anyone overhearing what they were talking about, no matter where they were.

"My place," he said.

Barclay's voice was higher when he asked, "Your place?"

His reaction was not a surprise. Barclay had never been to his place. Olly had never been to his place. Aryas either. Except for Whitney and a few other Dommes he'd let work him, no one had ever been invited to his place.

He wondered briefly what Evangeline would think of his place.

This was brief because he knew she wouldn't think much of it, not because she was that type of woman but because there wasn't much to think about.

"My place," he answered. "I'll text you the address."

"Uh, have I pissed someone off and you're asking me for a beer at this unknown locale so you can put a bullet in my brain and then cut me into little pieces, fit me in a suitcase and carry me out to your truck in order to dump my body somewhere?"

"Fuck no," Branch answered.

Hack up a body and put it in suitcases. Christ.

There were much better ways to make a body disappear.

"I'll get the beer in. Five?" he continued.

"I can be there at five, Branch. Text me the address."

"Right. Later."

"Yeah, later, bro."

Branch hung up.

Then Branch followed a moron for another hour, even though he had all the evidence he needed to present to Fred that one of his boys had gone dirty. Or, he was already filthy, working for Fred. So *dirtier*.

He was delaying. Fred was a slimeball of the variety that Branch didn't feel the need to shower after he'd met with him, but instead be sandblasted.

But he wanted to get paid and he wanted off this job.

So he met with Fred, reported his findings, got paid and didn't think for a second about the fact that the next time Fred called, there would be six jars on that shelf behind his desk.

He went to buy beer.

Barclay let out a low whistle as he looked around Branch's condo.

"Brother, you gotta give me the number of your decorator. Extreme minimalism. Inspired," he joked.

"Fuck off," Branch muttered, opening the fridge, taking out a couple of beers and turning to Clay, who he saw leaning to the side, looking into Branch's refrigerator and not hiding his curiosity.

Branch shut the fridge, turned and walked across the kitchen. He put the beers on the counter and slid the new bottle opener he'd bought at the grocery store his way. He uncapped the beers and slid one five inches across the countertop into Barclay's hand.

"Good you got a toaster, Branch. Least that's something. Though, nothing to put in it. Don't think I've ever seen a fridge that empty in a pad where someone actually lives." He was grinning at Branch. What he wasn't done doing was giving Branch shit. "Or do you just plug your bionic parts in and the government scientists who turned you from human to badass figured out a way you could exist without basic nutrition?"

He needed food but Barclay still wasn't far off.

He just gave his friend a look.

Barclay returned his look, his was amused, then he lifted the beer and took a deep tug on it.

He dropped his beer hand and when he did he didn't look amused any longer.

He looked sober with hints at concern.

"Everything cool?"

No it was not.

The extent of that Branch was not going to have a dialogue with Clay about.

"Got a question I need to ask, just you and me," Branch answered.

"Got that," Barclay said quietly and then his lips quirked as his eyes slid to the sectional. "Figured it out when you invited me to your couchatoriam. I'm glad it's you and not me putting that sad sectional out of its misery."

Branch ignored the ribbing.

"How long you owned the Bolt?"

Barclay's expression grew more alert even as he shrugged lightly and took another tug of his beer.

When he was done drinking, he answered, "Bought in when Josh and Pete were having troubles about four years ago. Why?"

"You know the scene," Branch declared.

Barclay nodded. "Yeah, being a sex club owner as well as a practitioner, why?"

Branch took a tug of his own beer before he asked, "You don't want to share, I get it. But between owning and practicing, you've seen a lot, yeah?"

"Done a lot too, Branch," Barclay answered openly. "May not have Aryas Weathers's money and style, but I own a scene because I'm into the scene and I wasn't big on some of the places you could find out there to get what you need. The Bolt was a dump when I bought in. Now it might not be the Honey, but it's a helluva lot better than it used to be."

"All you've seen and done, you ever know a Domme go sub?" Branch asked suddenly.

Barclay's body tensed up in surprise at the subject before he asked back, "Say that again?"

"You ever know a Domme, not a switch, go sub?" Branch repeated, then added, "During a scene."

His gaze watchful, his tone quiet and hesitant, he asked, "You tellin' me you went sub, brother?"

Branch stared at him.

Olly told Branch he talked openly about a variety of shit with Barclay. And Olly talked openly with Branch about a variety of shit too. The way they enjoyed getting off wasn't the only topic of conversation, but Ol didn't shy away from it, especially when he was trying to push Branch into finding something like what he had.

But when they were all three together, none of them talked about it. Branch only knew Barclay was in the life beyond owning a sex club because, before he knew the man personally, he'd seen him hanging from his wrists, up on his toes, getting flogged while Branch was on a job, being vapor at the Bolt.

Barclay and Olly made mention of things when they were all together that vaguely had to do with the life, but nothing deep and nothing revealing.

Branch never talked much regardless, so he'd never said anything.

And it was good to know, in all of his openness, that Olly didn't share when Branch wasn't around.

But it was interesting Barclay, in his business, hadn't read him.

It wasn't like this wasn't often mistaken, for instance, at a Pound. But Branch would guess some of those idiots didn't even know who was president so they definitely couldn't read on a fit, six-foot-two man he liked to have his ass spanked.

But Barclay was different.

"I'm a sub, man," he said quietly.

Barclay blinked before his brows went up. "Seriously?"

"Yeah," Branch confirmed.

"Didn't call that one," Barclay muttered before taking another tug of beer.

Branch didn't have a shot at saying anything because, once Barclay was done swallowing, he went on.

"And your Domme went sub?"

Branch nodded. "Scene was intense. She's talented. She's got her style. She rocks it. But no sign she had that in her. And giving you the honesty, never went there myself."

"But you . . . what?" Barclay prompted.

This was not where he'd wanted to go. What he and Evangeline shared was not anyone's business, especially details to that. It was too personal. But more, what they had and the way they had it, it was too precious.

Though to get what he needed, he had to give his friend something.

"Doing it vanilla, I top. Exclusively," Branch told him, though he didn't go on to say he hadn't had that yet with the woman he was talking about, nor that he intended to have just that, especially after last night. He had a new need with Evangeline, the need to get more of her pussy. And for as long as he had her, he was going to find his times to get more of that sweetness as often as he could. "In a scene, I bottom. Exclusively. She took me somewhere I've never been, got to that point, I took over. And she got off on it."

"Did you?"

"Fuck yeah."

Barclay was now looking perplexed. "Sorry, bro, not sure I get it. You seem troubled. If you both got off—?"

Branch had to give him more, so he did.

"Evangeline had a sub snap on her. It was—"

"You're seeing Evangeline?"

Branch shut his mouth and stared at Barclay.

Barclay correctly interpreted his stare. "I know her. Just met her recently. She's yours?" His lips tipped up. "I mean, you're hers?"

"Both," Branch grunted.

At least for a while.

Barclay's lips tipped higher. "Cool, Branch. She's pretty. And she's sweet. And she seems, from what little time I've spent with her, to have it together."

Barclay knowing Angie, Branch was no longer comfortable having this conversation.

So he declared, "You know her, this chat is done."

Barclay again looked perplexed. "Why?"

"I give you that part of me, my decision. She's not here to make that decision so I'm not giving you that part of her."

"I knew there was a reason I liked you," Clay muttered.

Branch ignored that.

"So I guess I wasted your time." He tipped his head to the bottle Barclay held on the counter. "But you can finish your beer."

Another smile came from his friend. "Thanks, bro, but just to put your mind at ease and so this isn't a waste of either of our time, you been hers awhile?"

To that, Branch just grunted, forming no words. Barclay could take that how he wanted.

He took it how he wanted, nodding. "Yeah, she cracked my whip, just hooked up with someone I dig a lot, I'd still consider it." His expression turned pained. "And she had a sub snap?"

"Clay, I dig you came here because I asked and I dig that you're obviously willing to help out but I already said we're not going there."

Barclay lifted his hand not wrapped around a beer. "Right. I get that. And it's cool, you giving that to Evangeline." He dropped his hand, and for one of the few times Branch had seen it do that, his mouth turned down. "But sucks, she had a sub snap on her."

"Yeah, it does," Branch agreed to that understatement, taking another swallow from his bottle.

Barclay wasn't finished.

"But, just so this isn't a bust for either of us, first, my advice is to talk to her about it. If you have concerns she's messed up because a sub snapped and she likes being jacked around because that shook something loose, best way to know is to go in gentle and get her to share where she's at." His expression lightened even as his gaze grew more intense. "That said, Branch, I think that's a leap. It says a lot about you and how you feel about her that you're concerned after that happened to her. Thinking, though, this is more about you being seriously sensitive that your woman has that in her history and not so much about her twisting that history."

His woman.

Branch was so caught on those two words, he said nothing, which was good with Clay because he wasn't done.

"I may not have read sub on you and I'm not sure many people

would think I should have my BDSM card taken away because you
don't exactly scream sub like Olly doesn't, even if it happens a lot,
men like you two swinging that way. But I do feel I got a good read
on Evangeline and she seemed to me to have her shit tight so . . ."

He shrugged again, took another sip from his beer and looked
into Branch's eyes before he kept talking.

"Relationships on the whole I am no master at navigating. Add
sex to the mix, shit can get messed up. Add *our* kind of sex to the
mix, all sorts of things could get whacked. That said, I know women
and Dommes who enjoy pushing their men or their subs' buttons
so they'll lose it and master the situation," he grinned, "for lack of
a better word. Doesn't make them no longer Dommes or make them
women with something screwy going on in their heads. Just means
the scene got out of control but in a good way. And truth of it is, that
could have been precisely where she was leading it. However, you
can't know that unless you ask her."

Barclay was right.

He couldn't know unless he asked her.

He just hadn't wanted to bring up Kevin. Not again. She seemed
over it. In fact, it seemed like it was Branch who had helped her take
the last steps to get over it (and since that felt too good, him being
able to help her in that, that was another thing he refused to think
about the last four days, and he'd succeeded in at least that).

But if she was over it, Branch wanted her to stay that way.

"It's cool you give this much of a shit about her that you'd call
me to try and look after her," Barclay noted quietly.

Branch focused on him again. "You just met her or not, you said
you got a read on her and your read is right. She has it together and
she's sweet."

"Like that you have that, bud," Barclay told him. "From what I
know of her, like she has you. Woman like that deserves a good man
in her life, just because she is who she is but especially because something awful like that went down with her. And already know, good
man like you deserves a good woman."

Branch made no response to that.

"But my new read is, you haven't been in the life very long," Barclay continued.

"That read would be wrong," Branch told him and took another tug of his beer.

"So you've not had a Leigh."

It took a lot but Branch schooled his features so he didn't show that Clay's words felt like a punch in the gut.

No, he hadn't had a Leigh. A woman in his life who gave him everything he needed, leaving him free to breathe, and not only that, making him straight-up happy without hassle, pain and over a decade of guilt that he'd played a part in ending her life.

He had an Evangeline.

But he wouldn't have her long.

"I have, in a way, but lost them. All of them," Barclay shared. "Either me fucking it up. Or them. But, you know, when the life is part of life, anything can go anywhere. And if it's good, like both of you getting something out of that change in roles, and the trust is there, that runs deep, maybe that just means she needs to switch it up every once in a while. Take you where you need to be to get something new and exciting that she needs. Or maybe she didn't plan it out but just dug how it went so she went with it. And if you both got off, that could just be it, brother. So instead of it being a result of something horrible happening to her, it's actually the opposite. She just trusts you."

Clay grinned again and didn't stop talking.

"Though, if you've been in the life awhile, I don't have to tell you to be careful with that. You do it when she isn't playing it that way, you might pay. Then again, maybe you'll wanna go too far because that's payment you like to make."

Branch hoped that was it because what they'd had the night before was fucking amazing, for him, and Evangeline had made it clear it was the same for her too.

He wanted her to have amazing.

What he didn't want to do was mess with her head any more than he already was, just being a weak, selfish motherfucker who was addicted to her smile.

"And you know," Barclay kept talking, "says nothing about you either, you went for it. Just says you got good, she can take you to that place, you go over that edge, and you both like it that way. It's just a scene, and if you have good, they're all different."

He'd had a lot of not so good and he'd a lot of totally shit.

So he knew that was the truth.

Barclay's smile went wired.

"Holy grail, Branch." He reached out with his beer bottle and tapped the neck against Branch's. "And as I mentioned earlier, I've met a woman that I'm thinking I might have found that with too. You, me and Olly all got the goods in all ways we want that, what with you having Evangeline and me finding a switch who's got a way with a flog *and* likes the way I got with one too."

So Barclay was a switch, giving and taking.

Branch hadn't read that either, but then again, he didn't put any effort into it. All the ways Barclay took it (or gave it) wasn't of interest to him.

The man lifted his beer and did a salute.

"To us. My guess is, Olly gets down to the business of popping the question, and I'd put money on the fact that's going to be soon, his best man will be Chad. But you and me'll give him an alternate bachelor party that Chad doesn't get to go to that Olly'll like a whole lot more than getting shitfaced and watching strippers gyrate in G-strings. So I'm putting my bid in, things happen with my woman, you boys take care of that for me and you can count on me to take care of that for you."

Branch didn't get into the fact there would be no bachelor parties for him at a strip club or other. He didn't need another friend breathing down his neck about how he should get his head straight when they had no clue he already had it straight. It was staying with Evangeline that was fucked up.

Branch lifted his bottle to return the salute before he put it to his lips but muttered around it, "Gotta admit, man, your idea of a bachelor party Ol would like kinda freaks me out."

Barclay burst out laughing.

Branch almost grinned before he took a tug of his beer.

Then he did something he had no intention of doing.

But Barclay was solid. He was decent. And he'd helped out.

So he did it.

"Right, that's done," he stated then demanded, "tell me about your girl."

If Barclay's smile had been wired before, it hit the stratosphere at Branch's demand.

And as he drank beer and listened to his friend talk about the new woman in his life, Branch thought, when the time came, since Branch probably wouldn't be around, he hoped like fuck Olly gave Barclay a bachelor party he'd never forget.

fifteen

Yes, It Was

EVANGELINE

The good news was that Branch's reply to her text that evening of *Done, handsome. Heading home,* was *Right. On it.* This meaning, she hoped (and not only because she was hungry) that Branch was at her house cooking

The next piece of good news was that Branch's truck was parked at her curb when she drove down the block.

However, when she walked into her kitchen, there was no Branch and no cooking smells.

Evangeline froze for a second, the dread that had eventually filtered into her system after four days of Branch being away illogically beginning to seep in, regardless of his text and his truck at the curb.

But this dread vanished when she saw Branch walk into the family room through the French doors that led outside to her backyard.

She let out a breath and smiled at him.

He didn't smile back, but that didn't bother her. He never smiled.

Something else she had to work on.

And she'd crack that too.

"Good timing," he said instead of offering her a greeting. "Chops'll be done in a couple of minutes."

He was grilling.

Branch Dillinger, mystery man, hot guy and alpha-sub extraordinaire, grilled.

Damn, she had come home to a beautiful man grilling chops for her dinner.

She felt the tingle of that go from her scalp to her toes.

She tossed her bags on the counter and moved his way, meeting him just beyond the island.

He stopped when she made it to him but he didn't reach out to her. He just stared down at her with that blank expression on his face that said he might be there, he might be grilling for her, but his guard was up.

She ignored it and moved in, fitting herself to his body, wrapping her arms around him and tipping her head back to hold his gaze.

"Chops?" she asked softly.

"Pork," he stated unnecessarily, since it was doubtful after her earlier litany of what she didn't like that they were lamb.

He hesitated a moment before settling his hands on her hips in a manner that was somewhat awkward, like he didn't know what he was doing, how to be in a casual embrace.

"Yum," she murmured.

He just stared down at her.

"If they're going to be ready soon, I'll run and be quick about changing," she told him.

He nodded.

She lifted up on her toes, sliding a hand up his spine on a trajectory to his neck to pull him down to her for a kiss but he moved much more swiftly.

Lifting his hand, he tangled his fingers in the ponytail she'd pulled her curls into and held her still in a way the rest of her went still.

"Need to chat about something," he muttered.

Oh no.

Evangeline didn't think she could handle another one of Branch's chats. Yes, sometimes when they were over, it was good they'd had them, fabulous, even awesome.

But they were draining and she needed a break.

At least a day.

"Branch—" she started carefully.

"Last night, babe, in your playroom you let me take over. It was good. Fuckin' great. We both felt that. Or my take was we both felt that. I just need you to share that's what it was for you."

She was confused.

How could he not know that it was great for her too?

"I, uh . . . last night?"

He dipped his face an inch closer to hers and he dipped his voice when he spoke too. "I took over. In a scene, never been driven to that. And you gotta know, I was driven to that in a good way. Came natural. Seemed you were happy with the flow but you've had a scene turn and . . ."

Her heart again leaped in her chest in that cartoon way that if she was nothing but a drawing, it would bound out of her chest and slam into him.

She wasn't a drawing but even so, the thump was so hard, she felt certain he had to feel it too.

He was worried about her. Looking out for her. Going over an experience that wasn't like any they'd had together, wasn't customary in the roles they both understood they held when they played, and he wanted to make sure she was all right with that.

". . . I don't want to bring him up again," Branch kept talking, "but I gotta know you were in a good place with that then and I gotta know, time has passed, shit can fuck with your head, you're still in a good place now."

"That was hot," she told him.

"Yeah," he agreed, but did it watching her closely.

Oh yes.

Her big handsome boy was clueless.

He was *so* into her.

So she melted into him and started stroking the skin at the back of his neck, her fingers drifting through his soft hair to do it.

"I'm okay with it, honey. I was then and I am now. That wasn't what I was expecting. But you didn't read it wrong. I was far more than okay it went down the way it went down so you don't have to worry."

Even though it didn't show in his face, his body relaxed in her arms.

God.

Branch.

She again slid up to her toes and tightened her arms. "That said, handsome, you were a bad boy." She gave him a squeeze. "I knew you would be. And I'm glad you were. But more, I figure when it comes time for the reckoning, I have a feeling you'll be glad you were too."

Heat infused his gaze but that was all he gave her before he muttered, "Right."

She grinned up at him.

A different kind of warmth mingled with the heat as he caught her smile.

Then he slid his hand in her hair to the back of her neck, the one at her hip to the small of her back, and sighed deeply, like a man who'd accepted his fate.

She knew he hadn't fully accepted it, he wouldn't make it that easy for her to get the win, but she also knew she'd get him there.

She knew that more when he dipped his head even further and gave her a brief, soft, closed-mouth kiss.

That was a far better greeting than "Chops'll be done in a couple of minutes."

When he lifted away, he ordered quietly, "Change."

She used his earlier words in reply. "Right. On it."

That earned her a hitch of his lips in a not-quite smile and he let her go.

When he did, Evangeline moved directly to the stairs, taking them slowly, but she hurried through changing because it was late and she was hungry.

And Branch had cooked her some chops.

Branch made love to her that night.

After thick, delicious, perfectly cooked pork chops that had been glazed in barbecue sauce that had earned its smoky flavor from more than just the bottle, a fresh salad full of greens, avocado, chopped red onion and Gorgonzola cheese, and fresh rolls slathered in soft butter, they caught an episode of *True Detective* (without his dick in her mouth) before they went up to bed.

Together.

As in, *holding hands* together.

She gave him no orders, wondering where he'd lead it.

And when the time came, he'd led it there.

Stopping her at the foot of the bed to take off her clothes and allowing her to pull off his.

Lifting her and putting her in the bed while kissing her.

Then touching her everywhere with his mouth. His lips. His tongue. His fingers.

It was not a race to an orgasm.

It was like he was memorizing the feel of her, her look, her scent, her taste. Drawing her in. Imprinting her on his brain.

And it wasn't *like* it was all gorgeous.

It just was.

Gorgeous.

This multisensory exploration wasn't just Branch's to have. He allowed her the same privilege.

Taking that from him while he was tied down for her was one beauty.

Taking it from him while he was giving the same to her was another one.

But when he finally rolled her to her back, opened her legs with his knee, settled between and slid inside, he was done taking while giving.

He communicated this by capturing her wrists in both of his hands, pulling them over her head and pressing them into the pillows. Having her in position, he angled slightly away even as he moved slowly inside. His eyes dark and roaming her body, watching hers take his, his gaze eventually roved up her belly, breasts and to her face.

And then it locked on hers.

Her lips parted, soft pants escaping with each thrust, Evangeline wrapped one leg around his ass, the other around his thigh and lifted her hips to get more.

"Pretty," he murmured and slid in deep, and she loved him there so much, her neck arched. "Always so pretty," he whispered. "Now beautiful, full of me."

"Branch," she breathed, pressing at his hands at her wrists to communicate she wanted to touch him.

His fingers held on tighter.

"No, baby," he denied gently, beginning again to move inside her. "When we have this, you're mine."

She felt her nipples contract.

"I want to touch you," she told him.

At that, he transferred both of her wrists to one of his hands and slid the other one down her side. Thumb extended and pressing in at her ribs, his hand moved in and up, where he cupped her breast.

"You want touch," he replied. "I'll give it to you."

"I want to do the touching."

His hand at her breast moved, his thumb slipping hard against the nipple, and it felt so freaking good, she arched into him.

"Looks like I got it covered."

She righted her head and tried to focus on him. "Baby—"

He started moving faster, thrusting deeper, and her soft pants weren't so soft anymore.

"Yes," she whispered.

His finger met his thumb at her nipple and gently rolled.

"*Yes*," she gasped. Her hips started rocking to meet his lunges and she found it more difficult to focus on him. "More, baby."

He gave her more, bending his head to take her mouth.

But that was it.

She took it, kissing him, tangling her tongue with his, reveling in the taste of him, tightening her hold on him with her legs, using him as leverage to lift up and meet his drives.

His fingers at her nipple ceased their gentle torture, his hand moved down over her midriff, her belly, between her legs, and his thumb slid in and hit her clit.

She gasped against his tongue and jolted in his hold.

He broke the kiss, moving faster, his lips brushing hers, his labored breaths skimming against her lips.

"More, Branch," she pushed out breathlessly.

"Of which, baby?" he asked tormentingly.

"Anything," she begged.

He gave it all to her, went faster, his thumb pressing harder, and God.

It was vanilla. Almost as vanilla as you could get in missionary position (except with her hands held down).

But it was *divine.*

"God," she breathed, her pussy tightening around him.

"Fuck, feel that," he grunted, going even faster, harder, his fingers at her wrists biting in, nearly causing pain.

Yes.

Her back bowed, she did her best to move her hips to meet his thrusts, gasping against his lips.

"Fuck, *feel that,*" he growled, now pressing her wrists fiercely in the pillows, seeking his own leverage to slam into her, his drives pounding against her clit adding delicious vibrations to the work of his thumb, and Evangeline was done.

Curling her fingers into fists, her body tightened under him, all around him, and she cried out against his lips as the slow, lazy orgasm swept her away. She almost didn't feel his mouth take hers so her noises filled it as his grunts filled hers, forcing her climax to linger, headily suspended in its grip, perfectly happy with the thought it might never let her go.

It was then his thumb went from between them but that hand went back to her breast, fingers squeezing and pulling her nipple so she moaned into his mouth, still cascading through her climax as his fingers bit brutally in her wrists and his grunted groans forced themselves down her throat.

He rode her through his climax and he rode her after it, gentling his touch everywhere, his tongue coming out to taste hers lightly before his lips slid away.

She lay under him, body liquefied, her breaths still coming shallowly, her legs still wrapped around him in the only embrace he'd allow.

Evangeline liked sex. She had her kink and she got off on it. But she liked it any way it came if who she was sharing it with was someone who could do it well and better, if they meant something to her.

But getting vanilla from Branch was a far sight better than simply liking it.

She was able to let loose. She did not have any hang-ups. Therefore she could get into sex, enjoy it, and had come in a variety of ways that didn't have to do with playing the Domme.

But she'd never climaxed that dreamily, that lazily, that amazingly during conventional sex.

God.

Branch.

And if that wasn't enough, she felt his lips skate along the shell of her ear before he whispered in it, "Okay?"

God.

Branch.

She turned her head so she had his ear. "Okay, baby."

He twisted his neck and looked in her eyes.

Before the languid beauty resting in the depths of the ice of his could fully penetrate, he let her wrists go and kissed her.

Finally free to do so, she circled him with her arms and kissed him back.

When he ended the kiss, he did it rolling them both to their sides, disengaging with his cock, but the rest of them he entwined.

"To make sure that's straight," he said quietly. "You take me, your game, your rules. I take you, both are mine."

"That's a deal," she replied immediately.

His expression changed, oddly growing soft even as it grew uneasy.

And then she lost it when he lifted his head and again put his lips to her ear.

"Fucks me to have to say it right now but I gotta keep you sharp, Angie. There's still a lot of this match to play and I'm thinkin' you don't get I'm conditioned to withstand pretty much anything."

"Wasn't me who just made love to you," she returned.

He settled back with his head on the pillow and his gaze on hers before he replied.

"Yes, it was."

She felt that like a blow to the stomach. It felt beautiful at the same time troubling.

But she didn't let it show.

"Just sayin', be careful, baby," he whispered.

She didn't feel like being careful.

"I will," she whispered her lie right back.

He looked like he didn't believe her.

But even so, he didn't caution her again.

He just rolled them both out of bed, led them to the bathroom, was hands-on with cleanup in a way that was so Branch (which meant in a way she very much liked), and then he led them back to bed.

Evangeline slept in his arms.

And she knew she'd won that game when, hours later, she woke up just the same.

sixteen

If It Was from You

EVANGELINE

Four days later, it was Sunday afternoon and Evangeline was in her Arizona room watering her plants, a task that took some time considering she had a ton of them, when she heard the kitchen door open.

She was in a bad mood.

It had been four days of life with Branch in it.

Though that was absolutely not what had put her in a mood.

During those days he worked.

She worked.

Twice, he had jobs that kept him away until late.

But one of those nights, while she was sleeping, he'd come to her bed, and when she'd woken in the morning, she'd left him there asleep.

Once she'd had to work late and she'd come home to his cooking, some TV and time to mellow out, and they'd gone to bed together, had sex, not missionary but still vanilla (and still fabulous).

And once she'd cooked for him, he'd come home at a decent hour, she'd planned to play, but he'd gotten a phone call that took him away before she could instigate it.

That was the only night when he hadn't joined her in bed and that had begun his time of late jobs where all she got was a drowsy wake-up when he joined her before she slid right back to sleep.

In that time there had been nothing intense. No heavy discussions. No games played.

Which meant no games won.

Just life. Food. Work. TV. Sex.

But they did it together with no sign Branch was retreating.

She hadn't earned a smile, or better, a laugh.

But that didn't mean she hadn't scaled a mountain.

He came to her home every night and he made himself at home when he did.

No more sitting on the edge of his seat, shoveling food in his mouth. No more holding himself awkward in the kitchen, staring out her back window.

If he was awake with her in the morning, he went down and made coffee for her (something she never requested, but she loved that he did).

When they watched TV, he rested back in the couch, his feet on the coffee table, her head on his thigh, his hand tangled in her hair.

And when she arrived back home after a day when she'd left him sleeping in bed, she'd come up to her room, finding he'd made her bed (not decoratively, the man could not arrange a toss pillow to save his life, and she had a lot of those, but he still made a mean bed, all straight covers, fluffed, precisely placed pillows and tightly tucked sheets—him knowing how to do this a curiosity she was dying to assuage).

And last, when he cooked for her, he moved around freely, knowing her kitchen, sharing an intimacy with her that she knew he didn't know he was sharing.

He hadn't left a toothbrush in her bathroom (though he didn't need to since he'd confiscated one of her toothbrush heads). And she hadn't cleared a drawer for him and told him to leave some boxers (mostly because, if they were normal, it was far too early for that, but it was especially since Branch was where Branch was in his head).

But progress had been made without her pushing it.

It was just happening.

And that was good.

However, this day was bad.

Because he'd come to her last night murmuring into her sleepiness while he pulled her into his arms that the job was done and she would have very much liked to have a full Sunday to have more time with him, make more progress with him . . .

And to play.

He'd helped her break the seal. She was back. And she had a sub who rocked it.

Not to mention, their last scene had been mind-blowing.

Branch was a phenomenal lover and she enjoyed every second when they had sex, his game, his rules. And importantly, if they were normal, it wouldn't always be about the kink. They'd have both, and if it worked (which it did, hugely), they'd get off on both.

But she was in the mood to crack a whip.

More, she wanted to use every way she could to show him what they had was something worth keeping. Something worth building. Something worth fighting for. And Evangeline wanted to use every way she could dream up to tie him tighter to her. So tight, he couldn't get loose even if the occasion came where he thought he should try, if only doing that to protect her from whatever it was that had all but destroyed him.

They were who they were. They liked what they liked in how they enjoyed playing. It was difficult to find someone in life you connected with in all the ways that were important. Add that crucial nuance, it made it exceptionally difficult.

She loved it that she had a man in her life who could throw a chop (or a steak, she'd now had both) on her grill and make her mouth water. And she loved that he'd fallen into a place where he could take off his boots and put his feet on her coffee table. She also loved it that he could make her feel what he made her feel with his hands and mouth on her.

But she was a woman who needed to wring a man's balls dry.

And he was a man who needed a woman to wring his dry.

So she'd hoped they'd have a time where they could take their time, fall into a prolonged scene and both enjoy the heck out of it.

And she'd wanted to do just that today.

That didn't happen because she had a job where she sometimes had to work Sundays. And she presently had an annoying client who knew more than she did about real estate (not even close) because he had a dick (though she suspected with his behavior that member was not all that much to write home about). And last, he wanted precisely what he wanted without buying his own damned lot and building the fucking thing himself.

So she'd shown him three (more) houses that day instead of spending it with Branch.

Branch had been cool with that. Another thing that worked for them that he wasn't noticing was that he was okay with her doing her thing the way she needed to do it and she gave him that same freedom.

He'd said he had things to do and to text him when she was heading home.

She'd done that, and within fifteen minutes, the time she was pulling into her drive, he'd replied, *Be there in an hour*

So now the day was more than half done and she'd spent the first part of it being irritated to an extreme and the last hour of it changing her sheets, doing laundry and watering her plants.

Not what she'd wanted to be doing.

That being reddening a fine male ass, that ass belonging to Branch.

Therefore, when Branch strolled into her Arizona room, eyes to her watering can before they came to her and he quipped, "Let me guess. With your jungle, you've been at that near on since you texted me," she was in no mood to giggle.

She was in the mood to bitch.

"Yes. And if the client I showed his fiftieth house to today, and

I'm not sure I'm exaggerating that, doesn't make an offer on something sometime soon, I'm going to take this watering can," she lifted it, "and shove it up his ass."

His mouth quirked and his eyes lit as he said, "You're good with ass, baby, but not sure that'd feel all that great."

She turned fully to him. "That's the point."

"Got that," he muttered, eyes still alight, standing where he'd stopped six feet from her and crossing his arms on his chest.

"He's driving me crazy."

"Got that too," he kept muttering.

"He works in tech sales," she informed him, even though he didn't ask, "although I have no earthly clue what that means, whatever it means, the only good thing about him is that he prequalified for a mortgage. But he also somehow knows every comp on every property within Maricopa County. Knowing this without looking a damned thing up, he can just rattle them off willy-nilly and, just to say, *inaccurately.*"

Branch said nothing.

She carried on bitching.

"And he's absolutely definite on what a seller should have listed a house for and this is always at least thirty percent less than the listing. *And* he has clairvoyance for he also knows precisely what a seller will accept as an offer and *that's* always at least *forty* percent below listing, which is *insane.* Though, I'll add, he knows this but hasn't offered *dick.*"

She took a deep breath as she watched his lips quirk again at her last, but she didn't shut up.

"*And,* with all of that genius at his disposal, he's also lived a past life as an inspector because all he has to do is glance at a roof and tell me the seller's agent lied on the listing's description. Because it isn't five years old, it's fifteen. And just to say, a, it's illegal to lie on a listing and, b, this guy is in *tech sales* not *roofing.*"

"I see your day hasn't been rough," Branch noted quietly. "It's been *rough.*"

She agreed to that with a sharp nod but didn't let up.

"And by the way, he's made it clear I don't know roofing, and a variety of other things, all having to do with my job, a career I've been engaged in rather successfully for seven years, and you know, say, simply *breathing*, not because I don't know roofing or how to breathe correctly. But because anyone with a vagina can't possibly understand something that complicated, and yes, that includes the proper techniques of breathing."

That earned Evangeline a thrilling scary look from Branch, which wasn't thrilling because it was scary.

It was thrilling because Branch looked pissed, he was hot when he looked pissed, and that was mostly because he was pissed on her behalf because he clearly didn't like a man disrespecting her.

"Usually, I love my job," she declared, alas, too irritated to fully appreciate Branch's pissed-on-her-behalf look. "I like houses. Mom and I would go to open houses on weekends back when I was in high school just because. She was a serial decorator. No room was ever decorated *quite* enough. So she went to get new ideas. For me, it was the houses. How they were laid out. The surprises you'd sometimes get. Imagining who lived in them. She wasn't surprised I got into the business. But when I got into the business, it became more. It's a thrill to be a part of finding someone a home, something that's fundamental to living your life. And it doesn't hurt if I sell enough that I make a good living."

His gaze wandering the room they were in, going so far as to look over his shoulder into the family room, Branch remarked, "Woulda thought you were about the decorating."

He was being funny.

And she thought he was funny.

That didn't mean she didn't snap, "Stop being a smartass, Branch."

He looked back at her and his mouth quirked again.

She ignored that and shared something more he'd already got. "Today, I did not love my job."

He finally became serious.

"You work too much, honey," he said softly.

"I know that, Branch."

"Said yourself you wanted to cut back," he reminded her.

"I know that too," she returned. "I just don't know how to do that without losing a client or the referrals they could bring because I might want to cut back but I still need to pay the mortgage."

"Far's I can see, you pay your mortgage and then some. Cut back a little on clothes, shoes and knickknacks, you could lose a client, especially a pain-in-the-ass one, and whatever referrals he might bring."

"I don't work hard not to be able to indulge in shopping sprees, Branch," she declared to another lip twitch. "And I like knickknacks. They're like physical memories."

He was back to muttering when he replied, "That wasn't lost on me."

"You're being a smartass again," she warned.

"No, Angie, that actually wasn't lost on me," he returned.

The way he shared that, Evangeline fell silent.

"Cut back, honey," Branch advised gently before she could figure out just what way he'd shared his last. "You got a pain-in-the-ass client, life's too fuckin' short to put up with his shit, scrape him off. You dig what you do but nothing in life is perfect all the time. Decide how much shit you're willing to put up with when it gets shoveled your way and cut it off when it goes over that line. That's a good way to protect your downtime because, even if you dig what you do, too much of it is never a good thing. And straight up, honey, if you protect your downtime, you'll have a lot more patience when an asshole crosses your path and shovels shit your way."

This was good advice.

And she was in the mood to take it.

But still.

"That doesn't get me back my Sunday," she pointed out. *With you*, she didn't say.

"You're right," he replied, moved her way and took her in his arms.

Yes, he moved right to her.

And took her in his arms.

She stood there, shocked and unmoving, but even so, she felt those two things still loving the feel of him holding her in a way no words could express how perfect it was.

It was just that perfect.

And then Branch made it better.

Holding her close to his tall body with one arm, sliding his other hand up in her ponytail, he murmured to the top of her head, "What can I do?"

"I'm in a bad mood," she shared, something else he definitely knew, curving her free arm around him, the other hand holding the watering can dangling at her side.

"Got that."

Yes.

He got that.

And he didn't balk, get impatient with her bitching or steer her in another direction because he didn't want to hear it.

He'd listened, advised, come right to her and *taken her in his arms.*

But standing in his arms, in this new place with Branch that *he* instigated, progress between them that *he* walked across a room to offer her, she didn't know how to proceed.

The part of their lives that was always a given from the very beginning should be the easy place to take him.

And a great way to burn off her mood.

But now with nearly a week with Branch where life was just life, they had the rest of their Sunday free, no work for her, no jobs for him, for some reason she felt shy in taking him there.

And more, standing in his arms, she wanted to do nothing but that. Especially since he'd put her right there, instigating something between them that was so precious, she wanted to hold on to it for as long as he was willing to give it to her.

"You want me to finish watering the plants?" he asked.

"I'm almost done," she muttered into his chest, now loving the fact that he'd made *that* offer because it was sweet.

"You wanna finish watering the plants while I get you a glass of wine?" he suggested.

Now she loved *that* offer.

Even so, she mumbled, "I feel more like a shot of tequila."

"You got tequila, I can do that. You don't, I can go out and get some."

Damn.

She'd been right.

So very *right*.

With each passing minute with him, she knew she wanted more of Branch Dillinger.

Even if it turned out to be just life and a whole lot of (really good) vanilla sex.

God, she hoped she could win their match.

If she didn't . . .

It wasn't worth contemplating.

Especially doing that standing in the warm sun streaming in through the windows of her Arizona room with his strong arms around her.

When she didn't answer, just snuggled closer, his fingers fisted in her hair, gently pulling her head to the side, and he bowed his back so he could put his lips to her ear.

"You wanna tie me up and do dirty things to me?"

Now *that* was motivation to lose his arms.

"You in the mood?" she queried in return, wanting to be sure he was but unable to keep all the breathy out of her words because she definitely was.

Absolutely.

"The way you give it, you really asking that shit?" he shot back.

She tried to turn her head so she could get a look at his face but his fingers tightened in her hair, stopping her.

He trailed his lips down the neck he'd exposed then back up to her ear, where he whispered, "Love taking your sweet, wet pussy. But you need to know, I'll likely always be in the mood for you to do the taking. You wanna get fucked, baby, I'll fuck that rough day away. But you wanna do the fucking, I'm open to that too."

Evangeline wasn't going to make him offer again.

"Then maybe you should go upstairs, get naked and position for me, on your knees at the edge of the pillows, hands behind your head, facing the headboard, handsome," she replied in her own whisper.

His arm around her slid down so he could cup her ass in his hand and press her into his hips as he ground into her body.

She felt his hardness against her belly.

It was safe to say he was in the mood.

"I'm down with that," he shared needlessly.

She turned her head so her lips were now at his ear. "Just a warning, my big boy, there's the matter of you being bad I'll be having to see to."

"Mm," he murmured, the hum of it gliding down her neck and exploding in her nipples.

He was right.

Mm.

"Might be best not to make me wait," she prompted.

She felt his teeth skim her earlobe before he replied, "Yes, ma'am."

That, she felt in her nipples *and* below.

He let her go, gave her the heat through the ice-blue of his gaze and then he sauntered out of the room as casually as he'd strolled into it.

God, even just watching him walk made her wet.

Branch disappeared and she watched him do it, going so far as to lean to the point she almost fell over not to lose sight of him.

But when she did, she forced herself to finish watering her plants. She then forced herself to go to the laundry room, put what was in the washer into the dryer and then start a new load.

And only then did she walk upstairs to start what she should have been doing all day.

Sharing it with Branch.

Evangeline just wanted to look at him.

He was magnificent, tied to her bed on his knees, his arms stretched out to his sides, bound at the wrists by silk ropes held high on her bedposts, his legs spread wide, his cock hard, his balls bulging, his ass red from the few crops he'd already taken, the muscles of his back, ass and thighs on display.

Oh yes.

She could look at him like that for hours.

She could just look at him for hours, tied to her bed on his knees, cooking in her kitchen, ambling into her house from the grill.

But now her pussy couldn't take just watching.

She needed to touch.

And other things.

So wearing nothing but a lacy black bra and panties, she walked on the bed on her knees and got close to his side at his back, running a hand flat down along his spine, feeling the warmth of his skin turn to heat at his ass.

"I'm afraid I've just broken you in, handsome," she whispered.

"Yes, ma'am," he replied.

"I wanted to spend all day playing with you, Branch," she admitted. "That means I'm going to have to pack a lot in in the time we have."

"I'm not going anywhere."

No.

He was not.

Now.

Or, if she got her way, maybe ever.

"Good, baby," she murmured, stroking his ass. "Now, I like it when you offer this to me." She gave his ass a squeeze. "You're going to take more from your crop. Be sure to tip for me so I'm sure you feel it."

"You got it, Angie."

He said the words and she felt his ass move into her hand as he carried out her order.

God, he was everything.

She moved back and grabbed the crop where she'd dropped it on the bed.

Then she went at him.

And she felt it drive up her pussy as he tipped for her, taking his crop, swaying forward with the blows, back to get more.

She gave it to him good and she gave it to him long but when the truncated grunt that surged up his throat shared he needed a break, as he swayed back, she didn't strike another blow.

She shifted in the bed, took the folded-over tip, slid it to his crevice right to his hole and pressed in.

He pressed back.

That drove up her pussy too.

"Remember being bad, Branch?"

His tone was rough when he replied, "I remember, Angie."

"You liked being bad, didn't you?"

"Fuck yeah."

She put on more pressure. "You liked making me say things, didn't you?"

"Fuck *yeah*."

She slid the tip of her crop up and down and said quietly, "I like making you say things too."

He didn't reply.

"How bad were you, Branch?"

"Bad."

She took the crop away and struck him with it, harder than she'd been giving it to him.

She watched his jaw get tight as he swung forward then tipped back.

Yes.

He was everything.

"How bad?" she pushed, landing another blow.

"Very bad," he forced out on a huff, rocking with the blow and again tipping back.

"Tell me," she demanded, lighting another crack.

"I've been very bad, baby. Crop my ass."

She did, ordering, "Tell me."

"More, Angie," he grunted. "Crop me raw."

She kept going, watching his fingers tighten on the ropes, the posts swaying the headboard with his movements, commanding, "Give me what I want, handsome."

"Been very bad, baby. Take my ass, it's yours. Crop it. Fuck it. Use it. Strip it raw."

She delivered another quick succession of blows before she dropped the crop and went in, fisting his cock at the front, spanking him skin to skin at his ass.

His head dropped back and he hissed out, "Yes."

Her big boy liked his ass spanked best of all.

And she liked spanking it just the same.

"Is this my ass?" she asked, still slapping it.

"Yes," he bit out.

She stroked him deep. "My cock?"

"Yes, Angie."

"I'm gonna fill that ass, baby. Offer it again to me."

He tipped back again immediately and she moved away, to the toys she'd already selected to choose from should she want them. She prepared the one she'd be using and moved in behind him.

"Stay in position," she ordered.

"Yes, ma'am."

She barely gave him time to rumble out those two words before she positioned the head of his toy where it needed to be, shifted in and, with one of her hands wrapped around his distended dick, her other hand on the toy, the base of it to her hips, she started gliding it in.

"Fuck, give me that," he growled.

"Stay in position."

She felt him straining, needing to thrust into her hand, shift back into her hips to take more of her up his ass, and she took it slow, stroking him and filling him.

Once she'd planted the toy fully inside, she cupped his balls in her free hand and whispered, "Stay in position, handsome."

"Fuck," he grunted.

She pumped his dick, lightly squeezing his balls, and he held for her.

She went faster, tightening her fingers in both places, and Branch, so damned perfect, held for her.

She watched him grit his teeth as she kept at him, a muscle jerking up his cheek.

And he held for her.

Finally, he broke.

"Ma'am," he ground out.

"Who's taking your cock?" she asked.

"You, baby," he pushed out.

"Who's filling you?"

"You, Angie. Untie me, I wanna come inside you with you up my ass."

"No, handsome. I like to watch it too much when you blow for me."

"*Fuck,*" he bit off.

"I'll let you eat me after I tie you to your belly. But first you'll give your cum to me."

"*Fuckin' fuck,*" he hissed, his hips slightly jerking. "Gotta do that now."

Not quite yet.

"You like me doing dirty things to you, Branch?" she pressed.

"Fuckin' love it, honey. Now let me blow, baby."

She went faster, squeezed harder, pressed closer to his back and put her lips to his skin.

"Missed being inside you," she whispered there.

"Me too. Fuck, Angie, me too. Nothin' better than havin' you buried deep. Now please, baby, fuckin' let me come," he grunted.

"Since you asked so sweet," she kept his dick pointed down to the towel covering the pillow, "show me what I do to you. You can move, handsome."

With that he thrust into her fist, his ass slamming into her belly, once, twice, three times, before his head shot back, his groan reverberated through the room and his cum gushed from his cock onto the towel as his body jerked and bucked in her hold.

She absorbed his orgasm, her clit humming, the hard buds of her nipples an agony of perfection brushing his back through her bra, and she gave his balls a gentle squeeze when the bucks turned to light spasms as his climax slid into the aftershocks.

She kept hold of him, fit close to his back, when he sagged into his bounds, his head falling forward.

And that was when she took them out of the simplicity of just living life, the natural progress that had earned her.

And she took a risk.

Releasing her hold on his balls, she swept her hand up until she found it.

The scar at his belly.

She felt his body still as she traced her fingers lightly across it.

"Angie."

His voice was low, gruff, sated.

But it still held a warning.

She ignored that warning and trailed her fingers up, to the scars at his shoulder, and she caressed them, a part of him, therefore doing it adoringly.

He felt her touch.

And he knew what it meant.

"Honey," he whispered.

"You know I want all of you," she told the skin of his back, gliding her lips across a scar there too.

"Babe—"

"You don't want to tell me, okay. I can't imagine the stories are ones I'll like hearing. But whatever made these, I don't care." She touched the scars and then down, to the one at his belly again, and down further, to the ones on his thigh, her fingers going right to them because she'd long since memorized their positions. "They're a part of you and I want them. I want anything that makes you."

She knew he'd turned his head to try to catch her eyes over his shoulder when she heard his "Angie," but she kept her mouth to his back, lining another scar with her lips, and she kept talking.

"But if you want to give it to me, Branch, I'll take it no matter what it is and I'll want it too."

To that, he said nothing.

She rubbed her nose against his back and slid both her hands up to his stomach, where she wrapped her arms around him.

"Now, I'm going to untie you and take away the towel. Once I do that you're going to lie down on your bolster and I'm going to bind you again for me because I'm not done with you. Then I'm going to slide out your toy and slide in your jewel because it's been a long time since I've seen me winking inside you and I want that back. Now after being filled this full, are you good to take that, baby?"

"Take anything from you, Angie," he replied, quiet and gentle.

She fought back a smile even though the tone of his words gave her more, more that wasn't just sweet, it was sad and sweet, she just refused to hear the sad part of it.

"Good," she murmured.

"Angie—" he started but stopped when she nipped his back with her teeth.

"No, Branch. We're playing my game now. And you know how it goes. My game, my rules."

He let that lie for long moments before he replied, "Your game, baby. Your rules."

"Mm-hmm," she mumbled against his skin then turned her head, pressed her cheek to his back and held him to her.

"Give you something," he said softly when she didn't move for a while.

"You give me everything, Branch."

He ignored her and carried on, "If I could give it, one woman on this earth I'd give it to, it'd be you, Evangeline."

At that, she let herself smile.

"But I can't give it, honey," he finished so low, she fancied if she didn't feel his words at her hands as well as at her ears, she wouldn't have heard them.

But she heard them.

"That's okay too, Branch. Since the beginning I knew I'd take what I could get from you and since the beginning I knew I'd be happy with that if it was from you."

He let another several moments lie between them in silence before he muttered, like he was talking to himself, "I'm a mother-fucker."

She put her chin to his back, looking to his head, seeing it again bowed, this time not from experiencing a hard climax.

Like he was experiencing defeat.

He would, eventually.

But not what he was right then thinking.

"Maybe," she replied. "But if you are, you're *my* motherfucker," she stated, giving him a squeeze on the word "my." "And I'll take that too."

"My Mistress is stubborn."

She couldn't stop her body from stilling but forced it to relax, hopefully before he noticed.

He'd said his Mistress.

Not his Domme.

Not "ma'am."

His *Mistress*.

More progress.

And yes, hell yes, she'd take that too.

She watched him turn his head, look down his back at her, and he guided them out of the moment.

"Want my jewel, baby."

She grinned up at him, watched his eyes get soft, then she kissed his back.

After that, she took care of him, tied him down on his belly and gave him what he asked.

And then some.

So in the end, when Evangeline fell asleep curled around her big bound boy at her side, their Sunday wasn't a bust.

It.

Was.

Delicious.

seventeen

Win or Lose

EVANGELINE

Evangeline was at her desk late the next morning when her phone rang.

She looked down at it, saw the screen telling her Branch was calling, and a slither of panic slipped through her belly because the last time Branch had called, he'd retreated, then she hadn't seen him in four days.

And she'd pushed him last night, reminding him what she wanted from them, thus reminding him where he was at in his head.

So this call could be not such a good thing.

But it was from Branch so she couldn't ignore it because maybe it would be.

She took in a deep breath, preparing for battle (if that was necessary), and snatched up her phone, engaging it and putting it to her ear.

"Hey, honey," she greeted chirpily.

"Angie—"

At least he was calling her Angie.

She didn't let him get further.

"Guess what."

A hesitation before, "What?"

"That client I was telling you about yesterday?" she asked.

"Yeah?" he prompted when she said no more.

"I called him. Told him that I had some family issues that would be taking my time so I needed to refer him to another agent. Then I referred him to a male agent here at the office who's kind of a jerk. So I'm done with him, and double the good, the agent who's got him now who I don't like all that much has to put up with his crap." She paused for a breath. "And that's that!" she cried the last excitedly.

"Good for you, baby, proud of you," he replied, sounding it.

And that sounded good.

"I'm proud of me too," she shared honestly.

"You should be," he murmured.

"I have to thank you, Branch." She smiled in order to put that in her voice so he could hear it because she knew he liked it. "You give good advice."

"More than welcome, babe," he returned.

She had nothing more to say and was scrambling to come up with a topic before Branch shared the reason he called, which might not make her day, when Branch spoke.

"Listen, I need a haircut."

She stared at the top of her desk, thinking, if she'd had to make a list of all the things he might have called about, that wouldn't be in the top ten.

Or the top one hundred.

"I, uh . . . okay," she mumbled.

"I need a haircut, babe," he repeated.

Evangeline was still confused.

"Okay, Branch," she said.

"Babe."

That was the only word he said but the depth in it, clearly, he thought communicated something to her.

"Sorry, honey, you might need to give me some more because I'm not sure what you want from me," she admitted.

"I'm yours."

She sucked in a breath that was so sharp, he had to have heard it.

"Yes," she whispered because she physically couldn't get her voice to go higher.

"And being yours in the way I'm yours, you might want my hair a certain way."

She let out her breath slowly.

There were Dominants and submissives that had certain kinds of relationships that could get into a whole bevy of things. This included the Dom requiring that their sub dress as they liked, even to the point of the Dom selecting what the sub was going to wear every day.

It also included Dominants demanding their subs doing their makeup or arranging their hair as the Dominant liked to see it.

Or having it cut like they liked.

Evangeline would not have guessed Branch was into the life that deep.

Outside of when they played and the infrequent times she'd left her mark on him with her lipstick, ordered him to leave holding her jewel inside, he was his own man. He didn't strike her as a man, or a sub, who would ask for that part of their lives to filter into his actual life.

Before she could get a lock on this information and process it, he spoke again.

"Just to say, you're mine too and if you wanted to do anything with that gorgeous hair of yours, it was extreme, I'd wanna be in on that discussion. And by saying 'wanna,' I mean, you did anything to your hair, like cut it off, it'd piss me off you didn't talk to me about it first."

At that, Evangeline had to force herself to quietly breathe deep.

All of her life her hair had been a boon and a drawback.

The boon part was that, except for putting product in it that would define the curls, she didn't have to do much with it. It was thick, naturally glossy and it gave great curl, bouncy, no frizz, the curls sleek and defined, her hair long. This meant style time was the time it took to dry. And that didn't stink.

But there was a lot of it and she lived in Phoenix where it could get *hot*. So simply the amount of hair she had could make her hotter. And it wasn't easy wrestling her mane just into a ponytail, much less anything else (but she'd become skilled with it and could manage a killer updo, if given the time).

Last, the style she had was the only style she could have. She'd tried different cuts but a short layering at the ends to give the curls more spring and stave off some of the weight was the only option available to her.

She loved that Branch thought it was gorgeous.

That was awesome.

But what had her deep breathing was the fact that he'd said, "You're mine too."

And not only that, he was talking future.

He didn't know when she intended to get her hair done.

He was just intimating that he'd be there when she did and if she intended to lose her mind and cut it off, he wanted a say in that.

"For you," he cut into her frenzied, delicious thoughts, "it isn't about me wanting to grab hold of it if I wanna do that, even though it is. It's that I like to look at it the way it is. For you with me, you wanna grab hold, babe, to do the things you do to me, I gotta know where you want me to go with it because I want you to have what you want. But I gotta take care of it. It's about three weeks too far in beginning to be a pain in my ass."

So it wasn't about him wanting her to take them to that place where she made demands of his appearance as her sub.

It was that they were in that place where he *was* her sub and she his Mistress and he wanted his Mistress to have him as she wanted him.

She liked that.

Not to mention, he was right. His hair was getting pretty long.

It looked good on him but she wasn't a man-bun or man-with-a-ponytail type of girl.

"I, you, well . . . you can tell them to cut it to the length it was when I met you in Aryas's red room."

His deep, rough voice held humor when he replied, "Not sure a barber will understand I say to cut it to when my babe first met me."

His babe.

Beautiful.

"Just brushing your collar, honey," she explained.

"That might work," he mumbled.

"Not too short," she kept explaining. "Because I'll want the opportunity to take hold."

"Gotcha," he replied and went on, "I'll be done at a decent hour tonight. If you don't have to work late, your turn to cook."

She would have liked him to say neither of them would cook. He'd take her out to dinner. Maybe a movie after. Do things normal couples would do out in public where people could see them, where she could show the world the handsome man who shared her bed.

But he was coming to her place so she'd take that.

For now.

"I'll need to hit a grocery store so I still might be a little late," she shared.

"I'll have time to hit a store sometime today. Text me what you need and I'll get it in."

She kept staring at her desktop. "Text you?"

"Yeah."

Carefully, she noted, "It'd be easier to e-mail you."

"I don't have e-mail."

More staring at her desktop. "You don't have e-mail?"

"No."

Evangeline was shocked.

"Who doesn't have e-mail?"

More humor in his voice when he replied, "Me."

"Branch, that's ... well, it's crazy. Everyone has e-mail. How do you function?"

He didn't respond and this lasted so long, she felt the need to call his name, worried they'd been cut off.

"Branch?"

"Here," he grunted, no amusement now.

Oh Lord.

He didn't have e-mail because ...

She didn't know.

But the reason was something that had to do with the fact that he didn't take her out to restaurants and he demanded she sign an NDA before she'd met him.

It had been so long since she'd been reminded of that last, she felt a chill slide over her skin.

She didn't know him at all, not really.

She knew him. She knew a lot about him.

But she still didn't know him at all.

"I sense you get me," he murmured.

She didn't.

She also did.

"Kind of," she replied quietly.

"I'm not everyone," he stated.

No, he wasn't.

"Yes," she whispered.

"My win," he said the same way, and she couldn't argue it was. Then he said the words she was experiencing. "And it feels shit."

Damn.

"If you ever knew, which you won't," he continued, "just sayin', you'd wish you didn't."

"I'm not sure that's true," she returned quickly.

"I'm sure for the both of us."

"Branch—"

"Text me what you need at the store."

"Honey—"

"Just text me, baby. Yeah?"

She closed her mouth and let the silence linger, but when he didn't break it, she did.

"I'll text you."

"Cool. See you tonight."

And there was that.

So she'd grab hold.

"Yes, Branch. See you tonight."

"Later, Angie."

"Later, honey."

He disconnected and Evangeline stared at her phone, feeling uneasy regardless of the fact she had the task of writing out a grocery list, texting the damned thing to Branch, meaning he'd be shopping for them and also home for her to cook for him that night.

Still, she had him.

But she didn't and he was holding huge things back from her.

It was coming clear he could be stubborn too.

She already knew that.

What she was sensing for the first time was that maybe they were evenly matched.

But in any game, *someone* had to win.

And for the first time since they'd started to play it, Evangeline was worried that she might be the one who would lose.

That afternoon, Evangeline was walking into the office after she'd been through an inspection with a client, when Mercy, the receptionist/assistant the agents used, greeted her.

"Hey, Evangeline," she said on a smile, and Evangeline started to smile back and offer her own greeting when Mercy carried on, "a Mr. Lange came in a few minutes ago. Since you were on the board scheduled to return about now, I asked him if he wanted to wait. He said yes so I showed him to your office."

For a second, she didn't know who Mr. Lange was.

"Mr. Lange?" she asked.

"*Mr. Lange*," Mercy replied, with emphasis, her smile turning huge, her eyes doing the same.

With that, she knew.

Stellan Lange, a Dom at the Honey, actually *the* Dom at the Honey, since Aryas often traveled the West to oversee all his clubs so he wasn't in town that much to take that role.

In other words, Amélie was queen, Aryas the king, and Stellan was prince regent, reigning over the club in the king's absence.

He was also a good guy. She liked him. And if she admitted it, she would have actually liked to have played with him, mostly because he was just that handsome.

In truth, until Branch, she'd actually never met a man as handsome as Stellan. Tall and dark, lean and fierce, Dom of Doms, in some of her fantasies pre- (and in most of them post-) Kevin, she'd imagined having a go at switching him.

And she didn't mean that in the way she'd use that tool on his ass (though that was part of the fantasy).

She meant convincing him with her awesome Mistress powers to switch sides.

This she didn't know at the time was foreshadowing of the fact that what she was looking for, but didn't know it, was an alpha-sub.

As strange as it might seem, however, she'd always thought he'd hook up with Amélie. Why she thought this, since they both were Dominants, she didn't know. They just suited each other with their mutual sophistication, and any time they spent together, which was often at the club, you could sense the chemistry. And as Evangeline well knew, two Doms could get what they needed, playing together with a sub or subs, ending that play with each other.

Although it was a definite surprise, it wasn't outlandish that he'd show at her office. When he'd met her, he'd thrown some business her way, friends and associates looking for homes. It was a nice thing to do, considering they all were wealthy so her commissions had been amazing. And he hadn't stopped doing this.

But she hadn't found his home for him, though she'd been to it a few of times for parties he'd invited her to, because he was a good guy. They were business networking parties and she'd been able to score some clients.

The other parties were of a different variety.

Stellan liked to play and he took that home with private parties he hosted that he was choosy about who attended.

It was an honor to get the invites, and although she didn't come to play, she'd definitely gone.

Stellan threw one heck of a party, in a number of ways.

So she'd enjoyed them.

This was mostly watching him work. With his demanding, affectionate style of Domination, she'd gotten a ton of ideas.

But now, smiling at Mercy and mumbling her thanks before heading toward the hall, she thought it would be surprising if he was looking for a new place. His house was close to Amélie's, though in a basin in Paradise Valley opposite Amélie's mountain. The streets leading to it were right in the city but they seemed to meander through massive lots that looked more like Southwestern desert ranches and not the veritable mansions they were.

When she'd first gone to his home, she'd pictured him riding up to her on a horse, one of those cool hats on his head that had a wide brim and not much curve, a whip coiled at his hip (of course).

But as far as she could tell, Stellan didn't even own a pair of jeans. He wore suits to the club, expensive, tailored ones. And when he worked a sub, he wore banded waistband or drawstring, low-slung, loose-fitting men's lounge pants, his chest and feet bare (if he wasn't nude).

In fact, remembering how Stellan's sculpted ass looked in those pants, Evangeline decided she needed to get some of those for Branch because Stellan looked amazing in them, but Branch would rock the heck out of them.

As she walked toward her office, Evangeline turned her mind from those pants and back to Stellan showing out of the blue.

He might be there (she hoped, she wouldn't refer *him* to another agent) because he was looking for a new place. His sprawling, ranch-style, Southwestern pueblo mansion with its slanted terra-cotta tile roofs, heavy, carved-wood doors and log-adorned back veranda was spectacular and oddly fit someone who looked more like he worked on Wall Street and owned a penthouse filled with leather and chrome.

But it had to cost millions, and if he was ready to trade up, Evangeline was ready to help him find what was perfect for him.

She turned into her office and saw him sitting in one of her desk chairs, his ankle on his opposite knee, wearing one of his elegant suits that highlighted the broadness of his shoulders (a broadness that had nothing to do with shoulder pads, she very well knew).

His dark head was turned to look over one of those broad shoulders, his hooded, midnight-blue eyes were on her.

Yes, she would have liked to have the opportunity to switch an alpha like him, in a number of ways.

But she had the most magnificent alpha-sub there was, so she'd gotten exactly what she needed.

She just had to find a way to keep him.

"Stellan, this is a surprise," she said with a smile.

"Close the door," he replied.

She felt a slither she didn't know how to read, not simply at what his command could mean but the way he delivered it, the blatant Dom coming from him. And even as a Domme herself, she noted that slither was nice.

It also was ominous.

She closed the door and, gaze to him, walked behind her desk. She sat.

He didn't make her wait.

"You were at the club a while ago."

"Yes," she confirmed.

"Rumor has it, you spent most of your time there in the booth with Dillinger."

He knew Branch's last name?

Which meant he knew Branch?

"You know Branch?" she queried.

"I know a lot of things," he replied, an answer but also not.

She powered through that because she had to.

Branch wanted things on the down low and she wanted to keep them there for him, and no longer just because she'd signed that document.

"I'd really rather not talk about that, Stellan."

"Have you turned?"

She wasn't following.

"Turned?"

"Against your nature," he explained.

"You mean, away from the life?" she asked.

"Away from you," he answered. "Who you are and how you like it."

She shifted in her seat and responded, "Stellan, again, I'd really rather not—"

"There are parts of me that might understand that. He's good-looking and it wasn't lost on anyone you had a fascination with Damian. Doms enjoying subordinate positions under the rule of an advanced Dom isn't unheard of. However, I've seen your work, at least what you'd show, and you're not a sub, Evangeline. So it concerns me you've turned from your nature after having Damian."

"You think Branch is a Dom?" she asked, not entirely surprised about this.

His brows went up briefly before he shifted out of his apparent surprise and returned, "We'll talk about Dillinger in a second."

She closed her mouth, knowing how she felt about that, and it wasn't pleasant.

It was just ominous.

"If you need to break yourself back in, and you're concerned about working with Damian and the extent you enjoy that, then I'll take a female and male sub and we'll work them together," he offered then shrugged. "If it goes somewhere that we share something together along with our work with our slaves, to be honest, this would please me. I've always found you more than attractive, so feeling that, it was regrettable, knowing your leanings. However, although I think you've made the right decision to steer clear of Damian as the extremes he needs in play don't coincide with your style, you'd be safer working with me in an effort to return to finding what you need rather than being with Dillinger."

"I . . . this offer is lovely, Stellan," she said softly, stunned in a nice way to learn he found her "more than attractive" even if that no longer factored in the slightest. "However, without sharing too much because it's private, I'll just say you've got nothing to worry about."

"Just you saying that, Evangeline, means I do. Because you're a real estate agent with a house in Willo and a talent with a switch. What you're not is the kind of woman who should be with the kind of man Dillinger is."

She felt her chest seize so she was forced to wheeze out, "Stellan—"

"He's not a good man," he declared.

"How do you know that?" she whispered.

"Because I'm not a good man," he answered immediately. "And the kind of man I am knows the circles a man like Dillinger doesn't quite run in because he doesn't quite exist, which is another reason you should be cautious. But something else I know is the kind of not-good I am is absolutely not the same as the kind of not-good Dillinger is."

Branch didn't "quite exist"?

What on earth did that mean?

She didn't ask.

She started, "I think this is something that we shouldn't—"

"Aryas sent Dillinger to deal with Kevin," he shared.

And she relaxed.

"I know that, Stellan," she informed him. "And I also know how he did that. Not because Aryas shared. Because Branch told me."

"Has he told you it all?" he asked.

Evangeline tensed again.

"What do you mean when you say, 'it all'?" she asked back.

"I've no idea. But you asking that means he hasn't shared it."

Damn it

"That's not your business," Evangeline declared.

"He hasn't," he again accurately deduced. "And I can't share because the kind of man Dillinger is, I don't know the extent of what there is to share. Which is another concern. However, just the not knowing is of greater concern, considering what we both know he's capable of."

Even if he was flipping her out, she was beginning to get angry.

"You do know I'm an adult and can make decisions for myself," she remarked.

He unhooked his ankle from his knee and leaned slightly her way. "What I also know, Leenie," he started gently, "is that you chose badly with Kevin. And it's my opinion you chose badly with Damian, even if Kevin explicitly requested him. It's not that Damian isn't in your league. It's just that Damian doesn't share your style and you should never have had anything to do with him."

She felt her face turn hard. "So, if you knew all this, maybe you could have shared *while* I was with Kevin or *before* we had our scene with Damian."

His face turned as gentle as his tone had been and it made him so handsome it almost hurt to look at him.

"I don't want to hurt you, honey. And I'm not saying this to cause harm to you. I'm trying to make a point and I'm using that in an effort to get you to listen to me. Like everyone, I was surprised at what Kevin did. The fact he wasn't good enough for you, I always knew. What he was hiding, I didn't. And I'm not saying you should have. What I'm saying is, we all need to learn from our mistakes. Including you."

"Branch isn't a mistake," she retorted.

"You might be right," he returned. "I don't know him. I just know of him and in that, I don't know much. I'm just here because you came to the club. You didn't partake. Rumor flew you were with one of Aryas's men. I was there that night so I know which man and what I know of him, and what I feel for you, with you again disappearing from the club and with what had happened to you there, I needed to reach out and urge you to be cautious."

"Don't you think I'd be that anyway?" she demanded to know.

"What I think is that Dillinger is a man with a certain manner that reminds me of Damian in the extremes he almost assuredly needs to get off," he replied.

Damn, he hadn't read that wrong.

"Branch isn't Damian," she asserted.

"No, I sense he's far more dangerous."

It was with those words that the memory hit her like a bullet.

The feel of Branch's strong arms wrapped around her, holding her to his tall, hard, warm body, and the sound of him asking, "What can I do?"

Branch Dillinger was not a bad man.

He was not a dangerous man.

He was a damaged man who lived the life he felt he needed to lead.

What he did to Kevin he did cognizantly, dispensing the justice he felt needed delivered, doing it with no regrets.

And Evangeline was in no position to judge him for that because she wasn't sure he should regret it and she didn't care what that said about her. Kevin might not get the help he needed but one thing she was certain about, with the justice Branch described he'd imparted, it was unlikely Kevin would ever harm anyone like he'd harmed her.

Aryas was not a bad man and she knew that to her bones. She also knew, even if he lived in a world where things had to be done she knew nothing about and didn't want to, he would not work with people he didn't respect, people who hadn't *earned* that respect.

Not to mention Branch called Olly friend. She didn't know Olly but no way would Amélie have anyone in her life, even through her partner, who hadn't earned the privilege of belonging there.

She could understand with what Stellan knew about Branch and with what had happened to her that he'd be overly cautious and want to counsel her to be the same. And it was sweet he'd acted on that.

She might have had the wool pulled over her eyes with Kevin, but so had Aryas, Amélie . . .

Stellan.

And she'd decided to go all-in with Branch, knowing what he was capable of, he gave that to her himself. She'd done this because she knew he was worth it and he'd done not one thing since to prove her wrong.

In fact, he'd done a great many things to prove her right.

But she'd decided to go all-in.

That was where she was and that was where she was going to remain until one of them won.

She just had to hope it was her.

"I know what I'm doing, honey," she replied to Stellan.

His blue gaze held hers for some moments before he dipped his chin and sat back in his chair.

"Now that we've got that relatively straight," Evangeline sought to change the subject, "Leigh said something about you two having a thing. Is that all good?"

"I wanted her," he announced bluntly.

She stared at him.

"Another lesson to learn, Leenie, this one you can learn from me. If you want something, don't play games, because it hurts like fuck when the person you're playing doesn't know how you're playing it, meaning you have to watch her fall in love with another man."

She ignored his warning about games because she couldn't go there.

But regardless, what he'd admitted about Leigh took precedence over all else.

"Oh my God, honey," she whispered. "I'm so sorry. I had no idea."

Though, she had.

Just not that the chemistry they had run that deep for Stellan.

"Apparently, neither did Leigh."

"Oh my God," she repeated.

He lifted one shoulder in an urbane shrug. "It doesn't matter now. He makes her happy and doesn't hide that she does the same for him. I wanted her but I fucked around and didn't win her. I still want to see her happy. I didn't like the man when he first came to the club but he's proved worthy of her in a variety of ways since. And it'd make my feelings for her a lie, not to mention make me the biggest form of asshole, if I wasn't happy for her once she'd found what she wanted."

"That's very sweet," she told him gently.

"Don't mistake me for sweet, Evangeline," he returned. "My subs do that often and they pay for making that mistake."

She grinned at him. "I've seen you work and I'm not sure they much mind."

"Yes," he replied, not grinning and not looking like that was something that pleased him.

She found that concerning, this prompting her to ask, "Is everything okay?"

Again bluntly, and without hesitation, he answered, "Although I'd do anything to erase what happened to you, and being the man I am, selfishly not wanting to live the powerlessness it made me feel and the remorse I experienced after not having read one single thing on Kevin so I could have saved you from that, I envy you one thing."

His words made her heart warm.

Yes, Stellan was a good guy.

"And what's that?" she queried.

"The break."

She raised a brow. "The break?"

"From the scene. I never thought I'd admit this, but it's beginning to get boring."

She grinned again. "Big, bad Dom needs a challenge."

"I need something," he murmured.

Evangeline leaned into her desk, her forearms crossed on top of it, and assured quietly, "You'll find it, Stellan."

"Perhaps," he replied. "And perhaps not."

"I think, maybe if you open your world a little bit, you'll be surprised."

To that, his dark brows went up. "Not hunt at the Honey?"

She sat back and shrugged. "There are subs out there who don't belong to the Honey."

"Not any who deserve to grace my playroom."

She bit back a laugh. "You're such a snob, Stellan."

"I've worked hard for that distinction, Evangeline."

To that, she smiled at him.

Her smile faded a bit as she felt her face get soft when she said, "Thank you for coming. Thank you for the reason behind why you came. This conversation might not have gone as you would have liked. But I still appreciate the thought behind it."

"You're one of the few worth it, Evangeline," he returned. "Unfortunately, you don't like to be tied down with your nipples clamped while I make you enjoy taking my cock up your ass, you prefer the other side of that coin, or I suspect you'd definitely be opening up my world more than a little bit and doing it for some time."

"I think that's a high compliment," she teased.

"There's no 'thinking' about it, sweetheart," he returned smoothly.

"Again, I've seen you work, Stellan. You're very right."

"I know."

That bold arrogance bought him her laughter and she watched his sensuous, full lips tip up, exposing openly he enjoyed it when he did.

Seeing how much more handsome he was smiling, she again wished she'd have that from Branch.

But she didn't linger on that thought too long.

She'd made a decision and she was all-in.

Win or lose.

That night when she walked in her kitchen door, she didn't know what to expect, seeing as Branch's truck was at the curb but their conversation that morning had gone the way it had.

However, in a million years, she wouldn't have expected him to meet her right at the door.

And right after she'd cleared it, before she'd even closed the door or put down her purse and attaché, he was in her space, his hands cupping her face, his head descending.

And he kissed her deeply.

She bowed into him, dropping her attaché and purse to the floor, rounding him with her arms and giving him freely what he was already taking from her mouth.

His hand slid into her hair, his other arm going around her, he bent her over it, deepening the thorough kiss, launching her straight to the heavens.

When he broke contact, she was excited, dazed, putty in his arms, open to him forming her into anything he desired.

She hazily caught his gaze to see he didn't look even close to the same.

"All right?" he whispered.

Evangeline had no idea what he was asking.

But she sensed he needed something from her, and as with anything Branch needed, she had only one answer.

"Yes, honey."

His hand gliding from her hair to the side of her neck, his forehead dropped to hers.

And that was when the haze cleared and she understood.

During his call that morning, he'd given her a great many cherished things.

And he'd kept from her things that she couldn't know because she didn't have them, but they could be far more precious.

And he knew it.

But more, he knew she did.

So he also knew she could think on all of that and come home having made a decision.

It was in her power to end this game a different way, asking him to walk out her door, something she knew, for her, he wouldn't hesitate to do.

And he didn't want that.

God, he didn't want that.

For him, not wanting that might include the words "not yet."

But he wasn't done.

And she was far from done.

So she had more time.

More time.

Exactly what she needed.

She just hoped like crazy she had enough.

"Flatbread pizza with my secret special something that will make you think you died and went to heaven," she whispered to take him out of a moment that he was probably not enjoying as much as she was.

"Secret special something?" he asked, not lifting his forehead from hers or loosening his hold in any way.

"Green olive tapenade and sun-dried tomato pesto brushed on the base before I add the sauce and toppings," she answered.

Branch finally lifted his head away, but only an inch.

"Now that you've shared that, do you have to kill me?" he quipped.

"I hope not," she replied. "I like seeing you tied down to my bed too much and who would give me good advice after they listened to me bitch for an hour?"

His gaze was soft and his thumb was moving, stroking the skin under her jaw. "You didn't bitch for an hour."

"Probably felt that way to you," she mumbled.

"Forty-five minutes, tops," he returned.

She grinned.

His look grew softer when he caught it.

But all of a sudden, his head came up, he looked over hers, something crossed his expression and he jerked up his chin in what appeared to be an alpha-man greeting.

He then pulled her into the kitchen, bent, picked up her things and closed the door, tossing her purse and attaché to the counter where she always threw them.

And her stomach grew warmer.

Because that was exactly where she always threw them.

"What was that?" she asked when he turned her way.

"Your neighbor just got home and she likes to watch," he answered, striding by her.

Ah.

"Jane," she informed him. "She's sweet but she's nosy. Her husband took off on her a few years ago. He got his strumpet, and according to Jane, a not-very-nice apartment since she took him to the cleaners. Obviously, she also got the house."

Branch was at the fridge pulling out the lavash bread and mumbling, "Mm-hmm," when she stopped speaking. Since she didn't start again, or move, he kept his body aimed to the fridge, only turning his head her way, and declared, "Hungry, babe."

She threw him another grin. "I live to serve."

"Unh-unh," he replied, straightening from the refrigerator with the bread, pepperoni and the ball of mozzarella she'd asked him to buy (and her stomach got even warmer) in his hands. "That's my gig."

With that, she walked up to him standing in her open fridge, got up on her toes and kissed his throat.

And when she was done with that, she rocked back on her heels, let her eyes roam his head, shot him a big smile and whispered, "I approve of the hair."

She saw his lips quirk, took that gladly and walked from the kitchen.

She needed to change.

Then she needed to feed her man.

And after that, she needed to do whatever she had to do to dig in deeper.

All-in.

In all ways she could be.

For the win.

eighteen

Promise Me That

BRANCH

Branch felt the bed move slightly as Evangeline slid away from his body.

He then felt her fingers working at the ties on his wrists, his ankles, and finally her hand fell light on his ass as her hair glided over the skin of his back and her lips were at his ear.

She touched the plug with her jewel planted inside him and whispered, "Baby, I've got that meeting this morning. Need to take care of you."

"Leave it," he grunted, not moving except to curl his arms around her pillow and pull it to his chest.

As he did this, he felt her curls skate across his skin as she moved away.

She had an early meeting that morning but he'd returned late-ish from drinks with Ol and Clay the night before, finding when he woke her as he'd joined her in bed that she was in the mood to play.

He had not said no.

In fact, often while she went at him, he'd said *fuck yes*

Now he'd had little sleep but the sleep he'd had he'd done with his balls empty, his cock jacked and his ass full so that sleep had been good.

And he wanted more of it.

She twisted the plug slightly, that drove through his dick, and he opened his eyes half-mast and slid them up to her to see she liked the idea of leaving him plugged.

"Unless you intend to do something about it," he mumbled into the pillow, "don't make me hard."

"You're already hard, Branch."

Morning erection with his ass full.

Fuck.

"Then don't make me harder," he demanded.

She stroked his crack.

"Angie," he growled his warning.

"Is my big boy sleepy?"

"You feel playful, baby, wait until your big boy recuperates and he'll give you the show you deserve. Now I'm still wiped from what you gave me last night."

She grinned.

So fucking pretty.

Her hand trailed over the cheek of his ass to the small of his back and she bent deeper, touching her lips to his jaw before she pulled away. "Sleep well, honey."

He gave her a look that was contradictory to the sweet her words made him feel before he turned away from her. He yanked the bolster out from under his hips and hitched up a leg so he wouldn't call her back because lying on his hard cock meant he needed it to have her attention. This effort made moot because his movements brought his attention to her plug up his ass and it felt fucking great.

She kissed his shoulder and left the bed.

He watched her walk to the bathroom, her purple nightie barely covering her ass.

His dick responded to that too.

But not enough to stop him from sliding back into sleep.

Showered, shaved and wearing nothing but the comfortable, stretchy pants that hung loose on his hips that Angie had given him after she'd come home from shopping with Amélie a week ago, Angie's bed made, his jewel cleaned and sitting in the nightstand where she kept it, Branch walked down the stairs.

He found the kitchen as he always found it when he slept in and Angie had to leave before he woke up, the last three and a half weeks since their uncomfortable phone call about texting grocery lists.

The kitchen was tidy and there was a big, square, neon Post-it note fixed to the coffeemaker that he knew was set up for him to flip a switch, and within minutes, he'd be caffeinated.

The note could say anything. When she intended to be home that night, if she was cooking, if she wanted him to cook, leaving him a list of shit she wanted him to pick up at the store, leaving him with vastly different instructions, or just saying good morning and telling him to have a good day.

He went to the coffeemaker, tore off the Post-it and flipped the switch.

Then he read the note.

MBB,
Recuperate well, honey. You left me in a certain mood. Get yourself fed. I'll text when I'm on my way home tonight and then I want to find you in the studio, like you always wait for me.
    I'll see you then.
    Can't wait for my show.
    Have a great day!

                         xxx E

It was Branch in a certain mood after he read the note, even not having a clue what was to come because Evangeline wasn't about routine. She liked to switch things up even if she clearly had a few of them she liked to repeat (like tying him down on the bolster). She also had a vivid imagination.

So he didn't know what was to come, he just knew without a doubt he'd get off on it fucking huge.

He also had to stop himself from thinking about it at all because just thinking about Evangeline wanting him in the studio waiting for her, which meant she wanted to find him naked, ass to the door, draped over her horse, was making his dick start to stand at attention.

Though she usually ordered it after they'd come home and had downtime. Not before dinner.

And he wasn't big on missing dinner with her.

For her, though, he'd do it.

As he crumpled the note in his hand and threw it in the trash, Branch was able to make himself stop thinking about it.

He'd received intensive training in a variety of skills.

And in the last three and a half weeks, he'd found he'd acquired a new one.

That being the ability to stop himself from thinking about a number of things.

Especially the fact that, the longer he let this last with Evangeline, the more deeply he was perfecting the art of being a motherfucking asshole.

They'd found their rhythm. Food. Sleep. Sex. Play. Communication. Relaxation.

Fuck, the last two weekends he'd helped her with laundry and had run the damned vacuum over the rugs covering her wood floors.

And he hadn't done it as her sub. He didn't get off on that kind of play anyway but it wasn't about that because he sensed she knew that, so it wasn't that she'd asked.

He did it because the sheets he'd put in the washer, he was sleeping on, and the rugs he was vacuuming, he was walking on, and she was cleaning a house he was living in, he'd been around when she was doing it, so he'd helped.

In the last three and a half weeks he hadn't once slept in his own bed, going to his condo only to change clothes, but he had a razor at her place, shave cream, a comb.

They lived their lives and they lived them together, sharing time, sharing space, sharing a bed.

Sharing everything.

Including their first fight . . .

No, not a fight.

An argument.

Something that started with him reminding her she hadn't bought the motion sensor lights he'd told her to get and her blowing him off, saying, "I'll get to it."

"What'd I say?" had been his response, to which—both of them engaged in preparing a meal in her kitchen because it was her turn to cook, but she'd asked him to grill—her eyes slid to him.

"It means something to you, I know that, honey, but I've been busy."

He'd looked away, paying attention to the fries he was pouring in the basket of her deep fat fryer, stating, "Then I'll get them."

"They have to work with the house."

He looked back to her. "Then buy them, Evangeline."

"I will."

"Tomorrow," he demanded.

She shook her head. "I don't have time tomorrow."

"Then tomorrow you'll come home to what I think'll work with the house."

She turned to him, not hiding she was losing patience. "We'll go out this weekend."

Anyone out there he might not want to see him, seeing *her with him*?

They would the fuck not.

"If you can't carve out time to go to the store, look online," he commanded. "When they arrive, I'll install them."

"I don't have time to look online either," she'd retorted.

"And *again*, I do have time to go out and get them so they'll be up when you get home tomorrow, babe."

"Just go to the store with me this weekend."

"That's not gonna happen."

Her mouth set and her eyes flashed blue fire. "Because you can't be seen with me."

He turned fully to her and stated simply, "Yeah."

"And you can't share with me why," she kept at him.

"Correct again, baby," he fired back.

She nodded her head repeatedly, still doing it as she looked down at the Asian slaw she was making, saying irately, "Then I'll go alone. You just have to wait for the weekend. It's, like, three days away."

"And that's, like, a month since I told you to get the fuckin' things in the first place," he returned, mimicking her speech pattern.

Her gaze shot to his. "Don't be an asshole."

"Already a motherfucker, beautiful. Well beyond an asshole. You know that and you still tie me to your bed."

Her face arrested but she didn't call him on a remark that was edging over the line.

She said softly, "You're not a motherfucker, Branch."

"You're wrong, Angie."

"You're not. You're mine."

He shut his mouth.

"I'll find time to go out and look tomorrow," she promised. "But, honey, if I don't find something I like, I'll need to look online so it'll take time for what I ordered to get here and I want you to be okay with that."

What Branch wanted was not to see the hurt she was trying to hide in the backs of her eyes when he took them out of the easy they'd had, the easy he was giving her when he damned well shouldn't, and reminded her exactly how it was between them.

What he also wanted was not to learn that she had a way with an argument and that was to nip it in the bud when it started to turn into something that could get ugly and cause damage they couldn't fix.

Yeah.

He wanted neither of those things.

He wanted reasons to go.

Not more reasons to stay.

"I'm okay with that," he grunted.

"Thanks, baby," she murmured.

He didn't reply.

He dropped the basket into the fryer, flipped its lid closed, went out to check the brats he'd put on the fucking grill like he was the modern-day Ozzie who liked his bare ass slapped to her modern-day Harriet, who got off doing the slapping.

Christ.

And then she'd given him better, which made it worse, because with that, it was done. She didn't settle into a mood, pout, act bitchy, give him looks, turn distant.

Nothing.

They'd had their words.

And when it was done, it was done.

Jesus.

She was a dream come true not just in reach but sitting beside him on the couch, tucked to him in sleep, and he still couldn't live the dream that was her.

He wasn't a submissive masochist.

He was just a fucking *masochist.*

Because just like everything else she gave to take him there, he was getting off on living a dream that he couldn't allow to be real.

Which meant now he was cooking her brats and coming home to her after going out to drinks with the guys, getting his kink better than he'd ever imagined he'd have it, and they'd slid so deep into normal, into easy, they were in discussions about whether she should get a cat or a dog.

Yes, they fucking were.

A cat or a dog.

And fucking fuck him, like they were normal, like they were easy, like they could have mutual friends that were a part of their lives, this was involving Amélie *and* Olly because it was Leigh who was pushing it with Angie, seeing as she intended to adopt from the vet where Leigh worked, and Leigh wanted her to get one of each.

Considering how often she was away from home, Angie just wanted a cat.

For her protection, Branch wanted her to get a dog.

Olly, colluding with his woman, was pressing Branch to push Evangeline into getting both.

This included Olly pushing it last night, right in front of Barclay, who motherfucking jumped right on Olly's bandwagon, doing it grinning like an idiot the whole time, like Branch and Angie were out with who they were and what they had together. When they were, both men knew about him and Evangeline.

They were also not.

And neither man knew that or, if Branch explained (something he didn't do), they wouldn't get it and would likely get up in his shit about it.

It also included Amélie texting his ass to try and convince him to convince Evangeline she needed to add a variety of species to her family.

All of this giving Branch ammunition he knew was weak to put off leaving her until he knew she'd made the right decision and got herself a dog, a scary one, even if she got one along with a cat.

Not to mention, once he'd accomplished that, he couldn't go until after she got the dog, he knew the beast was trained and would do his job, that being more than hanging around panting while Angie lavished him with her brand of love but instead after Branch was certain the canine would rip anyone limb from limb who might look at Angie wrong.

Yeah.

Fucking fuck him.

He shoved all this shit in his brain aside, made himself a bagel (also shoving aside the fact that the minute Angie knew he liked those in the mornings, she made sure to get some and then keep them stocked), poured himself some coffee and scowled through her abundance of plants at the window in her cozy, busy, homey kitchen out to the backyard.

He did this reminding himself he needed to check the levels on the pool like he'd been doing weekly after he caught her doing it and he told her to quit because he'd be doing it from then on.

Oh yeah.

Fucking fuck him.

His phone rang and to get him away from his thoughts he was happy to talk to whoever was on the other line, he didn't give a shit it was Pol Pot risen from the dead, so he nabbed it from the counter and looked at the display.

Unknown caller. No number. No location.

Gerbil.

Damn.

They hadn't spoken since Branch lost his shit with his friend weeks before.

He took the call and put the phone to his ear.

"Yo," he greeted.

"Brother."

Gerbil said no more but he didn't have to say anything, the whipped-dog tone of his voice said it all.

"Listen, man, I was a dick," Branch declared. "You didn't know and I threw it in your face like you did. Should have touched base, let you off the hook with that because I know you felt crap and you're my brother, deeper than blood. I owe my life to you and you saved it more times than getting me out of that hellhole, before and since. So you got my apology, Cameron. I left it too long but I shouldn't have let it happen at all."

"We all live our lives and the people around us, even those close to us, John, have to understand there are things they don't know and proceed thoughtfully and with as much grace as they can. Because we never know the demons people are battling, be it the reason why they're a pain in the ass in line ordering coffee or sitting homeless, baking in the sun, because they've lost touch with humanity. I didn't give you that. I went in hard and I should have kept my mouth shut. And for that, John, *you* have *my* apology."

He didn't deserve it but he knew Gerbil enough not to fight it.

"Then we're done with that," Branch muttered gratefully.

"We're done with that and I mean it when I say that, even when I end it by asking, you still with her?"

That surprised him.

"You don't know?"

"Disabled the GPS tracker on your truck and phone, man. Got no trace on you, like no one can get a trace on you. I know when she's home and everywhere she goes. You, no clue unless my facial recognition catches you and it doesn't when it does her, so no. I don't."

And so he was keeping her clean.

At least that was a relief.

"And just to say," Gerbil carried on, "you got a way with avoiding CCTV. At least you've kept that skill sharp."

The skills they'd drilled into him would stay sharp until the day he died and not because of the training. Because of the extent and extremity of the practice.

Regardless of what Gerbil said, he knew that so Branch didn't comment on it.

He said, "I'm still with her."

There was a long pause before his friend's reply of "Good."

"Gerbil—"

"Just good, John. That's all. It's temporary or you find it in you to take it further, even if you have a little bit of what you deserve, it'll make me happy."

"I need to end it."

It didn't feel good sharing that but he needed to say it out loud and do that giving it to someone he trusted.

Gerbil said nothing.

"I know I gave you reason to keep your mouth shut, but like we said, we're done with that," Branch told him.

"You giving me permission to ride your ass?"

Was he?

Was he asking his friend to give him more reasons to stay right where he was?

"Forget I said anything," he answered, lifting his mug and taking a sip of coffee.

Coffee he'd bought at the store.

With the Italian cream creamer Angie used that he'd learned he liked that he'd also bought when he saw they were running out.

Christ.

"You know where I stand with that," Gerbil reminded him.

"Yeah," Branch mumbled.

"And I'm glad we've worked this through, brother. I called to do that. I also called because things are going down and I couldn't delay any longer."

Branch grew alert. "What things?"

"Twice since we last talked, they nearly got a lock on Raines. I intervened. But I can't do that too often, John. They'll put two and two together and they might not get Gerbil, but it still puts me out there."

"Fuck," Branch murmured.

"So, you wanna play with him or you wanna get the deed done, it's time to get the lead out."

He thought of Angie.

He thought of coffee with Italian creamer.

He thought that he needed to clean her pool, check its levels, make sure it had enough chlorine.

He thought the motion sensor lights she'd ordered online were going to be arriving and he needed to put them in.

He thought he had to work on her to push her to get a dog and then he had work to do with that dog.

He thought all this would be happening with him in her bed.

And he had enough blood on his hands, he wasn't going to bring more into her house.

Not hers.

Not Angie.

"I wanna play with him. End game, they can have him."

"You got something in mind?" Gerbil asked.

"Pissed himself last time he saw a ghost. He'll lose his mind, everywhere he turns, that ghost is lurking."

Gerbil sounded like he was smiling when he declared, "Always liked the way you think."

"We need to plan it. I fuck with him, when I'm done, you lead them to him."

"I'll have that covered," Gerbil promised.

"Great."

Gerbil didn't miss a beat. "Permission to ride your ass, Lieutenant?"

Branch closed his eyes but his mouth moved. "What?"

"That deed gets done, that massive dickweed wiped from the earth, it's behind you, John. It's behind me. It's over. We can finally lay the team to rest. We can finally both move on. And when I say that, I'll hazard to say what I actually mean is, if you're still there because she's making you happy, I hope you move on with her."

Branch didn't reply.

"At least think about it, brother. Just promise me that," Gerbil pushed.

Maybe for himself, maybe for Angie, maybe out of guilt for losing it with Gerbil, maybe because he owed Gerbil everything, maybe because of all that, Branch gave it to him. "I'll promise you that."

"All I need."

He drew in breath and he didn't want to give Gerbil his next, but to organize maneuvers, he had to.

"I need some time with Evangeline. Need to tell her I'm going to be out of town. Once that's done, and I'll do it tomorrow morning, Gerbil, I'll connect and move out."

"Got it."

"Coming to you when it's over."

"Say again?" Gerbil demanded.

"We lay the team to rest. Together, brother. So I'm coming to you when it's over. When I decide a location, I'll tell you where to meet me."

"Don't know how to fold the flag, John."

"No one to hand them to so it doesn't matter, Cam. I've got Di, Piz and Rob's tags. Lex and Benetta . . ." He didn't finish that. Gerbil knew their tags were necessarily left in the mess that was made of their bodies when they'd been blown to goo. How he finished was, "We'll make do."

"That we will, my brother. Like we always do."

"Right."

"I'll wait for you to connect."

"Right. Later, Gerbil."

"Absolutely, John."

They disconnected.

Branch ate his bagel, drank his coffee, ran upstairs to change into street clothes, back down to make himself a travel mug, cleaned out the coffeepot and hit the road.

He went direct to his unit where he stored his gear.

And he collected Di, Piz and Rob's tags.

He grabbed another set of tags too.

He put them in his glove compartment, ready to roll when he was.

Then he went to his condo to change his clothes.

After that, he took on his day.

But he got home to her house in plenty of time before she'd get home in order to clean the pool and check its levels.

It needed chlorine.

So Branch fed it chlorine.

Christ, she could work him.

And he gave her that info by grunting behind the silk gag she had tied around his mouth.

That wasn't the only thing she'd tied.

He was motionless on his back on her spanking bench. His arms tied down to his sides, those bonds also securing him to the bench from hips to shoulders. She'd then shifted up his legs so they were high and tight, open against his sides, the sting of the stretch at the backs and insides of his thighs driving right down to his balls. And last, she'd trussed his calves from ankles to knees to the backs of thighs.

She'd also tied another scarf round his eyes.

He couldn't move at all. Touch. Speak. See.

Only feel.

And what he felt was the only thing she'd given him after tying him down, the entirety of her focus on his ass, balls and cock. She didn't touch him anywhere else. Not even a brush.

She'd started by taking all of them with her mouth. She'd also taken her time doing that.

When his breath was seriously labored behind his gag, she'd then harnessed his cock and balls, strapped his ass open and lashed it with a flog that felt like it had wide, black suede tails that were soft but packed a serious bite and had a wide range so she tagged his balls too.

Fucking amazing.

Only when his skin was burning, his balls were hanging heavy in their harness and his dick resting on his stomach felt ready to explode did she insert the lubed toy inside him and turn it on low, the thing filling him and thumping inside, forcing his cock and balls to push the boundaries of their restraints, an agony of beauty.

She'd done all this without talking.

Branch only knew how all she was doing was affecting her when she finally released his dick from its harness, grabbed hold and shifted the vibrations up his ass to overdrive.

His body bucked in its bonds, his hands fisted, his ass clenched in an effort to thrust—something that failed due to his restraints—this making all the brilliance he was feeling absolutely fucking phenomenal.

And he heard her whisper in the husky, reverent voice she got when she was seriously turned on, "God, you're amazing."

He was fucking thrilled she thought so.

But Branch needed her to jack his dick.

He needed to come.

All he could do was grunt behind his gag and convulse against his bonds, enjoying the fuck out of everything she was giving him.

"Hold it, baby." She was still whispering, stroking his cock like she'd just started the scene and had all night.

He growled against his gag, testing the limits of his ties not only with his body's natural reaction to her work but also reflexively trying to break free so he could get what he needed.

"Hold," she urged, her tone far past husky. She was close herself, he could hear it, and the straps started loosening even as she kept jacking his cock. "Good, handsome, hold," she ordered quietly, more bonds loosening, her hand at his dick going faster, tightening. "That's it, baby, keep holding for me," she cooed, and he felt the vibrations up his ass roll up higher, making magic.

His body jolted and his mind cleared of everything.

Everything but the toy thumping up his ass, her hand on his cock, his balls straining their harness.

So when he was only held down by two straps at his chest and shoulders, he slid under them, freeing himself, and heard her soft gasp.

He tore off the blindfold, yanked down the gag, and vaguely saw her bent over him.

He hooked her waist with an arm and lifted up, taking her with him. He turned and slammed her down on her back on the spanking bench. Hitching a leg over to straddle the bench and tower over her standing, he held her down with one hand tangled in her hair.

His other hand was at his cock, fisting it and pumping brutally.

"Baby," she breathed, her eyes gazing up at him burning, her hand gliding up the side of his hip, her other hand going to cup his balls.

"You want my cum down your throat or on you?" he grunted, still fisting his dick and now thrusting through his hand.

God.

Fuck.

Brilliant.

"What do you want?" she gasped.

"I wanna see me all over you."

"Then do it."

He gripped her hair tighter, pulling it back, bowing her neck, and heard her sweet whimper.

"Hand in your panties," he grunted.

She immediately shoved her hand down her panties and he hoped she was there because if she wasn't, he couldn't hold much longer so he'd have to take care of her after.

She was there.

The instant her hand slid into her panties, her entire sweet, little body arced off the bench and her moan rolled through the room with her orgasm.

It cost him, especially watching that, but he let her have it and only when her back relaxed and her hooded eyes hazily sought his did he blow all over her belly, chest and dark blue lacy bra, his spine arching, his head shooting back, his cum coming and coming and coming.

He thrust through it, grunting with each drive, until his body started to shudder with the aftershocks, his surges of cum weakened and he felt her hand glide along his hip and the toy up his ass stop vibrating.

He gave himself one look at her covered in his cum before he dropped down on her but only to gather her in his arms, roll them and land on his back on the floor with Evangeline on top of him.

She lifted up her knees to straddle him, giving him most of her weight, snuggling closer, nuzzling her face in the side of his neck.

In return, Branch wrapped one arm around her, the other hand he shoved in her panties and cupped her ass, and he lifted his own knees to take the pressure off the toy up his.

His voice came rough and grating when he declared, "You're getting a dog."

Her body stilled on his for several beats before it melted and she nuzzled her face closer. "Okay, honey. But can I have a cat too?"

"Just as long as you get a dog."

"Okay."

"A big one."

"Right."

"I'm gonna help you pick."

Again, he felt her body react to his words before she snuggled deeper, her hand gliding up his chest to his neck where she curled her fingers around.

"All right, Branch."

"We clean up, grab my cock ring before we go up, babe. I'm gonna do you vanilla with spice in the morning."

"The one with the tail?" she asked.

"Yeah," he answered.

"Okay, honey," she replied on a sweet shiver.

She wanted vanilla with spice.

He gathered her hair in his fist, tugged gently and bent his chin down to catch her eyes.

"You feel like playing when you get home, I'm obviously down with that. But not like tonight. You make it short. We can go back to it later, but I don't like missing dinner with you."

Her face was soft in that way he liked too fucking much, her eyes telling him things he loved to hear but still wished he hadn't made her feel. She pressed up and touched her mouth to his before she settled back.

"We'll play it that way from now on."

He shoved her face in his neck, lowered his head back to the floor and grunted.

"Can I tell you something in confidence?" she asked.

She could tell him anything.

"Yeah," he answered.

"You can't tell a soul."

"Baby, you think you can't trust me to keep my trap shut?"

She let out a little giggle, he got off a different way hearing it, and she wriggled on him, like she was digging into his flesh.

But she was actually digging deeper into his soul.

"Okay, then," she started, "so, you slamming me into a spanking bench and jacking off over me, not to mention *on* me, might just be the hottest thing I've ever seen *and* experienced."

She was telling him this so he wouldn't worry that she wasn't okay with what they'd just shared.

She didn't need to do it. Her coming that hard for him and snuggling him said it all.

But her doing it dug even deeper into his soul.

"Good to know," he muttered.

"It's not very Mistress-y and if anyone knew—"

"Leigh pushes Olly over the edge all the time."

Her head came up and he shifted his eyes to her.

"Really?"

"Yeah. Does it on purpose. He thinks she might get off on it more than he does."

"He told you that? Or did you see it on the monitors at the Honey?"

"Told me over beers a coupla weeks ago."

She tipped her head to the side. "Did you, uh . . . talk about us?"

He shook his head against the floor. "Olly lived his life before Leigh thinking his head was jacked the way he wanted it. With the freedom she gives him, he's now open about shit. *Very* open. Like the floodgates have been lifted so I know he had that pent in and needs a safe place to let it go."

"I'm glad he has that," she murmured.

"Me too."

"I'm glad you give him that part of it, to be able to talk about it, to someone other than Amélie, that is."

"Man's a brother."

She grinned at him. "Yes. And I'm glad you have that in him too."

Branch said nothing but he was glad too.

"As hot as what we just had was, handsome," she dipped closer, "I'm still gonna have to punish my big boy for being bad."

"You think I don't know what I'm buyin', and got no problem with it, you're wrong."

Her grin came back.

He tightened his arm and squeezed his hand at her ass. "Gotta get this toy outta me, babe."

"Right," she whispered and moved to get away.

He tightened his hold further and she stopped.

When he said nothing, even though she was lying right on him, she called, "Branch?"

"Thanks for rocking my world, honey," he said quietly.

That got him a big smile.

"More than welcome, Branch."

He brought her mouth to his and kissed her.

They did this for a while.

Then he rolled them to their feet, they cleaned up, she grabbed his cock ring while he pulled on the pants she'd bought him and they went into her house, up the stairs, to her bedroom.

And tangled together, like they always did if she hadn't tied him down, they fell asleep.

nineteen

Absolutely Right

BRANCH

She came still riding him and Branch watched as she offered her tits to him through her orgasm, her back curved, moving fast, pounding herself down on his cock hard, her whimpers slinking through the room, over the bed, along his skin.

He was torso and knees up, encasing her with his body, driving his hips up into hers to give her more, watching his pretty girl give him beauty as she came for him.

And when she was gasping, her eyes dazedly searching for his, he whipped her to her back, hitched up a knee and drove into her harder.

"Yes," she whispered.

The remote to the ring he was wearing in his hand, he hit the button to give them both more and grunted when he got it around the base of his cock, through his balls and at the bullet up his ass, making him power deeper into her.

"Branch," she panted out.

"Again," he growled.

"*Branch,*" she rasped, writhing underneath him.

"Fuck, Angie, *again,*" he demanded, lifting a hand to her tit, squeezing and pulling at her nipple.

Giving her that, she did as told, grasping onto his hair with both hands, yanking at it hard, her legs rounding him, and she held on tight as he rode her and took her to another orgasm.

He tossed the remote aside, wrapped his arm around her waist, drove her down into his thrusts and grunted his orgasm into the room as he filled her with his cum.

They were both shuddering when he reached for the remote, turned it off, hunched his back, rested his forehead against hers, and their breaths clashed as they came down.

She slid one hand out of his hair to curl it at the back of his neck, the other she gentled but left it where it was.

"I like vanilla and spice," she whispered.

Not even feeling what he was doing, Branch grinned at her.

Her body froze under his and the grin faded.

"Baby?" he asked.

She glided her hand out of his hair to his cheek and brushed her thumb along his lips while her eyes watched.

"You okay?" he pushed when she didn't respond to his call.

Her gaze lifted to his and she said quietly, "Definitely."

"You got—"

"I'm okay, Branch." She lifted her head from the mattress and gave him a light kiss. Dropping her head she said, "Totally, definitely okay."

He let it go but only because she looked exactly like her words said she was and asked instead, "Wanna untail me or you want me to take care of it?"

"I always want to take care of you, honey."

He took her mouth in a deeper kiss, but it wasn't a long one, before he slid out of her and rolled to his back.

She rolled with him, got to her knees and rested one hand on his stomach while her eyes went to his crotch. He felt her other hand working there, gently sliding out the bullet and lifting off the ring. She leaned over him, giving him an awesome view of her tits hanging in his face, as she tossed the cock ring on a washcloth on the nightstand.

Then she lowered himself to him.

It was time.

Shit.

"Got something to talk about," he announced.

He watched the wary look seep into her eyes and he wrapped his arm around her.

"It's not bad, baby, promise."

"Okay," she said softly.

"I gotta leave town."

She stared at him as he felt her get tense.

"Not long, a few days," he assured her quickly. "Maybe a week. I don't know how long it'll take to do what I gotta do but," he gave her a squeeze, "I'll be back."

"You'll be back?"

"I'll be back."

"I . . . are you going to be . . ." She paused for a long time before going on, "unavailable while you're away?"

"You wanna check in, do it. Text. Call. I'll have my phone, Angie, so you want it, just do it. I might be doing something that I can't answer right away, but I'll answer. And just to say, you can do that but I'll need to be focusing on what I'm doing so I'll answer when I can and I'll call you back when I can but it won't be me instigating either. Do you understand that?"

She nodded.

Of course she understood.

She was Evangeline.

"Are you down with that?" he pressed.

She relaxed against him. "Yes, Branch, I'm down with that."

He rolled into her, taking her to her back and resting his length down her side.

He lifted a hand and brushed her curls away from her forehead before he looked into her eyes.

"What I'm doing, you call, or I call back, I might not be able to talk long," he warned.

She nodded and whispered, "But you'll be back."

Christ, but he'd fucked with her head.

"Yeah, honey, I'll be back," he reassured.

"Can I . . . Do you mind if we talk about something else?" she asked.

"No," he answered.

"Okay." She bit her lip, looked to his shoulder, out the sides of her eyes toward the bed then back to him. "Can I ask . . . I mean, if it happens . . . if, you know, I don't . . ."

She trailed off, holding herself funny at the same time having difficulty holding his gaze, hers now on his chin. He gave her a squeeze with his arm still around her.

"Baby, say it," he urged. "You can give me anything."

Immediately, she looked directly into his eyes and shook his world straight to the foundations.

"If I don't win, if you feel you have to leave me, will you tell me?"

Before he could answer or even wrap his head around what she was asking, she kept talking and she did it fast.

"I just want you to tell me. I don't want you to just be gone. If I . . . if I lose you . . . I'll try to understand. If you need that, I'll try to let you go. But I don't want you to vanish. I want to be able to say goodbye."

Oh yeah.

He'd fucked with her head.

He pulled her to her side, into his body and both of his arms, stroking her back.

"I told you I'll be back," he said gently.

"I know . . . just . . ." She shook her head, wrapping both her arms around him, digging one under his body to do that, and she held on tight. "Just promise me that, Branch."

He was making a lot of promises.

Promises he knew were far more important to keep than the one he'd made Raines in that asshole's bedroom years before, even if that promise was for Rob. for Piz, for Lex, Di, Benetta.

And every single one of them would agree.

"Promise, Angie," he whispered.

She didn't look happy about it and the hold she had on his body didn't loosen because he'd given her what she wanted, but he'd also done the exact opposite, not sharing he'd not only be back, he wasn't really ever going to leave.

All she did was nod, tuck her face in his throat and hold on.

He put his lips to the top of her hair and drew in a huge breath.

He should tell her now. He should go back on what he said. He shouldn't come back to her. He should stop fucking with her head.

But fuck him, holding her in his arms in her bed, maybe especially because she was feeling what he was making her feel, weak and fucked in his own head, he couldn't do that.

Not to her.

Not to them.

Fuck.

"To get this done, I gotta get on the road, babe," he said into her hair.

She nodded again, her nose brushing his throat, before she moved, not looking at him.

She'd pulled out of his arms and started to crawl to the side of the bed when he caught her and tugged her right back.

She looked into his eyes.

"We can end this," he whispered.

She pressed into him, her beautiful blue eyes filling with dread.

Fuck.

"No," she whispered back

"I'm hurting you."

"I know the score."

"Baby, it isn't right."

"It's absolutely right, Branch. And I'll take what I can get of absolutely right for as long as I have it, fighting to earn more along the way, rather than not ever having it and never knowing how beautiful it feels."

He tunneled his fingers into her hair at her scalp, shoving her face in his throat again as he grunted, "Angie."

"If you're not ready to go, don't go," she said into his skin. "Do your thing, come back to me and give me more."

He didn't reply, fighting her pull, fighting the shit fucking with his head.

Fighting the need to give her what she wanted.

More.

"And anyway, you have to help me pick a dog," she reminded him.

Yeah, he had to do that.

He forced himself to relax, releasing the pressure he had on her head, and she tipped it back.

He looked down at her.

So pretty.

"You need to hit the road," she told him softly.

"Yeah."

"Kiss me, honey," she whispered.

He kissed her. He did it a long time.

Even after they were out of bed and going through the motions of him leaving, he pulled her into his arms and did it again.

Repeatedly.

And after he was showered and dressed and he had a travel mug of coffee in his hand, Evangeline in flip-flops, yoga pants and a tight little tee standing in front of him at the door to his truck that was at the curb of her house, he did it again for an even longer time.

He broke it but didn't pull away.

"See you soon," he murmured.

"Okay, Branch. Be careful. Stay safe."

He nodded.

She lifted up and touched her lips to his before Evangeline, always the strong one, pulled out of his arms.

She retreated to the sidewalk and stood there while he angled up into his truck.

She waited there while he pulled into her drive.

He caught sight of something to his right, glanced that way and saw her neighbor standing outside her car, watching them.

When she caught his glance, she lifted her hand and waved frantically.

Without thought, Branch took his hand from the steering wheel and flicked his wrist in return.

He reversed out and watched Angie walking backward up her drive as he started to roll away.

She blew him a kiss.

And that kiss landed way deep down in his soul.

He jerked up his chin at her.

He then watched in his rearview mirror as she turned to walk up her driveway, her eyes to his truck, until he lost sight of her as she reached the side of her house.

Branch drew in breath, engaged his phone and called Gerbil.

"Wassup?" Gerbil answered.

"Gonna hit my condo, change, pack a bag and go to the unit to grab some gear. Send me details of where I'm going. I'll be on the road in two hours."

"Done," Gerbil replied.

Branch disconnected.

And in two hours, he was on the road, heading to Pagosa Springs, Colorado, where Gerald Raines was renting a cabin in the mountains under a fake name.

twenty

Fools

EVANGELINE

Evangeline was in her bathroom, getting ready and wondering if she should be doing it, when her phone on the countertop rang.

She stopped applying mascara and snatched it up immediately when she saw Branch was calling.

It had been three days since he'd gone. She'd texted. He'd texted back. Short and uninformative for them both, but he'd kept contact.

But earlier, when Amélie had called and asked her out, Evangeline had told her she'd think on it and she'd called Branch to find out what he thought of it.

Now, although it had been over an hour since she left her message, he was calling back.

But he'd called back just like he'd said he would.

"Hey," she greeted.

"Hey," he said back.

"Everything good?" she asked.

"Yeah," he answered.

Okay, well, he didn't feel in the mood to share.

Not new.

"I called to ask you about something," she informed him.

"Shoot," he offered.

"Well, Leigh asked me to meet her and Olly at the club."

Branch said nothing.

"Just drinks," she told him. "And hanging with friends."

Branch still said nothing.

"You know I wouldn't do anything you didn't like, honey," she told him softly, shifting so she could rest the side of her hip against the basin. "But, well . . . I miss my friends. And that was our place to hang together where we could be with each other in a place that was ours. I guess I have to admit, I miss it."

"That asshole is there and he gets near you, you tell him to back off," Branch commanded.

She bit her lip.

He'd left.

But he was coming back.

Before he'd left, he'd grinned at her.

Grinned.

At.

Her.

She'd never seen anything quite so amazing.

If a smile from Stellan altered his face in way that made handsome exponentially more handsome, a mere grin from Branch was almost agonizingly beautiful.

Also before he'd left, he'd held her and kissed her beside his truck like it was him who didn't want to let her go.

Not to mention he was replying to her texts.

And now staking his claim.

Again.

She honestly had no idea where they stood. He was hanging on to where he was at in his head.

But he wasn't letting go of her.

He wasn't leaving.

No, he was taking care of her pool and demanding to help her pick out a dog.

Maybe he didn't even know what he was doing.

What she sensed was that she should just keep doing what *she* was doing. No pressure. Just showing him how good they were and how, if he let go of what was messing with his head, they could keep having that for as long as it lasted.

That being maybe forever.

Yes.

Evangeline was falling in love with Branch Dillinger. She knew it. She didn't fight it.

She had another battle on her hands and everything depended on her winning, most especially the fact she was falling in love.

She was hopeful.

And she was terrified.

"Of course," she agreed to his demand. "No Damian."

"You gonna go back to the playrooms and watch?" he asked.

She felt a little thrill that stunk to have because she wanted to do that. She liked doing that. She missed doing that.

But she wouldn't be doing it with him or be able to come back to him once she had

This being the part that stunk.

"Probably."

"Alone, babe, if Aryas is there, you can go back with him. One of your girls. Someone you know I'd trust. That isn't available to you, you go it alone."

"Okay, but, I'm kind of close to Stellan. He's there a lot and if—"

"Lange?" he cut her off to ask.

"Yes."

"You're not his flavor, and the guy might wear a suit but my take on him is that he's not big on putting up with shit and has his way to make that known, so if you're tight with him, okay."

He was wrong about the first (in a way) but she decided not to share that with him at that time.

For obvious reasons she'd not told him Stellan had paid her a visit. She figured they had to be in an entirely different place for her to do that.

"What you get from that, you save for me," he demanded.

She stared at the sink. "Um . . . sorry?"

"You come with me, be it me giving it to you or you taking it working me."

"Are you telling me to abstain from any dirty activities until my big boy gets home?" she asked.

"That's exactly what I'm telling you."

"You're such an alpha," she muttered, and it was far from a complaint.

"Take it out on me when I get back, which, babe, you worked up and pent up is the point of abstaining, as you know real well."

"Right," she mumbled, smiling.

"Go. Have fun. Thinking I'll be back in two days, maybe three."

Only two days.

Maybe three.

Good.

"Okay, honey."

"Right, baby. Talk to you later."

"Later, Branch. Stay safe and be good."

"I prefer being bad, Angie. But we'll see." She laughed softly and he whispered into it, " 'Bye, babe."

" 'Bye, Branch."

He disconnected.

Evangeline put her phone down on the counter and looked at her smiling face in the mirror.

She looked hopeful.

But she was still terrified.

"Is he making you happy?"

Amélie asked that question.

It was late. Evangeline had been at the Honey for a while.

And it had been *great*.

It was Saturday night so it was busy, everyone wanting to let loose from the week, burn off the stress, go where they'd wanted to be probably since last Saturday.

She'd chatted with Leigh and Olly (who, getting to know him better, she liked wholeheartedly) until Felicia had joined them and they'd gone back to the playrooms.

Felicia had been joined by Pascal. Felicia then found her plaything and took off. Pascal stayed and introduced Evangeline to a Domme called Talia who was an utterly gorgeous, tall, willowy African American with a hilariously smart mouth and a wicked sense of humor.

They'd all drifted away when Penn and Shane had joined her. She'd caught up with her favorite engaged couple when Marisol added herself to their party.

Penn and Shane gave her hugs before they went to the playrooms and Marisol had chatted only briefly before sending her sign to her subs and exiting the booth when Amélie got back.

Clearly, Olly needed some alone time and Evangeline grinned at her, knowing just that as Amélie slid into the booth beside her.

Now they were alone and Evangeline was buzzed just on being with good friends in her place that she missed and not on the champagne she'd been carefully sipping, since she'd driven there and wanted to drive back home.

After Amélie uttered her question Evangeline turned her head to look at Leigh and saw her friend studying her.

"I ask only, *chére*, because you've yet to give me the sign you're open for a dinner invitation at my house with you and Branch and me and Olly," Amélie said quietly.

"I've never been happier in my life," she confided.

Leigh smiled.

"And I've never been more terrified, because he's giving me everything and still nothing."

Leigh frowned.

"I don't understand this, Leenie," she shared.

"And I wish I could get deeper into it with you, Leigh, but I can't." Her eyes slid to the hunting ground of the Honey, which was the middle of the room where all the subs hung out, surrounded by the bar at the back wall and booths all around where the Dommes sat, looking over what was available. "Not here," she finished.

"Then we must do lunch again soon," Amélie stated.

Evangeline shook her head. "I don't know. Branch is, like, *super* private. That's so important to him, it's become important to me."

"I understand this, but first, you also need to look out for you. And second, do you not think you can trust me?"

"I trust you, Leigh," she told her, reaching out and curling her fingers around the hand Amélie had resting on the table. "But your boyfriend is one of Branch's good friends."

"Of course," she murmured, turning her hand and catching hold of Evangeline's. "Then all I'll share is, right now, you're saying these things to me. And weeks ago, you said essentially the same things. You're hopeful. And you're scared. But life needs progress, Evangeline, so it goes without saying, relationships need the same."

She nodded in agreement and assured, "We're progressing." She gave Leigh's hand a squeeze. "I just don't know *where*."

Leigh's finely arched brows drew together. "Where would progress take you except closer together if it's working?"

"Yes, that's where we're going. And I'm terrified of it only because Branch is *petrified* of the same."

"Ah," she breathed, also tightening her fingers around Evangeline's. "So what you're saying now is that you have more work to do."

Evangeline nodded again, relieved Amélie got it without her sharing much of anything.

Amélie lifted their hands from the table and gave them a light shake. "I have every faith."

She wished she felt the same.

She just gave her friend a shaky smile.

The return one she received was not shaky.

"Is this Mistresses only?"

They both looked up at Stellan's voice to see the man himself standing beside their table in another one of his impeccable suits looking dashing, gorgeous . . .

And impenetrable.

"Good, I'm glad you're here," Amélie said, letting Evangeline go and shifting out of the booth. "I must return to Olivier and I didn't want to leave Evangeline alone." She caught Stellan's gaze. "Now you can visit with her."

"My pleasure," he replied.

Amélie gave him a small smile, lifted her hand and curled her long, elegant fingers around his biceps for but a moment before she dropped her hand and threw her smile over her shoulder at Evangeline. She then floated to the door to the playrooms in that catwalk model sashay that Evangeline had always envied.

Stellan, she noted, didn't watch her go. He slid into the booth beside Evangeline and her attention turned to his profile to see him lifting his chin at somebody.

She looked that way to see it was a server.

"Do you need another?" he asked.

Her attention again went to him, she saw him tip his head to her glass and she shook her own. "I'm driving."

"Of course," he murmured. "And how are things?"

"Very good, Stellan. You?"

"They're always good, Evangeline, because I refuse to accept anything else. But you mistake my question. How are *things*?"

She held his gaze and repeated firmly, "Very good, Stellan."

He dipped his face closer to hers. "And if you were mine, that lie would earn you holding my balls in your mouth for an hour with a rabbit working inside you."

She wasn't going to share *that* with Branch either.

"Stop flirting," she admonished.

He smiled.

She tipped her head to the side. "Nothing striking your fancy tonight?"

He sighed, moving his attention to the hunting ground. "Aryas needs to return. New members aren't allowed in unless he interviews them personally and I'm thinking until there's something fresh to choose from, nothing will strike my fancy."

"Poor baby," she murmured.

His gaze cut to hers. "Now *you* need to stop flirting, sweetheart."

She grinned at him.

"I've heard Sixx is working in social," he remarked. "Fancy a stroll through the playrooms to watch her do her thing?"

She did.

She started to accept his offer but his head suddenly turned again. She felt something glide off of him that made a shiver race up her spine just as he slid out of the booth.

And when his deep, silky voice came again, it shocked her when it came in a growl.

"This is not happening."

Around his body, Damian stepped, coming into Evangeline's view.

Damn.

He might have stepped into her view but Damian's eyes were on Stellan. "She doesn't need a guard dog, Lange."

"*Master* Lange, friend," Stellan returned smoothly.

Damian's lip curled and he, too, was very handsome (though no match for Stellan, and definitely not Branch), unfortunately even doing that.

"I'd like a word with Evangeline," he demanded.

Of Stellan.

Lord, she was sitting right there.

"*Mistress* Evangeline," Stellan shot back.

"Stand down," Damian demanded, ignoring Stellan's words.

"I'd rather not," Stellan replied.

Damian gave up on him and looked at her. "I believe, pretty baby, that if you turned sub, I earned the right to be one of the first to know."

Her shoulders straightened in affront. "And if that ever happens, Master Damian, I'll see you get the news."

Stellan shifted, blocking Damian from her view, declaring, "And this ends here."

Again, Damian ignored his words.

"It's not on, she sends Amélie's stud to get up in my face and take her from me."

"It's my understanding it wasn't Evangeline who did that, but Amélie, and you know that's Amélie's prerogative and has nothing to do with her stallion. But regardless, it's Evangeline's prerogative to walk away and that's where that discussion begins and ends."

"Unsure why it's you standing in my way," Damian stated.

"I'm unsure I feel like explaining," Stellan replied.

"Just to say, Lange, as I've already staked my claim to her, you aren't in the position to do the same," Damian told him.

"Your memory appears to be faulty," Stellan retorted. "She's a Domme."

"She wasn't when I had my mouth up her cunt," Damian fired back.

Evangeline's head jerked in shock and anger.

"Making her come doesn't make her switch sides, Damian," Stellan returned.

"It wasn't you with your mouth between her legs, Lange, so you don't know how it was. But I do."

Everything about Stellan changed and Evangeline, who was about to open her mouth to intervene—heatedly—froze at seeing it.

And *feeling* it.

"It will be my hand twisting your balls off if you don't get the fuck away and do it *now*," he warned, that silk of his voice now silkier, the tone lower and downright scary.

She vaguely noticed the server arriving with Stellan's drink, but wisely reading the situation, the woman turned and retreated.

"Piss off," Damian clipped.

"I'll piss *on you* after I shove your balls up your ass," Stellan replied nonchalantly.

After that all she could see was Stellan's broad-shouldered back in his suit jacket and all she could hear was silence, but she felt the animosity roiling off both of them and she knew she wasn't the only one. The hum of chatter in the room had dimmed significantly.

Wonderful.

Everyone who'd been a member back then knew what had happened to her and everyone who hadn't had probably been told.

Now this.

"Gentlemen," she started, sliding her behind across the seat.

Stellan twisted at the waist and pinned her with his eyes.

"You get nowhere near this piece of trash," he bit out and she froze. "Stay where you are, Evangeline. Please."

She nodded slowly.

He turned back to Damian.

"You're done," he informed Damian.

"Her pussy was sweet but not worth your hassle."

"And this is why you won't earn it again, for every good Master knows sweet pussy is worth *any* hassle," Stellan returned.

And Evangeline thought *that* was sweet because she sensed it meant much more than the simple words he used to say it.

Stellan carried on.

"I won't tell Aryas about our conversation, although it's been witnessed by others who might, and I don't have to tell you how he'll feel, you brought this to his club *and* to Evangeline. What I will tell you is that, if I hear Evangeline has difficulties again with you, you'll not only deal with me, and Aryas, you'll also deal with someone else who's staked their claim to her and I can assure you that you actually *don't* want my hassle. You know you don't want Aryas's. But the man you really need to fear is not Aryas or me."

"I'm quaking in my boots," Damian said flippantly.

"Smart," Stellan rejoined. "Though you catch what you earned tonight from who she's made hers, you'll be shitting in your pants."

"Aryas's security guy?" Damian puffed out in disbelief.

"Tell me, where is Kevin?" Stellan asked casually.

Evangeline rolled her eyes to the ceiling.

"Fuck you," Damian spat.

"Please, no," Stellan murmured sardonically. "Then again, you already know I do the fucking and your ass is not to my taste."

There were several moments of silence that lengthened before the hum of conversation began again, far more animated than it had been, and Stellan turned, offering his arm to her.

It was then she saw that Damian was gone, stalking across the hunting ground toward the front door.

"We were going to social?" he noted.

She looked up at him and burst out laughing.

Then she reached out a hand and curled it around his arm, finishing sliding out of the booth to take her feet.

He shifted his arm to tuck her hand to his side and started her across the hunting ground as she remarked, "It's good he left the building. A sub caught that mood from Damian, they might be in bed for a week."

"Mm," he murmured noncommittally, moving them toward the playroom door, knowing, just as she did, that no Dom brought their attitude into a playroom unless the sub knew precisely what they were getting.

That didn't mean a Master like Damian wouldn't play it anyway.

And even only getting his murmur, she knew Stellan not only didn't play it that way, he wasn't big on anyone doing the same.

She waited until they were through, the door closing the hunting ground off behind them before she said her next.

"It'd be good you didn't talk about Branch and me."

He kept them walking as he looked down at her. "If you think it's a secret, honey, it's my sad duty to disabuse you of that notion."

"Still, throwing him in Damian's face—"

He stopped them and looked down at her. "What would Dillinger do if he knew that had happened?"

She couldn't control her shiver.

"Right," he whispered before he drew her closer and dipped his face toward hers. "Leenie, a part of me understands his caution when it comes to what you mean to him and how he's striving to protect you. Probably more than even you understand it, though it's clear you're trying to protect it too."

She felt his words settle in her chest in a way that was arresting.

Not like her breath had stopped.

Like she'd been holding it and she was again breathing.

Part of me understands his caution when it comes to what you mean to him.

And just like that, part of Evangeline understood the same thing.

Not entirely.

But having just a hint of it gave her something extraordinary.

"However," Stellan carried on, "of the very few positives I can think of in terms of you being with him, and of others knowing you are, the fact that no one will ever harm you in any way, physically or verbally, is one of them."

She felt her face get soft. "And what are the other positives?"

"That tall piece of lean meat?" he asked and shook his head slightly. "I'm afraid, sweetheart, that since you shared the things you shared in your office I've enjoyed thinking of the things he lets you do to him. I'd pay a good deal to be a fly on the wall of your playroom."

She grinned and teased, "It's my sad duty to inform you that will never happen."

"It's my sad duty to be informed, Leenie. Because even if I can let my imagination loose, I'll bet the reality is a far better thing."

He was a master at being a Master. He might be wrong. She'd seen the results of his imagination.

But the way she saw it, he was very right.

She just kept grinning at him.

He then started them moving again.

And Evangeline was allowing her mind to turn over his earlier words so she didn't quite take it in when Stellan stopped them at the window to Shane and Penn's playroom long enough for them to watch Penn fucking Shane's face while his partner, sub and fiancé was on his knees, wrists tied behind him with the bindings also tied to his ankles.

She also didn't get much out of Marisol lashing a female sub's back while she was tied in a fetal position on the floor, her face in the pussy of another female sub who was shackled spread-eagled, also to the floor.

And she almost didn't let it filter through when Stellan stopped them to watch Amélie with her Olly.

When it did, as she would normally have done if it had penetrated she'd been watching Penn with his Shane, her body grew tight and she tried to draw him away.

He stood firm as well as lifted his hand to curl his fingers securely around hers at his arm.

"That's what I hope you have, Leenie," he murmured and her gaze went to his profile.

The way he was watching what was happening in Leigh and Olly's playroom, her eyes drifted back there.

"That's what I imagine when I think of you with your tall, lean piece of meat," he went on quietly.

Leigh's preferred playroom was set up with a stall and Olly was in it, arms lifted high, wide and manacled, his legs set far apart, also manacled. She saw the long, stunning pony's tail swaying between his legs behind him that Leigh had had to have made custom for Olly because it matched the hair on his body perfectly. His large balls were harnessed. His massive body was oiled. His cock was enormous, hard and hanging low. His face was harsh with hunger and the effort at holding back for his Mistress. And she was standing in front of him and slightly to the side, a crop in one hand she was using on his thick flank while he fucked her other fist.

Leigh's adoration and admiration of her stallion was written all over her face, along with the hunger she shared with her sub, and Evangeline felt some surprise when her friend didn't drop to her

knees and take that huge, handsome, well-hung, rutting cock in her
mouth.

She felt her fingers curl tighter into Stellan's arm as she shifted
as if to move, but she couldn't quite tear her eyes away, and regardless, Stellan kept her where she was.

"They want you to watch," Stellan whispered.

"I don't think—"

"They want to show off."

She closed her mouth.

"They want you to have what they have, Leenie."

Now he was murmuring right in her ear.

She felt it trail down her neck and she was missing Branch in
her life, her bed.

But she was also seeing the error of her ways, coming to the club
when he wasn't at home to return to.

"You must watch him make his offering to her, Evangeline,"
Stellan urged. "I'd kill to give that queen my cum and it cuts, knowing she'll only have his. But even so, I never fail to find it magnificent
when I watch him erupt for her."

With Stellan's sleek voice purring in her ear, what was meeting
her eyes, no longer able to move, she watched Olly focus slightly on
Stellan. And then she watched his lips curl back in an arrogant sneer
she felt drive right to her pussy.

Seeing that, she knew Olly not only liked being watched but it
was his way of staking his claim to his woman in a manner that could
not be mistaken was intensely possessive and deliciously assertive,
even if he was manacled in a stall.

It was one of the most affecting things she'd ever seen.

And she knew Branch gave her that even if no one was looking.

Then she watched Olly's mouth move.

And then his head jerked back as his large, powerful body surged
forward and his cum streamed across the room as Amélie milked him
and cropped his flank, a cat's smile curving her lips, her eyes hooded,
her face flushed with want.

Oh yes.

She was seeing the error of her ways, coming to the club when Branch wasn't at home to return to.

Suddenly, with a gentle tug, they were moving again and Stellan was talking.

"She'll make him come again almost just like that two, three times tonight. It's a wonder the man can walk her to their car, much less drive his woman home."

If she wrung that out of him three or four times a night, Stellan was right.

She looked up at Stellan, and half curious, half teasing, she asked, "Would you have turned sub for her?"

He looked down at her, still keeping them walking. "I think you heard me say before that sweet pussy is worth any hassle. But to earn the attention of a queen . . ."

Good Lord.

What he was saying was . . .

Stellan?

She pulled at his arm. He stopped for her and turned into her.

"Why are you sharing all this with me, honey?"

He lifted a hand and tugged at a curl she'd let fall around her face when she'd done her updo that evening before going out.

"I can count on one hand the people I trust," he said softly.

Evangeline held her breath.

"Because I can count on one hand the people who've earned that trust," he continued.

"Stellan," she whispered, moved by what it seemed he was saying.

"And so I've learned there is not a single thing on this earth more precious than having those you can trust."

"You can trust me," she told him.

"I know."

Yes, she was moved at what he was saying.

She swayed into him. "You must know that means a great deal to me, honey."

He shook his head slightly. "You're not understanding. I'm show-ing you my trust so you know you can give me yours, Leenie." He bent closer to her. "You had your trust broken. I just want you to be very aware that you can still offer that gift to someone who will take care of it, as I can assure you I will."

"I kinda wish you'd start flirting with me again because you're doing me in," she told him the truth through a joke.

He grinned, turned from her and set them moving again. "Ex-cellent. Then should I share with you all the ways I'd allow you to earn my cum?"

"I've changed my mind," she muttered.

Stellan laughed softly.

Then he opened the door and led them into the social room.

Aryas's social room was like the rest of the club.

Gorgeous.

Blue lighting set dim. Smaller and more intimate than the hunt-ing ground, though also lined with curved booths but with the ad-dition of several raised, lit platforms along the middle where Doms could take subs to make them perform.

Play occurred anywhere, however, not just the small stages in the middle, but also at the tables, at the bar, in the corners, wherever a Dom felt like working.

Right then, though, no one was working anything. Subs might be sitting at their Doms' feet or with their faces tucked into a crotch (sadly, for they couldn't see what was happening on the center stage).

And no one was working because Sixx was.

Stellan shifted them through the crowd and she heard him say, "If you would," this meaning the Doms that were standing in their way shifted themselves and their subs aside, for the prince regent had arrived and he wanted an unadulterated view.

They got one just as Sixx, wearing a fabulous, skintight, supple, black leather jumpsuit that covered her, ankles to neck to wrists, the curve of the sole of her shoe at the top of the ass of a male sub positioned before her, naked and folded completely into himself,

forehead to the floor of the stage, slid the spiked heel of her platform pump up his ass.

"Thank you, Mistress, fuck me with that," the slave huffed out.

"Are you missing something?" Sixx asked.

"Thank you, Mistress, fuck me with that. Please."

She fucked him with her heel.

She kept doing it as she turned and latched onto the dick of a
sub standing behind her with his hands linked behind his head.

"He needs his mouth filled," she demanded.

"Yes, Mistress," the sub murmured and moved.

He got on his ass in front of the sub taking his fucking from
his Mistress's heel and lifted the sub's head by his hair. He slithered
under him and forced the sub's mouth to take his cock.

"Make him take you," Sixx ordered.

Using the first sub's hair, the second sub forced the other to
give him a blowjob, though "forced" wasn't exactly the right word
since the man's cheeks hollowed, going for the gusto, and his face
grew enraptured.

Evangeline's gaze wandered to the bar as her mind wandered to
the fact that she could probably have one more drink before she drove
home.

"Champagne for Mistress Evangeline. Scotch for me," she heard
Stellan say before he guided her to a booth.

The booths were empty as the crowd had formed around Sixx's
platform, which couldn't be seen from their booth.

Evangeline slid in and Stellan followed right at her side.

"It does nothing for you," he noted and she tipped her head back
to look at him.

"I trained under her. Her talent goes without saying. It's always
interesting to see what she's doing. But no, although she's creative,
and a lot of the time that's inspired, sometimes, like tonight, there's
just something about her work. She—"

"Doesn't connect," Stellan finished for her.

Evangeline nodded. "I get many subs don't want the connection, just someone to take them into the zone, to let go, hand power over, it just..." she trailed off.

"You need to connect."

She shrugged but kept hold of his gaze. "I've watched you work and you sometimes hold on to a sub awhile, sometimes not, but always, you connect too."

He dipped his head in agreement.

God, only Stellan could look cool doing that.

Her eyes wandered back to the platform, still hidden from her as the crowd had closed back in.

"I wonder what she gets from it."

"She didn't tell you in training?"

The way he asked that made her attention cut back to him.

"No."

He sat back and looked across the room, murmuring, "Too bad."

"Interested?" she asked.

Stellan smiled devilishly at her. "To earn the attention of a queen..."

Evangeline giggled. "She *is* a queen."

"No, sweetheart, in our world, any true queen needs her king. But Sixx refuses to bow to him in the only way any good Dom should bow to their sub, so she's no queen. You and I both know, we can force a slave to their knees, but it's their desires that reign over us. If you think Leigh's stallion is just her stallion, you'd be wrong. He's king to her queen. Sixx is talented, you're right, it goes without saying. And there's a beauty in detachment, especially her form of detachment, which she's perfected to an art. But in the end, she's going through the motions. So in the end, does she get what she wants?"

Before Evangeline could answer his question, he answered it.

"She does not because she doesn't know what she wants."

"Do you?" she asked.

"Know what Sixx wants?" he asked back.

"Know what you want?" she clarified.

"And she shifts the conversation, my pretty little cat, maybe too curious for her own good."

"And this would be opening your world a little bit to find out what she wants and give it to her," she pointed out.

His brows shot up. "And have her force-feed me cock while she slides her spiked heel up my ass?"

"To earn the attention of a queen . . ."

He leaned into her. "None of them, not even Sixx, are going to get anything out of that," he jerked his head toward the platform, "but an orgasm, and they'll get it only if she allows them that. And I think we both can agree that's nothing like what Leigh just gave to her stallion."

Yes, they both could agree to that.

After the server set their drinks on blue cocktail napkins in front of them, Evangeline turned more fully to Stellan.

"Is that what you want? What Amélie has with Olly?"

"Isn't that what anyone wants?"

He had a point there.

"Maybe not Sixx," she told him.

"Hmm," he murmured, reaching for his drink.

"Sometimes that's not what people look for," she shared and he focused on her again.

"If you think Sixx isn't searching for something, honey, you'd be wrong about that too. We all are. It's just that what Sixx is searching for remains a mystery."

She studied him in the dim blue light.

Then she whispered startlingly, "How often do you watch Sixx, Stellan?"

And as she was understanding was his style, he replied bluntly, "As often as I can, Leenie."

She scooted into him like he was a girlfriend and advised, "You should go for that."

"I'll repeat, and be force-fed cock with a Domme's heel up my ass?"

"Amélie doesn't share."

He said nothing.

"I don't share."

He remained silent.

"You don't share either, honey," she told him, something he knew.

"I haven't seen Sixx work with only a single slave since she returned to Phoenix."

"And I've never seen Sixx work with a male Dom *ever*. Be her first," she encouraged.

"She needs something else," he noted.

"Then be her first for that."

"Fools in love want everyone to be just as foolish as them," he retorted.

That was when she fell silent.

"That wasn't a cut, sweetheart," he said gently. "If you're happy with him then I'm happy for you."

She believed him.

She still worried she was a fool in love, or a fool falling in love, with the operative word being "fool."

She lifted her glass and took a sip.

"You want to get drunk, I'll drive you home," he offered.

"Thanks, that's sweet. But not tonight," she declined.

He let quiet lie between them for long moments before he spoke again.

"We all want to be fools, Leenie."

She looked from her glass to him.

"Dying to turn fool, honey," he said softly.

She hoped he found that.

She gave him a small smile. "News at eleven if I find it's all it's cracked up to be."

"I'll wait for that news, sweetheart."

To that, she gave him a bigger smile.

"Please, Mistress,' split the air and both Stellan and Evangeline looked toward the platform, seeing only the backs of bodies, *"please don't make him stop sucking my cock!"*

Stellan sighed, sat back and took a drink of Scotch.

"Maybe we should go back to the hunting ground," Evangeline suggested.

"I couldn't agree more," he murmured, slid out of the booth, again gave her his arm, they both grabbed their drinks, and Stellan led her back to the hunting ground.

It might have been only five minutes after she'd turned out her light, but she still wasn't asleep, when her phone rang.

She reached to the nightstand, looked at the screen and quickly took the call.

"Everything okay, honey?" she asked Branch.

"You home safe?" he asked back.

She settled into the sheets, closing her eyes.

He'd called.

He said he wasn't going to call.

But he'd called.

To make sure she was home safe.

"I'm home," she told him. "Just got in bed and turned out the light."

"Okay, Angie. Have a good time?"

"How do you feel about a pony's tail?"

Her body turned to stone when she heard his rough, rusty laughter.

"Let me guess, you watched Leigh working Olly," he deduced.

"Yes," she forced out, his laughter searing in her brain and she liked the burn, but she wished she'd heard it at the same time seeing it.

"Like the tail I got, baby," he murmured.

She did too. It looked fabulous, circling his cock, cutting through his balls and leading into his ass.

Still, Olly rocked the pony.

"You good with watching them?" he asked.

"Not really but they didn't mind."

"Olly's a big fuckin' show-off," he muttered.

She grinned then lost it because she knew she had to share, "You need to know, Stellan was my escort tonight."

"Like I said, got no problem with Lange."

"I'm trying to get him to have a crack at Sixx."

"How's that gonna work? That woman is made of stone and she swings his way, not the way he needs."

"I don't know I've just . . . got a feeling."

There was quiet, clearly while Branch was considering this, because his next was, "Can't say I wouldn't be interested in watching how he'd attempt to break through her granite."

"Mm," she mumbled, knowing a thing or two about what it would take to break through.

Just wishing she held the key to finally solve that mystery.

"So you had a good night," he said, but it was a question.

Now she had to share something else.

"I saw Damian."

"And you steered clear," he stated like he could make it so just with his words even though the event had already happened.

Lord, he was hot when he was alpha.

Which meant all the time, even if he was getting his ass spanked.

"Well, I didn't know he was there. But he saw me and he had a few things to say."

"You're shitting me," he rumbled and it wasn't a good rumble.

Far from it.

Okay, maybe she shouldn't have shared.

"Stellan was with me and he made a few things clear," she assured him.

"Good," he bit off.

"And, just to say, Branch, without using names, but he wasn't vague about it, he threatened Damian with you."

"Good," he repeated sharply.

She blinked into the dark.

"Good?"

"Fucker doesn't back off, it's not like he wasn't warned."

"But you—"

"Babe, we're out. No shoving us back in. And not too concerned about that if I gotta make something clear to an asshole."

"Right," she whispered.

Fool falling in love.

Part of me understands his caution when it comes to what you mean to him.

Damn it.

Fool falling in love.

"You okay that went down?" he asked.

"Outside of wishing I'd never met him, and that wasn't the first time, just not for the reasons that he was a big jerkface, then yes. I'm fine."

She heard humor when he repeated, "Jerkface?"

"Okay, fuckface."

"Better," he muttered, still amused.

"Did you call just to tease me?" she queried.

"No. I called to make sure my babe was all right. She is so I'm wiped, she spent the night watching people do dirty shit to each other so she's probably more than all right, outside of needing me about now to eat her pussy. So I'll let you try to get to sleep even though you're thinking about my mouth on your pussy."

His babe.

God.

And all the rest.

God.

"Not fair, Branch," she whispered.

"Warm up your switch, baby, you think I've been bad."

"That's not fair either."

"Then go to sleep, Angie. And I'll talk to you later."

"All right," she grumbled, not wanting to let him go but needing to if he was doing something that required "focus" and he'd said he was wiped. "Talk to you later."

"Sleep tight, Angie."

"You too, honey."

" 'Night."

" 'Night, Branch."

They hung up.

She put the phone on the nightstand and stared into the dark thinking she was a fool.

She was also thinking, with his call, and everything else that was Branch, Stellan was right.

She'd die to be a fool.

In love.

With Branch Dillinger.

twenty-one

Taking This Ride Until It's Right

BRANCH

The next morning, sitting in a car in the parking lot of a convenience store, watching through the windows as Raines checked into a motel in Bumfuck, Nevada, Branch's phone vibrated against his thigh.

He took it up and saw it had a Phoenix number, which could mean anything. But with the way he gave out his number (meaning he didn't give it out unless there was a reason), it probably meant business, and he always needed business, so he took the call.

"Yo."

"Dillinger."

"Who's calling?"

"Stellan Lange."

Branch went more alert than he already was and asked, "Angie okay?"

"Angie?"

Shit.

"Evangeline."

There was a pause before Lange replied, "As far as I know, she's fine."

Branch's neck got tight. "As far as you know?"

"When we parted in the parking lot of the club last night, she'd had a good night and seemed relaxed, but tired, so yes. As it's only been nine hours since that time, I'm sure she's fine."

The muscles in Branch's neck loosened and he asked his next pertinent question.

"Right, then how did you get my number?"

"I asked Aryas for it. I told him I had some business you might wish to help me with."

Raines and the guy in reception seemed to be having heated words, but Branch wasn't surprised by this.

Since he'd flipped that fucker right out, appearing in crowds, there and gone. Standing at the counter of a crowded coffee shop long enough to catch Raines's glance, only to disappear half a second later when someone crossed Raines's sight line. Raines had left his cabin and hit the road.

Branch had followed him.

And he'd learned along the way that apparently not a lot of motels, no matter how bad they obviously needed the business, liked the idea of four Rottweilers checking in.

"Aryas didn't tell me you'd asked for my number," he told Lange.

"I suppose he trusts I'm someone you'd want to speak to," Langue replied.

"Not his choice to make," Branch pointed out.

"The deed is done, Dillinger," Lange sighed.

It was for now. He'd be chatting with Aryas about this later, though.

"So this business you got to talk to me about," Branch prompted.

"That was a lie. I don't have any business for you. At least not right now. I wished to discuss Evangeline."

Branch fought sitting up straighter in the beat-up sedan he'd picked up for a couple hundred bucks to switch out for his truck, to assist him with Raines not spotting his tail. Slouched, he could be seen, but barely, and you had to be looking hard. He didn't need to be totally visible unless he wanted to be.

"You've wasted your time. Not talking about Evangeline."

Lange ignored him.

"You do know, she has other people who care about her, not just you."

Branch knew that so he didn't feel it worth the energy to confirm.

Though he wasn't real big on Lange calling him to inform him of that fact.

Lange didn't need Branch to confirm. He kept talking.

"So you do know that, if she finds someone that makes her happy, and that discovery means the effort needs to be made, and I think we both can move right to it since you know exactly what I'm talking about, that someone wouldn't be the only one who'd assure she's safe. She has others in her life with a fair amount of means and influence who would help."

His focus shifted off Raines to center on what Lange said.

And Lange kept giving it to him.

"To be clear about that, Aryas, for certain. And I would assume with your relationship he'd know this might be in the cards should you find somebody and already be positioning to assist. However, since it's Evangeline, not only would Aryas see to it, so would I."

"Thanks for the offer, but we're good."

"I've no doubt, with your reputation, or more accurately, your near-prevailing lack of one, that you are. It takes a good deal of skill to be known of but not known, a Phoenician ghost. Though I suspect if you care about her, care about her enough to demand she be taken from a Dom like Damian and delivered to you simply because you're monitoring the halls of the Honey and don't like her being with a man who's tasted her, you'll never really feel like you're *good.* I'm simply sharing you have added insurance, whether you want that or not."

"Appreciate the share, but just to say," he focused on Raines again to see him stomping out of the reception area, "I'm in the middle of something so you said what you had to say, now we're done."

He moved his hand to the ignition, not wanting to fire up the

car until Raines had pulled out because it was clear he hadn't secured a room and Branch didn't want engaging his car to capture
Raines's attention, when Lange continued.

"She wants you at the Honey."

God damn it.

"Evangeline said you two were tight and for her, I gave you my
time. But that's none of your fuckin' business," Branch returned.

"Not to show off, she doesn't enjoy that," Lange said like Branch
hadn't spoken. "But after she enjoys other things, she'll want to go
direct to a playroom, direct to you."

Raines pulled himself up into his big Cadillac SUV and Branch
kept his eyes locked on him, his thoughts on that, and not the fact
his balls were drawing up.

Angie turned on by what she could see at the Honey and being
primed to walk right into a playroom to him?

Shit.

"I need relationship advice, Lange, I got your number now. I'll
call."

"So you and Leenie are in a relationship."

Fuck.

"We're finished," he bit out.

"She cares deeply for you."

Fuck.

"Like I said, we're finished."

"I understand your need to protect her from you, Dillinger, but
you're underestimating our Evangeline. She knows what she wants.
She always did. Good for her, or bad, she goes for it. Takes the risk.
And accepts the consequences." He paused but not long enough for
Branch to say anything before he finished, "Make those consequences
worth it this time."

And with that, he hung up on Branch.

Branch growled, tossed his phone on the seat and started up the
car when Raines had pulled out.

He gave it a beat. Two. Four.

Then he shoved the conversation with Lange to the back of his head and pulled out to follow Raines.

Ten minutes later, trailing Raines, he hit the number and hit speakerphone, then set the phone on his thigh.

"You got me," Aryas said.

"Not feelin' real good about you giving my number to Lange."

"Shoulda bet someone five K you'd be making this call. I'd come out even," Aryas muttered.

He had no clue what that meant.

Still, Branch clipped, "This isn't a joke."

"You're still with her," Aryas noted.

"Yes."

"There's a reason you're still with her," Aryas continued.

"Yes."

"Stellan wants her to be happy," Aryas told him. "I want you both to be happy. Stellan calls to say he's in to help make sure you're in a place to give her all she deserves and he wants to share that info with you, I'm not going to stand in his way. I'm going to give the man your number."

So Lange hadn't called Aryas about a job.

He'd given it to Aryas straight.

And Aryas had still given Lange his number.

"My trust ran deeper than that with you, Aryas," Branch informed him.

"No, Branch, it ran just that deep because that's as deep as it gets and you fuckin' know it so don't fuckin' give me this shit because you can't pull your head out of your ass. Pull your head out of your ass, son. You are not alone. Not anymore. You have people who give a shit about you and you have a woman who does it for you. Don't fight it. Rejoice."

The call dropped because Aryas dropped it.

"Fuck," Branch hissed, took the phone from his thigh and threw it in the passenger seat.

Then he ignored what was happening in his chest, shoving the feel of it to the back of his head.

And he focused on Raines.

Almost an hour later, due to the fact there was nowhere to position in order to keep an eye in his car, Branch stood hidden behind a building, watching Raines checking into another motel, when his phone vibrated again.

He pulled it out of his pocket, checked it, saw it was a text, and he pulled it up even though he didn't want to.

Evangeline needs this furry darling.

Amélie, and at the end of her text was a picture of a little dog that looked more like a stringy, dirty mop.

Jesus.

His thumb moved over the screen and he hit "Send" before his eyes went back to Raines.

Add a hundred pounds to that beast and we'd see.

He watched Raines leave reception and he watched Raines take his one bag and four dogs into a room with its door right to his parked car.

Another text came in and he looked down at it.

You're being very picky, Branch.

His thumb moved over the screen.

Strap in, Leigh. We're taking this ride until it's right.

When he saw Raines close the curtains over his window, Branch bent, picked up the bag at his feet, moved out and went right to reception.

He was checking in when Amélie texted back, *I wholeheartedly agree. We'll keep looking!*

"Christ," he muttered.

"Sorry?" the clerk asked him.

He looked the man in the eye. "Room nineteen."

"Uh . . . no problem."

The clerk took way too long checking him in.

But he got his key and he'd already stashed his car so he took the long route behind the L shape of the building to hit his room.

He got in without being seen.

"You're getting to the point you're done playing, John, gonna need you to re-enable his GPS. He disabled it. It'll make it easier for me to track him and make him blip back online for the team that's tracking him, which again makes it easier for me to lead them to him," Gerbil told him as Branch lay on his back in his motel room.

Raines's room was in view from Branch's motel window, the curtains on his window closed but with his knife he'd made a slit in them that gaped partially. However, it looked like something that motel might have, instead of looking like someone had jacked the curtain open so they could see out.

This made it so, even in his position, he'd see it when Raines took off but Raines might not clock he was being watched. And bonus, he couldn't see Branch.

"I'll let you know when I get to that point."

"Gotta make it look like Raines's work is faulty, brother," Gerbil advised. "They'll wonder why he slid back on the grid. They check, and if they're like Rifle Team, they'll check, so you've gotta make it look like Raines fucked up and the jimmy he did on his GPS somehow reconnected."

"You're not popping my cherry on this, Gerbil," Branch reminded him.

Just like Gerbil, he easily slid right out of stealth-maneuvers-strategy mode and into giving-shit mode.

"Yeah, right, all your cherries been popped a while ago."

Branch didn't respond, just kept his head turned and his eyes out the window.

"Speaking of popping cherries—" Gerbil kept at him.

"I wasn't," Branch stated.

Gerbil ignored him. "You keeping in contact with your girl during this mission?"

Evangeline was miles away but she was also in his piece-of-shit car and his motel room.

Damn.

"Permission withdrawn to ride my ass about that, Gerbil."

"You are," Gerbil said low.

"Not sure we're going to last but it isn't over and I'm out of town. Evangeline and me have been together for a while now. I'm not gonna take off and not keep in touch," Branch growled.

"Now you're not sure you and Evangeline are going to last when before you communicated it was totally sure that this wasn't going anywhere," Gerbil remarked.

Branch looked to the ceiling then directly back to the window.

"It was my understanding that once Raines went down," Gerbil kept at him, "you were off to parts unknown to live in a hut and cultivate your wardrobe of Hawaiian shirts and cutoffs."

Christ.

"Just the cutoffs," he muttered.

"No, now you're going back to her, with Phoenix not yet in summer, but still hot, cutoffs optional."

"Gerbil, for shit's sake—"

"Let me enjoy it too, John, for as long as it lasts," Gerbil said quietly.

Branch shut up and sighed.

"Just so you know, I've been keeping an eye on her and she's good," Gerbil told him.

"I know she's good," Branch replied, having had three texts from her that day saying nothing, but just hearing from her, knowing he was on her mind and she missed him, they meant a lot.

"Yeah, you do, since you're keeping in touch."

"I'm feelin' we're done talking," Branch told him.

"For now. Though I'll want you to share all about that sex club she belongs to."

Branch closed his eyes.

"You meet her there?" Gerbil pushed.

"In a way," Branch replied.

"Know you do work for the big man at that place. Know that man's got his shit together since not one computer with anything juicy is networked even internally so no one can get dick on members. Only know she went because her car was parked there. And am not surprised you went for that honey you saw at the Honey."

Branch was done sharing so he kept silent.

"Fuck, you knew she went last night, right?" Gerbil asked.

Apparently, Branch wasn't done sharing.

"She asked if it was cool she went, so yeah. She's got no secrets. It's just me who's the motherfucker."

Gerbil was surprisingly quiet.

Was he going to share this?

Shit.

"She didn't partake, man. She's mine. She's got friends she hangs with there and she likes to watch."

"She isn't alone," Gerbil murmured.

"So now, we're done talking. And I want to be done with this Raines shit. It's not as fun as it was when it started," Branch told him.

Translation: He wanted to get back home to Evangeline.

He sighed again.

"Right, so I'll expect you to give me that heads-up on the GPS," Gerbil said.

"Yeah. Maybe tomorrow."

"Cool. Good. Then I'll see you at the rendezvous point on Monday."

"Yeah," Branch confirmed.

"It's good this is gonna be done, John."

"Yeah," Branch repeated.

"Later, my brother."

"Later."

They disconnected and Branch knifed up from the bed to go sit by the window.

It took twenty minutes before Raines, his four dogs on leashes, left their motel room for a necessary evening walk.

It was too bad he couldn't confiscate one or two of those beasts to give to Evangeline.

But he didn't want anything to remind him of Raines or anything of Raines to touch Angie, so that wouldn't be happening.

When the man turned the corner and went out of sight, Branch moved.

He was across the lot, picked the lock and was in Raines's hotel room within three minutes.

He went direct to the bathroom, pulled on his nitrile gloves and stood on the toilet to disable the bathroom fan.

He moved to the sink. He pulled the slim bar of soap out of his pocket, wet it and lifted it to the mirror.

He wrote twelve words.

Then he pulled a bunch of tissues out of his pocket and traced over the words until the soap residue disappeared.

He ran a towel in the sink to wipe up the wet he'd put there and checked the space to make sure he hadn't dropped a Kleenex or left anything else behind.

He then left the room, locked up behind him and strolled back to his own.

An hour later, his phone rang. He looked from the window to it and took the call.

"Yo, Ol," he greeted.

"Yo, bro, how's things?" Olly replied.

"I'm out of town on a job."

There was a beat before he heard Olly chuckle and his friend said, "That doesn't tell me much, Branch."

"You like work?" Branch asked.

"Most the time, yeah," Olly answered.

"Well, sometimes I like mine but most of the time it sucks."

"Like, I'm guessin', now," Olly deduced.

Branch let his silence be his answer.

"Probably this time it's mostly about the fact it isn't fun the first time you're away from Evangeline," Olly noted semi-accurately.

Mostly his work just sucked.

Or at least who he did it for.

His answer to that was, "I'll be back soon."

"Yeah," Olly muttered.

"Man, if you're calling to talk about that breathing mop Amélie wants Angie to adopt—"

"No, brother, Evangeline told us last night she's gonna get a dog and a cat so Leigh's good to cool her jets on that."

"Excellent," Branch replied.

"Now she's on about bein' worried you and Evangeline haven't asked us to dinner or opened it up for Leigh to ask you two to our place. So give a brother a break and get your ass over here for her cooking. I barely survived her campaign to get you guys some pets. I'm not sure I can make it through an all-out offensive to get you over here to eat her food."

Get you guys some pets.

"Trust me," Olly kept on, "you'll wanna eat her cooking. I'll talk her into making you her chili. She uses filet mignon instead of ground beef. And Branch, man, it's staggering."

Get you guys some pets.

"Branch?" Olly called.

"Damian showed last night," he stated.

Ol's voice went low. "Yeah, I heard. I was tied up, literally, or I would have intervened. But Leigh and I waited. She told me Damian usually comes early and has a few drinks before he picks his victim. We were on the lookout so by the time we went back, we thought it was safe. Sorry it wasn't. Though, I heard Stellan took care of her."

"He did."

"No way we woulda hit a room, Branch, if we knew we were opening her up for that," Olly promised. "You can trust we have her back if she's there and you're not there too, monitoring the situation.

That said, Talia was in the next booth, she heard everything and she called Leigh today to report that Stellan was pretty fuckin' thorough with his message."

"Good to know," Branch murmured.

"Still sorry it wasn't me, brother," Olly said quietly.

"Not a problem as long as she was looked after," Branch told him. "Shouldn't have laid that on you. Shouldn't have let her go. I knew it was a possibility. She asked if I was down with her going, I should have made her wait until I got home."

"She's got friends there, Branch. Not just me you can trust to look out for her," Ol shared.

He was right.

Apparently, they *both* had friends who would look out for her.

"Yeah."

"Tables turned, two men I'd trust to take Leigh's back. You. And Aryas. So I get you," Olly went on.

He got him.

Get you guys some pets.

Yeah, Olly got him.

"So, you get back to town, you comin' over for chili?" Ol asked.

"I'll let you know," Branch told him.

"Brother, I get that time when it's new and it's fuckin' amazing and you want to keep her just to yourself. Or possibly more accurately, you want her close because she's strapped you to a horse and has something jacking your ass so you need her around on the off chance she'll let you shoot for her. But you gotta remember, shit went down with her and she checked out. Her friends want her back."

"I'll let you know, Ol," Branch repeated.

"Right, be selfish and keep her for a while. Totally get that. But don't make that last too long. Leigh gets what she wants, and you know that, seein' as soon you'll be breaking in a feline *and* a canine at *casa de la* Evangeline. But regardless, you're just plain stupid, you hold out much longer before you experience Amélie's chili."

"I hear you," Branch replied.

"Cool, let you go. Drinks when you get back. Later, brother."

"Later, Ol."

Drinks when he got back.

Branch put down his phone and briefly allowed all that had come at him that day to fill his brain.

When he was done allowing that, he shoved it aside, got up and went to his bag.

He dug out the dog tags.

He positioned them in his palm by prodding them with his finger until he could read all the names.

"Almost there," he whispered.

He closed his fist around the tags, walked them back to his bag, carefully tucked them inside and went back to the chair by the window.

Branch stared out of it at Raines's room. He did it until he saw the thin streams of light around Raines's curtains go dark.

And he did it longer.

When all was dark and quiet and had been for some time, Branch went to bed.

He woke up early, dawn far from arriving, and went out to re-enable the GPS on Raines's truck.

He got back to his room and phoned that in to Gerbil.

Then he again hit the bed and slept.

RAINES

The next morning, after Gerald Raines took a shower, he slapped open the curtain and stood stock-still.

Written in the steam of the mirror, clearly, he read:

Robert Baker

Diane Collins

Lexis Mitro

Louis Pizale

Benetta Rodriguez
John Wright

In his haste to exit the bath, and the hotel, Raines slipped and slammed his head against the basin, tearing open his skin.

He got his bag and dogs in the car and drove out of the parking lot with blood streaming into his eye.

But at least he'd left his urine in the bathtub this time.

Branch's lips quirked when he saw Raines, blood streaming from his forehead into his eye, load up his bag and dogs and haul ass.

When Raines was out of sight, Branch gathered his minimal shit, loaded it up in his car and checked out.

After that, he started the long drive back to his truck in Colorado.

He'd meet Gerbil on his way home.

twenty-two

Double Whammy

EVANGELINE

Late the evening before...

After taking in a movie with Felicia, Evangeline let herself into her kitchen, turning to unarm and then rearm the alarm for doors and windows.

She locked the kitchen door, and since they'd caught a movie after dinner and it was late and dark, she didn't bother turning on the light as she dumped her purse on the counter by the door and moved across the kitchen to go direct to bed.

The night before she'd gone to the club and had her time with her friends and had her revealing time with Stellan.

That night she'd had a fabulous girl date with Felicia, getting right back into the groove with her friend.

But even though she'd had fun, and she swore to herself (and Felicia) that she'd do it more often, that day for Evangeline was just another day gone before Branch got back.

He'd said two days, maybe three.

Now it was one, maybe two.

Which was better.

She hit the family room, turning toward the living room, but stopping dead when she heard a man's deep voice say, "Please don't be scared. I'm not here to hurt you."

Her panicked immobilization lasted a split second before she spun around and started to sprint toward the kitchen door.

Strong arms closed around her, one hand covered her mouth, but both jerked her back into a hard body, and that deep voice was at her ear.

"Seriously, Evangeline. Don't be scared. I'm a friend of Branch's, he's my brother, deeper than blood, you're his so I'd never hurt you."

New panic assailed her and she whipped around in his arms to face him.

"Is Branch okay?" she demanded.

"Peachy," the tall, shadowed man in front of her said casually, hesitating only a moment before dropping his arms and taking a step back.

"Then why are you lurking in my family room in the dark?" she asked.

"I wasn't lurking. I was taking a nap."

She stared up at him, noting through the dark he was black and tall and seemed built (that last part she'd experienced to be true when he'd grabbed hold of her), but not much else.

"Do you mind if I turn on a light?" she requested.

"My guess is, if Branch has given you anything, which he has, seeing as you're not flipped right the hell out right now, you'll get it when I say, yeah, darlin', I do mind."

Oh my God.

The fact that she'd unarmed and rearmed her alarm suddenly hit her. This fact meaning he'd somehow unarmed and rearmed it too.

Oh my God.

"So you're *really* a friend of Branch's," she whispered.

"Best he has still breathing."

Those odd, terrible words clogged in her own throat.

"What does that mean?" she asked, her voice suddenly hoarse.

"Can we talk?" he asked back.

"I think so," she said hesitantly.

"Sit down, darlin'," he ordered gently.

Staying right where she was, she watched his big shadow move through the living room to the chair situated in front of her French doors.

He sat.

She walked to the couch, slowly lowering her behind to it where Branch usually sat, which was the farthest she could be from the shadowed man.

When he didn't say anything, she asked, "Do you want to tell me what this is all about?"

"Been practicing this since he first told me he found you in case I needed to make this visit, and now, sittin' here, got no clue how to play it," he replied.

Branch was telling his friends about her.

His *friend* friends.

"How about just starting anywhere and we'll go from there," she suggested.

He let moments slide by where he didn't say anything.

There were so many of them, she was about to prompt him, when he spoke.

"You're his first."

She tensed (or tensed more).

"His first what?" she asked.

"His first after Tara. The, uh . . . woman he was livin' with who, well, she—"

Evangeline helped him out, speaking softly, "Was murdered."

"He gave that to you?" he asked disbelievingly.

"Sadly, and that not being the fact he gave it to me, but the facts he gave to me."

And her name was Tara.

It was a beautiful name.

"Well, fuckin' fuck me, uh . . . pardon my language, darlin'."

"Branch doesn't apologize for having a flair with the f-word so don't worry about it."

He sounded slightly amused when he muttered, "Right."

"And I'm his first . . . what . . . after Tara?" she asked.

"Woman. That being one he spent any time with. Or, I probably should say any breathing being he gave a shit about who wasn't a member of the team."

The team?

What team?

His *first woman*?

"That was a long time ago," she replied, not able to process the fact Branch had had this Tara lady in his twenties and now he was thirty-eight and since then he'd had no one.

He'd said Tara was his only real relationship.

But *no one*?

God.

No one.

Except her.

"Woman you love loses her life like that, probably not so easy to bounce back, especially if you're blamin' yourself she got taken out."

"Yes," she agreed, did it whispering and with her heart beginning to hurt.

She tensed again when his shadow moved but it only did it so he could lean forward and put his elbows to his knees.

And her body turned solid when he said, "Here to ask you not to give up."

Oh God.

"I—"

"Please, Evangeline, don't give up on him. He's the finest man I know. He's the finest man you'll ever know. He's earned his peace. This house. That pool. A pretty girl like you walkin' in the door. He'll try to push you away. All I'm askin' is, don't let him, and I can promise, you get through, he'll make it worth it."

She couldn't do this without knowing something about this man. Or, him being a *friend* friend of Branch's, at least trying to.

"Can I have your name?"

"You can call me G."

That wasn't much but this was a friend of Branch so it was actually more than she expected.

She'd expected him to refuse to give her anything.

So as she did with Branch, she took what she could get from G.

"Okay, G," she drew in breath, "this is very sweet, in a totally insane, terrifying way, but if you know Branch, you know he's not going to like it that you're talking to me."

"No, he isn't. But he owes me his life, my count, nine times over, so he finds out, he'll have to get over it."

Owes his life nine times over?

"And babe, no joke," G went on, "I said that, you repeat it, I'll have to kill you, but more, Branch will kill me not only because I told you, then I had to kill you, but I said shit at all. He's that good of a soldier. And getting deeper into you-know-you-talk-you-die, those missions were classified, Evangeline. So you'll never know. Not from him. He'd have shoots shoved under his fingernails and he still wouldn't say dick. And darlin', I think right about now you might be getting how, but I know that as fact."

He knew that as fact.

He knew Branch could take shoots driven under his fingernails and not say dick *as fact*.

God, Branch had been a soldier.

He knew how to make a bed so well because he'd been a soldier.

And he'd been on missions, classified ones, so she'd never know. Never know what he did. Never know what he saw. Never know what tortures he'd endured (apparently and heartbreakingly literally).

She'd never know what happened to him that tore him apart.

Not from Branch.

His scars.

The extremes he'd needed in play to take him out of his head and send him someplace he might find some minimal amount of respite.

Evangeline realized she'd started trembling.

She leaned toward G. "You have to tell me."

"Evangeline——"

"He won't tell me. Now I know why. But *you* have to tell me so I can put him back together."

"Dar——"

She scooted down the couch his way and did it talking. "I won't say a word. I won't breathe a word of this, uh . . . G. Not to Branch. Not to anyone," she assured quickly. "You weren't here. I'll never tell. But if I don't know what tore him apart, I can't know how to put him back together."

"I'm a soldier too, baby," he said gently.

God!

She hit the end of the couch and reached out to him, putting her hand on the arm of his chair. "So he's yours. And he was yours before he was mine. But he's also mine. We can do this together. You have my word. I won't say one, single thing. Swear it to the heavens. So please tell me and help me take care of our boy."

"Wish like fuck I could but you have to get it's to protect Branch, me, *you*, that I can't."

"He's withholding it from me, G, and I'm worried that I'll lose. He'll let whatever is tearing him apart tear him away from me and I'll never get the chance to put him back together."

"Evange——"

She shook her head and scooched further to the edge of the seat, talking.

"You don't know me but I can assure you I'd never do anything to harm him. Never. Not Branch. And if he's yours, you're his, so I'd never do a thing to harm you either. Heck, I'd never do a thing to harm *anybody*, but especially not Branch. Or you."

"I sense that, babe, but——"

Damn!

She needed to get through!

"He told me from the beginning he's going to leave me and *you know it.*" She lost control in the end, spat out her last, leaning deeper toward him but taking her hand from his chair, putting it in her lap. "That's why you're here. You know he's going to do it. Eventually. Thinking he's protecting me from," she flipped her hand in the air and returned it to her lap, "*whatever.* He's going to go and I'll move on, maybe," and maybe not, but she didn't share that, "but he won't. He'll never move on and you know that too."

"I do, darlin', and that's why—"

She finished for him.

"You're here to tell me not to give up but you won't *give* me the ammunition I need to *break through.*"

G said nothing.

Evangeline waited.

G made her wait longer.

Damn these men.

"Right," she stood, "thanks for scaring the pants off me and a whole lot of nothing."

He stood too and she fought taking a step away.

"He lost his team," he announced.

Her body locked, all but her mouth.

"Wh-what?"

"On a mission, his last mission, he watched every member of his team die."

"Oh my God," she breathed.

Her legs failing her, she plopped back down on the couch.

G towered over her long seconds before he sat again too.

"Handpicked. Elite. Trained in munitions. Explosives. Reconnaissance. Amphibious recon and attack. Urban combat. Surveillance. Intelligence. Assault. Jump. Search and rescue. Combined applications. And that's just the surface. These guys were the guys they sent in when the mission was forecast to fail and these guys were the guys that went in and kicked ass. But to do what they did, they didn't exist. *He* doesn't exist and he hasn't for a lot longer than before he became Branch Dillinger."

Before he became Branch Dillinger.

So that wasn't even his real name, who he'd been.

Who he'd been before.

Before now.

Before her.

Evangeline feared her knees would knock so she clamped her hands on them to stop them from shaking.

"He's the badass motherfucker the baddest badass motherfucker *wished* he was," G whispered.

Branch's words of weeks before came to her.

What can I do?

Apparently everything.

But none of it he thought was any good.

"Branch," she whispered back.

"And one day his team, and it was *his* team, Evangeline, he was their lieutenant, became more valuable dead than alive. So they were set up to go down. He didn't know this because he was set up to go down with them. And they did. All of them but Branch."

She felt the tears spring to her eyes but she said nothing.

"So he survived," G told her quietly. "He survived his woman being murdered and he survived his team being wiped out. Now, I don't know but I'm thinkin' that's the double whammy of survivor's remorse it's not too easy to shake."

It was her voice shaking when she agreed, "No."

"That's all I can give you and that's more than I should have given you. Much more, darlin'," G told her.

"I don't . . . I don't know . . ." She cleared her croaky throat. "I don't know how to fix that, G."

G had no response to that.

They sat in silence, Evangeline doing it feeling the hot tear that ran down her face.

She lifted a hand and dashed it away, turning her head to look out the French doors at her pool lit by moonlight with all its potted plants, her fire pit, the lounge chairs, all so normal. Prettier (in her estimation, but she was a real estate agent, she'd seen a lot of pools, so she felt a relative expert in that) than most, but normal.

A pool in a house in a city where a woman lived who was getting a dog and a cat and falling in love with a handsome, protective, funny, kind man.

Another tear coursed down her cheek.

"I . . . I have to find a way to fix that," she said to the pool.

G again had no response.

She looked to him. "Doesn't the VA have programs for PTSD? Don't they—?"

"Baby, he's dead," G said gently. "Even before they thought they took him out, they killed him. He's not off the grid. The minute he signed on, knowing direct close contact with the enemy is a guarantee upon acceptance and if captured or killed, missions assigned might have knowledge they exist denied by the government, he ceased to exist. But to stay safe after they took out the team, he needed to *cease to exist.* There's no VA program for him. There's nothing for him. There *is* no him, and if they ever found out he survived, we'll just say they wouldn't arrange a welcome-home party."

And it all finally made sense.

"Can he . . . Is it safe for him to be with me?"

"He doesn't think so."

"God," she pushed out, looking back to the pool.

"It is, though, Evangeline. I . . . *fuck*," he bit off and she looked back at him. "I have certain skills and I made that happen," he shared something of himself, "so if he wanted it, he could have you. A life. Be on the grid in a way he could do that and no one would know. Before, he didn't slice back on because he thought his life was over, he didn't think he had a reason to. Now, he's earned himself a life, meeting you, and he's not sliding on to protect you."

"But you can make him safe?"

"I already have."

"Then I don't understand why—"

"Your woman gets dead then every member of your team, *your* team, darlin', under *your* command on *your* watch gets dead, my take, you get a wee bit overprotective."

Her stomach burning, she started laughing uncontrollably.

Leaning forward to put her face in her hands, her elbows to her knees, her shoulders wracking, the laughter switched to hiccupping tears.

She felt G sit down beside her and put his hand on her back, stroking and murmuring, "Hey," and she twisted and forced her face in his chest, lurching in his arms with the force of her tears.

Those arms closed tight around her and she burrowed deeper.

The man she only knew as G and that for not very long stroked her back and held her close.

All of a sudden, she tore free and took her feet. Swiping her hands on her cheeks, she rounded the coffee table and started pacing.

"No. Fuck that. *Fuck that*," she snapped, stopped and turned to G. "Fuck that, G."

"Fuck what, baby?" he asked quietly.

She didn't know, but fuck *something*.

Then she knew

So she shared.

"I told myself even *before* I was in love with him that I was all-in to win. He's not going to leave me. Not because of that shit, shit he couldn't control. Shit other people infested his life with. No way. Fuck *that*."

"What are you gonna do?" he queried.

She tossed a hand high in the air, beginning to pace again. "I have no friggin' clue. But it'll be something." She stopped, looked back at him and announced abruptly, "I have a guest room. Are you staying?"

"Uh . . . say what?"

"It's late. Do you want a glass of wine or something? We can kick back. Kill a bottle. Maybe three. Then you can crash here."

"Evangeline, I haven't spent the night in a home for seven years," he said quietly.

God!

These men!

"Then you're due," she snapped, lifted her hand and jerked her finger at him. "And, you know, I'm a little overwrought about this stuff about Branch. But it isn't lost on me *you* have issues." On her "you" she jerked her finger at him again. "So once I fix him, you're Branch's *friend* friend. You're here to look out for him. If you can fix it so he can be on the grid, then you can fix it to put *you* on the grid." Another jerk of her finger. "So once I've done that, I'm going to fix *you.*"

She ended that on yet another jerk of her finger at him.

"You *are* a little overwrought, darlin'," he agreed, his voice shaking with laughter. "And you're a little bitty thing. But I'm still thinkin' I believe you."

She lifted her head. "He's falling in love with me, G."

"I'm a little in love with you too," he muttered.

"Sorry, honey, I'm taken."

At that, his booming laughter filled the room.

She wouldn't have thought it possible, but hearing it made her smile.

He stood and walked around the coffee table to get to where she'd paced.

He stopped in front of her, bent low to be able to grab her hand (he wasn't as tall as Branch but most everyone was taller than Evangeline) and he lifted it to press it against his chest.

"I knew, when she hit him, if he picked her, she'd hit hard and she'd be worth it," he whispered.

God, that was *so nice.*

"Don't make me cry again. I *detest* crying."

"Sorry, baby."

It was time to move on.

She'd strategize later.

Now it was time to drink.

"Do you want wine?" she asked.

"You got vodka?"

"Absolutely."

"Then get the glasses."

She turned to move away from him but he kept a firm hold on her hand so she stopped and turned back.

"I'm Cameron. My friends call me Cam."

Tears filled her eyes again but she fought them back, even if they filled her voice when she replied, "Lovely to meet you, Cam."

"You can turn on the lights now, beautiful."

She swallowed and nodded.

He let her go.

She moved to the table at the side of the couch and turned on the light.

That was when she looked to Branch's friend.

And she was not surprised to find he was utterly beautiful.

twenty-three

My Name Is Branch

BRANCH

Branch rounded the rock and saw what he expected to see in the distance.

He moved there slowly, because the terrain in the dark was dicey, not to mention it wouldn't be good to surprise the man he was meeting.

Therefore he let out the whistle the man would recognize before he even got close.

He saw the figure hunched beside the fire straighten and turn his way.

Branch walked right to him, and when he arrived, he dumped his pack and they clasped forearms, pulled each other into their torsos, rounded backs with their other arms and pounded.

The pounding stopped and they stood just like that for long beats before they broke away, still clasping forearms.

They looked through the dark cut only by moonlight and firelight to catch each other's eyes and stood that way for several more beats before Gerbil said, "Target neutralized."

Branch drew in a deep breath.

They let each other go and turned to the small fire. Both of them hunkering down beside it, Gerbil grabbed a long twig he'd been using and poked at the flames.

"Team communications reported target acquired at one seventeen yesterday afternoon. At one twenty-two p.m., they reported target neutralized. GPS on Raines's truck blipped out at three thirty-two. My guess, they compacted it. Best way to leave no trace," Gerbil shared. His voice became a mutter when he finished, "Wonder what they did with the dogs."

Branch knew what they'd done with the dogs. If that team was like his team, they had enough wet work on their job descriptions. Taking the life of an innocent, two-legged or four-legged, was avoided if at all possible. If those dogs posed no threat, they'd be caged and sitting outside a no-kill shelter for the staff to discover when they showed in the morning.

"Feels weird, it bein' done," Gerbil noted quietly.

"Yeah," Branch agreed.

Branch kept his eyes to the fire even as he felt Gerbil's aimed at his face.

"Figure, you picked this as the rendezvous point, you remember that weekend of leave."

Branch lifted his gaze skyward, the auburn Technicolor of the variegated walls of the Grand Canyon shadowed and looking fogged in the moonlight, leading up to an inky sky filled with trailing clouds and dotted with stars.

That weekend.

That weekend when Gerbil was still with them and the team had hiked down to the Colorado River together and spent it doing nothing. Nothing but shooting the shit and kicking back, drinking beer and eating hot dogs, laughing at crap only they got and no one else would think was funny. No bullets flying, nothing exploding, in the presence of the only six people in the world any of them trusted.

In the presence of family.

"I remember."

"Lex was in love with Benetta," Gerbil whispered.

Branch looked back to the fire.

"They got it on about a klick from here," Gerbil told him.

Even though the temperature was mild, Branch lifted his hands, palms toward the fire.

"Benetta was hard to read," Gerbil continued. "But the way she went more gung ho than her usual gung ho in Venezuela when Lex got his ass in a sling, my guess is, she was feelin' it too in more ways than getting loose and getting her some under an Arizona moon."

He wasn't wrong. Branch had known why they'd taken off that night. The entire team knew. Fuck, Branch had caught them going at it in the tactical room at their mobile base in Korea four months before their weekend of leave.

He'd walked right back out.

None of them had ever said a word.

But Branch knew that shit had started way before their trek through the Grand Canyon.

He also knew it never ended.

And Gerbil was right.

Lex wasn't the only one who'd taken that fall.

"I think about it a lot, John," Gerbil whispered, "and what I think is that it's good they went together. Just the thought of one of them seeing the other go first . . ." Gerbil let that thought trail.

"Yeah," Branch agreed.

"Lex had good taste. She was a beautiful woman."

"Benetta was fucked in the head. Lex was butt-ugly."

He heard Gerbil's chuckle before his friend replied, "Some women go for those giant-sized, bald-headed fucks who look like they eat nails for breakfast."

"Obviously."

They were silent a few beats before Gerbil murmured, "Good they went together."

Branch felt his throat close.

"You asked him, Rob would have said it no hesitation, he would have died for you," Gerbil said quietly.

Branch kept his eyes to the fire. "We all felt the same way about each other."

"Yeah, but you know it was more with Rob. He worshiped you, John. Hero-type shit. Best thing that happened in his life was working beside you, able to call you his best friend and knowing he had that in return."

He knew.

He'd felt that too.

"Best man I knew," Branch finally turned his head and looked at Gerbil, "other than you."

To that, Branch knew what those words meant to Gerbil when he looked to the fire.

"They aren't dead, not really, not until we go," Gerbil whispered. "Until their memory dies with us, we still got them."

"That's the truth, Cam, but I'm still gonna hang on to being pissed off with how we lost them because they didn't deserve that."

"I'm with you."

"Raines is gone and I got no regrets the hand we played in that but always knew, he was out, that wouldn't erase what he took from us."

"I hear that too."

Branch looked back to the fire. "But yeah. We're here to be with them and you're right. They'll always be with us. So even with time and vengeance behind us, it still fuckin' sucks. But reason we're right here is to be with them so let's do that."

"Hiked down fifteen hundred feet then navigated six klicks of beautiful but difficult terrain to break the law, start a fire and illegally camp, brother. In other words, don't gotta say I'm all-in with that."

Branch turned, opened his pack, dug in and pulled out the Scotch.

Piz's favorite brand.

It cost a fuckin' fortune. Piz had always been about quality, not giving a shit about a price tag.

Most of the crap he dropped a wad on, Branch thought he was insane.

But that bottle of Scotch would be worth every penny.

He broke the seal, looked to Gerbil and lifted the bottle.

"Team," he said before he threw back a mouthful, swallowed it and felt the burn slide down his throat and warm his stomach.

He handed the bottle to Gerbil, who lifted it Branch's way.

"Team," he replied and threw back his own swallow.

He handed the bottle back to Branch and they both looked at the fire.

"Syria," Branch murmured.

Gerbil emitted a quiet laugh.

"Christ, that was fucked up," he declared.

"Di was a fuckin' lunatic," Branch muttered.

"Woman had bigger balls than any man I know," Gerbil returned.

Branch felt his mouth form a smile and he didn't let it fade.

He yanked his pack under him, rested his ass to it and sat in the moonlight by the Colorado River, kicked back and shooting the shit with a man he knew was family.

RIFLE TEAM

At dawn the next morning, the two men stood at the base of the Grand Canyon on the banks of the Colorado River.

They stared at the tranquil flow of the water before the tall, white man started it.

"Benetta Maria Rodriguez," he said.

They both let that name settle in the canyon walls before the black man kept it going.

"Lexis Artemas Mitro."

They waited for that name to settle too, before the white man closed his fist around the tags in his hand.

He lifted them to his forehead, then touched them to his heart and finally to his lips before he said, "Diane Rose Collins."

He then threw them into the middle of the river.

They saw the small splash the tags made, the ripples floating out and disappearing.

The black man touched the tags he held to his forehead, his heart and his lips before he said, "Louis Anthony Pizale," and he threw the tags into the river.

The ripples disappeared and the white man took a visibly deep gust of oxygen into his lungs before he transferred the tags in his left hand to his right, touched them to forehead, heart, lips, and he said, "Robert Alan Baker."

He threw the tags into the river.

And like the others, they were gone.

He turned his gaze to his black brother.

His brother was watching him.

The white man nodded.

The black man lifted the tags in his hand, touched them to his head, his heart, his lips, before he called out the words "John David Wright," and threw the tags into the peaceful blue.

They let them sink into an eternity before the white man looked again to the black man. He waited until his friend ducked his head, lifting his hand to dig into the back of his tee, the tags clinking quietly as he pulled them loose from his shirt.

He handed them to his friend.

The white man took them and lifted them to head, heart, lips, before he called, "Cameron Drew Reed," and threw them in the river.

The sun rising in the east like it always did, they stared at waters that had been flowing for six million years through canyons that were seventy million years old, both of them now a part of that sacred place in a way they would be until the sun stopped rising.

They did this until Gerbil said, "Right. Let's hike out, get somewhere and order a huge fuckin' breakfast. I'm starved. You feel me, John?"

Branch looked to his brother.

"My name is Branch."

As the sun rose over the canyon, Gerbil held his gaze before his white teeth cut a slash in his handsome face.

Then he whispered, "You feel me, Branch?"

"I feel you, Gerbil."

"Tavis."

"Come again?"

"Tavis Warren."

That name, and what lay behind it, settled way down deep in his soul.

Regardless.

"Are you serious?" Branch asked and Gerbil's chest puffed up.

"It's a shit-hot name."

Branch shook his head, turning from the river, heading back to their packs, muttering, "You suck at making up names."

Gerbil followed him, asking, "What's wrong with Tavis Warren?"

"We only got a six-kilometer walk and a fifteen-hundred-foot ascent for me to say all the things wrong with it and that's not near enough time," Branch gave him shit.

"A pain in my ass," Gerbil muttered. "For years, that's all you've been, a pain in my ass."

Branch allowed himself a small grin as he hitched up his pack.

Although they'd already done it, he again made sure the fire was out while Gerbil pulled on his own pack.

Then, Branch leading, Gerbil following, they headed through one of the most majestic locations on the planet, trekking down the riverbank to the trailhead that would take them to the top so they could have breakfast

The last mission of Rifle Team.

That evening, Branch parked at Evangeline's curb.

After leaving Gerbil at the diner where they'd had breakfast, he'd texted to let her know he was returning and about the time he'd be doing that.

He found it weirdly surprising, angling out of his truck while looking at her house, that even though it had only been days, nothing had changed.

But in those days, it felt like the world had shifted. The colors were different, even the air tasted strange.

He moved up her drive, seeing her girly-assed Fiat under the carport, and heard, "March."

He looked right and saw Evangeline's neighbor in her own drive holding a filled trash bag.

The Branch Dillinger who was still John Wright would have pretended he didn't hear or said a low "Hey," and kept walking, making his point, trying to be forgettable.

The Branch Dillinger he was with Di, Piz, Benetta, Lex and Rob at peace stopped.

"Sorry?" he asked.

"It's March. April's around the corner. Which means May is coming so we better enjoy it as long as we can before Hades rises in Phoenix again," she said through a huge smile.

"Yeah," he replied, wondering why everyone in Phoenix always talked about the weather. It wasn't a secret. It wasn't sprung on anyone. Hell, he had no clue the origins of the city's name, but something arising from ashes, which always indicated there'd been fire, it didn't take a huge leap, so it was actually all-in the fucking name.

"So you're seeing Evangeline," she noted.

Branch fought his spine straightening.

No, John did.

But John was at the bottom of the Colorado River.

Which meant Branch relaxed and said, "Yeah."

"Best neighbor ever," the woman declared. "She's so sweet and she always takes care of my cats when I'm away. I come home and I'm never sure if they're happy to see me or sad that me being home means they won't be seeing Evangeline. Then again, they're cats.

They're finicky. And they act like they don't give a stuff about anything. Still, it's nice to know when I'm gone someone's taking good care of them." She stopped jabbering, took a step toward him and halted before announcing, "I'm Jane."

Branch stared at her, history, instinct and heart at war inside him, before he forced out, "Branch."

Her huge smile got even bigger.

"What a neat name!" she cried.

"Thanks," he muttered.

"I have a farewell party every Memorial Day," she proclaimed for reasons unknown. Then she made them known. "You know, farewell to being able to be outside without melting to goo. Evangeline comes every year. I hope you come with her this year."

He did nothing but jerk up his chin to that.

"Great!" she exclaimed like he'd given her an "Of course I'll be there, and we'll be announcing our engagement then too."

Before she could say more, they both heard Evangeline's door open and Branch locked that way to see her racing out wearing a pair of little shorts, a little tee and no shoes.

She kept coming his way and he only realized she wasn't going to stop when she did just that, but only to launch herself into his arms, her legs curling around his hips, her arms curving around his neck, the fingers of one hand going into his hair to pull his head down to her.

And she was making out with him.

Audience forgotten, Branch didn't hesitate to curve his fingers around her ass and participate.

She broke it suddenly, shifting both hands to either side of his head.

"You're back," she declared breathlessly, her blue eyes shining, her smile even bigger than her neighbor's.

And Branch was lost.

"Yup."

She squeezed him with her legs.

And Branch was done.

He started walking her to her kitchen door.

Her attention shifted over his shoulder.

"Uh . . . hey, Jane," she called.

"Hey, sweetie. Glad your man's home," the neighbor called back.

"Me too!" Evangeline cried, not hiding her excitement.

Yep.

Done.

"Babe," he growled and her gaze went from over his shoulder to him.

The instant it did, he took her mouth and he kept taking it even after he got her through the door, kicked it closed with his boot and planted her ass on her kitchen counter.

She immediately pressed her crotch into his growing erection and he grunted into her mouth.

Feeling her sweet pussy grind into his dick . . . he wasn't done before.

It was *then* he was done.

Burying a hand in her hair, using it to pull her back over his arm, he went at her harder, taking more.

She gave it, squirming against him, and her hands went into his tee, pulling it up.

Branch lifted his arms and only at the last minute did he disengage his mouth for her to tug the shirt over his head.

He took over, yanking it free and tossing it aside before he hauled her to him again, slamming his mouth down on hers, his hands going up her tee, hitting hot, soft skin, and he ground his groin against her.

"Baby," she breathed against his lips and he felt her fingers leave his hips and she was shifting a different way, her hands at her fly.

"Yeah," he growled.

Missing her, hungry for her, seeing her just as hungry for him, he took a step back, his hands going to his belt.

They kept eye contact as she swayed cheek to cheek, yanking

her shorts and panties down, every movement making his cock harder.

She kicked them off as Branch tore his shorts and jeans down his hips to his thighs, his dick jumping free.

Her eyes dipped to it, the tip of her pink tongue wet her lip, her eyes dilated, her little hand circled his cock, and she pulled him to her, widening her thighs.

She positioned him, her hand disappeared, and eyes to eyes, lips to lips, he drove into her wet pussy.

She latched onto his hair and whispered, "God, yes, Branch."

His hands anchored at her hips, holding her steady for his pounding, Branch pistoned inside her, their escalating breaths colliding, gazes locked.

"Fuck me," she begged.

He cupped her ass in both hands and took her to the edge of the counter so she could get more and so could he.

Her lids lowered.

"*Yes*, fuck me, baby." She pulled his forehead to hers with her hands in his hair, panting against his lips. "Keep fucking me, Branch."

Her legs around him spasmed, drawing him deeper, her ass in his hands clenching in an effort to rock into his thrusts, she suddenly gasped and tugged at his hair, her head falling back.

"Yes," she whispered, her pussy convulsing around his cock, her little body trembling in his arms.

Christ, she was coming.

Christ.

Angie.

He yanked her off the counter, turned, kept his dick buried inside her and went down on a knee, the other one. Falling forward, he took her to her back on the floor and slammed into her.

Damn, she was beautiful when she came, every way he could see it.

And feel it.

"My God. Oh my God. *God*," she pushed out.

Her nails scored down his back, he arched against the pain that traveled his spine from scalp to ass to balls to dick and groaned as he ground into her, shooting deep.

Still experiencing aftershocks, thrusting faintly inside her through them, Branch shoved his face in her neck.

She wrapped her arm around his back, her other hand starting to stroke his hair.

Angie waited for him to calm before he felt her turn her head and whisper, "Welcome home, honey."

He lifted his head and looked down at her soft face and eyes, which had a look that was warring between sated and happy.

"Dinner's ready," she announced.

Christ.

Angie.

The chuckle that rumbled out of his gut beat gently into her and her body, soft, warm, relaxed and loose, melted under him.

"You hungry?" she asked, her beautiful voice low, husky, sweet.

"Not anymore. But I could eat."

She grinned up at him.

"We, uh . . . might have just given Jane a show," she shared before she warned, "as I told you, she's nosy and the curtains are open over the window at the kitchen door."

"Angle of your carport, babe, and that bougainvillea between your two houses that's so fuckin' huge it's got to have been there since the dawn of time, she'd have to be standing at the bumper of your Fiat to see in your kitchen door."

"As I told you," she said again, "she's nosy."

He dipped his face closer and whispered, "She's that nosy, and her man left her, then hope she enjoyed the show."

Her grin got bigger. "Fortunately I was part of the show so I know *I* enjoyed it but can't imagine just watching it wasn't almost as hot."

"Definitely hotter being part of it," he grunted.

"I agree."

"You gonna stop being cute long enough to feed me?" he asked.

She tipped her head to the side. "Can I be cute while I feed you?"

In Branch's experience, she couldn't *not* be cute.

"Sure," he allowed.

"Then get out of me, big boy. I need to clean up and feed my guy."

He touched his mouth to hers before he slid out and started to move to bring them both up to their feet.

He stopped when she held on in a way he couldn't ignore and he looked back to her face.

"I mean it, Branch. Welcome home," she said softly.

He'd never had a welcome home. Not in his life.

Fuck, he'd never even had a home, not since Tara.

And Evangeline had earned it. She deserved it. .

And fuck it all, so did he.

So he whispered in reply, "Good to be home, baby."

She gave him another smile.

Branch took it in before he pulled them both up to their feet, held her until she was steady, and only then did he let her go so he could yank up his jeans and she could head to her shorts and panties. He reached for his shirt as she nabbed them, separating them, sliding her panties up her legs and following them with her shorts while he tugged on his tee.

She was still zipping her fly when her head turned to him.

"Be right back."

He nodded and watched her walk out of the kitchen.

Branch kept his eyes to where she'd disappeared.

But she'd be right back.

And he'd be right there.

I hope you come with her this year.

The words sounded in his head as Branch smelled garlic.

He drew in the smell of Evangeline's cooking and when he did he drew it in deep.

Then he moved, topping off the wine in the glass she'd left sitting by the stove.

And he grabbed a beer.

He was wedging off the cap when, as always when she promised something, his Angie came back.

twenty-four

Soft Against Hard

EVANGELINE

The next morning, Evangeline woke before Branch.

She didn't move.

She lay in his arms in the early morning dawn coming through her sun lights and studied his handsome face, the hard lines still there, even in sleep.

She wanted to touch him, to make some effort to smooth them away, especially now, after the little she knew of what put them there, just knowing that little was too much for him to carry, but she didn't.

In the short time she'd had since Cam had left and Branch had returned, she'd thought of practically nothing except how to find a way to break through with Branch Dillinger. She'd spent a ton of time on the computer learning about PTSD and survivor's guilt (another form of PTSD) and what family members could do to help.

The answer to that question was frustratingly what it was in all things like this: not much. Understand the conditions so you can understand your loved one's behavior. Listen actively. Communicate clearly. Be positive. And encourage your loved one to do the things that could help him or her to get some relief.

A symptom of PTSD was withdrawal, and Branch had that in spades, so urging him to spend time with people he cared about was a way to help. That meant she'd decided to try not to make it too obvious when she encouraged him to spend more time with Olly and Barclay, even Aryas. Help him to see his place in this world, or simply the fact he still had one, and there were those around him who cared about him.

She wished she could help bring Cam more fully into his life, not only for Branch but also for Cam, but for obvious reasons (since Cam had made her take a vow of silence about his visit), she couldn't.

Or at least, not yet.

But she hoped one day she'd have that opportunity.

Exercise was important too and Evangeline figured she had that down, in the way she could with the physicality of their relationship.

She knew it couldn't only be that, though. She had to find a way to make that a part of their lives, but Branch had used his sexuality as a way to escape the garbage infesting his head. Although she could make that safer, more intimate, more loving, more a part of being in a healthy relationship, she had to find other ways to accomplish that too.

But she also knew Branch took care of his body. He'd never mentioned going to the gym but there was no way he was that fit without making an effort to stay that fit. He just didn't, as with a great many other things, share how he went about doing that.

So she might ask and she might see if there was something they could do together that he'd be comfortable with. Taking hikes in remote places in the mountains. Using some of her vacation fund to buy some fitness equipment so her playroom studio could multitask in offering two ways where she could help Branch clear his head.

The only other way she could come up with was that she knew a knife could slash through skin, a bullet could tear through flesh, but the hard, sharp and strong that Branch was, and the woman Evangeline was, the only weapon she had in their war was to combat all that hard and sharp with soft.

She had no idea if giving him soft after he'd had so many years of hard would take him where he needed to be. He might see her soft, mistake it and think she couldn't handle the hard.

But, first, he'd had enough hard times. So she was not going to go at him that way.

And second, if she could take him over that edge, she needed to make sure she'd created a soft, safe place for him to land.

That was her mission.

And she could not fail.

Determined to succeed, she slid a hand up the skin of his side and watched his dark, curly eyelashes flutter before his eyes opened and he gave her the warmth of his ice.

She wondered if he knew how beautiful he was.

She wondered, even if he knew, if he'd care.

Probably the latter.

But overwhelmed with loving having that right there, that close, back in her bed after he'd been away, and all that loomed ahead for her in keeping it right there, Evangeline ducked her face into his throat.

"Morning," she whispered.

His arms tightened around her and he bent his neck, forcing her temple to slide along the stubble at his jaw so he could put his mouth to her ear.

"Mornin'," he murmured.

She pressed closer.

His hands started roaming.

She pressed even closer.

"You gotta get to work?" he asked.

"I cleared my schedule today."

His hands stopped roaming. "Sorry?"

She tipped her head back and he lifted his so she could catch his gaze.

"You texted to say you were coming home. So I cleared my schedule today so I could spend it with you."

His eyes warmed, his arms gathered her closer and she felt like punching her fist in the air because there it was.

Early indication soft could beat out hard.

"If you have things you need to do, you know, since you're just getting back, I can putz around while you—" she began.

"Got nothin' to do, Angie."

She melted into him and smiled brightly. "Great. Then we're starting with a big Evange-English breakfast."

His lips curved up slightly.

Gorgeous.

"An Evange-what?" he asked.

She slid her hands to his chest and pushed him to his back, coming up over him, still smiling in his face. "An Evange-English. Have you ever been to England?"

A guard slammed over his eyes, but she gave it her all to ignore it, finding it funny in a not ha-ha way, which meant finding it incredibly sad that this was the first, direct, personal question about the everyday experiences of life she'd ever asked him.

He shocked her out of her thoughts by replying, "Yes."

And that was the first direct, personal question about the everyday experiences of life he'd ever answered.

Evangeline felt like crying.

She did not.

"I have too. Twice," she shared. "Once on a family vacation when I was in high school, and again with a girlfriend one summer when I was in college."

Branch's hand lifted her nightie over her ass so he could start to circle the skin at the small of her back with his fingers, but he didn't answer.

"When you were there, did you have an English breakfast?" she queried.

He nodded. "But I still got no clue what an Evange-English breakfast is."

"Did you like English breakfasts?" she pressed.

"Sausage, eggs, bacon, hash browns, mushrooms, beans and toast, not sure what there is not to like."

She grinned at him. "Then trust me. You're gonna *love* your first Evange-English. *I* love them so much, sometimes I have them for dinner."

"I trust you, baby," he murmured, staring at her mouth. His gaze lifted to hers. "What's after breakfast?"

She rested her torso on his to get closer. "What do you want?"

He shook his head. "Thinkin' my babe took the day off to spend it with me, she has plans."

"I've never had a whole day with you, Branch, and I have to admit, that thought was so good, I couldn't get past the Evange-English."

His fingers drawing on the small of her back drifted to curl around the top of her hip as his other arm lifted so he could cup the back of her neck and he noted, "Thinkin' you got a better imagination than that."

"Mm," she mumbled.

"A whole day, babe," he prompted.

"I picked breakfast," she whispered. "You get to pick what we do next."

His arm around her back tightened as he slid her up his chest and his hand at her neck pulled her face closer to his.

And his eyes dropped again to her mouth when he whispered back, "Anything I want?"

She kept up with the whispering. "Anything."

"Then want my babe to take her time doin' dirty things to me."

Of course he'd want that. His safe place. *Their* safe place. Where their connection was assured.

But that meant he wanted their connection.

She'd give him that.

Absolutely.

But she'd also give him more.

She hoped.

Starting with an Evange-English.

"We can do that," she breathed.

His eyes lifted to hers. "My choice?"

"Anything you want, handsome, I'm in a good mood so I'll give it to you."

"Then feed me, Angie. And after, I'll tell you what I want you to give to me."

"You got it, Branch."

She made to roll over him in an effort to get to the other side of the bed, which was closest to the bathroom.

She accomplished the rolling-over part only to be rolled to her back and find herself kissing Branch.

She was not a morning kisser. She always worried her breath was awful. Worse, his would be.

But she didn't mind morning kisses from Branch because Branch always tasted like Branch, warm and rich and amazing, and he took the kiss deep and made it long so he must have liked her taste too.

When it was over, Branch did the rolling, giving her no choice but to go with him because he pulled her there, out of bed, setting her on her feet.

She tipped her head back. "I'll brush my teeth, go make coffee and start breakfast."

His brows drew together.

"In your nightie?" he asked, like that was outlandish.

"Do we have a reason to get dressed today?" she asked back.

His face relaxed. "Fuck no."

She leaned into him. "Then yes, baby. In my nightie."

He stared at her a second, his eyes moving over her face in a manner that made her think he was going to do that for ages, studying her, memorizing her, before he abruptly turned her toward the bathroom and swatted her ass.

"Then get moving, babe. Been existing on road food nearly a week. Dinner last night was your usual awesome but I'm nowhere near topped up."

He was nowhere near topped up.

She hoped he never was. Never *quite* full of her cooking. Never *ever* full of her.

Still, she muttered, "I aim to please," as she strolled to the bathroom.

"A skill you got in spades," he muttered back.

She entered the bathroom smiling.

She couldn't stop.

And she hoped he didn't give her reason to.

Not for a long, long time.

"Okay, I'll say it, never had a better breakfast than the ones I got in the UK, but you kicked an English breakfast's ass."

Branch was sitting opposite her at the table in the window of her kitchen. She'd ordered him to plant his backside there as she'd set his coffee mug on the table the minute he'd sauntered into the room wearing the lounge pants she'd bought him weeks before (and she'd been right, he rocked those pants, totally looked better in them than Stellan).

At first, he'd looked like he'd balk at her order. They'd never eaten there, across from each other, with nothing like the TV to ease the way, divert attention.

But he'd gone for it. And as his reward, she'd bent and kissed his jaw after he'd sat down and before she rounded the counter to get back to the kitchen.

And anyway, she was armed and ready so he wouldn't retreat back to a former position, become uncomfortable, get awkward.

The weapon she pulled out to accomplish this was chattering.

She told him about the movie she'd seen with Felicia.

She told him that she'd sold Mira's house, Trey's was getting good interest and she predicted a sale soon, but they'd both found a place they wanted, they'd put in an offer and it was accepted.

And as she set his plate in front of him, piled high with buttered toast, hash brown on top, fried egg on that, sautéed mushrooms on *that*, covered in baked beans and sprinkled with sharp cheddar cheese—an Evange-English—she told him about her night at the Honey. That she'd contacted them to renew her membership. And she went deeper into the conversation she'd had with Stellan about Sixx.

That was where they were when she sat down across from him.

He'd started tucking in at the same time he remarked, "If Lange wants a challenge, that woman will give him one. Like I told you before, she's stone cold."

"I trained under her, honey, she's good people," she replied.

His eyes came to hers. "I don't doubt you, Angie. But in a playroom, shit leaks out. I've seen them both work. Lange is about sugar and spice, liberal on the spice. She's about fire and ice, *very* liberal on the ice."

"That's a good analogy," she murmured.

"What I'm saying is, they don't sync in more ways than they're both Dominants." He shook his head and turned his attention to his plate, scooping up some of his Evange-English and lifting it, but before putting it into his mouth, he finished, "Man takes on that, might be biting off more than he can chew. Lange never struck me as someone who likes to bang his head against a wall." Then he took his bite.

"Can I tell you something and you won't tell Olly?"

He looked to her, chewed, swallowed and replied, "Definitely."

"He was in love with Amélie. Stellan, I mean."

"He didn't hide that from Olly, babe," Branch shared surprisingly. "My boy didn't like it much when things started with Leigh. But he's in a place he feels more magnanimous about the situation so Leigh and Lange had been giving each other a wide berth, but that's ended, and Olly's cool with it."

So that was what the thing was that Leigh and Stellan had that was making them distant.

"That explains the arrogant smile Olly aimed at Stellan when we were watching them in their playroom," she observed.

"I'm thinking a whole lot of other things make his night when she's at him, Angie. But know for fact, Lange takes in the show, Ol fuckin' loves it. It's like spiking a ball after a touchdown with the defenders standing around, but a fuckuva lot more in your face."

"I'll say," she murmured.

Branch's lips tipped up again.

Taking that in, it felt much better than her Evange-English filling her belly.

And Evangeline mentally spiked her own ball.

"The point I'm trying to make," she went on, "is that Stellan *does* want a challenge. He also wants to find his queen. And he's a snob so only the best will do."

Branch looked back to his plate, digging in. "He's a solid guy so I hope he finds that." He took his bite, chewed and swallowed, before he again gave her his gaze and warned, "But baby, don't get too wrapped up in that for your friend. Like Amélie, and probably times a thousand, Sixx likes her toys on their knees and Lange is not a man who finds that a comfortable place to be."

She quirked him a grin. "It's not meant to be comfortable, honey."

His lips just quirked, but his eyes were serious when he returned gently, "I still think you get me."

She nodded and returned her attention to her plate. "I do."

Conversation flowed from there and Evangeline watched closely without letting on she was, but she saw no indication that Branch hadn't settled in, comfortable at her little table by her kitchen window, eating breakfast with her.

Now he'd said what he'd said about her kicking an English breakfast's ass and she saw from his plate that this was no lie.

She looked to him. "Glad you enjoyed it."

"You could probably feed me coconut and I'd like it," he replied.

She perked up but tried not to look like she was perking up.

"You don't like coconut?" she asked.

"Hate it," he answered.

And there was more everyday stuff from Branch.

She rejoiced.

Silently.

"So noted," she muttered, going back to her plate, still struggling with not smiling, or more to the point, whooping with glee. "It's hard to improve on perfection, but it wouldn't suck if I could add English sausage and black pudding," she noted.

"You score an English sausage or black pudding in Phoenix, babe, and you don't tell me where you found that shit, it'll be me doing the spanking."

At that, she allowed herself to throw him a smile.

He took it with a warm gaze and focused again on his plate.

She continued to eat.

She did this until she realized they'd fallen into silence.

When she did, she lifted her head quickly, her mouth open to fill the silence, keep him occupied, keep him with her, but seeing him, she snapped it shut.

Because he was finished eating, leaned back in his chair casually, long legs stretched out in front of him, elbow on the arm of the chair, mug of coffee up, eyes aimed out the window.

Her throat closed and tears gathered behind her eyes.

Even though she wanted to take him in, memorize him at ease in her kitchen looking out the window, she swiftly returned her attention to her plate and concentrated on eating before she lost it and had to find a way of explaining why she was suddenly crying, sitting in the sun with him, eating breakfast.

She only looked up again when she had it together, which was when she felt him move.

He picked up his plate and came to her, bending over her to touch his lips to the top of her hair.

God, he was killing her.

"You get done, baby, just put the dishes in the sink," he ordered. "You cooked, I'll clean up. I'm gonna go get the things you're gonna need."

She tipped her head back and nodded, scared if she spoke what her voice would reveal.

He bent deeper, brushed her lips with his and straightened away.

She watched him walk to the sink, and since it was at the counter that delineated the seating area from the kitchen, she smiled at him while he rinsed his plate.

Then she took up another forkful of food and turned her eyes to the window as she chewed it.

It was working.

It was working.

Please, God, let it be working.

She felt Branch leave the kitchen and she drew in a deep breath.

Then she forced herself to take her time and finish breakfast.

After she was done, she left her dishes in the sink.

Evangeline wasn't sure if in the future she'd again allow Branch to pick their dirty activities.

Of course, standing beside her couch, seeing him on his knees over a towel in the seat, his arms tied behind him at the wrists, his forehead planted on the cushions, a dark blue silk gag around his mouth, his ass in the air, his cock hard, balls full, it wasn't like he didn't look amazing.

He totally did.

But he always totally did (though, having him trussed and offered up for her, it was arguable, but that might be the best look he had, or at least in the top twenty).

There were a great many things she could think to do to him in this position and they might include what he'd asked.

But it wouldn't be just what he'd asked.

Still, she'd given him permission to choose.

So she had to go with it.

It'd be awesome, she was sure.

She just hoped he was up to keep going after, so she'd have a chance to get creative.

She smoothed a hand over his ass, down his flank and then entered the couch on her knees between his calves.

And seeing him before her, hers to do with what she wanted, Evangeline couldn't help but get into the swing of things.

So she bent.

Digging her nails into the back of his thigh, she then dragged them up and murmured, "So fucking amazing, all that is you offered like this to me."

She put both her hands to him, sliding them flat over his arms where they were bound behind him, then up the sides of his spine. At his shoulders, she spread them out, curling them around, running them down the outsides of his biceps, along his forearms and gliding them down. She slipped one over his ass, through his cleft, and cupped his balls.

"I've neglected my paddles," she whispered, lightly squeezing.

She felt his thighs tense around her and that feeling hit her pussy.

Okay, perhaps this wasn't as unimaginative as she'd thought.

"Tie you just like this, see how much you can take."

She dipped down, grasping his cock and stroking.

He made a noise behind his gag and she ordered, "No moving, Branch."

His body stiffened.

She kept stroking.

"Paddle you. Get your ass red for me," she went back to whispering. "Then make you stay still and milk you until you blow for me."

She continued stroking him until she felt the effort it took for him not to move with her.

Only then did she let him go, slide her hand back over his ass, to the small of his back. Her other one joined it and she moved them back up, over his bound arms, his back, to his shoulders, going down with them until her breasts and hair brushed his back.

She braced herself with her hands in the couch on either side of him and ordered, "You hold for me."

He grunted behind his gag.

She took that as his acquiescence.

So she put her lips to his skin, trailing them down his spine. She kissed the flesh above his bound wrists, both of them, liking more than a little bit the sight of his strong, calloused, square-fingered hands tethered for her. She touched her lips to the small of his back and then slid out her tongue, gliding it down, to the top of his cleft, and just a bit farther.

Branch's big body trembled and he made another noise behind his gag.

She slid her tongue back in and grinned.

Her big boy liked being eaten out.

He hadn't asked for that.

When his Mistress was in a good mood, he'd have to learn to be more thorough in his instructions.

She lifted away and reached to the coffee table to grab what Branch had brought.

If it was anyone else but Branch, she'd have a discussion with him about his selection.

The cock was huge. She wouldn't be able to play with his ass for days.

But he wanted it.

And she knew he could take it.

So she prepared it, doing this far more liberally then she would normally, and she was normally liberal with the lube.

She also coated her fingers with it, running them along his cleft, up and down, then in.

She heard his suppressed puff of breath when she continued to press the gel from the tube to her finger working inside him, preparing him, adding a finger, going deep.

His ass cheeks were clenching, his thighs tense, his hands in fists when she slid her fingers out and took hold of the toy.

"You're going to take my cock now, baby," she cooed.

He didn't move or make a noise, just remained offered to her in front of her on the couch.

She licked her lips, aimed her gaze at his ass and positioned the toy.

Okay, yes.

He knew what he was doing.

Evangeline understood just that as she shifted closer. The palm of her hand against the end, placing her pelvis against that, she put pressure on and watched him open for her, his fingers flexing then again fisting. Smooth, slow, she gave him more and watched his head come back, planting his chin in the seat. And then she heard his low, stifled grunt as she took her time and seated herself deep.

God, *God*, he was *amazing*.

"Ready to get fucked?" she asked breathlessly.

He put his forehead again to the couch and tipped his ass only slightly.

Oh yes.

Her Branch knew exactly what he was doing.

Fingers wrapped firmly around the rim, with her hand and her pelvis, she started fucking him.

His head jerked back again, chin to the seat, and he took it, his body straining, quivering, his deep grunts muted. His hips began to tip, welcoming her thrusts, as muffled noises came from behind his gag, words she couldn't make out, mingled with the grunts he couldn't bite back while taking and seriously getting off on his fucking.

She added what he'd asked, slapping his flank, and she felt him tense against the blows, and the noises behind his gag came faster.

Damn.

Evangeline was getting off on it too, as she would do.

But too much.

He was just that magnificent.

After a while, she couldn't take it. Her clit pulsing, her pussy drenched, as he kept taking it, glorious before her in his submission, it was her who broke.

And when she did, she slid the toy inside him, fast and deep, his body jerking with the thrust. Then she tore down her panties, dropped to a hip to drag them off and tossed them aside.

With that, she fell to her ass. Guiding her legs quickly through his, she slithered down under him, forcing him to lift his face up from the couch.

She reached out with one hand, driving her fingers into his hair, the fingers of the other hand went to his gag, which she dragged down to his neck.

She then slammed his face in her pussy and only just managed to force out a husky, "Eat."

He went at her, his mouth buried deep, and she kept one hand in his hair, holding him to her, as she used the other one to lift herself up, making his knees slide back, and then she had him.

She sucked in his cock.

His head shot back.

"*Fuck*," he groaned into her cunt.

She bobbed under him, taking him deep. Her hand slid to his toy, grasped it and she started taking his ass again.

"Goddamn *fuck*," he grunted, straining all around her. "Fuck, *fuck.*"

She put pressure on his head, forcing him back to her, and he ate, his mouth working magic, making her body shudder. She lifted a leg and threw it over the back of the couch, using it as leverage to pump her hips up into his mouth.

He went at her harder.

She returned it.

And it was so beautiful, she got lost in what she was doing. She was just body and feeling and instinct. Moving under him. Sucking his dick. Fucking his ass. Rocking into his mouth.

He dragged his teeth along her clit and she cried out against his cock, bucking under him, slamming into his ass.

His teeth sunk into the skin of her inner thigh before he growled, "Fuck yeah. *Fuck yeah.* Take my cock. Take my ass. Fuck me hard, Mistress. Suck me off. Bury your cock in me."

She gave it to him and he went back to her pussy, devouring her, the sensations he created taking away body and instinct, she was nothing but *feeling*, and Evangeline's hips drove faster into his mouth. Her hand gripping his hair tightly, the orgasm overcame her and she ground his face into her sex and whimpered against his cock, spasming under him, coming in his mouth, and coming, and still coming.

It became too much and she yanked his hair to pull him away as she tried to focus on what her mouth and hand were doing.

"Yeah, Mistress," he bit out. "Fuck, your mouth is fuckin' beautiful. Fuckin' love the way you fuck me, baby."

She took her hand from his hair, put it to his ass and dragged her nails across the cheek to his hip then slapped his flank.

His face necessarily still shoved up her cunt, he started fucking her mouth with his cock.

"Fuck yeah, Angie, take that, *fuck*, gotta blow."

She slapped him again.

"*Fuck*," he hissed, reading correctly she didn't want him to stop, and he sucked in her clit.

She jolted under him, suddenly done. She seated the toy up his ass, latched onto both cheeks with her fingers and dug her nails in.

"Yes," he growled, drove into her mouth, and his whole body trembled and strained as he shot down her throat. "Yes," he groaned, forcing his dick deeper, "take my cum, baby."

She took it, almost drowning in it, swallowing at the same time trying to milk him with her mouth.

She loosened her hold on his ass, soothing the flesh, and he kissed her clit and adjusted so his head was lying on her thigh.

She glided him out of her mouth and he helped, sliding up on his knees.

After, they both lay there, breathing hard, being close in the way their nature gave them the privilege to be.

Evangeline gave it time before she reached out again and stroked his hair, saying softly, "Going to take care of you now, honey."

His answer was to turn his head and kiss her thigh.

It was a nice answer.

He lifted up his head and she slid out from under him. Then she took care of him, slipping out the toy and setting it on the towel on the coffee table. He pushed up to his knees using she didn't know what muscles you had to use to do that without the use of your hands. She got on her knees behind him in the couch and untied his hands.

She'd barely dropped the silk ropes to the table before he twisted, hooked her at her waist and pulled her to his front, dropping with her so he was on her, but her back was slightly pressed into the back of the couch.

She moved her hands to his chest.

He stared into her eyes.

"Okay?" she asked quietly.

"Can I tell you something?" he asked in return.

Could he tell her something?

She'd commit a felony and do the time for him to tell her *anything.*

"Yes," she replied simply.

"Last bitch I let have me, before you and not including the one at the Pound because she doesn't count for anything, she did me that way."

Evangeline stared up at him, not certain how to take that.

"Her idea," he declared. "Our gig was I'd just get naked and she did her thing. She never got inspired during a scene and that's what she did. Bound my wrists. Gagged me. Bent me over in a couch. And took my ass."

"I . . . well—"

"Didn't get near my dick."

Evangeline felt her eyes get wide.

"Still, I blew for her."

"Oh," she whispered.

"Because Aryas had offered you up, and while she was doin' me, I blew for her because I was thinking of you."

She felt her hands automatically curl on his chest as her lower body pressed into him.

"Branch."

He kept his body tight to hers as he took his arm from around her and started to slide his fingers through her hair at her hairline from temple to ear and back again as he shared, "I don't want this to upset you, what I'm gonna say. But she sucked. I took her shit scenes because my choice was limited and she sucked less than the rest."

Good God.

Seriously?

He kept talking.

"I wanted you to do that to me to see how you'd do it. How I'd feel when you were doin' it. Where you'd take it."

Okay.

What?

Was he saying he was testing her? Seeing if she could do him better than someone else?

Hadn't she already proved that?

"So you'd do me how you alone can do me and it'd erase her," he finished.

Oh Lord.

She was fighting tears again.

"Honey," she whispered.

"Didn't erase it," he muttered. "Nothing erases dick."

Nothing erases dick.

Oh Lord.

He was killing her.

She slid her hand down and around his back to hold him to her.

He smiled.

She froze solid.

"Still, I might have that memory of a shit scene, but now I got the memory of fucking your face and coming down your throat with your huge, black cock buried up my ass so it's all good."

She heard his words but she was caught in his smile.

She couldn't move. She couldn't speak.

Then something hit her so violently, she was surprised she didn't jolt with it.

"You called me Mistress."

His smile faded as his expression turned perplexed.

"You are my Mistress," he noted in a way he clearly thought making that effort was unnecessary.

She pulled him deeper into her. "You've never called me that."

Not during a scene. He'd said it. Once.

But not during a scene.

The smile came back and that didn't hit her, it charged through her like electricity.

"You never sucked my cock while forcing my face in your sweet, wet pussy and taking my ass," he replied.

She arched a brow. "So you're saying I earned it?"

He brought his lips to hers. "Baby, you earned it the minute you tagged my belt and dragged my ass through the filth at the Pound wearing a pretty, lacy blouse, a dark angel striding through the earthly dregs on a pair of sexy-as-fuck pumps. If that didn't do it, which it did, you would have earned it when you yanked my pants down with my hands on the hood of my own goddamned truck and made me take your spanking." He brushed his lips side to side on hers before he whispered, "But I'm tellin' you shit you know, don't you?"

Even though he'd never given it to her, she did know it.

But now he'd given it to her.

So she had it.

And what was left unsaid was that he might be saying these things (the dark angel part was especially nice), but he knew the difference just as well as she did.

She was just hoping that he meant more in giving it.

As usual, Evangeline took what she got and didn't make a big deal of it.

Instead, she squirmed against him, murmuring, "Stop turning me on with memories."

"Baby, my balls are empty, you swallowed it all down, and I'll add, you kept sucking me off even as you sucked me dry. But you feel like delivering a spanking, swear to fuck, I'll rally."

She smiled at him.

His eyes dropped to her mouth.

And then she was alone on the couch.

But only for a second.

After that second she was thrown over his shoulder and he was walking across her family room.

She latched onto the sides of his waist and snapped, "Branch!"

"Time for a bath," he muttered.

She closed her mouth.

She could do a bath.

Absolutely.

Evangeline nuzzled Branch's neck, then lower, sweeping her lips across his collarbone.

"Thanks for dinner, honey," she whispered at his shoulder and went down.

His hands curled around her ribs slid to her ass and he started stroking her lightly along the outside of her cleft.

"You got breakfast, Angie, my turn," he whispered back.

She kissed his nipple, his other one, then went between his pecs and tipped her head back, putting her chin to his chest, giving her eyes to him.

He was on his back in her bed, dark head to the pillows, unbound, and she'd just finished riding him to a vanilla climax that didn't rival the scene on the couch, but it didn't stink either. Especially watching his face and feeling his hands share how much he enjoyed watching her bounce on his cock.

"Not a big fan of our day being over," she told him.

"Come here," he murmured on a squeeze of her ass.

She slid up him so they were face-to-face.

"Don't make plans all weekend," he ordered, keeping hold of her ass with one hand but trailing his other up her back so he could tangle it into her hair.

She liked the feel of him touching her.

But all she could think was that she had at least until the weekend to wage her war, soft against hard.

"You got it, Branch."

"Good," he muttered, using his hand in her hair to bring her mouth to his.

He kissed her.

She kissed him back.

When he was done, he maneuvered her face into his neck.

She snuggled it deeper there.

But her thighs straddling his hips clenched in when his hand at her ass went up then down, his middle finger digging in to fit itself snug in her crevice.

"Same toy, though smaller, if they got it, jewel a lighter blue, baby, you tell me where you got mine, I'll get one for you. Have it made if I have to. And you wear it while you work me," he stated.

She stared at the skin of his neck.

He was going to buy her a toy?

Stake his claim in her while she did her work with him?

She hoped he didn't feel how hard her heart was beating.

"So you, uh . . . got the significance of the color of the jewel."

"You inside me, you work me, I get a toy so I'm inside you too."

She tried to control the thump of her heart.

He got the significance.

And he liked it.

His finger pressed deeper and his next question shared he'd mistaken her.

"Do you not like to be plugged?"

"I like it," she forced out.

"Like to get fucked?"

She nodded.

He sifted his fingers through her hair then tangled them back in, saying, "Mental note to take my babe's ass."

She pressed against him and smiled.

He wanted more of her. More of her time. More of her body. Him inside her in different ways.

Just more.

Soft was kicking the shit out of hard.

Evangeline felt his stubble scrape her forehead as he dipped his head to her.

"Come in every part of you," he whispered.

She lifted her head, their mouths met and they kissed again, Branch wrapping both arms around her and rolling her to her back, taking the kiss deeper.

They made out lazily but thoroughly for a long time before Branch broke it and dipped his own face to bury it in her neck and nuzzle her there.

Evangeline gloried in the feeling as she stared at the ceiling, moving her hands on him and hoping to God that beautiful taste on her tongue wasn't just Branch.

But also a hint of victory.

Then she declared, "I want ice cream."

He lifted his head and looked down at her. "I didn't fill you up?"

She cupped his cheek in her hand and smiled at him. "In more ways than one. I still want ice cream. Do you want some?"

"Babe, it's nearly ten."

"Is there an international cutoff for ice cream I don't know about?" she asked.

His lips twitched. "Not that I know."

"So do you want ice cream?"

He got close, something moving over his face she couldn't quite describe.

But she knew it was beauty.

"Yeah, Angie, I want ice cream."

She grinned.

Branch rolled them out of bed.

She cleaned up then put on her nightie and panties.

He tugged on his lounge pants.

And together they walked down her narrow stairs to get some ice cream.

twenty-five

Played

BRANCH

That next evening, hearing her car pull up in the drive, Branch hit "Pause" on the TV, hauled his ass out of the couch and started moving into the kitchen.

He stopped when she threw open the kitchen door and he got a look at her face.

She tossed her shit aside and skipped, actually *skipped* on her high heels his way, burning a huge smile right through him, not stopping when she reached him, instead throwing herself in his arms, giving him a tight hug and jumping excitedly in his hold.

"They . . . look . . . *great!*" she cried.

He grinned down at her. "See you like the lights."

"They look *great!*" she repeated.

Branch just kept grinning.

"Are they all up?" she asked.

"Yup," he answered.

She let him go, pulled out of his arms and walked quickly to the back doors, declaring, "Saw the ones in the front and at the kitchen door. Want to see the one out back."

He'd seen the motion sensor lights she bought had come in while he was gone so he put them up.

They were all the same style. In Branch's estimation, you saw one up, that was all you had to see. But obviously Evangeline didn't agree.

He stood where he was, crossing his arms on his chest and watching her.

She was outside and he heard her shout, "It looks *great!*"

And he was still grinning.

But he called, 'Babe, you wanna get over it and get on with cooking? You're on tonight and I missed lunch so I'm hungry."

Her head turned his way and she looked to him through the window before she hurried back through the door and came right at him, showing she wasn't a big fan of him missing lunch and she was intent to do something about it.

Branch felt that hit his chest.

Then he shoved that feeling to the back of his head.

She put her hand to his gut and lifted on her toes, but Branch still had to help her, so he bent his neck.

She touched her mouth to his and pulled back, saying, "I'll get changed and get on it."

"Appreciated."

She scorched another smile into his soul and moved away, walking quickly toward the stairs.

Branch watched her go until she disappeared.

Then he walked to the couch and threw himself on it, lying on his back, one leg thrown over the back of the couch. He nabbed the remote, pointed it at the TV and hit "Play" to continue watching the news.

The next morning, Branch fell on the floor beside the bed, landing on his back with a grunt, this because of the fall and the fact Angie's weight landed on him.

"Babe," he huffed.

"Here?" she asked, her fingers moving on him.

"Babe," he growled.

"Here," she mumbled, her pretty face wearing a determined look.

"Baby," he said, his voice now shaking with laughter.

Her head jerked back and she looked in his face.

"Was it there?" she asked.

"I'm laughin' because you're a goof, not because what you're doing is working. I'm not ticklish."

She gave him an annoyed look. "Everyone is ticklish, Branch."

"I'm not."

She went at him again and he took it, lying under her as she straddled him, trying not to laugh because she was just too cute.

She kept glancing at his face through it before she gave up, slapping both hands on his bare chest and snapping, "I can't believe you aren't ticklish."

He moved fast, and she let out a screech when she flew through the air, landed on her back and took his weight.

Then she took his fingers moving on her sides, flailing under him, pushing at his forearms, her head thrashing, shouting through uncontrolled giggles, "Stop it, Branch!"

"I guess you're right," he murmured, not letting up. "Most everyone is ticklish."

She stilled, so he stopped, and she shot him a glare.

She surged back into squirming and giggling as he went back at her.

"Stop it, Branch!" she yelled.

He gave her more, smiling doing it, until he decided she'd had enough. She let out another shriek when he angled off her abruptly and pulled them both to their feet.

"Right, Angie, time to quit fuckin' around. You got houses to sell."

She smacked his upper arm, half irritated, half playful, then immediately turned and flounced in her short little nightie to the bathroom.

He enjoyed the show before he followed her and found her at the sink, pulling her hair into a ponytail.

She sent him another glare through the mirror and, finished with her ponytail, she snatched up the electric toothbrush, nabbing her toothbrush head that was resting in the holder beside his and snapping it on, muttering irately, "Don't think that didn't earn retribution."

He fit his front to her back and dropped his mouth to her neck. "You said it the first night you worked me, Angie. But now you know from experience I like being bad."

She shivered against him.

Branch smiled against her skin.

"Well, *that* is not going to get you a spanking. *That* is going to get you a paddle, handsome. And I'm a frigging *virtuoso* with a paddle."

He put his chin to her shoulder and looked into her eyes in the mirror.

"Bring it on, Mistress."

"Stop turning me on," she clipped. "I have houses to sell."

He grinned into the mirror then kissed her shoulder before he shoved her out of the way so he could splash water on his face.

Branch confiscated her toothbrush when she was done with it and stepped aside so she could wash her face.

He thought she needed another basin.

Then he thought he didn't mind sharing the one she had.

After he had that thought, he shoved it into the back of his head.

Then, together, they got in her shower.

"No fucking way."

"But, Branch."

"No . . . *fucking* . . . way."

She set her face.

Branch just stared down at her.

It was that afternoon and Amélie had called them in, declaring they'd made their decision, there was no reason to wait any longer, it was time to add to the family.

He should have demanded to see photos of what was available. He had not.

Big mistake.

"We think he's a bichpoo, that's bichon frise and poodle. Obviously you can see he's light brown," Amélie stated, not at all helpfully.

Because to that, Evangeline cried, "A bichpoo! I've always wanted a bichpoo."

"You have not," Branch declared.

She frowned at him. "If I knew they existed, I would have." She swung an arm toward the cage in Amélie's vet's building and the little mop of a dog who was staring out at them with black eyes that, fuck him, looked curious, intelligent . . . and sad. "I mean, look at him."

Branch was already looking at him, but when she demanded he keep doing it, he looked to her and slowly shook his head.

Her frown became a glower.

"A neighbor heard him whining and not stopping," Amélie put in. "She knew the people in the house were on vacation so she called the police. They went in, found him in a pen with a lot of food that he'd kicked outside the cage and water bowls he'd turned over, caked in his own excrement. When Dr. Hill got him, he was only mildly malnourished, but severely dehydrated. However, he's quite all right now."

Shit, fuck.

Angie's face melted.

Shit, *fuck.*

"That client has three dogs or she would have kept him," Leigh went on. "So she brought him to us."

"Branch," Angie whispered.

Shit. Fuck.

"Baby, that dog is gonna get adopted in no time. He'll get a good home. You need something bigger that can keep you company but also that can keep you safe," he said gently.

"He hasn't been adopted yet and he's been here for days," she replied.

Branch looked to Amélie.

She studiously avoided catching his gaze.

Right.

He drew in breath.

"Fine," Evangeline muttered before he could say anything and looked to Leigh. "Can I just snuggle him for a while?"

Shit.

Fuck.

"Of course," Amélie stated quickly, moving to the cage.

"Angie, that isn't a good idea," Branch warned.

She tipped her eyes to his. "Just a little snuggle. He's barely more than a puppy and all puppies need snuggles."

"Dr. Hill thinks he's around six months," Amélie shared, pulling the dog from his confines. "So definitely still a puppy."

Christ.

Before Branch could intervene, Leigh gave him to Angie and she held him close, cooing to him while he wriggled enthusiastically in her arms.

And through it, Branch watched his babe fall in love.

Jesus.

"Give the thing to me," he ordered.

Her gaze shot to him and he would almost swear he saw her fighting the urge to curl protectively over the animal and hold him away.

"Branch."

"Give it to me, Angie."

Looking like she was Sophie making her choice, she handed the dog to Branch.

He took it, held it up to his face and the thing wiggled in his hold, not trying to get down, trying to lick Branch's face.

Shit, fuck.

He tucked the dog in his arm, curled his fingers around the dog's scruff and started massaging.

The dog began panting and settled in.

"You get him, you also get another one, a bigger one, one *I* pick, and no cat," he announced.

Her face lit with joy and that look crawled right into his soul.

Even so, she declared, "But I want a cat."

"Then get a cat. But you're getting another dog too, Angie."

She fell on that instantly. "Deal!"

"Wonderful!" Amélie exclaimed.

Branch looked to the ceiling, and as usual with Evangeline, even though this time it was irritating as hell and had the addition of Amélie joining in, he enjoyed the pain of being played.

The dog twisted its neck and started gnawing on Branch's fingers.

Branch looked down at it, and when the animal felt his attention, his head snapped back and he stared up at Branch, panting and looking like he was smiling.

"Shit. Fuck," he muttered.

Angie giggled.

Amélie emitted a laugh that sounded like a purr.

Branch looked to Olly's woman and ordered, "Get the papers."

She inclined her head, shot Evangeline a happy look and hustled out on her high heels.

Angie got close, her hands out. "Can I have him?"

"I got him," Branch replied and looked to her. "You need to fill out the paperwork."

She was staring up at him, not blasting him with a smile but her eyes were burning right into him.

"Right," she whispered.

"Papers, babe."

She nodded, got closer, scratched her new pup's head then stretched up.

Branch gave her his mouth.

She took it in a soft kiss and then strutted out, hips swaying.

When she disappeared, or the view of her ass did, Branch cut his attention back to the dog.

"You're a lucky fuck," he told him.

The dog yapped exuberantly.

Yeah, that dog was not dumb.

Branch pulled the pup up his chest, buried his hand in its fur again and followed the women.

Branch's eyes opened to see Angie leaning over him.

"Time to go to bed, honey."

Damn, he'd conked out.

He felt warmth at his chest, saw Murphy curled there asleep, so he wrapped the pup in an arm and did an ab crunch to pull himself out of the couch.

When he headed to the big crate they'd brought him home in, Angie spoke.

"I've puppy-proofed the laundry room," she told him. "You can put him in there. I don't want him in another cage."

"Good idea," he muttered.

He took him to the laundry room, saw he had plenty of food, water, his new dog bed, some toys to gnaw on, so he put him down and gently held him back with a foot before he shut him in.

He turned to see Evangeline close so he tossed an arm around her shoulders and guided her to a light switch to turn it off.

"He's so cute, I can't wait until he's used to his new home and he can sleep with us."

When she was curled into his arms, that'd work.

When she had him tied down, it would not.

He didn't share that. He held her to him as he moved around the house, switching off all the lights and glancing at all the doors to make sure the locks were turned.

Only then did he guide them to the stairs.

"You're cute with him," she noted as he led them up.

"Whatever," he muttered.

"You like him, Branch," she said, laughter and happiness in her voice.

He grunted, hit the landing with her and turned them to the next set of stairs.

"Don't fight it," she advised.

He felt those words hit his gut and chest and immediately shoved them to the back of his head.

He got naked. She put on a nightie. They got in bed. Branch turned out the lights.

Then he turned into her and gathered her close.

She snuggled closer.

"Thanks for letting me have him," she murmured, giving him a squeeze.

He'd let her have him but the dog had claimed Branch and she knew it.

This was likely because Branch had claimed the dog and both of them knew that.

He shoved that into the back of his head too and gave her a return squeeze.

"Not a problem. Now go to sleep."

" 'Kay. 'Night, baby."

" 'Night, Angie."

She gave his throat a nuzzle with her face and within seconds was asleep.

Seconds later, Branch had followed her.

"Mistress," Branch growled.

It was the next evening.

He was on his knees bent over his spanking bench. She'd pulled his tee over his head but left it stuck around his biceps, his arms stretched out in front of him, fingers curled around the edge of the bench.

She'd also pulled his jeans and shorts over his ass and down to his thighs, where she forced his legs apart so his clothes caught on them, biting in.

And she'd slid up his cock ring, inserted the bullet at the end of the tail up his ass, turned it on low and then she went at him with her paddle.

She had not lied.

She rocked it with a spanking. She didn't mess around with a flog or a strap. And she killed it with a switch.

But she was genius with a paddle.

She had not tied him down. After being bad, he now had to take his paddling, proving he could be a good boy.

That was only part of how she aced the paddle.

She stopped whacking him and rubbed the flat of the paddle over his ass.

He drew in deep breaths to force some modicum of a recovery.

"Has my big boy had enough?" she taunted.

Taunted.

He twisted his neck to look up at her, and at one look, his aching cock pulsed.

He was a bad boy on his knees with his pants bunched at his thighs.

She was the Mistress teaching a lesson still wearing the tight skirt she'd worn to work, the see-through blouse with the little polka dots on it and a cami underneath, and she'd slipped her high-heeled pumps back on after they'd had dinner and she'd ordered him to the playroom.

Her hair was up in a mess at the top of her head, curls trailing down her neck.

His babe.

His Mistress.

His Evangeline.

Perfection from head to toe.

"Give it," he challenged.

She lifted the hand not holding the paddle but holding the remote to his tail.

"Take it," she whispered and the thing thumped harder up his ass, vibrated deeper through his balls and around the base of his cock.

His neck arched back, his chest pressed into the bench, and his ass automatically tipped for her.

She walloped it with his paddle.

Branch stayed arched. He couldn't help it as the pain burned through his ass, his hole to his swaying balls and down his swinging dick, the cockhead slamming against the underside of the bench with each blow.

It was *outstanding*.

"Who's my bad boy?" she asked.

Whack!

"Me," he grunted.

"Are you going to be good?"

Whack!

"No," he hissed between his teeth.

"No?"

Whack!

Braced to the point he was straining, Branch focused on not coming instead of focusing on speaking.

"My bad boy needs more," she murmured.

Whack!

"Yes," he forced out.

"More?"

Whack!

"More, Mistress, please," he bit off.

Whack!

"*Fuck yeah*, baby, yeah. Give your bad boy his paddle," he growled.

Christ, he was going to blow.

Whack!

Branch grunted and his cock slammed into the bench so he grunted again because that hurt so fucking, *fucking* good.

She rested the paddle along the small of his back but didn't let up on him. She dug her fingernails into the flesh at the backs of his thighs and up over his ass.

Fuck, he loved it when she did that, anytime, but especially after she'd given his flesh the heat.

He clenched his teeth before the pressure left and then he huffed out a breath.

"You going to be good, handsome?" she asked quietly.

"I like being bad, Mistress."

"Good," she whispered, drove her thumb up his ass and his body jolted.

Oh yeah.

"Fuck me with that," he groaned.

"Oh, I don't know," she said, even as she slid it out but slid two fingers in and did just that.

Sensational.

"I think I want to see if I can make my big boy come taking his paddle," she finished.

She glided her fingers out, took up the paddle again and he curled his hold tighter around the edge of the bench and locked his legs.

Then the vibrations up his ass and at his balls and cock hit the max and Branch automatically started humping the air for her, the paddle landing on his ass each time he swung out.

Yeah.

She was a magician with a paddle.

He only had it in him to give her a warning, groaned, *"Mistress,"* before he bucked on the bench, shooting his cum under it, hips thrusting convulsively head back, jaw hard, growls rumbling through the room.

He vaguely heard the paddle thud to the floor but the feeling wasn't vague when she latched onto his balls and his dick, squeezing the former and milking him dry with the latter.

When he was slumped on the bench, forehead to it, hips flexing faintly, his cock jumping with the aftershocks in her hand, she stroked the final spurts out of him. She turned the toy off and soothed the heat of his skin with her mouth, massaging his balls and gently fondling his dick while she did it.

She bit lightly into the flesh of his cheek and his body gave a weak jolt before she brushed her lips softly along the skin of his lower back and he felt the bullet glide out, the ring slide off, the toy thudding quietly when it hit the ground.

Evangeline moved over him and he felt her tits pressed to his back as she rested against him, bent over him.

"Stay there, honey."

Not hard to do. At that moment, he wasn't sure he could move.

"You got it," he muttered.

She kissed his back and left him.

When she returned, he was too spent to do much but let out a low, pleased grunt when she slid his jewel up his ass.

She resumed her position bent over him, lying on his back, and said into his skin, "Feel like tying you down tonight so you can eat me while I stare at my jewel winking up your ass and then I can play with you again in the morning."

Even empty, he knew when he felt her words in his dick that he felt like that too.

"Yes, ma'am."

She trailed a hand over his hip, between his legs, skimming his junk, making him jerk, before she wrapped her arm around him at his lower abdominals.

"You're everything."

Branch froze at her words.

She wasn't done.

"It's like I wrote out a wish list and whatever powers at work who got hold of it made you just for me, ticking off all the boxes."

He closed his eyes and whispered, "Angie."

She gave his abs a squeeze. "It's the truth."

He knew that.

He knew exactly that.

Except the other way around.

"Baby—" he began.

"And you should know the truth."

He started to press up but she pushed him down with her torso, and her arm left him so she could cup his cock and balls.

He stilled.

"It's still my game, my rules, Branch," she reminded him.

Played.

Again.

She rubbed her nose against his back and then whispered there, "Get up. Pull down your shirt. Pull up your pants. Go upstairs and position how you know I want you. I'll be up in a bit and you can take care of me."

"Help you clean up, baby," he murmured.

"You have your orders, handsome."

He let that sit a beat before he sighed.

"Yes, Mistress."

"Good." She was back to whispering, rubbing her nose on his back, and she did that awhile and Branch loved every second of it before she moved away.

When she did, Branch did as told.

He was at the door and she was at the sink when he turned to her.

"Angie?" he called.

She looked over her shoulder at him. "Yes, honey."

"You're everything too, you know," he said gently.

He watched her frame lock before she turned fully to him, a wet towel in her hand, a soft smile on her face.

"I hope so, Branch. I really fucking hope so."

He knew she did.

Fuck him.

He knew it down to his soul.

They stared at each other across the room and when Branch knew he couldn't shove that expression on her face into the back of his mind, he lifted up his chin to her and left her studio.

When she was out of his sight and he was looking in on Murphy in the laundry room, checking he was all right, he realized he could accomplish the superhuman feat of not thinking about all that had happened after he'd returned from dealing with Raines, putting the team at peace. Hell, all that had happened before that.

All that had happened since Evangeline came into his life.

But as Branch lay naked on her bed, arms and legs spread, hips on the bolster, jewel up his ass, waiting for her, it all came crashing back.

All of it.

Every infinitesimal detail.

And he knew what he had to do.

He had no choice.

He'd never really had one.

He just had to go about it the best he could so, in the end, it worked for Angie.

Late the next morning, their Saturday starting their weekend together, after she'd worked him and then untied him, while Angie was outside with Murphy, Branch made the call.

Olly picked up.

"Hey, brother."

Branch didn't ease into it.

"Remember when you offered to listen to my shit?"

There was only a beat of hesitation before Ol replied, "Yes."

"Need that, Olly," Branch said.

"Tonight?"

"Yeah."

"Come to our place."

"Leigh—"

"She'll be there but she'll give us space."

Branch didn't like it.

But he took it.

"What time?" he asked.

"Six?"

He had to tell Evangeline he'd need to be gone on a day they were supposed to spend together.

But she wouldn't care.

Just as long as he came home to her.

Fuck, he hoped he knew what he was doing.

"See you at six," he agreed.

"I'll get the beer."

"Thanks, Ol," Branch muttered.

"Any time, man," Olly replied.

They hung up.

Branch tossed his phone onto the kitchen counter and looked out the windows to Evangeline.

And one last time, he shoved it all into the back of his mind.

Tonight, he'd let it out.

And then it would be done.

They sat out by the pool on the end of lounge chairs next to a kickass statue Leigh had on her deck of a curvy woman on her knees with her arms raised above her in what looked like the shape of a heart.

There was shit Branch couldn't give Olly because he just couldn't, but more, he didn't want to mire his friend down in that massive quagmire of crap.

But he told him about Tara.

And he told him what he could tell him about the team and how that ended and where he was at, who he was, or more accurately, how he wasn't anything.

He also told him about him and Evangeline, the game they'd been playing, how she was playing it dirty, how he was playing it even dirtier, and how he wanted that to end.

And last, he gave him the dangers that lurked for him, which didn't matter, and the same that lurked for Evangeline, which did.

When he was done, not having looked at Ol the entire time he spoke, he continued to keep his eyes to their view of the Valley spilled out below them on their mountain.

Olly didn't say anything and this lasted a good while.

Branch still didn't look at him.

He let it rest between them, fetid and stinking like the pile of shit it was.

Then he muttered, "Maybe I should go."

"No, you absolutely should not."

Branch cut his eyes to Olly.

Olly looked pissed, his mouth tight, his eyes wired.

"Buddy," he sounded choked. "Christ. Fuck. Buddy."

Suddenly, he reached out and Branch started to move away but Olly caught him around the back of the neck and swung Branch to him, swaying in himself. The tops of their heads collided with a thud and Olly moved his hand up and cupped the back of Branch's head as he pushed their craniums together.

Branch sat still, staring at Olly's knees, knowing in that moment he had another member of his family.

Finally, he found it in him to say, "Ol, just—"

"I have no words. Got no magic. Got nothin' to help you with all that shit, brother. Except to say I'm so fuckin' sorry, I can't even express how fuckin' sorry I am you lived through all that."

Branch shut his mouth.

Olly pressed their heads together even harder before he let go and sat straight, looking to the Valley.

"Guts me," he muttered.

"I shouldn't have given it to you," Branch replied and Olly's gaze sliced to his.

"Keep it to yourself? Are you insane?"

"It's not easy to know."

"You're right," Ol agreed. "But it's still a privilege to know it."

Branch again shut his mouth.

"You've made the right decision," Olly told him.

Branch shook his head. "I'm not sure I agree."

"Well, bro, you're straight-up wrong."

"I follow through with that decision, let her win, take the life she's offering, what kind of life can I give her in return?"

"The kind she wants."

Branch shook his head again. "Not thinkin' I'd ever be down with a trip to Disneyland with my babe and our kids."

"So don't take them to Disneyland," Olly fired back and leaned into him. "And she won't give a shit. Take them to a cottage by a lake in the middle of nowhere where there's nothing to do but fish, cook out and fuck when the kids are asleep. You're there and you're together, Disneyland ll never be better than that."

A cottage by the lake in the middle of nowhere.

Fucking when their kids were asleep.

Have his babe offer him something soft and sweet and delicious after he took care of her, his cum still inside her, and they go downstairs to get some ice cream while their kids are asleep under his roof.

Kids.

Under his roof.

Asleep.

Shit.

He might be able to do that.

Shit.

He *wanted* to do that.

With Angie.

Still.

"You give up enough of what you want, you never forget you gave it up and that can fester, man," he informed Olly.

"You get everything you want, you'll forget what you thought you wanted before because you not only got everything you really wanted, you got everything you need," Olly returned.

Branch looked away.

Ol didn't let it slide.

"And I see you fuckin' know it."

"She deserves better. A man like me in her home, her life?" Again he shook his head and repeated, "She deserves better."

"You're the best she's ever had, suspected it before but know that for a fact with all you just gave me, but bet she knows it better, not even having that shit. The only one who doesn't know that's the truth is you and the way you don't, no way I can talk you into getting it. So, my advice, Branch, just let her have a chance at the promise of a lifetime of showing it to you."

Branch glanced over his shoulder at his friend. "When we first started, I could barely stand in her kitchen, Ol. That's not the man I am anymore. To stand like I belong in a home like that owned by a woman like Evangeline. But I brought my shit into her house. Now you think I should settle it into her life?"

"You already did that and seems to me she doesn't care."

Branch turned fully to him. "She doesn't know."

"This shit," Ol flipped up a hand, "my advice, don't give it to her. Not ever. You need to let more out, give it to me. Just let her have the man she knows has the baggage you've already told her and she totally doesn't give a shit."

"How do I get past where I'm at in my head?"

"Eat her cooking. Take her spankings. Get her the dog you want her to have so you'll feel she's safe. Come over to our house for chili. And sleep with her in your arms."

"You think it's as easy as that?" Branch clipped.

"No," Olly shot back. "What I think is, you should die. In your mind, you should die in that place where you lost your team. And then you should come back and see the one who lived. See him or her livin' the life you're making yourself live. And feel what they feel, Branch. Feel how fuckin' goddamned, motherfucking," he leaned deep into Branch and kept growling, "*pissed* they'd be that you were throwing away the life they didn't get to live."

Branch felt his jaw clench.

"Your woman," Olly kept at him. "The one you lost. She saw this, she loved you. How would she feel?"

"You think it's *that* easy?" Branch ground out.

"Yeah, for that, brother, I think it's *that* easy."

"You're wrong."

Olly shook his head. "I see you're takin' on the responsibility of what happened to them. *All* of them. But it isn't yours, Branch. And the only way I can help you get past that is to say what I just said. If that shit went down with you and you were the one who was lost, would you blame them? If that doesn't penetrate, think of it this way. With the shit that happened to Evangeline, is it her fault? Did *she* make that guy do what he did? Was that her responsibility?"

"Fuck no," Branch clipped.

"So why is it yours when other people did crazy, awful crap that ended with tragic consequences?"

Damn him.

He had a valid point.

Seriously valid.

Branch shifted in the lounger so he was facing Olly dead-on.

"I'm not just a PI like any PI, Olly, I deal with filth."

"You break the law?"

"Only ones I think need broken. Not ones I get paid to break."

"You got no problem with that, she won't either."

"That's the man in her home, her bed," Branch reminded him.

"That's the man she's falling in love with."

Unable to take the truth of that while looking in Olly's eyes, Branch looked down to his knees.

Olly's voice came quieter when he said, "Scrape off the filth if you don't want that to infest your life. She doesn't care. But you don't want to bring that to her, then scrape it off. And then there's nothing, bro. You said your bud can keep you both off the radar so you're safe. She's safe. So you got no excuse except just to be fuckin' happy."

He looked into his friend's eyes.

"I want it to be that easy."

That's all he'd ever wanted, growing up with his family, he just wanted easy.

After Tara, after the work he did with the team, after the team bought it the way they did, he lost all hope for easy.

Until Evangeline.

Olly reached out again and hooked him around the back of the neck.

"Then let it be that easy."

They looked at each other long beats before Olly grabbed hold of the neck of his shirt, swayed him a couple of times and then let go.

"You there?" he asked.

"She's the world I always wanted the world to be," Branch answered.

Olly's face split in a huge fucking smile.

"Then you're there."

He wasn't.

But he was right then beginning to think he could be.

OLIVIER

Olly closed the door on Branch after flicking two fingers his way while he was driving through their semicircular drive.

He turned and saw his Leigh-Leigh leaned against the wall at the end of the foyer, her cat Cleo in her arms, her eyes on him and they were talking.

"Has he made the right decision?" she asked softly.

"I'm thinkin' yes."

"It seemed difficult."

She'd given them their space.

But she'd watched.

That was his Leigh-Leigh, looking out for Olly. Looking out for Branch.

He started moving to her as he answered, "'Difficult' is not the word. 'Practically impossible' is. But think I got him there."

"Please stop moving, darling."

He halted.

And when he did everything about her penetrated and his balls drew up.

She spoke.

"I would very much like to reward you for your recent efforts on behalf of your Branch and my Evangeline, so, *chevalier*, your choice. Take me to our bed and make love to me. Or position for me as you know I wish it so I can give you your tail and then give you much more."

He knew which way she was leaning just by looking at her so he walked to her, cupped her beautiful face in both of his hands and dropped his mouth to hers.

He kissed her deep and wet.

Then he said, "Think your beast has earned not waiting too long to get his shit jacked and good."

Her lips curved up. "We'll see."

He grinned at her.

Then he dropped his hands, one going to Cleo to rub her head, before he turned away and strolled down the hall to position for his Mistress so he could get his shit jacked like she always jacked him.

Really fucking good.

BRANCH

Sitting in his truck in the parking lot of a fast-food restaurant, Branch heard the click, the pop and two more clicks before Gerbil answered, "Wassup?"

"You still going with Tavis?"

"Pain in my ass," Gerbil muttered.

"You can make her safe," Branch declared.

This got him a sucking void of silence.

"Gerbil, vow it to me, man. I get a life with her, you can make us safe."

"I can make you safe, Branch."

"Then make us safe."

He disconnected.

TAVIS WARREN

After Branch hung up on him, he stared at the six computer monitors in front of him.

Suddenly not in his control, his head dropped, his chin hitting his throat.

He drew in a deep breath.

He lifted one hand to the back of his neck and scrubbed it over his head, the other one, and repeat with both.

He dropped his hands and lifted his head.

"Right, so maybe this world isn't the shithole I knew it to be," he said to his monitors.

Then he grinned a lunatic grin and put his fingers to his keyboard.

ARYAS

"Talk to me," Aryas demanded when he picked up Branch's call.

Branch didn't fuck around.

"There are going to be changes, Aryas, and I need you on board with those changes or I'm going to have to refer you to somebody else."

Aryas went completely silent.

"Know a couple of guys. They're assholes but they get the job done. That said, you'll have to keep an eye on them because they like their work. Too much."

Aryas ignored his last.

"Well thank fuck, son. 'Cause, see, I just made the decision to open a club in Tahoe so a lot of my time is going to be tied up in that for the next eight months. But doesn't matter. All work and no play makes Aryas a horny boy. Need a man I can trust who knows his shit to oversee operations with a focus on membership approval and security. I'll give you a bonus, you don't make me place an ad."

There was only a moment of silence before Branch asked, "What's the start date?"

"Yesterday."

"Right. Good you didn't give me an office during orientation because I don't need one. And I'm down with travel. But I got a woman here in Phoenix so you need me to go, I'll go, but I can't be gone for long because I'll want to get back home to her."

Well thank . . .

Fuck.

Finally.

Aryas's voice dipped low. "You owe me, Branch."

Branch's voice was just as low. "I know, Aryas."

"Paid in full, you make her happy and you find some of that yourself."

"We done, boss?" Branch asked.

"For now."

"Later."

"Later, Branch."

They disconnected.

And Aryas Weathers exploded with laughter.

STELLAN

His phone rang and Stellan's mouth got tight at seeing it was an unknown caller.

He almost ignored it.

In five minutes, he would be glad he didn't.

For two reasons.

"Yes?" he answered.

"Lange," Branch Dillinger said.

Concern filtered through him as he asked, "Is everything good with Evangeline?"

"She's fine. Just called to say, you're up."

Stellan was silent.

"Anything goes down," Dillinger went on, "it's on me. But just to say, if you're in, you're up and if you can keep an eye, it'd be appreciated."

"I'm in," Stellan told him immediately, wondering how soon it would be before Leenie called to share that it was, actually, all it was cracked up to be. He let that go and continued, "It's good I have you on the line. I've got a job for you."

"I'm out of the business, Lange, found alternate employment."

Stellan smiled.

Yes, he suspected it was all it was cracked up to be.

He was actually counting on it.

So he persevered.

"I'll make it worth your while to do some moonlighting."

There was a pause before Dillinger asked, "What's the job?"

"I want to know everything there is to know about Mistress Sixx."

Another pause before, "Give me a couple of days."

"To decide if you want to take the job?" Stellan asked, not a big fan of waiting, at least not for something like this.

"To get you everything there is to know about Sixx."

Stellan stared at the marble of his kitchen counter.

"A couple of days?" he asked.

"You're in a hurry, I'll have a report to you by tomorrow afternoon. It will be comprehensive, but not as comprehensive as it would be if you gave me a coupla days."

Holy fuck.

"You can take your time, Dillinger," he shared. "I'll be doing the same."

There was another pause, this one longer, before Dillinger said, "You didn't ask for it but you're doing me and Angie a solid so I'll give one back. You take that on, man, you might be in for a world of hurt."

"I'm counting on it," Stellan replied.

There was amusement in his voice when he muttered. "Right. Welcome to the dark side, brother. You got it in you, I suspect you're gonna enjoy your stay. Now, we done?"

"We're done."

"Meet soon."

"Yes."

Dillinger disconnected.

Stellan tossed his phone on the counter and smiled a very slow smile.

BRANCH

Branch stood in his condo and looked around.

He should let her sell it.

But he figured that was a commission she didn't need.

He hefted his bags up, walked five feet and dumped all three of them beside the door.

Ready.

Waiting.

It was early for them. He didn't intend to move in.

What he did intend to do was move the fuck out.

But his next place, he'd be renting.

He went to the kitchen and grabbed his bottle opener.

On his count, she had three.

But he liked his.

So he was keeping it.

Pocketing the thing, Branch walked out the door.

And then he was on his way to Angie.

twenty-six

Match Point

EVANGELINE

Evangeline was pacing with Murphy at her heels.

She had her phone in her hand, cued up to call Cam because she was worried.

Branch had been gone almost all day.

A day he'd told her would herald the beginning of a weekend they'd share with no plans, except to be together.

When she'd come in that morning after spending time outside with Murphy, he'd told her he had "something to do."

Not a job, "something to do."

"And I might be late, babe," he'd shared.

He'd done it with one of his hands cupping her face, the other arm engaged in holding an active Murphy against his chest.

She'd let him go. He had something to do, she wouldn't hang on. That wasn't how she was going to win this war.

She needed to hang on without *hanging on*.

It still cost her because when he'd told her that, he hadn't hidden the conflict in his eyes.

Now it was late, after nine, and she hadn't heard anything from him the entire time he was gone.

That was not like Branch. He might not share his every move but he didn't keep radio silence when he was away from her.

She also hadn't texted him, hoping she was making the right play with that, giving him some space.

She looked down at her phone for the fiftieth time that day and made the decision she'd made the other forty-nine times.

She set it aside on the kitchen island.

She'd only engage Cam if it was an emergency.

She had no idea what Branch did when he was away from her but they both lived their lives and he was often away from her.

This was no different, she told herself.

Not at all.

Murphy yapped and dashed away.

She looked in the direction he was heading, the kitchen door, to see lights illuminating her driveway.

Her sigh of relief was audible.

Branch usually parked at the curb.

Unless they were in for the night and she had nowhere to go. Then he penned her in, in her drive.

She took it as a good sign he was penning her in.

On that thought she rushed to Murphy so he wouldn't make a run for it when the door opened, even though she knew this wouldn't happen.

Murphy hadn't been with them very long but she knew he wanted one thing.

His daddy.

He liked his mama.

But if he had the choice, he was a daddy's boy.

She scooped him up, seeing Branch easily in the motion sensor light through the window.

Her relief took a hit when she saw the look on his face, but she forced what she hoped looked like a genuine grin at him and flipped the lock on the door.

She stepped back as he stepped in.

"Hey, honey," she greeted.

"Hey," he returned, his eyes only holding hers briefly before he reached out and plucked Murphy right out of her arms.

That made her grin turn natural.

"Hey, buddy," Branch said quietly to Murphy, pulling him up his chest, letting Murphy lick his neck and bounce in his arms as Branch gave his ruff scratches.

"He missed you," Evangeline shared softly, and unnecessarily, saying more with her words than sharing about their dog's emotional state.

Branch didn't miss it and his gaze cut to hers. "Can we talk?"

She looked right into his eyes.

Oh God.

Oh no.

God, no.

"Yes," she answered, her voice sounding scratchy.

Branch looked to her mouth when he heard it then down to Murphy. "Has he been walked?"

"All good," she said.

"No accidents today?" he asked, still looking at Murphy.

"No."

God, she needed him to get on with it even though she sensed she totally *did not.*

"Right," he stated, gave Murphy one last scratch, then bent and put him on the ground. He straightened and turned to her. "You need wine?"

"I, uh . . . have some. In the other room."

"Right," he muttered.

Then she watched him go to the fridge and do something strange.

He got a beer.

But that wasn't the strange part.

The strange part was that he had a bottle opener in the pocket of his cargo pants.

He used it to flip off the top of his beer, pitched the cap in the trash and then, casually, he tossed the opener in her drawer with the others she had.

She stared at his hand closing the drawer, feeling something weird start fluttering in her belly. She just couldn't figure out if it was a good flutter or, with the look on his face and his distant demeanor, a bad one.

"Babe."

His call made her look at him, and when she did, he jerked his head toward the family room.

She went there.

She sat where she used to sit on her end of the couch before she'd made them the them she was making them and her position had changed. Head on his thigh with his hand in her hair or drawing circles on her hip or just holding her at her waist. Cuddled with her back into his front if he was stretched out.

That flutter turned bad when he sat on his side of the couch and didn't give her any indication he wanted her closer.

He took a sip of beer.

She'd left her wine on the coffee table in the middle, too far away right then to grab without shifting. Her body felt so fragile, she thought any movement might make it shatter. So she left it where it was even though she had a feeling she would need a hefty sip, or to gulp the whole glass.

"I've made a decision," he told the blank TV.

Oh God.

Oh no.

God.

"Yes?" she whispered.

He didn't lead into it easy.

"You don't need my shit."

Oh God, no.

"Branch, honey—"

His gaze sliced to her and he ordered tersely, "Let me finish."

They said on the websites for PTSD that you had to listen and you shouldn't interrupt.

So she shut her mouth and tried not to focus on the fact her heart was slamming in her chest and that flutter in her stomach felt less like something good and more like she was about to vomit.

He leaned to put his beer on the coffee table, and although he straightened, he did it sitting like he used to, on the edge of his seat, like he was going to get up and take off at any moment.

"You got a lot of knickknacks," he declared to his beer, and at that, she stared.

As he could do, Branch surprised her, taking her somewhere she didn't know he was leading and she had no clue where he was in his head, thus where he was guiding her.

He knew, though. She'd learned that.

So she kept silent and waited for him to take her there.

"Can see it. Everywhere. Except for what that fuck did to you, you've lived a good life. Got stuff all around to remind you of the good times. The people you spent them with."

She said nothing and not only because he was right.

"When Aryas offered you up to me, I knew you," his eyes finally came to her. "I was there that night so you know that. But it was more. He offered you up so I investigated you. Told myself it was about seeing if I wanted to take you on. Mostly it was about seeing how bad you taking me on would fuck up your life. So I looked into you. Your financials. Work history. Education. Even went so far as to download the floor plan to your place. Came one night when you were asleep, broke in, checked out your studio, walked through your house, saw you in bed."

"Oh my God," she whispered, unable to hear that and not speak, even if what he was saying wasn't a surprise—that was very Branch—it was still a shock.

"Knew even then, if I made the decision to take you on, it was a big mistake. Not for me. For you."

Evangeline pressed her lips together and he watched.

Then he continued talking.

"Barely could do my search, but not because I was an intruder and no one needs that, especially not you. Because I couldn't stand to be in your space."

She tried to keep her breath even but it was far from easy.

He shook his head. "This place, fuck," he kept shaking his head, "all of it was so far away from who I am, the life I have, didn't belong here not just because I broke in. In a way I felt it crawling over my skin. This house and the woman who made it a home were not for the likes of me."

She felt the tears sting her eyes and was concentrating so hard on not letting them flow she couldn't stop herself from reaching out to him.

The look on his face, his detached manner, none of it giving her an opening, she let her hand drop.

She'd lost.

Now he was telling her he could take no more and he had to go.

So she had a decision to make.

And she had to make it now.

She hated it but that decision was clear. It had always been clear. She just wouldn't let herself see.

For him, because that was how much she loved him, holding it together just barely, determined to fall apart when he didn't have to watch, she whispered, "Branch, honey, it means a lot to me that you're giving me this. But I see now I shouldn't have asked for it. So I think to make it easier on you, that you should just—"

He cut her off. "Make it easy on me."

"Yes, so you can—"

"You make everything easy, Angie."

Evangeline shut her mouth again.

He turned more fully to her on the couch, lifting up a cocked leg to rest it in the seat.

And the flutter in her belly shifted.

"I was a soldier."

Oh God.

She did nothing but nod, though it took some effort not to do it enthusiastically.

"You'll never know anything about that, babe."

She kept nodding.

"Not a thing. You can ask. I won't tell. The shit I did," he shook his head, "I can't tell."

"Okay, honey," she whispered.

He stared at her like he'd just noticed she was there.

She felt some guilt about this because he didn't know what she knew.

But she didn't feel much.

All's fair in love. Not war. Nothing was fair in war.

But all was fair in love.

"It fucked with me," he said softly.

She started nodding again.

"I lost some people. They meant a lot to me. They didn't go in good ways."

"Honey," she breathed, trying to figure out what to do, go to him or give him space.

"I didn't handle that very well," he admitted.

"I think you're doing fine," she told him gently.

"Baby, they lost their lives. In response, in a way that was fucked up, I took my own even if I was still breathing."

"You needed to process," she shared.

"I needed vengeance," he declared.

She went still.

"I got it, babe," he told her bluntly. "I got blood on my hands, I was a soldier so I think you might get that. But at least with that last, I didn't bring it into your home. I didn't bring that to you. How I needed to put them to rest is done. That was what I was doing while I was away. But how that vengeance went down was not on me. I just did what I needed to do to put my people to rest. It's important to me you get that."

"Okay, baby. Good. I'm glad you could do that."

Murphy, who was done doing whatever he'd been doing after Branch put him down (that "whatever" she hoped wasn't decimating something that wasn't one of the twenty toys they'd bought him or making a lie of her saying he was all good with his bathroom business), made a jump to join them on the couch.

And failed.

Branch helped him out, lifting him up to the seat.

And watching that, everything settled for Evangeline, inside and out. So much, it was a wonder she didn't sink into her couch, into the floor, becoming a permanent part of that house, permanently fixed in that time she was spending with Branch.

Murphy dashed to her and let her get one pet in before he dashed back to Branch and sat in the crook of his knee, right where he wanted to be, but he gazed at Evangeline, panting happily.

"It's done," Branch announced and her eyes shot from Murphy to him.

"Sorry?"

"That. What I was. Where I was. How I was. It's done."

That flutter went berserk.

"I . . . are you——?"

"There's shit, that shit I mentioned earlier that you can't have, Angie, that will always be there. For me, it'll always be lurking. I'll always feel I have to stay vigilant to keep you safe from what's in my head and all I think that's out there that might hurt you. But I wouldn't be sitting here if I didn't think I could give you that already. It's just that I've come to terms with the fact I always really knew that, I just didn't believe I deserved what you were offering."

"Branch," she whispered shakily, starting to scoot toward him.

"Baby, just a few more seconds, yeah?" he whispered back, the distance out of his face.

It was warm.

Soft.

Hopeful.

She felt her heart thump and stopped moving.

"That shit you can't have, Angie, like I said, it'll never go away."

"Okay," she replied immediately.

That made his mouth go soft.

"You can take anything, can't you?" he asked.

"If it comes with you, yes," she answered.

"Fuck," he whispered.

"Can I come to you now?" she asked.

"You gotta know all you're getting," he told her.

"I already know."

"Babe, it's over. All of it. Aryas offered me a job working at his clubs. I took it. The shit I do, or did, shit I don't want to bring into your home, your life, more shit you can't know, that's over too. But it was there. It was who I let myself be. The people I worked for. The things I did."

"Okay. But I don't care."

"Babe—"

Right, it was time, she felt, to interrupt.

"Branch, I know who you are," she stated. "I didn't know you before but my guess, you've always been just who you are. What you did, how you coped, whatever happened, it is what you say it is. It's shit. And it's over. Now you're here with me. That's all I care about. You being here with me. Whatever you bring with you, I can take it because I *want* it if it's part of you. And I knew from the beginning I'd take whatever I could get from you. So if you can't give it all to me, if that's something you need, then I'll give that to you too and I'll take what I can get."

"Now, babe," he growled, his expression no longer warm or soft or hopeful, but harsh, "you can get over here."

She got over there.

Branch scooped up Murphy, twisting the dog behind him on the seat as he surged into her, meeting her halfway, taking her back into the couch and landing on top of her.

Murphy thought they were playing so he yapped and raced up

Branch's body, jumping into the side of the couch by their heads to snuffle into their faces and lick them both.

Evangeline felt it and didn't.

Because she was getting another kiss, and she loved her new puppy, but she loved the kiss Branch was planting on her a whole lot better.

Branch ended it abruptly and rested his forehead on hers.

Murphy tried to push into their bodies so Branch lifted up, giving his boy what he wanted (like always, he was going to spoil the pooch rotten, but she didn't mind) and Murphy pressed in, settling at Evangeline's shoulder but doing it licking Branch's neck.

"Never had knickknacks," he said quietly.

And again Evangeline gloried in knowing more about Branch even if what she knew broke her heart.

"Honey," she replied simply.

"Even before life turned shit, life was shit. Grew up in a home without things like knickknacks, babe. My dad was barely around but took off for good when I was eight. But when he was around, he knocked my mom around and he didn't feel much of a need to hide that from his sons. Treated her like dirt. Didn't treat his boys much better. Mom was a mess. Never kicked his ass out. Acted, when he'd disappear and then come home, like we were getting a visit from a king. After he left for good, she never sorted her shit out, just sank deeper in her own crap. She drank, before he left and after, and she was a sloppy drunk, Angie. When she was thirty, she looked fifty. When I left at age eighteen, she looked half dead."

God.

Branch.

"Oh, honey," she breathed.

"She didn't protect us from Dad, she didn't protect us from life. She leaned on us. Twice, I tried to intervene when he was having a go at her. Twice, he backhanded me, knocked me into a wall. Second time, stunned me so bad, think I might have lost consciousness for a while. But I remember, when I came to, she was just staring at me like she was taking in a show. That was, she did that until it hit her that Dad was yelling at me, his attention turned, and she got the fuck out. Leaving me with him. I never intervened again and felt shit about it. Luckily, not long after that, he took off and didn't come back."

"Oh, *honey*," she forced out, her eyes prickling.

But she held it together because she had to.

He wasn't done.

"My brother took the dark path, started dealin' drugs when he was in high school. He was a mean motherfucker and one you didn't mess with . . . *in high school*. That included me. He was a dick to me. Until I got old enough he thought he might be able to recruit me into his business."

She bit her lip, staring up at him, unable to believe this amazing man on her couch had endured all he'd endured and the only thing he did was check out not lose it completely.

"I couldn't wait to get out," he told her quietly. "Enlisted the minute I could. It was torture, finishing high school. Putting up with my brother's shit. Watching my mom waste away. Best day of my life was packing up for boot camp. I left and never went back. Twenty years, never went back. But I've kept tabs. She's still a mess. He's in prison. Strike three. He'll be there awhile."

She tightened her hold on him with her arms around his back and gave him what he needed.

Closeness.

He watched her and remarked, "That's more of what you let in your home."

"Think I said I'd take would I could get," she reminded him.

He shook his head like he couldn't quite believe she was real before he lifted a hand, rubbed Murphy's ears but then held the dog closer to them with his forearm as he slid his fingers into the side of her hair.

"I just wanted easy," he said softly. "And everything I did, everyone who crossed my path, it wasn't easy, Angie."

By God, she was going to make his life easy if she dropped dead doing it.

"It's going to be easy now, Branch," she vowed.

"It's gonna be life, baby. What's gonna be easy is not having to put up with the shit without someone at my back."

She stroked that back, whispering, "Well, you've got that."

"I know."

She smiled at him, it was soft and slow, but she knew he liked it when he watched it form and the ice in his eyes melted.

"Peace of mind, Murphy's the shit, but you need a bigger dog," he declared.

"You already know I'm happy with that."

"Decal in your front window that says you've got an alarm."

She closed her mouth because those were ugly and she didn't want one in her front window but she forced her head to nod.

His lips twitched. He knew she didn't want it.

But he didn't relent because he wanted more to find as many ways as he could to keep her safe.

And she was good with that.

He bent closer and the humor fled from his expression.

"This keeps working, we take it further, baby, I can't promise a normal life with shit like Disneyland and you'll never meet my mom."

Disneyland?

Did he mean . . . ?

She didn't press that.

"Can you meet mine?" she asked.

He nodded.

She'd take it.

"I have a dad and two brothers too," she shared.

"Meet your mom, can't dis your dad and brothers."

She smiled up at him.

He shifted his hips so she had no choice but to round his thighs with her legs.

"Disneyland?" she whispered.

"It goes that way with us, you want that?" he whispered back.

Beautiful boys with ice-blue eyes, long bodies, black hair, fierce protective streaks, good senses of humor and kind hearts?

"Disneyland with . . . um, kids?" she asked tentatively.

He shook his head and her stomach took a dive.

Then he said, "No Disneyland. I'm not good in crowds. Too much to keep an eye on. But yes. Kids."

She was not tentative with her answer to that.

"Absolutely."

"No soccer, babe."

She frowned.

"Pop Warner," he stated.

She grinned.

"Girls can have dance classes," he allowed.

"What if they want to play soccer?"

"They can have that too."

God, were they actually discussing this?

They were.

She, Evangeline Brooks, and Branch Dillinger were talking about kids and soccer and dance classes and . . .

Everything.

"I'm thinking you already get this, honey, but I may have a house filled with knickknacks and a really cute car, but I'm not normal and I've been good with that since forever," she shared. "My man works at a sex club, that's not what some would consider normal either. Just as long as it's good and we're happy, I don't give that first fuck."

"That's my Angie," he murmured.

His Angie.

She'd take that too.

Oh yes, she would.

"That first fuck?" he teased.

"I'm embracing the f-word."

Finally, that earned her a big, beautiful, white smile.

Trapped, Murphy didn't fight it but settled in, jaw to her shoulder, after having the shit in his short life that wasn't easy, finding a home where he was safe.

And happy to settle in with that.

Just like his daddy.

But although she felt her pooch rest easy, her attention was on the other man in her life.

"Baby?" she called.

"Right here," he said.

She smiled before she took an arm from his back and curled her hand around his neck, stroking his jaw with her thumb.

"There's something I need to say."

"Say it."

"I don't want to upset you."

He looked guarded but he urged gently, "Say it, Angie."

She shifted her hand to cup his jaw.

After that, she lifted her head from the couch to get her face closer to his.

Through all that, she didn't lose hold on his eyes.

And once in position, she whispered, "Match point."

Instantly she discovered something new about Branch Dillinger.

He was a really good loser.

epilogue

Jungle of Plants

EVANGELINE

"Can we have a minute?" Evangeline asked.

"Sure," the apartment complex manager replied and moved to stand in the kitchen.

That wasn't far enough so Evangeline grabbed Branch's hand and dragged him out to the tiny balcony off the living room.

The complex was close to her place. It was gated. It was well kept. It had a gym and a great pool, big trees all around so it was shady and the unit came with two parking places under a carport.

She hated it.

She slid the sliding door to after she got Branch outside and looked up to him.

"I don't like it," she declared.

"Babe, fifth place we've seen today and the best place yet. You've hated them all. I understood with some of the others but not this one."

"I don't get it," she stated.

He looked into the great room area with its cathedral ceilings and a big L-shaped kitchen with a massive island that fed off of it (which was all actually quite lush) and back to her.

Then he asked a pertinent question.

"What don't you get?"

"I need to understand, you know, if we're looking at a joint custody situation with Murphy."

Branch grinned but turned his head like he was trying to hide it from her. When he turned back, he'd gotten control of his grin, which she thought was too bad.

He also got closer, pulling her into his arms.

"Murphy's home, honey, and he's staying home," he told her.

She nodded smartly.

"So now the part I don't get is that you said you have a condo."

"I'm selling it."

Her eyes got big.

He read her reaction and turned them so she was still in his arms but he had his back to the sliding glass doors and he bent his face close to hers.

"And the way I bought it, Evangeline, you're not gonna have any hand in me getting rid of it."

Oh.

Well, that explained that.

She decided it was prudent to say nothing.

About that.

"Which brings us to you getting rid of your condo but getting an apartment."

"Need a place."

"You have a place."

She knew he got what she was saying when his expression softened and he trailed a hand up her spine and tangled it in her ponytail.

"Babe, we barely been together two months," he told her something she knew.

"I'm aware of that, Branch. And perhaps not officially, but unofficially you've been living with me that whole time."

"Yeah, but we need this."

"We need you unnecessarily renting an apartment when you've already got a home?"

He drew her closer and his face got even softer.

She had him.

She fought smiling in triumph.

"It's probably going to be the same," he said. "Be cool, I could leave some clothes at your house so I don't have to swing by here to get changed. But we're doing this, you and me, building on what we got, and we should do it smart. Your space. My space. We each have that, should that time, however unlikely, come if we need it. Not moving too fast. Get to know each other better. Make the unofficial official when we're at that place and we know it's right."

All this meant she actually *didn't* have him.

She frowned.

"I already know it's right, Branch."

He smiled.

"I'm getting that, Angie."

"So?" she prompted.

He got serious.

"I need to know I'm doing it right with you. I need to know I'm giving you that. I just need to know I'm taking care of you."

Damn.

She looked to his shoulder and gave in ungracefully with a muttered, "Whatever."

The humor was back in his voice when he said, "Thanks, baby."

She looked up at him and took one more shot. "Waste of good money since I'm down with making unofficially official just plain official."

"At this point, with the salary package and 401k Aryas offers, the nest egg I built, got a friend who's got certain skills. If he can turn that into legitimate cash, when we make the unofficial official, we can pay off your house and probably put the first couple kids through college, and in between times, seriously rest easy."

The first *couple* of kids?

Her heart started beating faster.

She didn't get into that.

She got into the other bombshell he'd dropped.

"What you're saying is, you're rich so you can blow unnecessary money on rent in an expensive apartment complex," she noted.

"That's what I'm saying."

"So you're also saying when I won, I didn't just win a hot guy, master alpha-sub who likes little dogs, I got a *rich* hot guy, master alpha-sub who likes little dogs?" she asked.

That earned her another smile.

"And again, that's what I'm saying. That is, that's what I'm saying unless you keep the drips on your plants like they are. If you do, we'll be blowing millions just paying the city to keep your flowers outside from dying. And that's not getting into the jungle you have on the inside," he teased.

"They make my house pretty," she retorted.

"Yeah, they do," he muttered, bending to touch his mouth to hers. "They totally do."

She melted into him.

"So, babe, the apartment?" he prompted.

She leaned slightly to the side and looked into the space.

He'd said his condo was a dump and his bed was lumpy.

That place wasn't a dump, and even though he wasn't going to spend any time in it, just him knowing he had space that was decent space was okay with her.

She looked back at him. "If you like this one best, then take it."

His fingers fisted in her hair. "First thing I'm gonna do when I move in is eat you out on the kitchen island."

"Then you're definitely taking it," she breathed.

He grinned.

After he did that, he kissed her.

And after that, he walked her back into the apartment and took it, negotiating a six-month lease.

Evangeline sat on her knees, held onto the headboard and bit her lip.

Then she closed her eyes when she got it.

All of it.

Did it feel that beautiful for him?

It had to.

From the very beginning.

She felt Branch's stubble scrape her cheek before he murmured against her jaw, "Okay?"

"Yes, baby."

"*Fuck* yes, baby," he corrected.

She opened her eyes, turned her head and caught his heated gaze.

"Fuck yes, baby." she whispered.

Then she stifled a cry when he pulled her away from the headboard, tossed her onto her back and shifted around, coming over her.

His mouth bore down on her between her legs and her hips surged up at the same time his surged down and he thrust his dick into her mouth.

She saw her jewel winking as he fucked her face.

And then she moaned against his cock when he kept eating her as he twisted the plug with the ice-blue jewel he'd just planted up hers.

"What'd I tell you?" Olly asked Branch.

Branch didn't answer Olly. He looked to Amélie.

"Never had better chili in my life."

Leigh smiled her classy smile at him. "I'm delighted you like it."

Evangeline was listening but mostly she was leaned back in her chair, twisted to the side, looking under Amélie's dining room table, seeing Stasia, Amélie's very shy kitty, lying on Branch's lap.

Branch was eating.

He was also petting.

Stasia, she heard, was purring.

Apparently, those who hadn't had easy and understood just how precious it was when they got good gravitated to each other. Evangeline hadn't even seen Stasia sit on Amélie's lap like that. Heck, Evangeline had barely seen Stasia *at all*.

When she righted herself at the table, about to return her attention to the utterly delicious bowl of chili in front of her (and the homemade corn bread, which was moist and *just that touch* sweet . . . forget about it, it was a wonder she didn't shove the whole piece in her mouth after the first bite), she felt something and looked Amélie's way.

Her friend was smiling at her.

It wasn't a classy smile.

It was a happy one.

Evangeline gave her a happy one back.

Later, when she and Olly were relaxing outside next to Leigh and Olly's fire pit with after-dinner drinks and Leigh was some distance away, standing with Branch chatting while he threw a ball for Leigh and Olly's dog, Chevy, Olly noted, "He's good with the kids."

She turned her head his way.

"The kids?"

"Stasia. Chevy." He grinned. "Our kids."

"Your kids," she murmured, thinking that was cute.

"Got furry ones," he looked away and lifted his beer to his lips but didn't take a sip before he finished, "for now."

To that, she grinned, looked at the fire pit and lifted her cool glass of champagne to her lips.

Soon, they wouldn't be able do this. The heat was going to hit the Valley. It'd be all about air-conditioning and pool parties.

But they had this.

For now.

And Evangeline had learned she enjoyed living life, taking the goodness it gave her moment to moment, conscious of every second of it, aware of how remarkable it was.

She looked back to Olly when she felt his boot hit her high-heeled sandal.

He was looking across at Leigh and Branch.

She turned her attention that way and saw Branch smiling at

Amélie while she had her hand wrapped around his biceps, leaned into him, and she appeared to be gazing at him, quietly laughing.

He seemed content. Relaxed.

Right at home.

Yes, she'd take each moment of goodness as it came, aware of how remarkable it was.

She turned back to Olly when she felt her hand suddenly taken in his.

And she watched as he lifted it and touched his lips to her knuckles.

He dropped their hands from his mouth but kept hold of hers.

"Thank you," he whispered.

She swallowed back the tears but replied softly, "Nothing to thank me for."

"I think you know there is."

He loved his friend.

She loved that.

She held his gaze and twisted more fully to him, leaning in.

"He needs us. That won't stop but my guess is, you know that. So we need to keep an eye out for him."

Now she was whispering.

He nodded. "We will."

She squeezed his hand. "Thank you too."

"Nothing to thank me for."

"I think you know there is."

The grin on his attractive face was part sad but mostly content.

She didn't like the sad part.

But she'd take that too.

Evangeline decided it was time.

So she stopped reading her book in her corner of the couch and looked over the top of it to Branch in his corner.

He was naked, spread for her as she'd positioned him, one calf over the back of the couch, other knee cocked, his foot in the couch, knee dropped to the side.

His eyes were lazy and aimed to her. His cock was hard because he'd been ordered to stroke it to keep it that way.

And his balls were resting on her toes where she'd settled them, digging under, resting the ball of her foot so the cool of her jewel touched her skin there.

She wriggled her toes, something she'd been doing randomly and repeatedly for the last hour.

And she watched Branch's jaw get tight.

So, *so* pretty.

Gently, she slid her foot away but she watched him come alert as he watched her move, putting her book aside, turning her legs under her and crawling over to him in the seat of the couch.

Seeing all of him, his jewel winking at her, the wet between her legs pulsed wetter.

When she came close, she put a hand to the inside of either knee and slid them up his inner thighs.

One she left at the juncture of his hip.

The other one she put to his jewel.

Gently twisting it, she watched his teeth bite his lip as she slid it out and started slowly fucking him with it.

"How you doing, baby?" she asked softly.

"Good, Mistress," he rumbled.

He looked good.

He looked *hot*.

And he was all hers.

"Wanna be better?"

His eyes flashed.

"Anything you want, Angie."

She filled him. "Then turn to your knees, handsome. Hands to the arm of the couch. I'm going to fuck my big boy's ass a little bit before I guide you upstairs by your cock and do a number of dirty things to you."

Another flash. Hotter. Longer. Burning deep.

"Yes, ma'am."

She shifted back so he could position.

She moved back in when he had so she could do as she said.

When he'd dropped his head and a languid, purring growl rolled up his throat, she asked, "How's that feel?"

"You know I love how you take my ass."

"I know, baby. But are you ready to get dirty?"

"You give it, Angie, you know I'm ready for anything."

She slid his jewel inside, pressed her chest to his back and kissed his lat.

There she whispered, "Then let's go, big boy."

She got off the couch and then she drew him off with her, tugging him by his cock.

She led him to their bedroom.

And she enjoyed every second of it as they got dirty.

Evangeline barely got through the door before she had a dog attacking her feet and a man sweeping her into his arms.

Branch kissed her.

She wasn't sure (and didn't care while Branch was kissing her) but she had a feeling Murphy was trying to eat her spiked heel.

He took his time but Branch eventually ended the kiss.

Lifting his head slightly away, Evangeline opened her eyes and whispered, "Hey, honey. I'm home."

Branch smiled, big and beautiful, and replied, "Thank fuck. I'm hungry and it's your turn to cook."

He then took her stuff, tossed it on the counter, and when he noticed she hadn't moved, he put a hand to the small of her back, shoved her into the kitchen and ended that with a swat on her ass.

"Daddy's annoying," she shared with Murphy as Branch sauntered out of the room.

Murphy just looked up at her with his big, black, happy eyes before he trotted off behind Branch.

She watched as Branch threw himself on his back on the couch and disappeared.

Then she hustled to the stairs so she could change and feed her man.

Evangeline was riding the high she always rode whenever she and Branch went out together.

These days, it happened more. They'd been to a couple of movies (she'd noted he wasn't a big fan of being in a dark room with other people, however, so she'd stopped suggesting that). They'd been out to dinner (something he didn't seem comfortable with at first, but he'd settled in, so she didn't ask often, but she was still going to push that). Breakfasts were better. Meeting for quick lunches he didn't mind at all, not even in the beginning. They didn't work out together, however. He went to a boxing gym and she'd tried it with him once, but she needed her treadmills and rowing machines, not the testosterone-fueled eye candy of men sparring and punching bags distracting her, even if it made Branch smile.

And just now, running errands and going through a drive-thru of a coffee place to get a coffee, like normal people.

Because that was what they were.

Normal people.

With a delicious twist.

He no longer asked what she wanted to order.

He just pulled up in his big SUV (that was so much roomier than her Fiat, it wasn't funny, she loved her little Fiat but his truck reminded her of him, big, solid, built tough—it *rocked*) and said into the speaker, "Iced chai latte and a nonfat iced mocha."

She was happily sipping it when Branch made the turn to pull into her drive behind her Fiat.

Summer was almost on them.

And her carport held only one car, even if that car was a tiny Fiat.

"We should look into having the carport extended so it can cover your truck," she noted.

"It'll fuck with the look of your house," he replied.

"We'll get a good designer," she told him.

"Trees offer enough shade, Angie."

She turned to him. "And they also offer a crap ton of bird poo."

He parked, turned off the truck and looked to her, smiling, "Good point. And I got the cash so I'll ask around. Aryas probably knows someone who does good work."

"I have the cash too. My vacation fund is out the roof."

"So take a vacation. But I'll do the carport."

She felt her mouth turn down.

He watched it then looked into her eyes.

"Baby, told you," he started gently, "you need to slow down. You've been doin' that but that also means sometimes allowing yourself an even bigger break."

She didn't want a break. That meaning she wanted a break, she needed one, just not one from him.

"I can't think of anywhere I want to go," she muttered, turning to open her door so she could hop out.

"I can."

She froze a second before she turned back to him. "You can?"

"Not exactly been kicking back the last, I don't know, 'bout twenty years," he remarked.

This was sadly very true.

"You mean you want to go on vacation with me?"

His brows snapped together. "Not gonna let you go on your own."

Her heart flipped.

Still, she asked, "Not gonna *let*?"

"No, babe. Not . . . gonna . . . *let*. You wanted an alpha, you got him and not just the good parts you like. You want time away with a girlfriend. Cool. But the first vacation you take when we're together, you take with me."

She smiled. "I can do that."

He smiled back. "Cottage on a lake."

She frowned. "House by a beach."

His face changed. "Beaches are always busy. Cottage on a lake."

Her voice dropped. "Cottage on a lake."

When she gave in, he reached out to her, hooked her behind the neck and brought her to him.

He touched their mouths together, let her go, then turned, threw open his door and angled out.

She was going on vacation with Branch to a cottage on a lake.

On this thought, she hopped out of his truck and did it smiling like crazy.

"Got the shit, you just get inside," Branch ordered from the back of the SUV.

Her alpha wanted to carry in all their stuff, she was not going to argue.

But she stutter-stepped when she saw Jane working in her front yard and stopped fully when Jane saw her.

She lifted her hand to wave.

"Hey, kids!" Jane called, garden gloves on, coming their way, waving back at her maniacally.

"Hey, Jane!" Evangeline returned, sensing Branch coming up the other side of the car so she started to move again.

She rounded the hood only to be claimed by Branch with an arm thrown over her shoulder, the handles of the plastic bags they'd accumulated during their errands dripping from the fingers of his other hand (all five of them).

"Yo," Branch grunted as greeting.

Even if that was grunted and not-so-vaguely Neanderthal, Jane smiled at it like *she* was crazy.

"You hitting my party next weekend?" she asked.

"Wouldn't miss it," Evangeline told her.

"Can we bring something?" Branch inquired, and Evangeline tried not to show how much she loved the total beauty of the normalcy of that (not to mention the politeness) by not melting into him.

But she didn't try too hard because she loved it and she decided it wasn't a bad thing that Branch knew it.

"Just yourselves. And if you have something specific you want to drink. I'll have beer. Wine. And margaritas."

"Great," Branch said, putting pressure on and tugging her toward the house, clearly done with chatting with Jane.

"See you then!" Jane cried.

"See you, Jane. Can't wait!" Evangeline called back.

Branch got them in the door, immediately dumped the bags on a counter and turned to the laundry room, saying, "I'll let Murphy out then go grab the mail."

"Thanks, baby," she muttered.

She went to the bags.

Murphy bounded out to say hi by sniffing her foot then he bounded after Branch as he headed to the front of her house.

He came back and dumped the mail then led Murphy out back.

She put the stuff away and sifted through the mail.

As she did, one piece caught her eye and she snatched it from the rest, ripping it open and sliding out what was inside.

Then she dashed to the French doors, threw them open and exclaimed while continuing her dash outside, "Guess what?"

Branch had the pool skimmer resting net down to the pool deck, long handle to his shoulder, his head bent to his phone.

He seemed to jerk out of some shock as his head snapped up and he appeared distracted when he asked, "What?"

Murphy nearly sent the skimmer sailing when he collided with the net but Branch grabbed it as she walked to him, fighting a sour feeling hitting her belly at whatever might be distracting him and making his face look like that.

"Everything cool?" she asked.

"You first," he demanded.

She lifted the cream, heavy-stock, perfectly hand-calligraphed invitation in her hand. "Penn and Shane's wedding invitation."

"Awesome," he muttered, gently propelling Murphy back with a foot and taking up the skimmer again.

"Your turn," she said, getting closer.

He was eyes to the pool, but he spoke.

"Got a text. Friend's in town."

She waited.

He didn't make her wait long.

His blue eyes came to her. "He wants to . . ."

He trailed off.

She waited again.

That time, she had to prompt, "He wants to what, honey?"

"His name is Tavis," he stated, instead of answering her question.

"Okay," she replied.

"Or it might be. It might be something else."

Evangeline fell silent.

He put the skimmer net to the deck again and gave her his full attention.

"You get me, baby?" he asked carefully.

She nodded.

"He wants to meet you."

"Do you think that's safe?" she queried.

"Absolutely."

To that, she smiled. "Then I'd love to meet him."

"He's . . . ," he shook his head, "he's like me, except more of a pain in the ass."

Evangeline let out a breath.

One of *those* friends.

She knew *those* friends.

So she stated, "Then I figure I'll love him."

Branch went totally still.

At that, Evangeline realized what she'd just said.

And she did not care.

"Don't pretend you don't know," she whispered.

"Baby."

"Fell in love with you in the red room the first second I laid eyes on you," she informed him.

"Fell in love with you looking at you, beat to shit, finding it hard to breathe, not listening to Aryas telling me what he wanted me to do to that guy, just fighting the urge I already had when I got him not to kill him," he fired back.

Oh my God.

He loved her.

Loved.

Her.

And he'd loved her since the very beginning.

She smiled up at him but noted, "That's not very romantic."

He shrugged.

"But it's totally you," she finished.

"That it is."

"Thank God."

"Am I gonna kiss you or are you gonna kiss me?" he asked.

"Way it goes with us, I think it'll be both."

Branch lost patience.

"Get over here, Evangeline."

She got over there.

He kissed her. She participated. But with her alpha, the way it went when she was his Angie, it was mostly all Branch.

She loved every second.

When their mouths broke, she didn't make more avowals of love. Branch wasn't that way.

They had it.

They knew it.

They didn't need to go over it.

They just needed to be easy.

So she asked, "Do you think your friend will want to have dinner with us?"

"I think he'd kill to eat your food and sit in your house with you while he was doin' it."

"I think it's probably that he'd kill to do that with you, but that's okay, honey. I'll play second fiddle."

Branch grinned.

She pressed closer a second before she pulled away.

She located their dog, found him looking like he was snuffling an ant on the pool deck, and asked Branch, "You want him out with you?"

"Yeah."

She knew that answer too.

She gave him another smile, seeing he had his phone out, before she turned to walk away.

She wasn't too far when she heard him say, "Yeah, Gerbil. Wanna come for dinner?"

Gerbil?

She didn't ask.

She went in and did an inventory to decide if she needed to pop out to the grocery store so she could wow Branch's friend during dinner.

Fell in love with you looking at you, beat to shit, finding it hard to breathe, not listening to Aryas telling me what he wanted me to do to that guy, just fighting the urge I already had when I got him not to kill him.

She finally had something to thank Kevin for.

She'd never have the opportunity.

Because there was a man who loved her who would not allow that.

She giggled with glee and decided to make lasagna.

"Hi, nice to meet you."

"Hi, you too. Name's Cam."

Early that evening, she stood with Branch at her front door and stared up into Cameron's beautiful brown eyes, trying not to laugh her head off at both of them pretending they hadn't stood right there not too long ago when she'd given him a hug goodbye the morning after they'd gotten drunk on vodka and he'd crashed in her guest room.

G.

For Gerbil.

And it all came together.

"Cam?" Branch asked.

Cam looked at his friend. "Decided to go vintage. 'Least for you two. I'll be someone else tomorrow."

Branch rolled his eyes to the ceiling.

"Would you like a beer?" Evangeline inquired.

"You got vodka?" he asked back.

At that, she knew he was making an inside joke but she didn't want to laugh.

And at *that*, her heart beat a little harder, she could swear her cheeks were getting pink and now she was trying not to weep at the expression on his face.

He was there.

He was going to try too.

And he was going to be with them when he did it.

So she was going to guide him to winning too.

She knew it.

Because so far, she had a great track record.

"Absolutely," she said. "Please," she swept out an arm, the one that wasn't around Branch's waist as his was again thrown around her neck. "Come in."

Branch moved them aside. Cam strode in.

Branch shut the door, gave her a squeeze and she broke off, murmuring, "I'll just get drinks. You boys settle in."

"Thanks, honey," Branch murmured back.

She moved off.

Murphy bounced around Cameron's feet.

"Cute dog," she heard him rumble.

"Shut up."

"Cute girl."

Nothing from Branch.

"Great ass," Cameron said.

"Do you want a throat punch?" Branch asked.

"Not really," Cameron replied.

"Then no more about my babe's ass."

She'd never get tired of being his babe.

She was moving around in the kitchen when they continued a conversation in the family room neither of them tried really hard not to let her hear.

"Want some good news or some bad news?" Cam queried.

"Good," Branch answered cautiously.

"Someone you know who's a lot prettier than you is moving to Phoenix."

"Fuck, seriously?" Branch asked.

"Seriously."

"What's the bad news?"

"Someone you know who's a lot prettier than you is moving to Phoenix."

Branch busted out laughing.

God, she loved that.

She grinned at the vodka gliding over its ice.

"Lucky for you, you got a cute babe. So it won't gut you when I take all the rest," Cam remarked.

"You can have them."

That made her grin bigger.

"Brother."

At the tone of that from Branch, she put the vodka down and didn't move.

Neither of the men said anything more but she could feel the atmosphere around her turning warm and beautiful.

Branch's voice was gruff when he finally broke the silence.

"It'll be good to have you around."

"Friend of mine recently slid over the edge. Never thought he'd get there. That fucker was far, *far* away. But he made it and he took the fall. Reckon, he could do it, since I'm better than him in just about everything, but the art of kicking ass, I could do it too."

"Just sayin', you better brace for second place, man. There's only one Angie."

"I know."

She looked out through the jungle of plants around her kitchen window at her pool, which was a gorgeous pool in a normal home where a woman fell in love with an amazing man.

She would never guess that was what the farthest edge looked like.

But it was perfect.

Evangeline drifted through the halls of the Honey with a glass of champagne in her hand.

She was alone.

And she was taking her time.

The gang was all there, Penn and Shane doing their thing, but behind silhouetted shades, so she knew they were in their favorite playroom, but they were feeling the need for a bit of privacy.

She understood that.

Their wedding was happening the next weekend, now it was private time before the big celebration.

She couldn't wait.

She figured they were more excited.

She didn't watch Marisol long with her two subs because she never watched Marisol long. Marisol was talented, it was just that female on female wasn't her thing.

She watched Talia work for longer. That Domme was relatively new but obviously no longer a newbie and she clearly enjoyed what she did.

Her sub, clearly, did too.

Mira and Trey didn't offer up much of anything. Since she'd sold both their houses, they'd moved in together and Mira announced

their engagement at the next book club meeting; they kept the silhouette blinds down when they played.

But Felicia was feeling playful, Evangeline knew, mostly because
she came out of her scene with her handsome boy long enough to
give Evangeline a wink.

As usual, when she saw Amélie at work with Olly, she skimmed
right by.

It would be beautiful, she knew, but she still felt the need to give
it only to them, even if they didn't feel that same need. She would have
done the same with Mira and Trey, Penn and Shane, if they'd kept
their blinds open.

On the way to where she was going, she took a detour that would
take her deeper into the playrooms and in the opposite direction to
where she was going to end up.

When she arrived at her destination, although it was one of the
playrooms that was out of the way, like Aryas's room on the other
side of the Honey, there was still a rather large audience.

Even though she knew what she would find in that room and it
would normally have made her skim it, she found a place to stand
and gazed in, instantly licking her lips at what she saw.

Sixx was working.

Her sub was spread-eagled and spread-armed, lashed to a table,
on his stomach. His balls and cock were harnessed, both tightly.
His ass was strapped open, the crease glistening visibly. He had a
jaw harness on, forcing his head back, the chain leading from the
back of the harness looped around the baton that was planted firmly
up his ass.

And she was stroking him.

Not his cock. Not his balls. Not with his baton.

His body. Legs. Ass. Back. Shoulders. Arms. Hair.

Everything.

And she was doing it slowly, lovingly . . . reverentially.

She also did it looking like she was cooing to him, the expression on her face softening her usually remote beauty in a way that it was almost unbearable to look at her.

"God, he's switched her," Romy, standing beside her, murmured in awe.

"He has," Evangeline whispered, doing it happily.

Sixx moved from him looking like she didn't want to.

And she didn't once cast a glance at a single member of her audience as she walked to the control panel by the door and they heard the whirring start as the blackout shades started to float down.

"Damn, would kill to see where she was taking that," Romy grumbled.

Evangeline turned to her friend. "The queen needs privacy with her king."

Romy stopped looking miffed and smiled. "Have you been around to see when he works her?"

She shook her head.

"The way he works her, totally go sub for him. *Toe-tah-lee*," Romy declared.

"Stellan's always been a king. He just needed to find his queen."

She looked longingly at the blackout shades. "Wish he'd broken me into the splendors of being a switch."

Evangeline watched her do that and did it smiling, knowing no way that would happen. Stellan was hot. He looked like an amazing sub. He just *was* an amazing Dom.

But Romy was a dyed-in-the-wool Mistress.

Romy's attention came back to her and her head tipped to the side. "You know she had that in her?"

She shook her head.

"You know he had that in him?" she went on.

"I know that love allows you to go places you never thought you'd go and like being there a heck of a lot," Evangeline answered.

Romy's face got soft with happiness for several of her friends,

Evangeline knowing she was one of them. "Yeah." More happiness came in when she asked, "Leigh tell you Olly popped the question?"

That, Evangeline knew, made her own face get soft.

"They had us over to dinner last week. Gave us the news."

"The ring is impressive," Romy remarked.

"It was his mother's," Evangeline told her.

"God," she whispered. "How sweet."

It was. Amélie had shared Olly was close with his mom, who had sadly died. So it was tremendously sweet.

As luck would have it, the ring was also beautiful. Elegant. Very much Leigh. And the rock wasn't anything to sneeze at.

"You're not going to play?" Evangeline asked and Romy looked down the hall.

"Right. Damn. Best get back to my well-hung boy." She shot Evangeline a wicked look. "He's probably tired of waiting."

Evangeline just shot her another smile.

They gave each other quick hugs and Romy went one direction, Evangeline the other.

She ran into Aryas on the way to her final destination.

"Good, there you are," he said, coming right to her.

Damn, after seeing Sixx with Stellan, she was impatient to get where she was going.

"Aryas—"

He interrupted her. "Got the matter of a bet to settle and you keep dodging me."

"You gave me free membership for a year," she reminded him. "And that's more than our bet."

"No, I didn't," he returned. "Family of staff get membership gratis."

"That's not true," she guessed, because she didn't know if it was and Branch didn't share a lot about work because it was nearly as confidential as all the other jobs he'd had in his life.

Aryas had chosen well.

"Okay, so the woman of my operations manager gets member-ship for free because he's so fuckin' good at his job, I'm afraid I'm going to open a random new member file and see the pictorial results of a recent colonoscopy."

She giggled.

"I'm not joking." Aryas said in all seriousness.

She tried to stop giggling and didn't manage it so her next was shaking.

"Okay, then, just consider us even."

"I cover my debts."

"My man's stupid six-month lease is up on the apartment he's spent approximately forty-five minutes in since he signed it"—and that forty-five minutes had been as long as it took him to give her an orgasm with his mouth while she writhed on his kitchen island before he took his own climax with his cock, giving her another one along the way—"so he's moving in next week. In other words, like I said, my beautiful, beautiful man, consider us even."

Aryas's eyes warmed and he pulled her into one of his big, strong hugs.

But into the top of her hair, he said, "Don't bitch, you get a shit-hot wedding gift."

She arched back over his arm in order to look into his face. "I'd never bitch about that."

He lifted a finger to touch it to her nose before he fully let her go, gave her a lift of his chin, and strolled away.

She strolled to where her mind had been the last half an hour.

The red blinds were down, blocking out the view to what was inside.

She took the key out of the cleavage of her little dark blue dress, inserted it and unlocked the only door in the Honey that had a lock.

She looked left, right and again before she opened the door and quickly slipped inside the only room that was occupied that had no camera running.

She locked the door again behind her.

Then she looked to the bed and drew in a deep breath.

Branch was naked on his back in the middle of the red satin sheets. His arms were lifted over his head, wide, wrists lashed with silk cords to the bedposts.

She'd gotten fancy and tied his lifted bent knees spread wide to the top posts, also swinging out his feet in stirrups that were secured to the bottom posts.

His eyes had a blindfold over them. His mouth was gagged with a black silk scarf.

His ass was lifted on pillows covered in red satin, his cock ringed, the tail running through his balls, the bullet up his ass, all of this working, set on medium low.

His nipples were tightly clamped with the chain running between them, dragging them down, as it was hooked around the end of her jewel, which was winking.

She went to the side of the bed and watched him turn his head to follow the noise of her movements.

She took a last sip of her champagne then set it aside.

After that, she unzipped her dress and pulled it over her head. She tossed it on the bed, the soft sound of it landing drawing Branch's attention.

Then off went her panties and her bra.

She kept her high-heeled, strappy sandals on.

She entered the bed on her knees and rested a hand light on his chest as she bent her lips to his ear.

"I want you watching."

On that, she pulled off his blindfold.

His heated gaze met hers.

She smiled at him and bent close, brushing her lips against his gagged ones, feeling the touch as it was with his gag throb through her clit.

Then she shifted down him, ducking under his leg, and getting between both.

She put her hands to his abs, flat, gliding them up, until her fingers touched the chain just under the clamps on his nipples.

She gave it a sharp tug and gloried in the grunt, the blaze in his eyes as it stayed locked on her.

She let the chain go and slid further up him, tipping her ass.

That was when she lost his gaze. It went right to the mirror over the bed.

She knew what he saw.

Ice blue winking.

And she knew he liked it when the fingers he had wrapped around his bonds yanked at them.

"Me inside you," she whispered. "You inside me."

She heard what sounded like a muffled, "Angie."

She ignored it.

"You're going to watch me fuck you now, Branch."

The noise that came from behind his gag was not a word, just a stifled growl.

She rubbed a thumb hard across his nipple, watching his jaw clench and a muscle jump up his cheek.

So . . . *fucking* . . . pretty.

"Ready to slip over the edge with me, baby?" she asked.

He made no noise to that but the ice of his eyes burning through hers told her everything.

Her Branch no longer surfed the edge.

He lived the one they shared.

And he loved it there.

As did she.

She moved down, kissed his throat, nipped hard on each nipple and felt the pulse of the jolt of his body each time race up her pussy.

Then she moved down.

And she took him over the edge.

He watched in the mirror, his body straining, bucking, swaying the posts.

But he lost sight when he went over, taking her with him, his head digging back into the satin as his cum arced in a stream over his chest.

BRANCH

Branch's eyes opened to see nothing but dark and his body froze.

It relaxed when he felt Murphy stop roaming and settle on their big bed at Branch's feet.

But he heard Elsa, their German shepherd, who slept sprawled behind Angie's legs, give a soft woof.

"It's okay, girl," he murmured quietly.

Another soft woof and then he felt Elsa settle in.

Loki, he had no clue. The damn cat was probably in the secret control room he'd created through a panel of one of Angie's walls, communicating with his cat brethren in his effort to take over the world.

Alternately, he could be single-mindedly shredding the wicker of one of the chairs in the Arizona room, a favorite nocturnal *and* diurnal pastime.

Angie's warm, soft little body was pressed to him, and through all this, she didn't move.

She hadn't felt a thing.

She slept and she slept deep, having no clue what terrors there were out there that were real.

And she never would.

He carefully gathered her closer so he wouldn't wake her and closed his eyes.

Branch heard a big dog sigh.

And the harsh smoothed out of his face when he fell right back to sleep.

Stay tuned for the next book in the
Honey series coming soon

Check Kristenashley.net for details.

Enter a decadent, sensual world
where gorgeous alpha males are committed
to fulfilling a woman's every desire...

—— ENTER THE HONEY SERIES ——

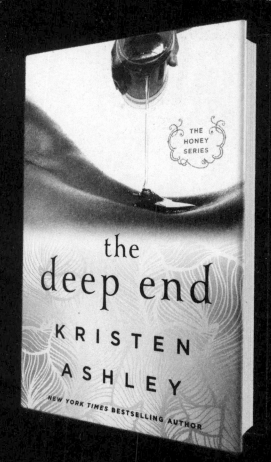

THE
HONEY
SERIES

the
deep end

KRISTEN
ASHLEY

NEW YORK TIMES BESTSELLING AUTHOR

"KRISTEN ASHLEY'S BOOKS ARE
ADDICTING!"
—Jill Shalvis, *New York Times* bestselling author

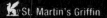 St. Martin's Griffin